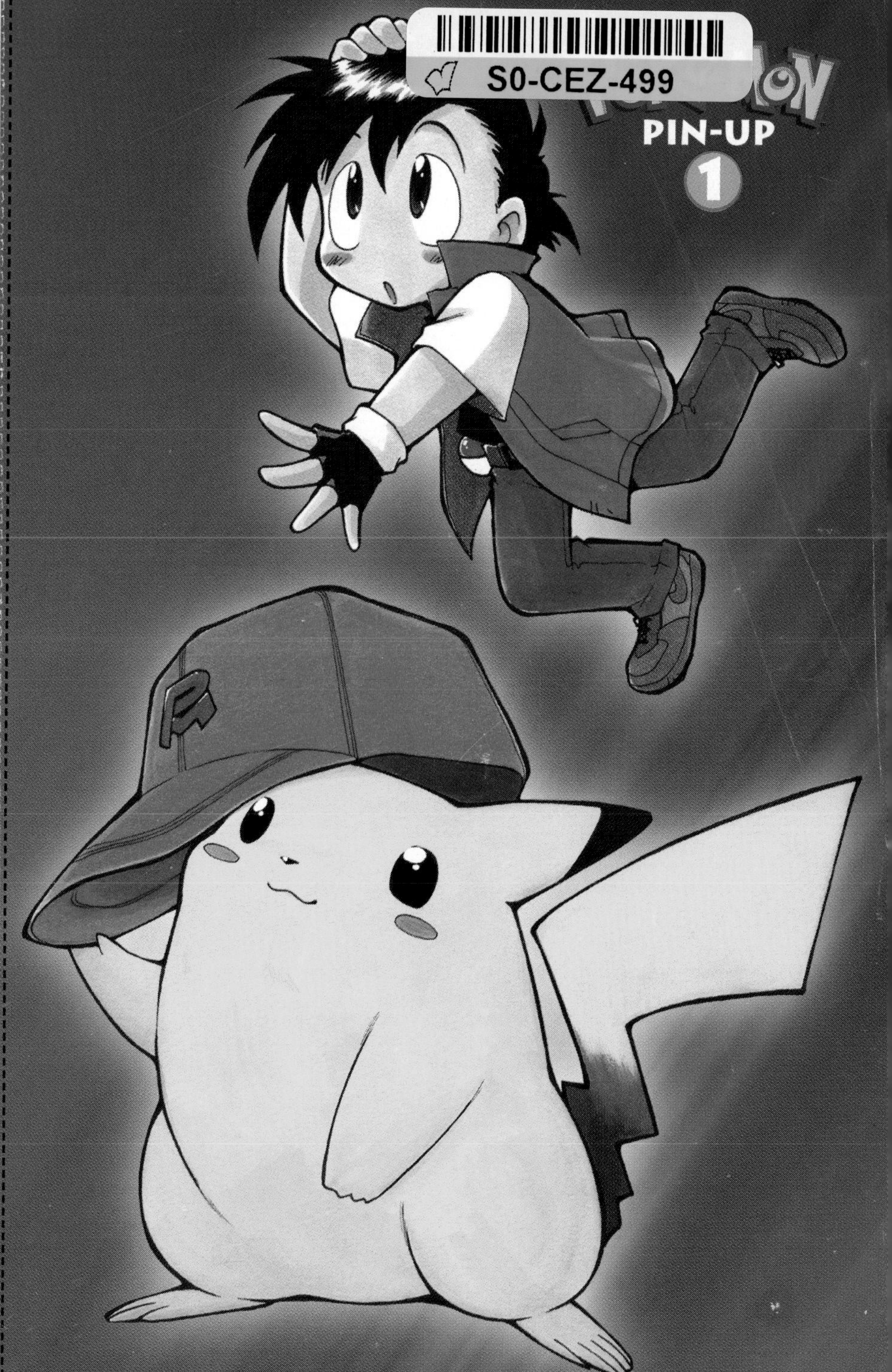
PIN-UP
1

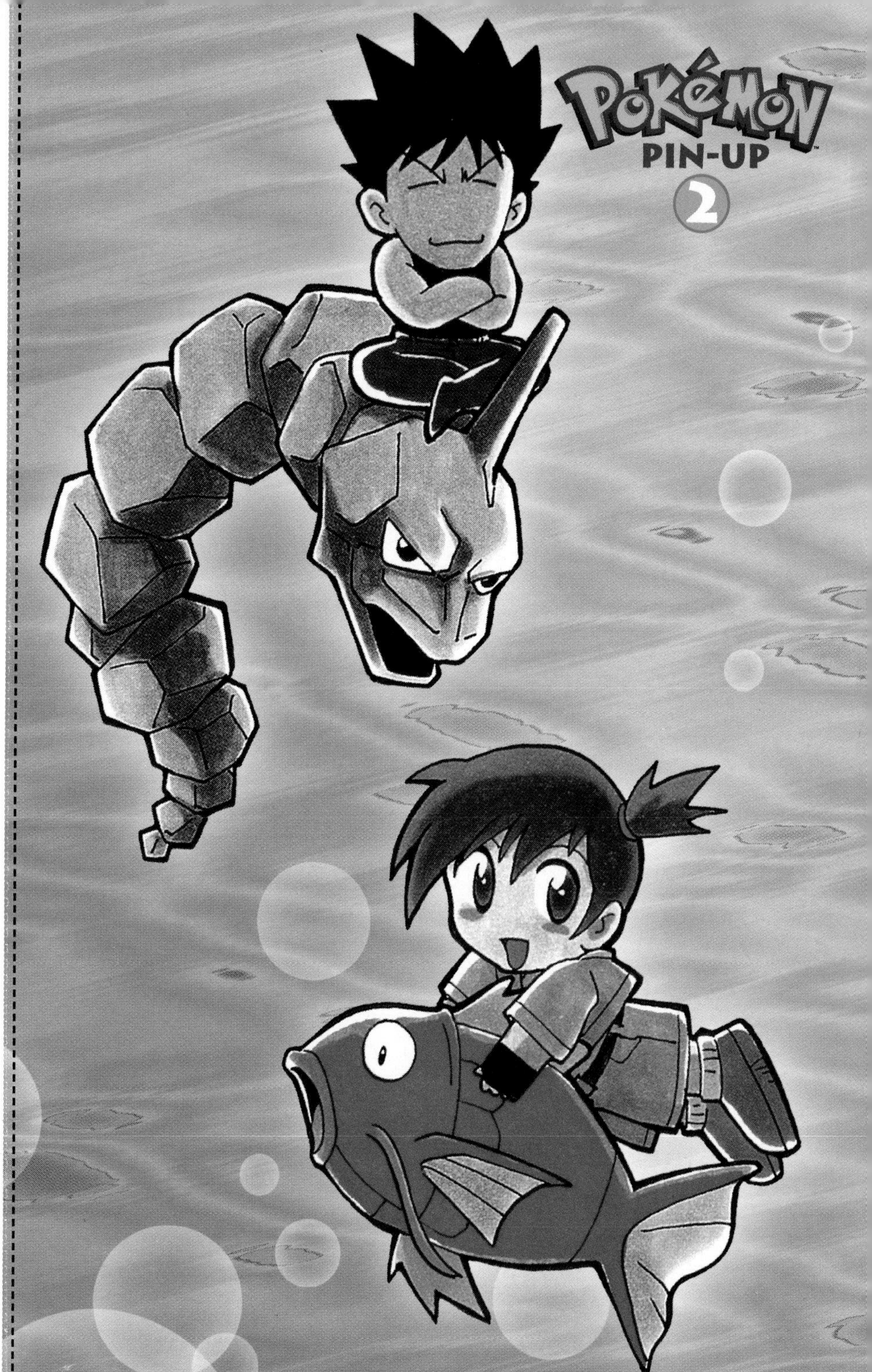
POKéMON™
PIN-UP
2

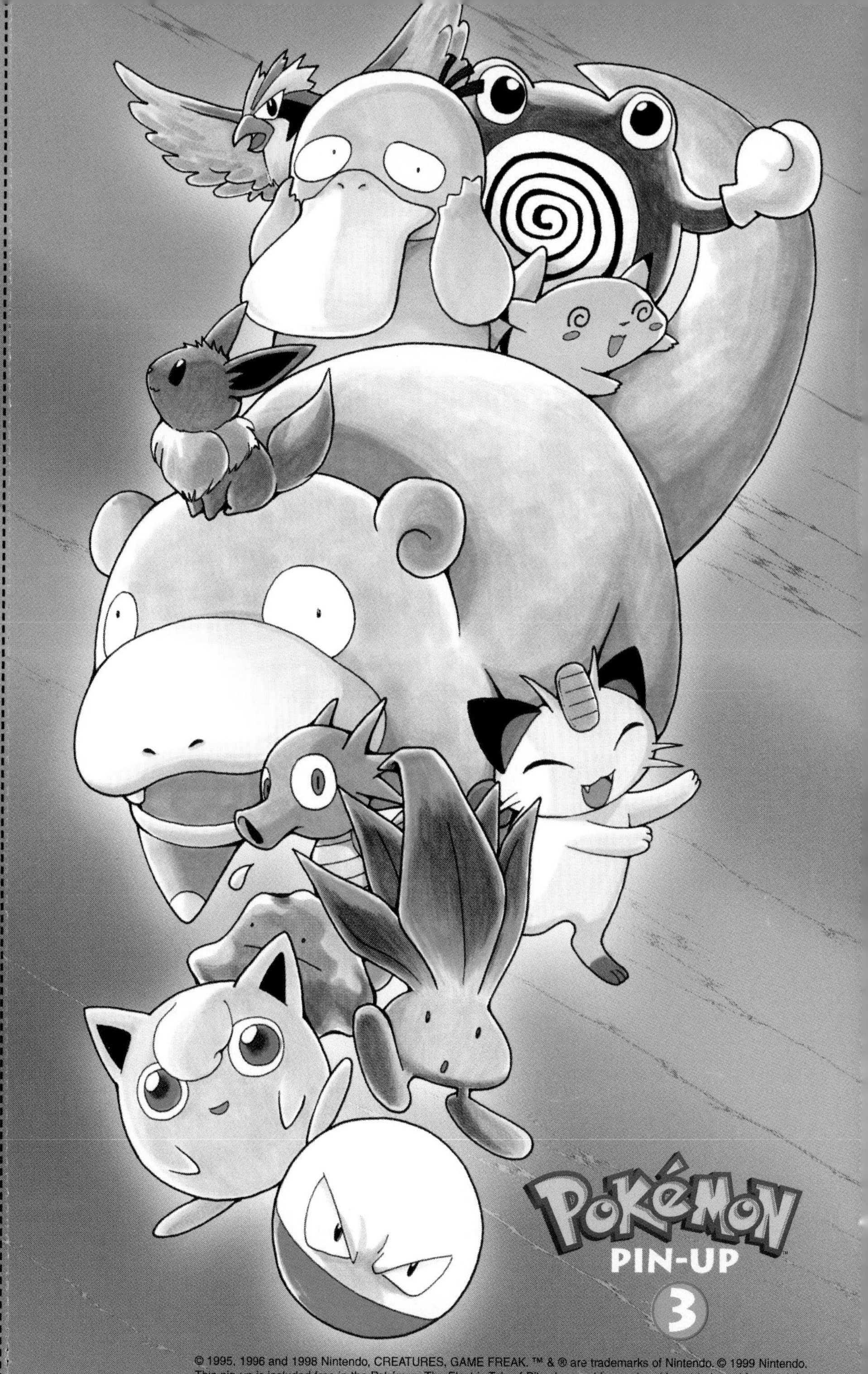
POKéMON
PIN-UP
3

TALES OF PIKACHU IN THE WILD

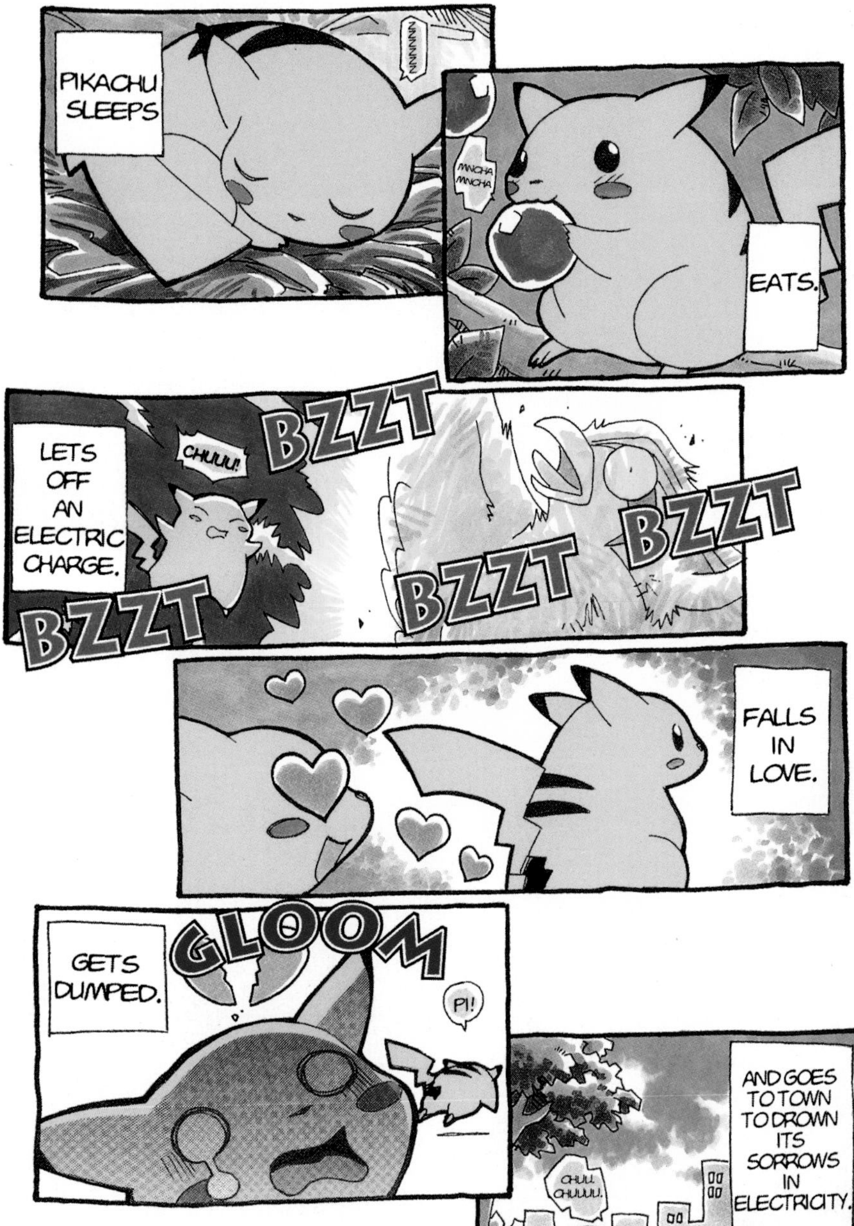
PIKACHU SLEEPS
MNCHA MNCHA
EATS.
LETS OFF AN ELECTRIC CHARGE.
CHUUU!
BZZT
BZZT
BZZT
BZZT
FALLS IN LOVE.
GETS DUMPED.
GLOOM
PI!
AND GOES TO TOWN TO DROWN ITS SORROWS IN ELECTRICITY.
CHUU. CHUUUU.

TO BE CONTINUED IN THE COMIC...

The Electric Tale of Pikachu

Story and Art by:
TOSHIHIRO ONO

Based on the animated series by
Tsunekazu Ishihara & Satoshi Tajiri

OUR HEROES

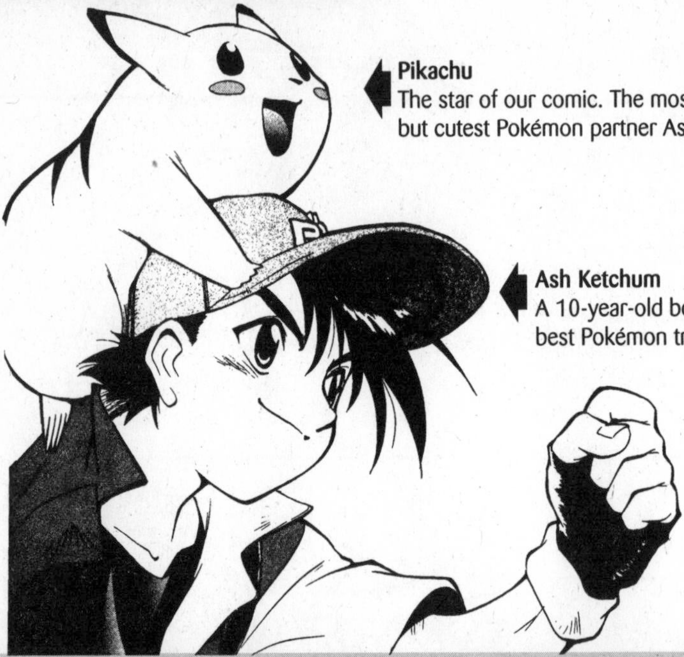

Pikachu
The star of our comic. The most capricious, but cutest Pokémon partner Ash could have.

Ash Ketchum
A 10-year-old boy striving to be the best Pokémon trainer in the world!

THE HUMANS

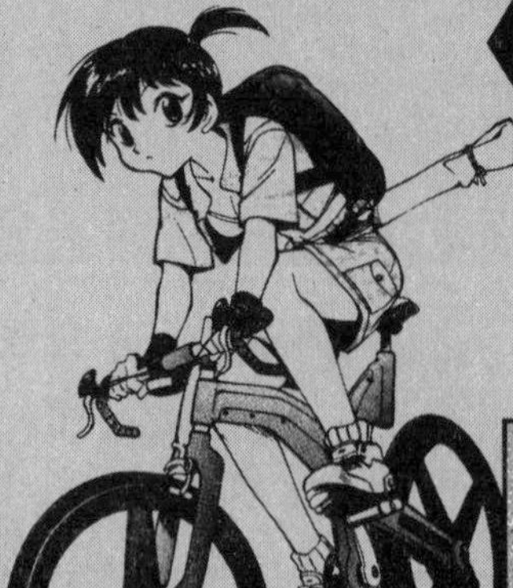

Misty
A 12-year-old trainer who seems to be an expert with water Pokémon.

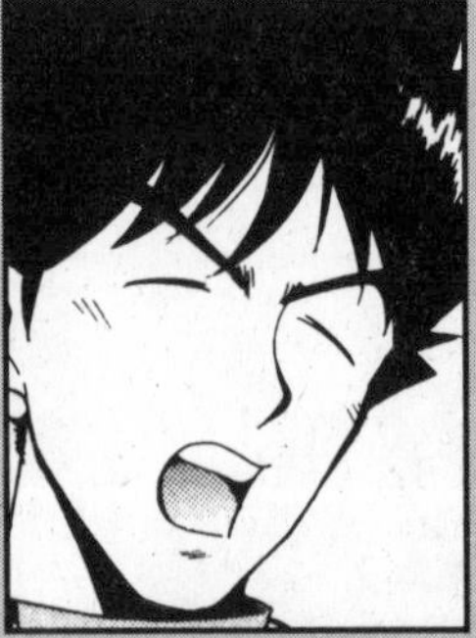

Brock
A rock Pokémon expert and the leader of Pewter City Gym.

Gary
Gary always seems to have accomplished more than Ash.

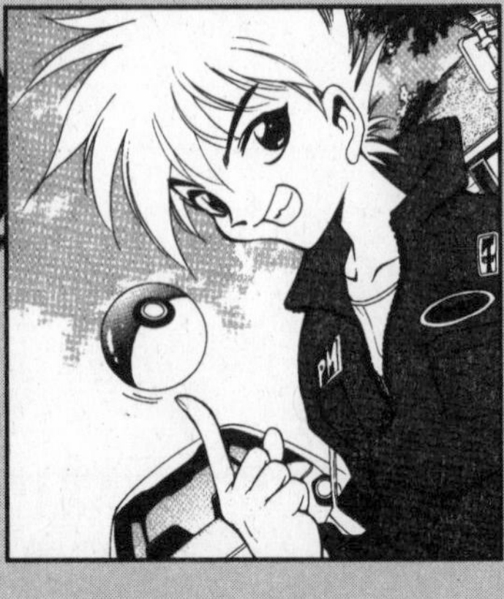

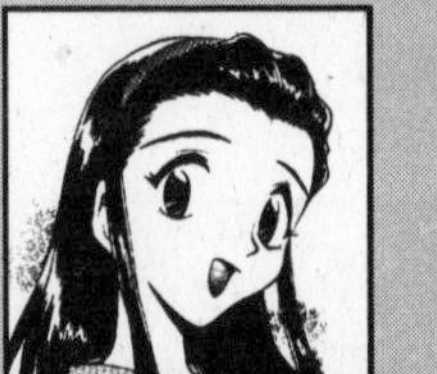

May
Gary's sister, who Ash secretly has a crush on.

THE POKéMON

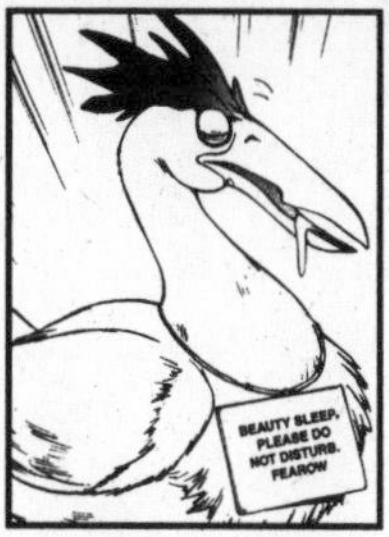
BEAUTY SLEEP. PLEASE DO NOT DISTURB. FEAROW

Fearow
The first Pokémon Ash and Pikachu ever captured.

Pidgeotto
Has a vicious Sand-attack.

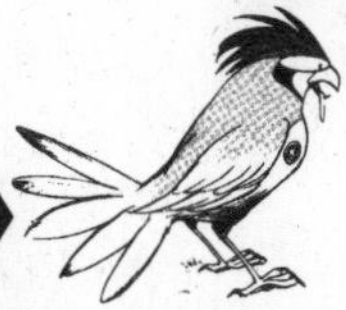

Clefairy
A very rare Pokémon with the mysterious Metronome attack.

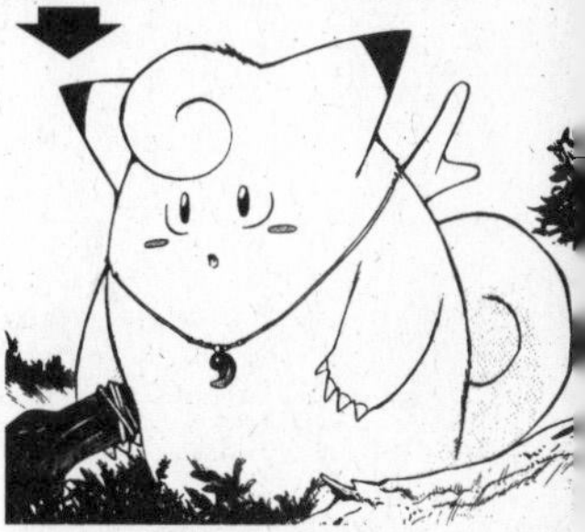

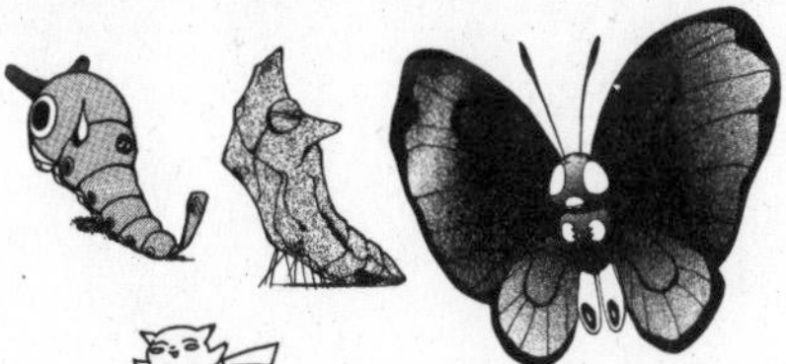

Caterpie, Metapod and Butterfree
The fastest evolving Pokémon in the Pokémon world.

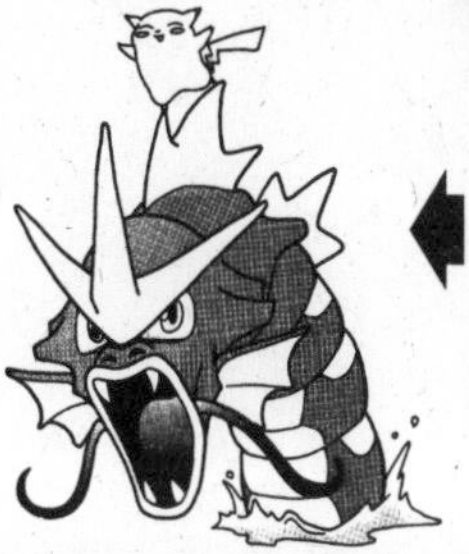

Gyarados
One of the largest and most terrifying water Pokémon.

Haunter
An ancient Pokémon that can use the Dream Eater attack.

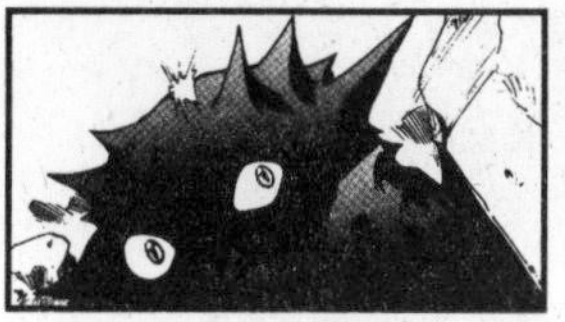

(and many, many more!)

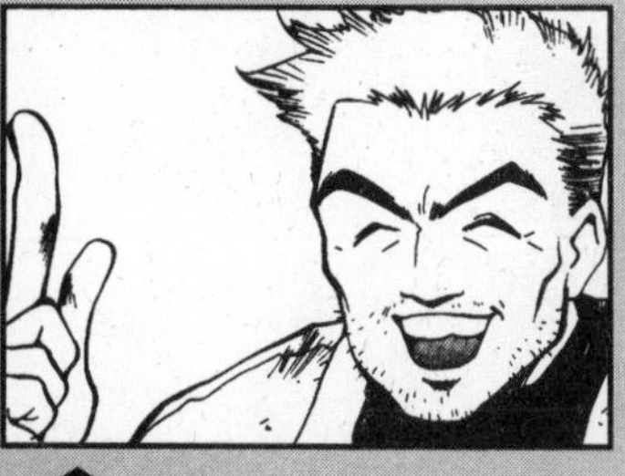

Professor Oak
A leading Pokémon expert and inventor of the Pokédex.

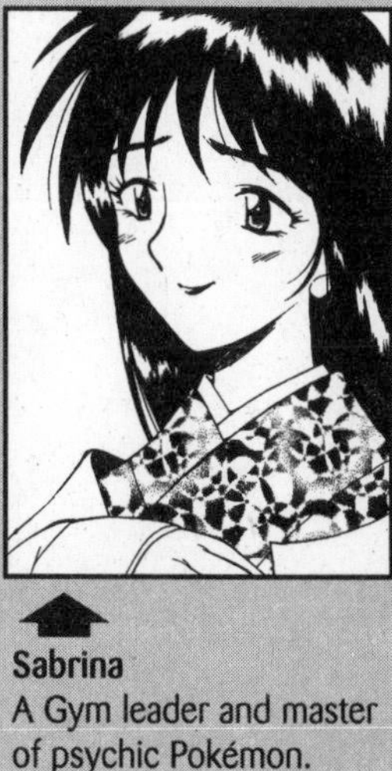

Sabrina
A Gym leader and master of psychic Pokémon.

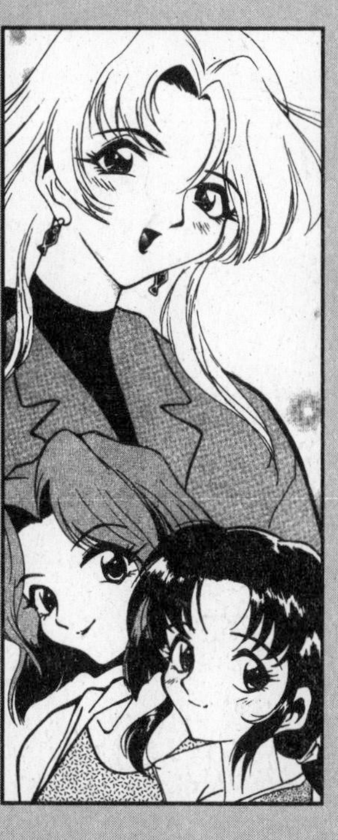

Daisy, Violet, and Lily
The Sisters of Cerulean City, all three are beautiful Pokémon gym leaders!

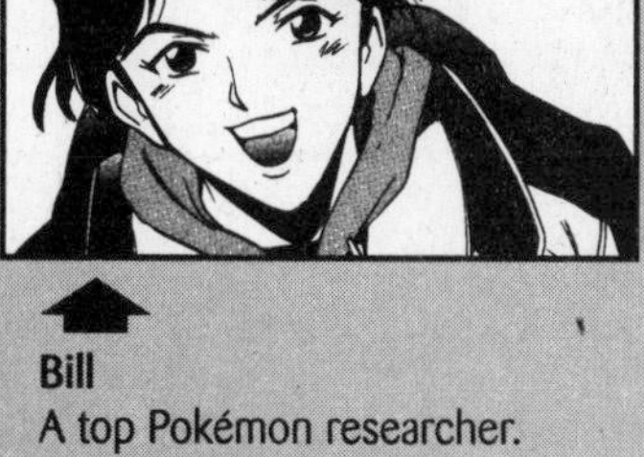

Bill
A top Pokémon researcher.

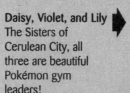

CONTENTS:

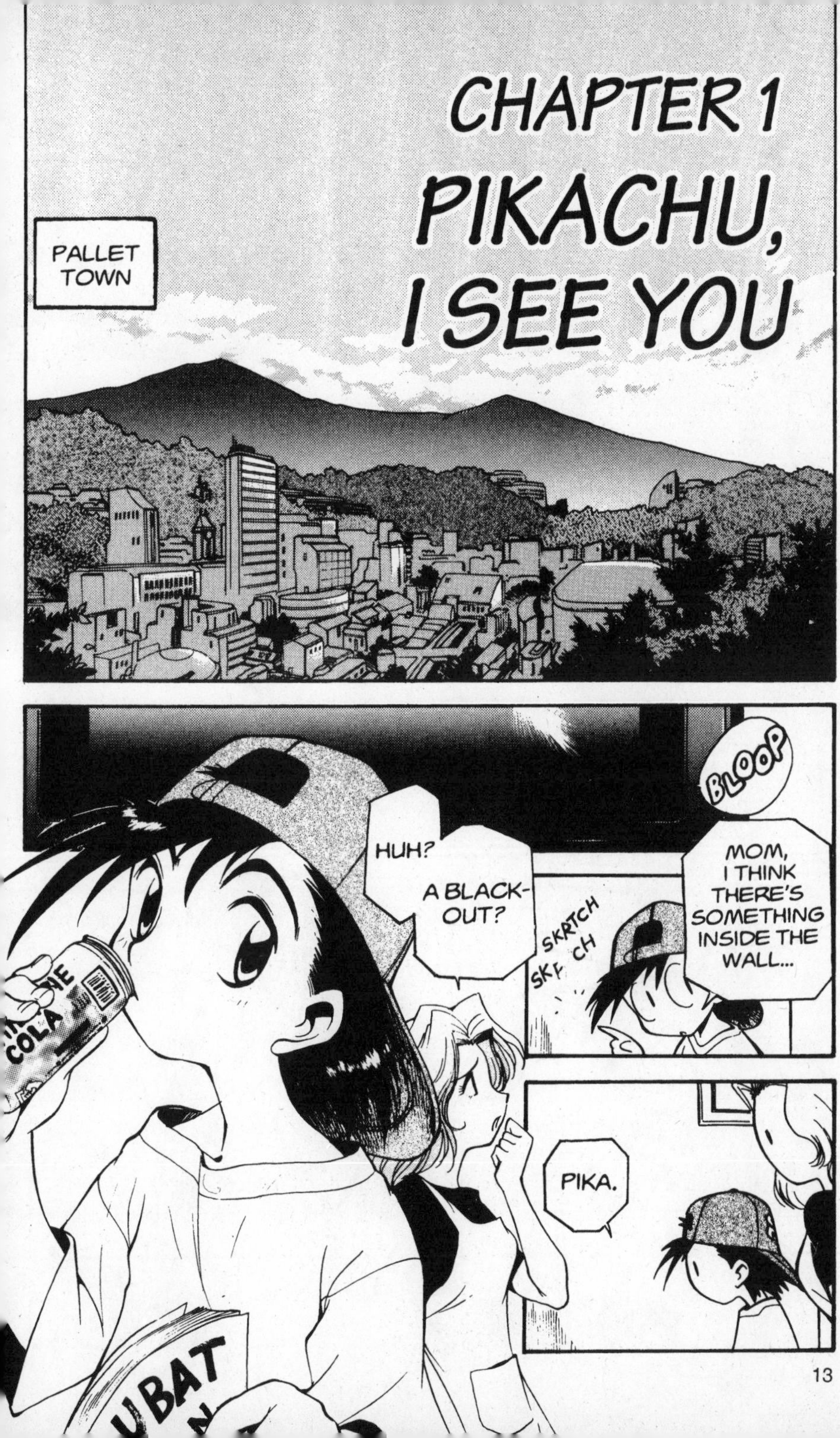
CHAPTER 1
PIKACHU, I SEE YOU
PALLET TOWN
HUH?
A BLACK-OUT?
COLA
BLOOP
MOM, I THINK THERE'S SOMETHING INSIDE THE WALL...
SKRTCH
PIKA.

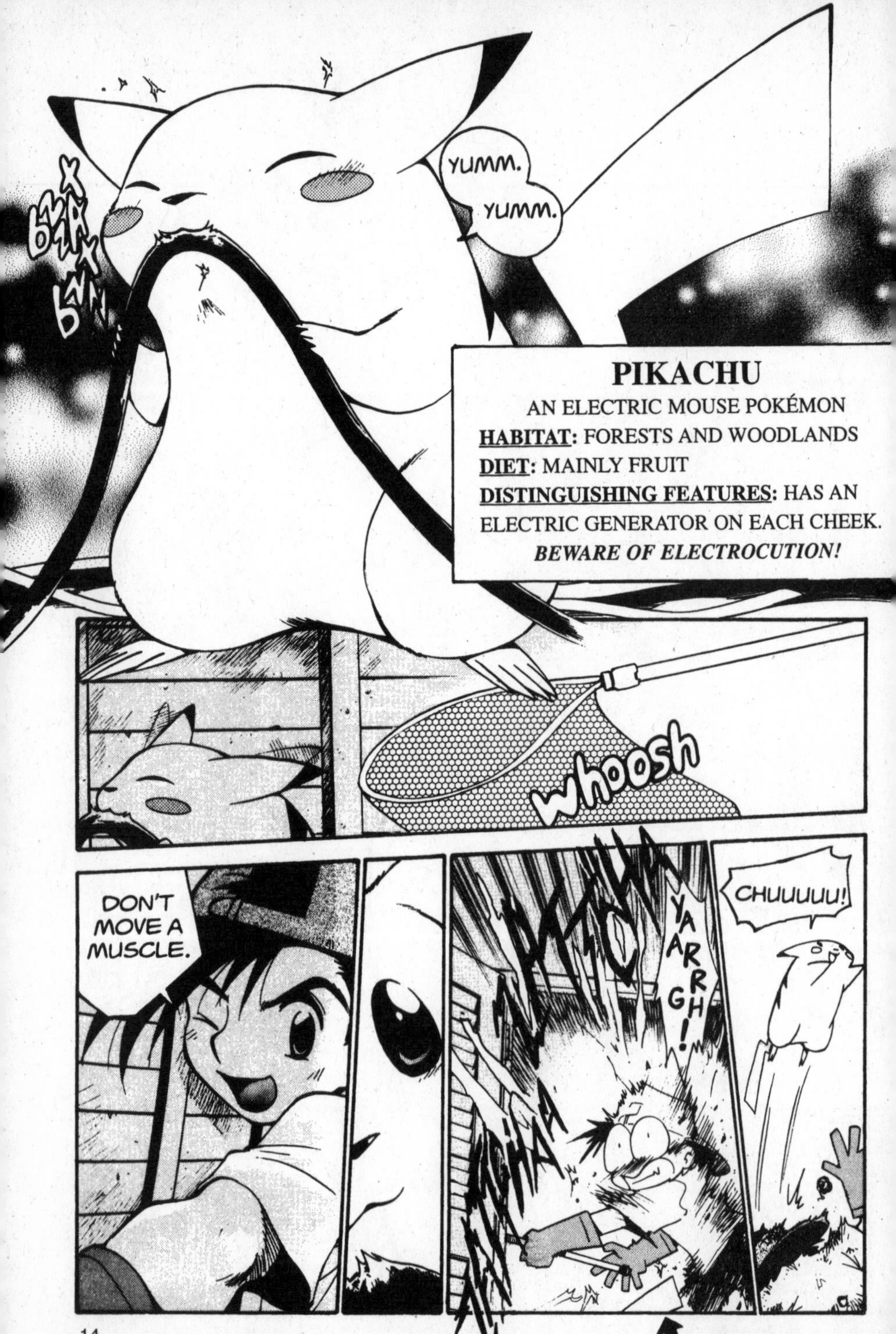
YUMM.
YUMM.
PIKACHU
AN ELECTRIC MOUSE POKÉMON
HABITAT: FORESTS AND WOODLANDS
DIET: MAINLY FRUIT
DISTINGUISHING FEATURES: HAS AN ELECTRIC GENERATOR ON EACH CHEEK.
BEWARE OF ELECTROCUTION!
whoosh
DON'T MOVE A MUSCLE.
YAARRGH!
CHUUUUU!

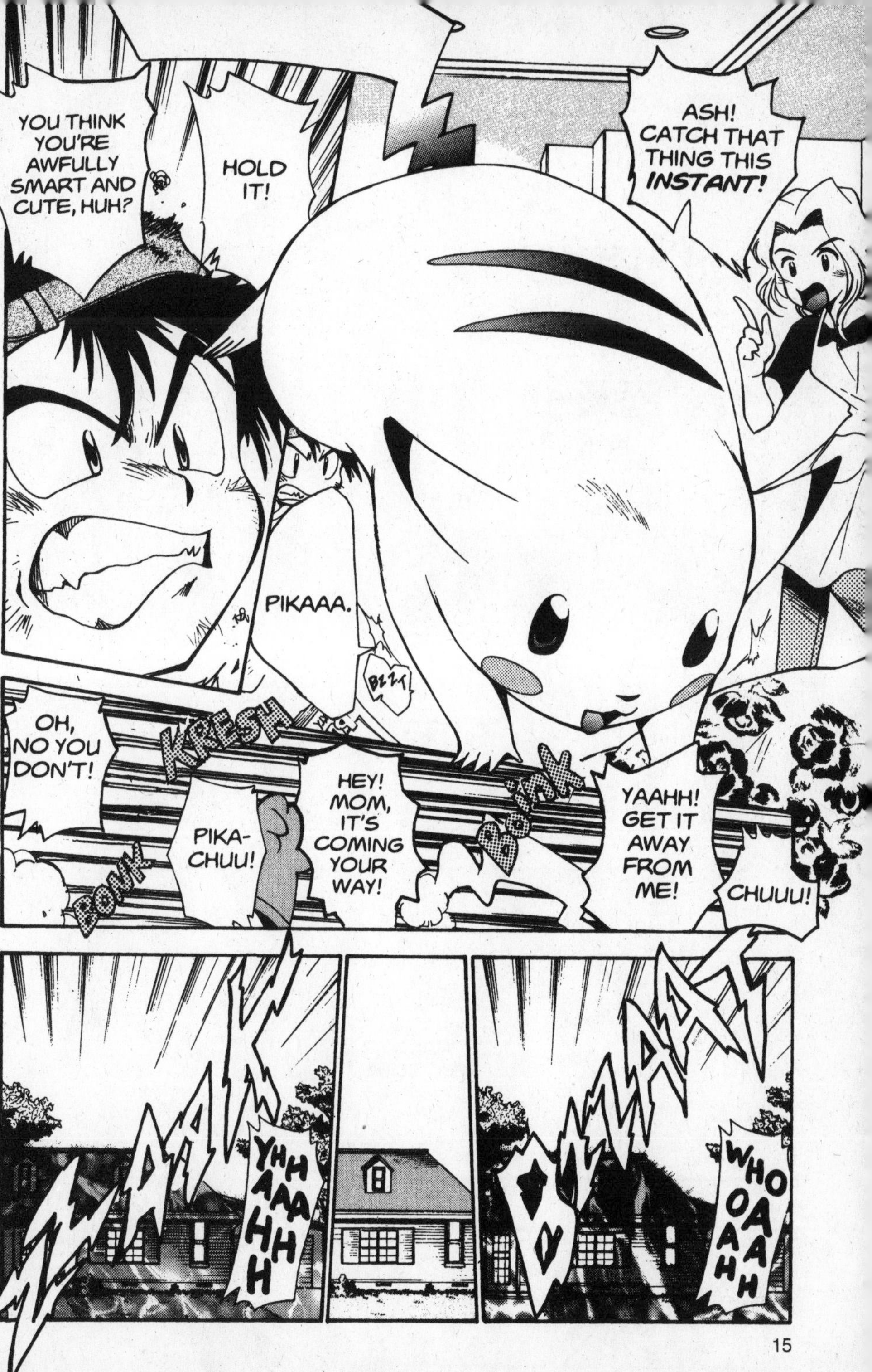
YOU THINK YOU'RE AWFULLY SMART AND CUTE, HUH?
HOLD IT!
ASH! CATCH THAT THING THIS INSTANT!
PIKAAA.
OH, NO YOU DON'T!
KRESH
BONK
PIKA-CHUU!
HEY! MOM, IT'S COMING YOUR WAY!
YAAHH! GET IT AWAY FROM ME!
CHUUU!

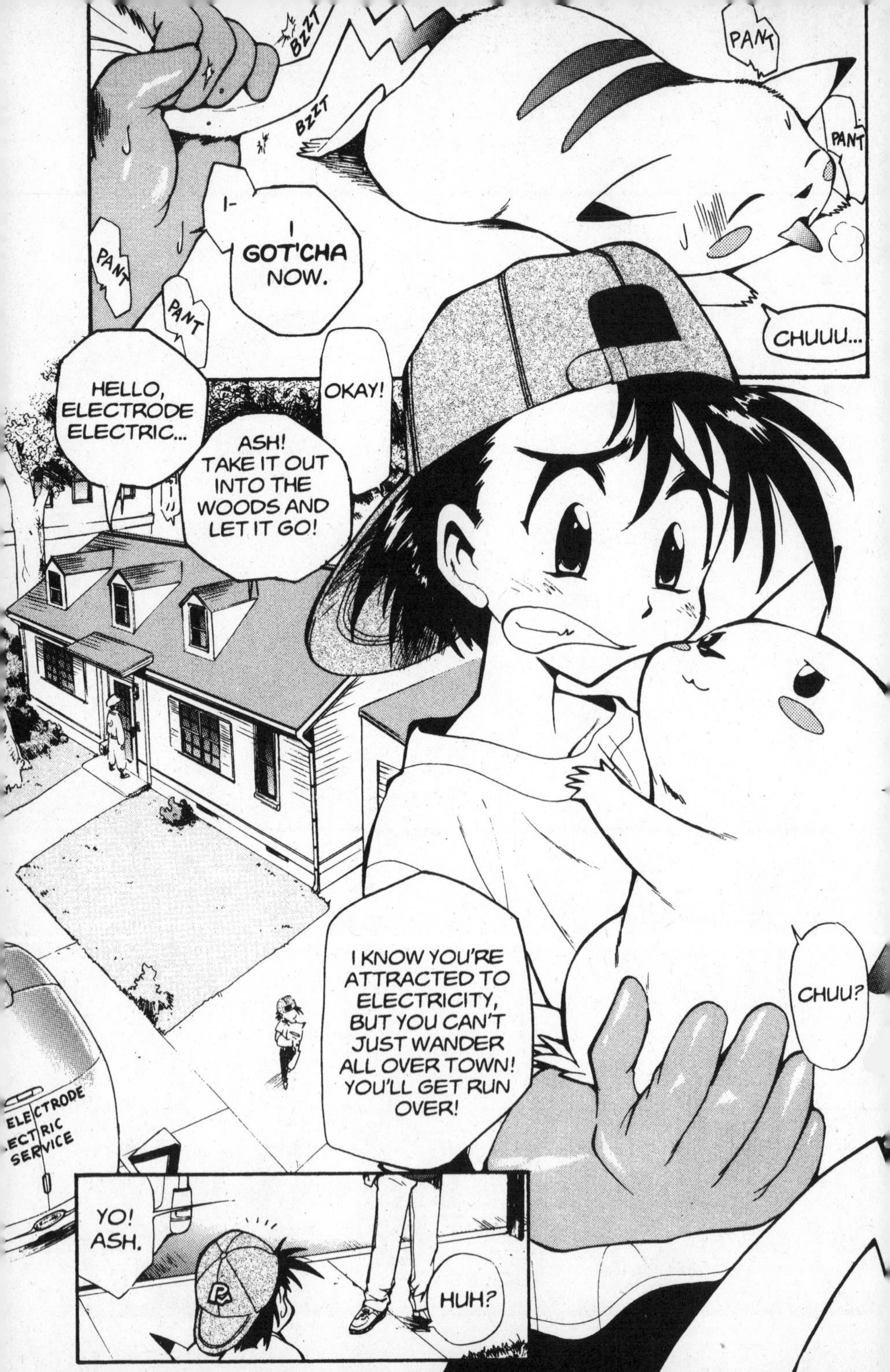
BZZT
BZZT
PANT
PANT
I-
I GOT'CHA NOW.
PANT
PANT
CHUUU...
HELLO, ELECTRODE ELECTRIC...
OKAY!
ASH! TAKE IT OUT INTO THE WOODS AND LET IT GO!
ELECTRODE
SERVICE
I KNOW YOU'RE ATTRACTED TO ELECTRICITY, BUT YOU CAN'T JUST WANDER ALL OVER TOWN! YOU'LL GET RUN OVER!
CHUU?
YO! ASH.
HUH?

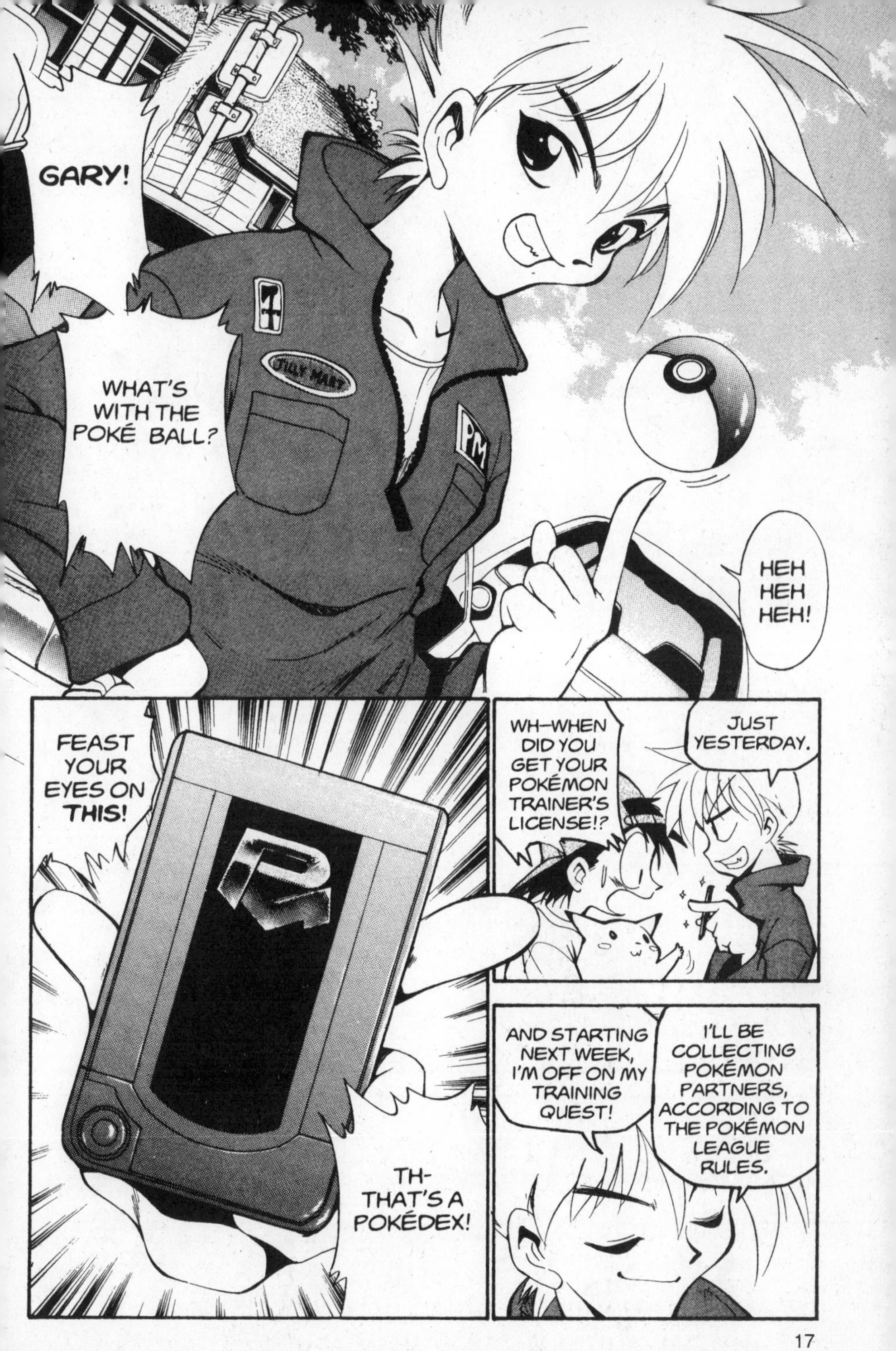
GARY!
WHAT'S WITH THE POKÉ BALL?
JILLY MART
PM
HEH HEH HEH!
FEAST YOUR EYES ON THIS!
TH- THAT'S A POKÉDEX!
WH-WHEN DID YOU GET YOUR POKÉMON TRAINER'S LICENSE!?
JUST YESTERDAY.
AND STARTING NEXT WEEK, I'M OFF ON MY TRAINING QUEST!
I'LL BE COLLECTING POKÉMON PARTNERS, ACCORDING TO THE POKÉMON LEAGUE RULES.

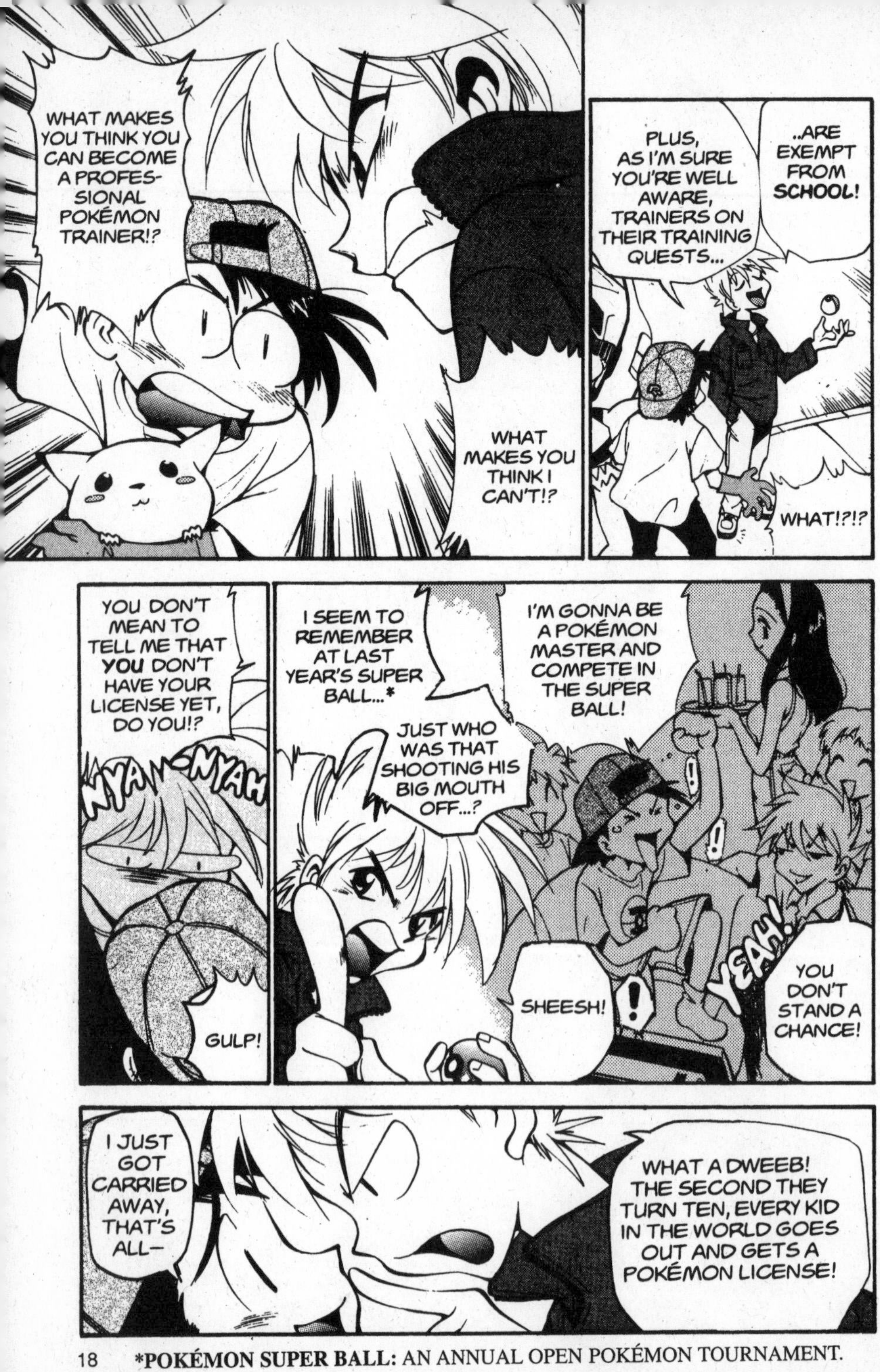
WHAT MAKES YOU THINK YOU CAN BECOME A PROFES-SIONAL POKÉMON TRAINER!?
WHAT MAKES YOU THINK I CAN'T!?
PLUS, AS I'M SURE YOU'RE WELL AWARE, TRAINERS ON THEIR TRAINING QUESTS...
..ARE EXEMPT FROM SCHOOL!
WHAT!?!?
YOU DON'T MEAN TO TELL ME THAT YOU DON'T HAVE YOUR LICENSE YET, DO YOU!?
NYA-NYAH
GULP!
I SEEM TO REMEMBER AT LAST YEAR'S SUPER BALL...*
JUST WHO WAS THAT SHOOTING HIS BIG MOUTH OFF...?
I'M GONNA BE A POKÉMON MASTER AND COMPETE IN THE SUPER BALL!
SHEESH!
YEAH!
YOU DON'T STAND A CHANCE!
I JUST GOT CARRIED AWAY, THAT'S ALL—
WHAT A DWEEB! THE SECOND THEY TURN TEN, EVERY KID IN THE WORLD GOES OUT AND GETS A POKÉMON LICENSE!

*POKÉMON SUPER BALL: AN ANNUAL OPEN POKÉMON TOURNAMENT.

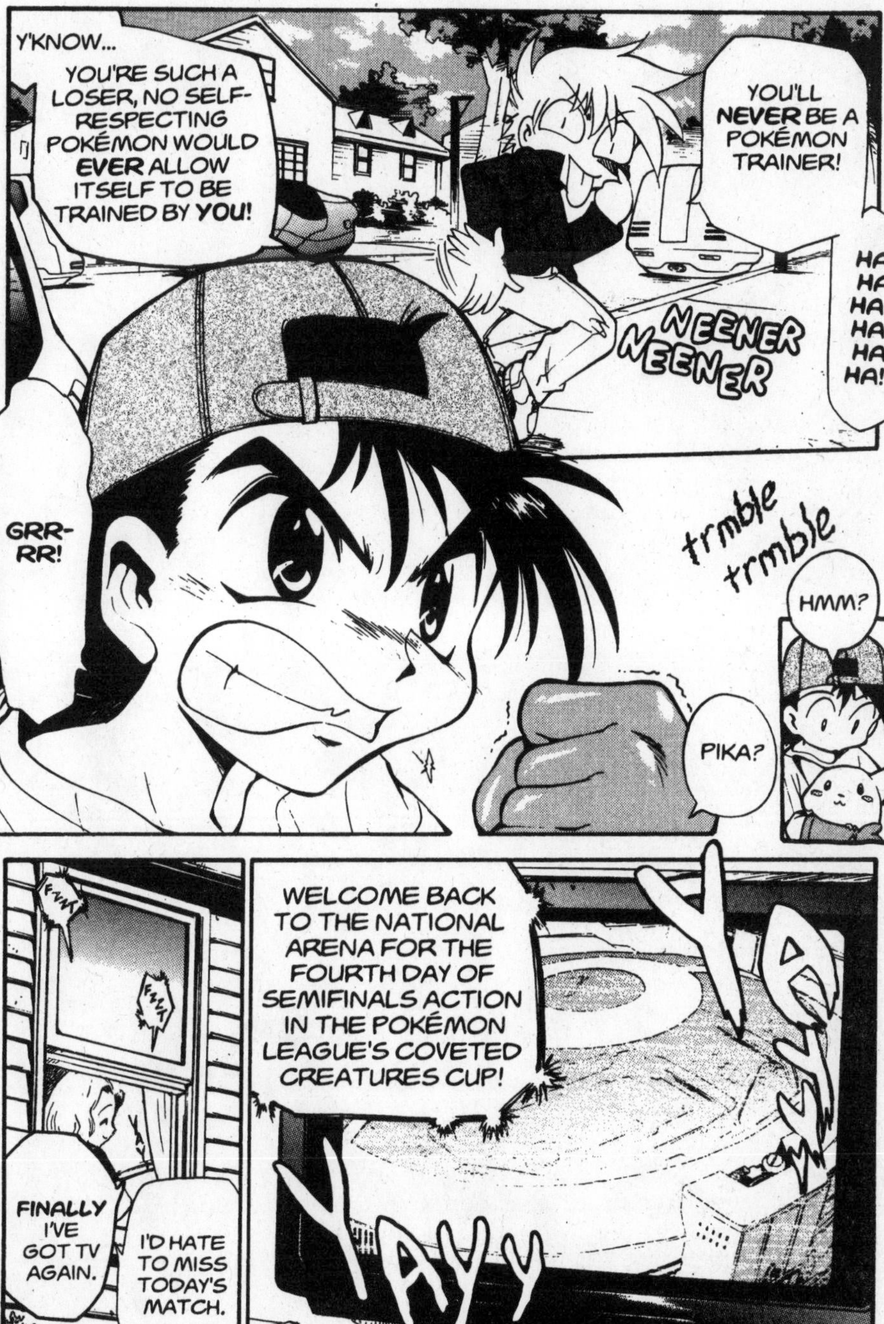
Y'KNOW...
YOU'RE SUCH A LOSER, NO SELF-RESPECTING POKÉMON WOULD EVER ALLOW ITSELF TO BE TRAINED BY YOU!
YOU'LL NEVER BE A POKÉMON TRAINER!
NEENER NEENER
HA HA HA HA HA HA!
GRR-RR!
trmble trmble
HMM?
PIKA?
F-Z-Z-T
FZZT
FINALLY I'VE GOT TV AGAIN.
I'D HATE TO MISS TODAY'S MATCH.
WELCOME BACK TO THE NATIONAL ARENA FOR THE FOURTH DAY OF SEMIFINALS ACTION IN THE POKÉMON LEAGUE'S COVETED CREATURES CUP!
YAYY
YAYY

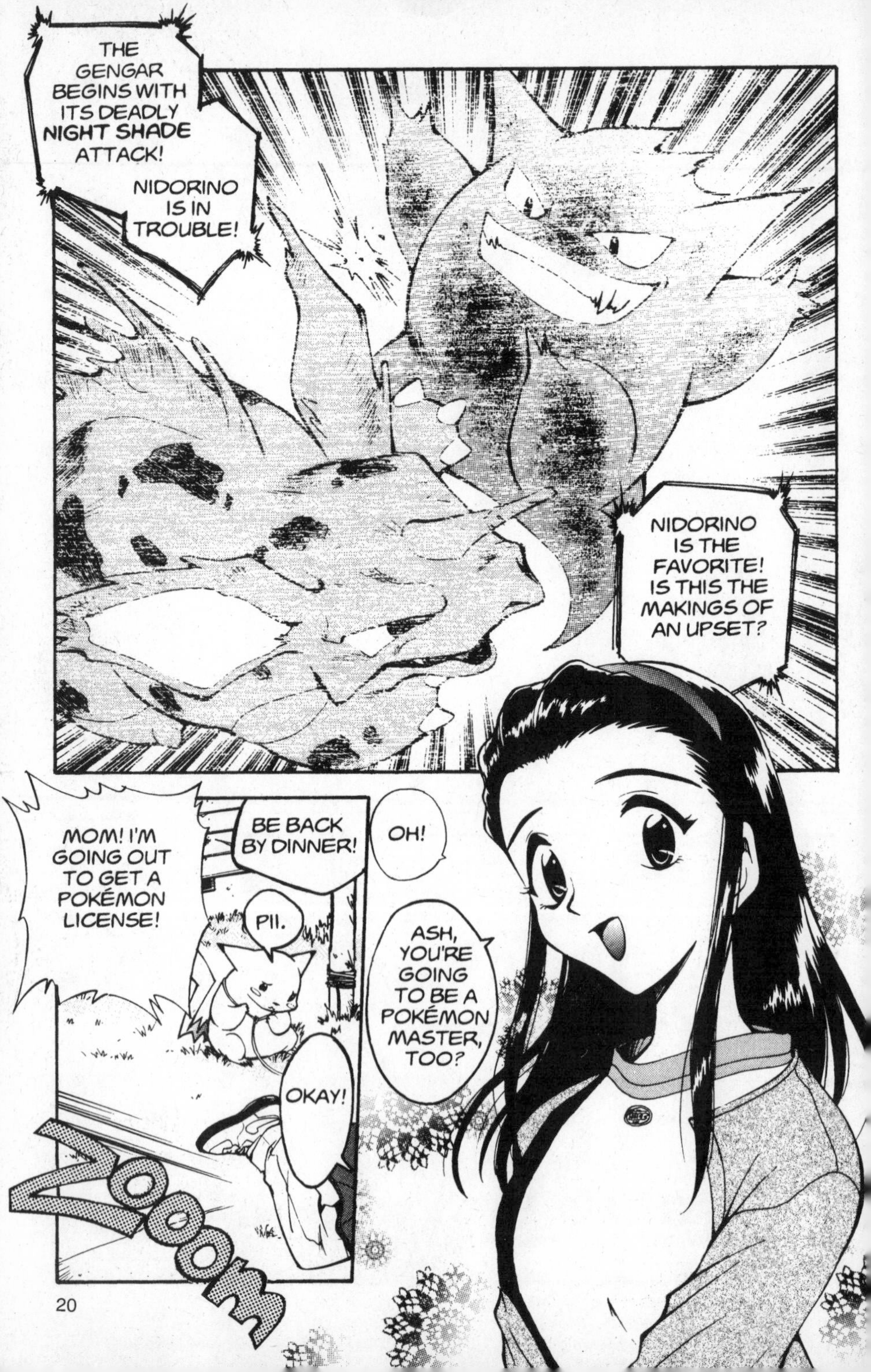
THE GENGAR BEGINS WITH ITS DEADLY NIGHT SHADE ATTACK!
NIDORINO IS IN TROUBLE!
NIDORINO IS THE FAVORITE! IS THIS THE MAKINGS OF AN UPSET?
MOM! I'M GOING OUT TO GET A POKÉMON LICENSE!
BE BACK BY DINNER!
PII.
OKAY!
VOOOOM
OH!
ASH, YOU'RE GOING TO BE A POKÉMON MASTER, TOO?

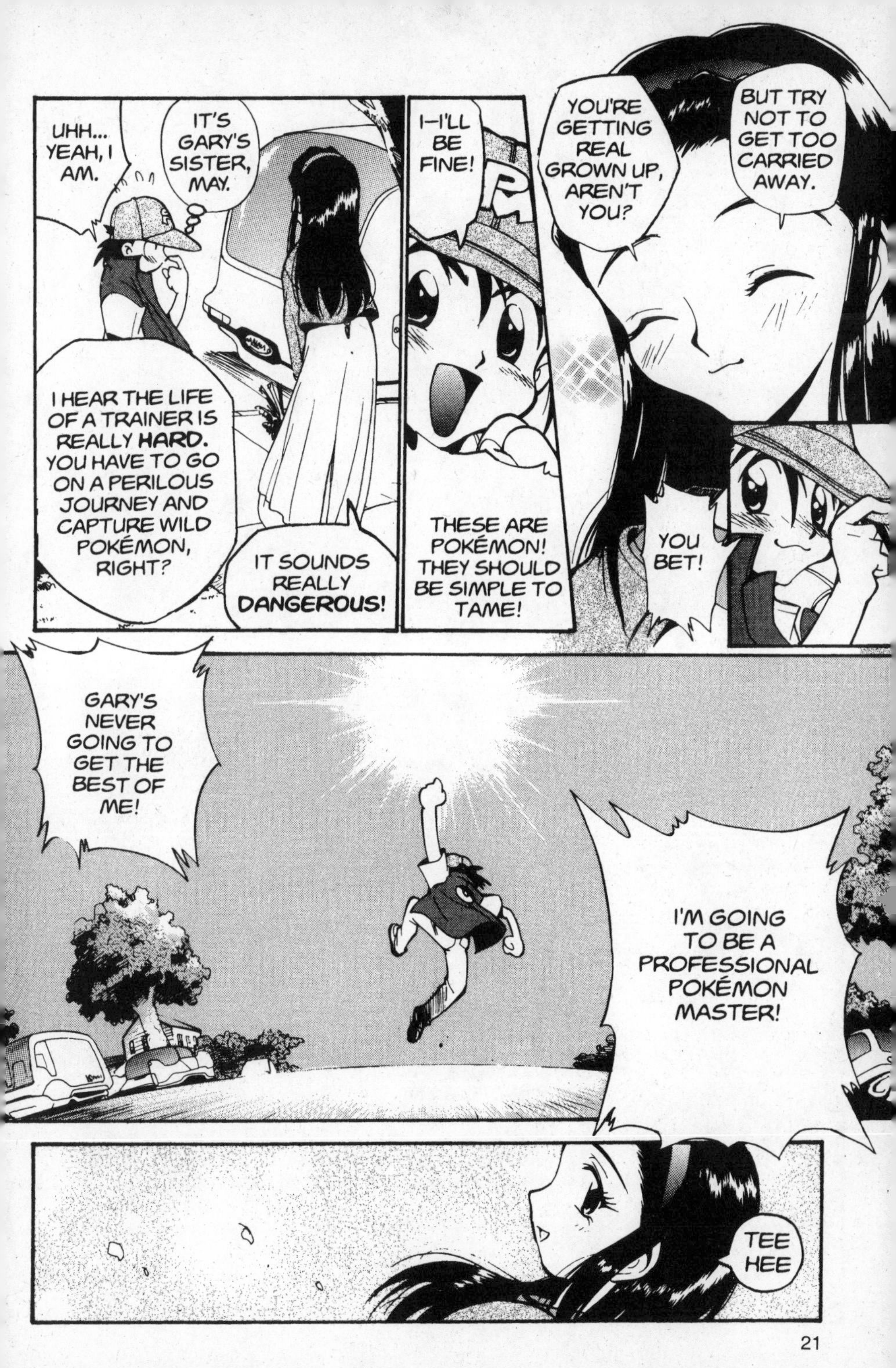

UHH... YEAH, I AM.
IT'S GARY'S SISTER, MAY.
I HEAR THE LIFE OF A TRAINER IS REALLY **HARD.** YOU HAVE TO GO ON A PERILOUS JOURNEY AND CAPTURE WILD POKÉMON, RIGHT?
IT SOUNDS REALLY **DANGEROUS!**
I-I'LL BE FINE!
THESE ARE POKÉMON! THEY SHOULD BE SIMPLE TO TAME!
YOU'RE GETTING REAL GROWN UP, AREN'T YOU?
BUT TRY NOT TO GET TOO CARRIED AWAY.
YOU BET!
GARY'S NEVER GOING TO GET THE BEST OF ME!
I'M GOING TO BE A PROFESSIONAL POKÉMON MASTER!
TEE HEE

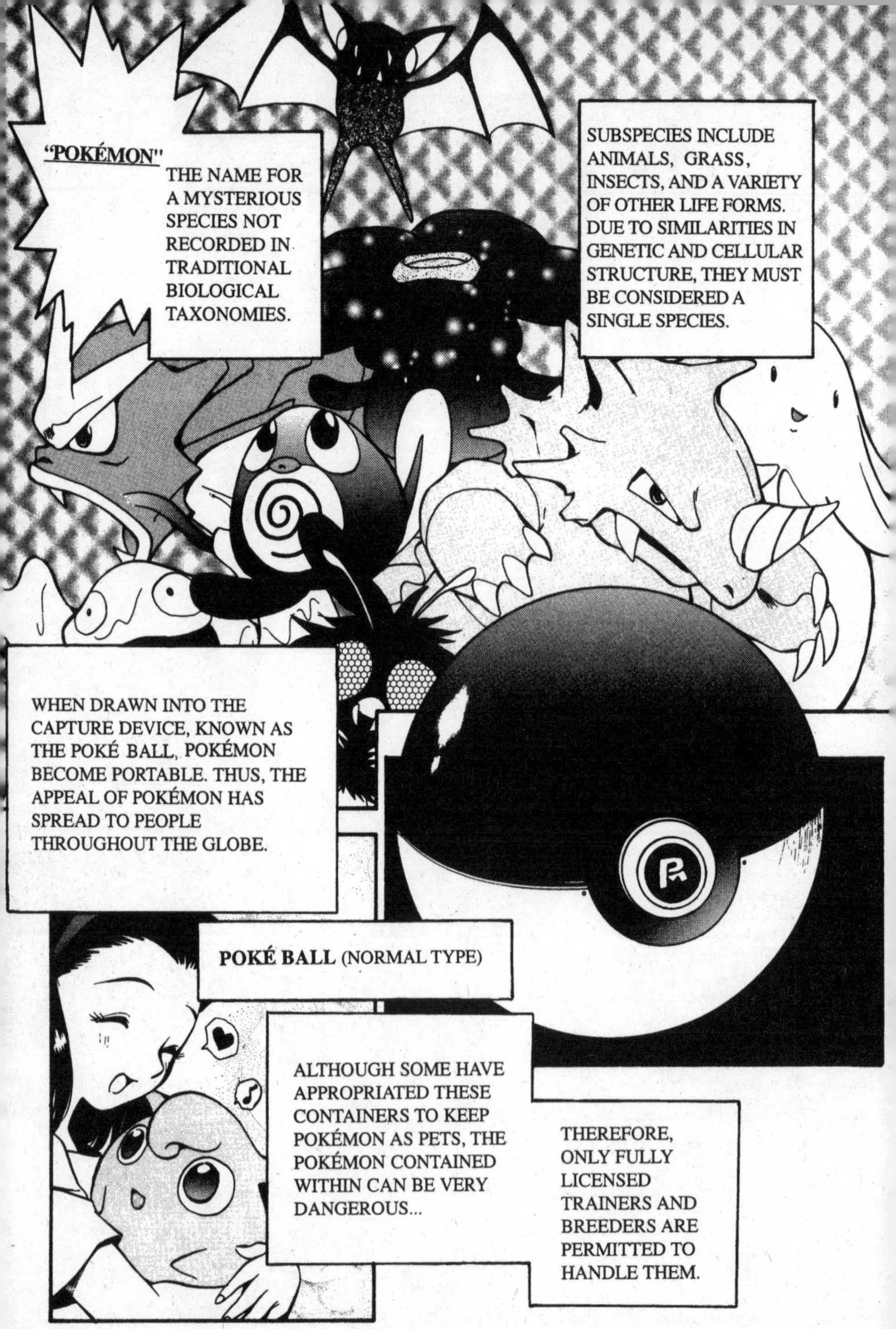
"POKÉMON"
THE NAME FOR A MYSTERIOUS SPECIES NOT RECORDED IN TRADITIONAL BIOLOGICAL TAXONOMIES.
SUBSPECIES INCLUDE ANIMALS, GRASS, INSECTS, AND A VARIETY OF OTHER LIFE FORMS. DUE TO SIMILARITIES IN GENETIC AND CELLULAR STRUCTURE, THEY MUST BE CONSIDERED A SINGLE SPECIES.
WHEN DRAWN INTO THE CAPTURE DEVICE, KNOWN AS THE POKÉ BALL, POKÉMON BECOME PORTABLE. THUS, THE APPEAL OF POKÉMON HAS SPREAD TO PEOPLE THROUGHOUT THE GLOBE.
POKÉ BALL (NORMAL TYPE)
ALTHOUGH SOME HAVE APPROPRIATED THESE CONTAINERS TO KEEP POKÉMON AS PETS, THE POKÉMON CONTAINED WITHIN CAN BE VERY DANGEROUS...
THEREFORE, ONLY FULLY LICENSED TRAINERS AND BREEDERS ARE PERMITTED TO HANDLE THEM.

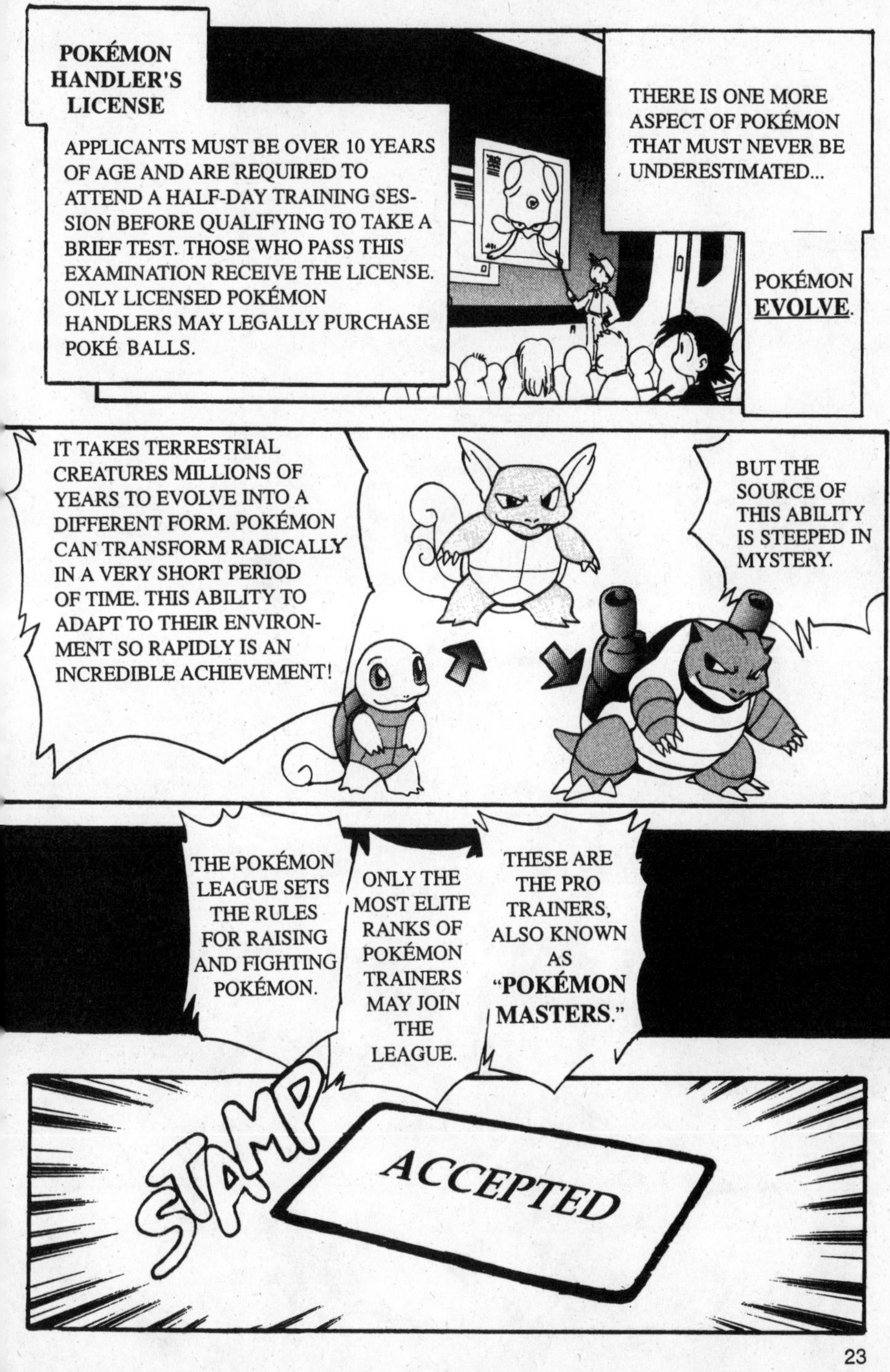

POKÉMON HANDLER'S LICENSE
APPLICANTS MUST BE OVER 10 YEARS OF AGE AND ARE REQUIRED TO ATTEND A HALF-DAY TRAINING SESSION BEFORE QUALIFYING TO TAKE A BRIEF TEST. THOSE WHO PASS THIS EXAMINATION RECEIVE THE LICENSE. ONLY LICENSED POKÉMON HANDLERS MAY LEGALLY PURCHASE POKÉ BALLS.
THERE IS ONE MORE ASPECT OF POKÉMON THAT MUST NEVER BE UNDERESTIMATED...
POKÉMON EVOLVE.
IT TAKES TERRESTRIAL CREATURES MILLIONS OF YEARS TO EVOLVE INTO A DIFFERENT FORM. POKÉMON CAN TRANSFORM RADICALLY IN A VERY SHORT PERIOD OF TIME. THIS ABILITY TO ADAPT TO THEIR ENVIRONMENT SO RAPIDLY IS AN INCREDIBLE ACHIEVEMENT!
BUT THE SOURCE OF THIS ABILITY IS STEEPED IN MYSTERY.
THE POKÉMON LEAGUE SETS THE RULES FOR RAISING AND FIGHTING POKÉMON.
ONLY THE MOST ELITE RANKS OF POKÉMON TRAINERS MAY JOIN THE LEAGUE.
THESE ARE THE PRO TRAINERS, ALSO KNOWN AS "POKÉMON MASTERS."
STAMP
ACCEPTED

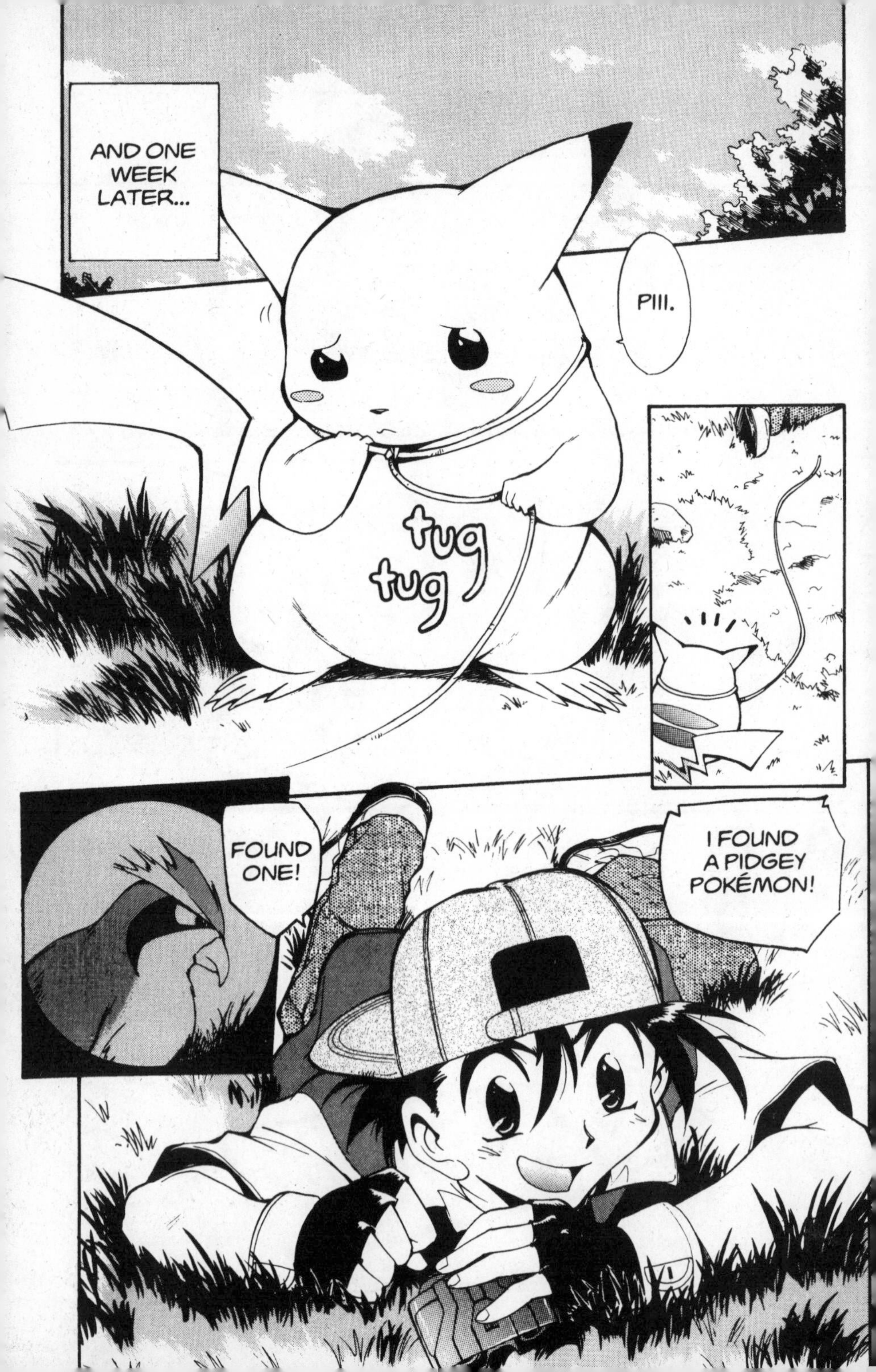
AND ONE WEEK LATER...
PIII.
tug tug
FOUND ONE!
I FOUND A PIDGEY POKÉMON!

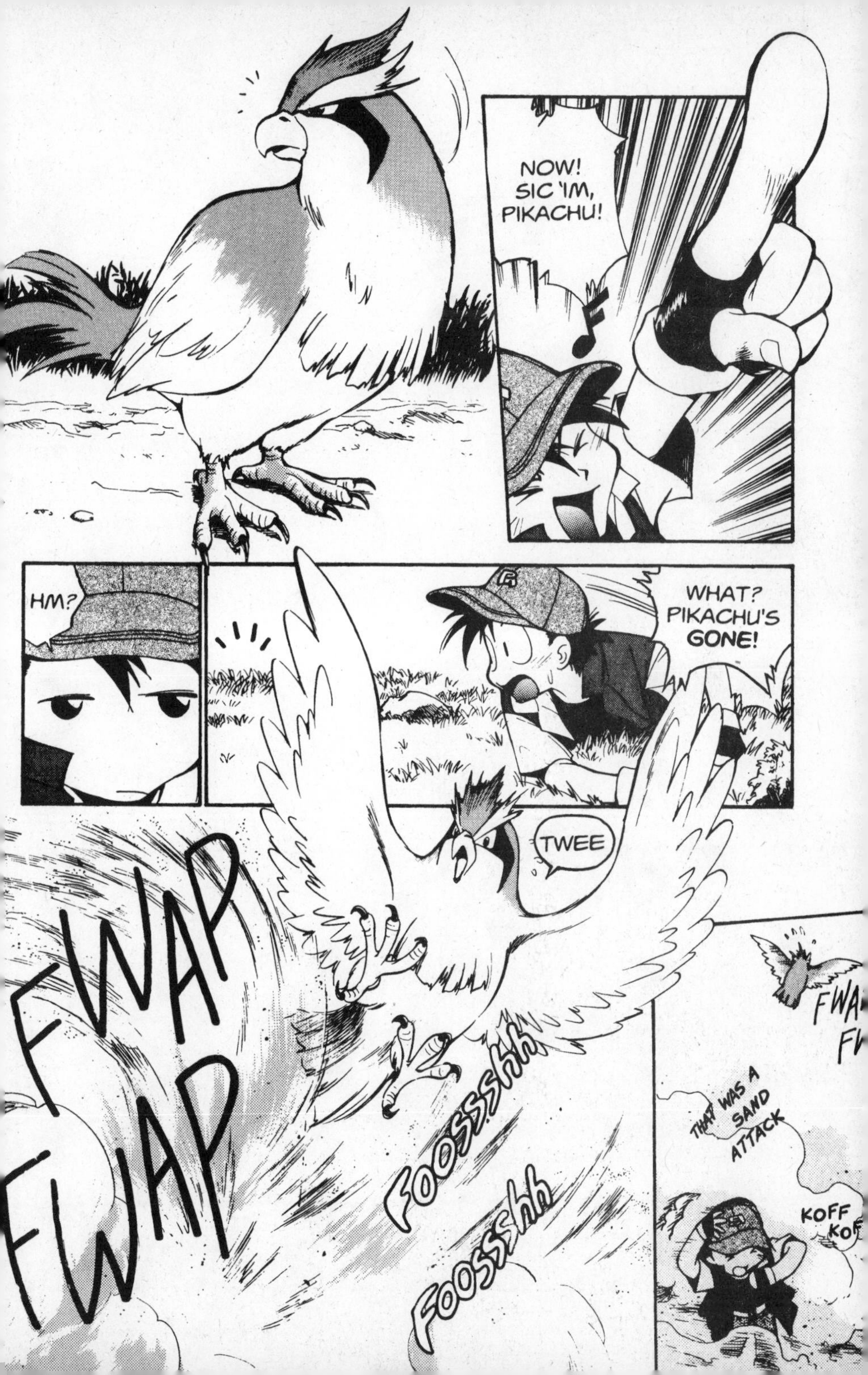
NOW! SIC 'IM, PIKACHU!
HM?
WHAT? PIKACHU'S GONE!
TWEE
FWAP
FWAP
FOOSSSHH
FOOSSSHH
THAT WAS A SAND ATTACK
KOFF KOF

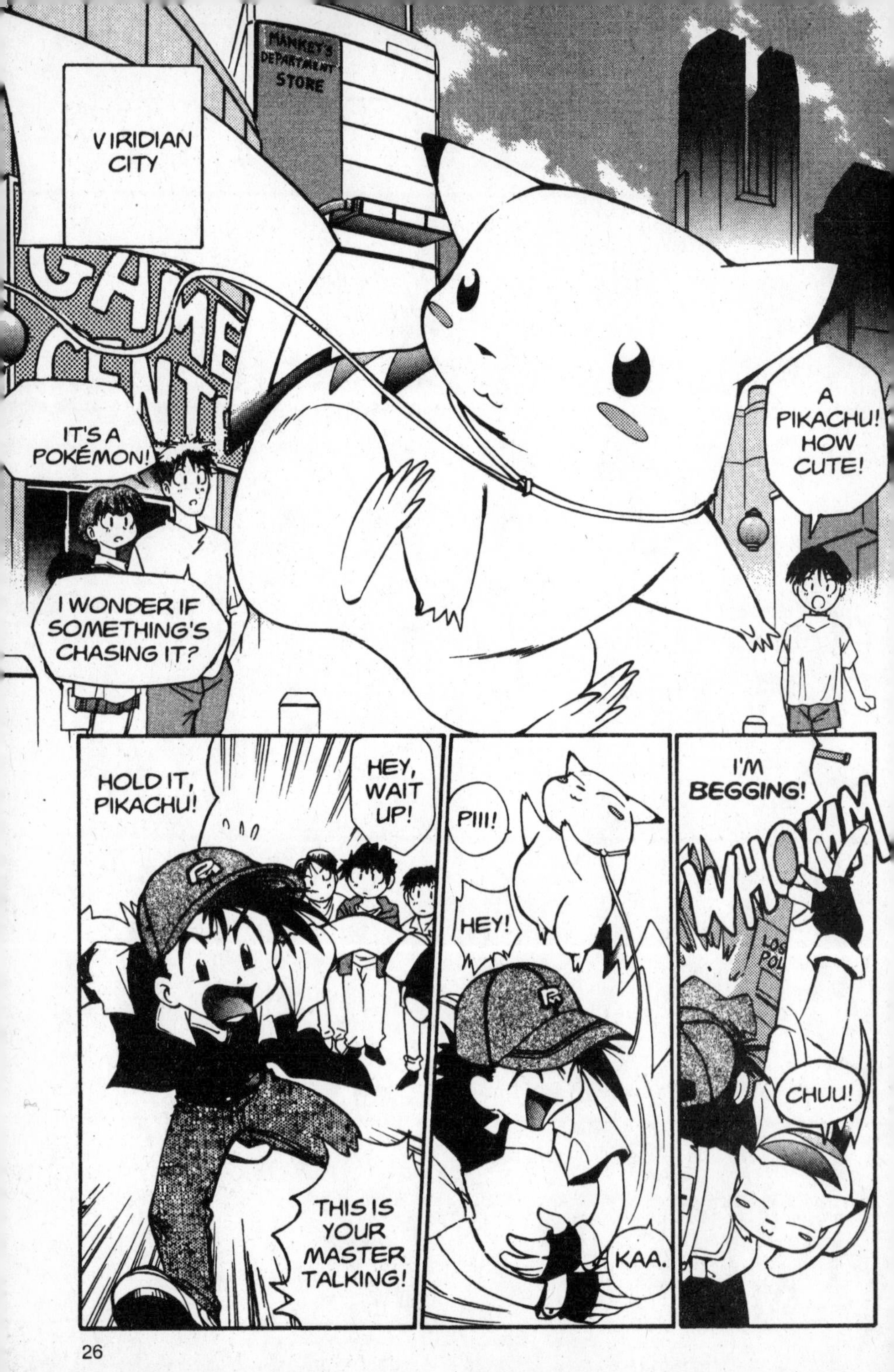
MANKEY'S DEPARTMENT STORE
VIRIDIAN CITY
IT'S A POKÉMON!
I WONDER IF SOMETHING'S CHASING IT?
A PIKACHU! HOW CUTE!
HOLD IT, PIKACHU!
HEY, WAIT UP!
THIS IS YOUR MASTER TALKING!
PIII!
HEY!
KAA.
I'M BEGGING!
WHOMM
CHUU!

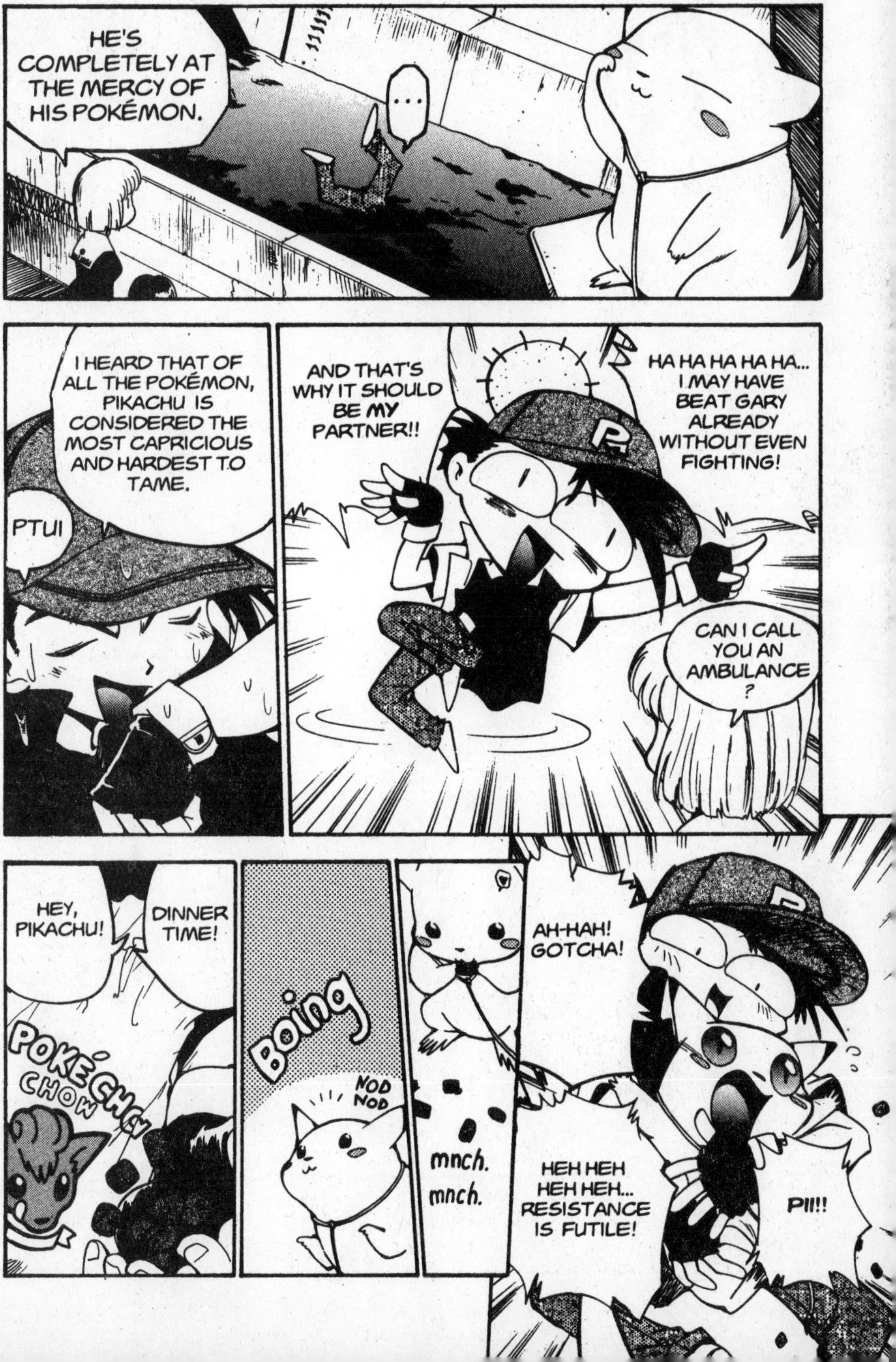
HE'S COMPLETELY AT THE MERCY OF HIS POKÉMON.
...
I HEARD THAT OF ALL THE POKÉMON, PIKACHU IS CONSIDERED THE MOST CAPRICIOUS AND HARDEST TO TAME.
PTUI
AND THAT'S WHY IT SHOULD BE MY PARTNER!!
HA HA HA HA HA... I MAY HAVE BEAT GARY ALREADY WITHOUT EVEN FIGHTING!
CAN I CALL YOU AN AMBULANCE ?
HEY, PIKACHU!
DINNER TIME!
POKÉ CHOW
POKÉ CHOW
BOING
NOD NOD
mnch.
mnch.
AH-HAH! GOTCHA!
HEH HEH HEH HEH... RESISTANCE IS FUTILE!
PII!!

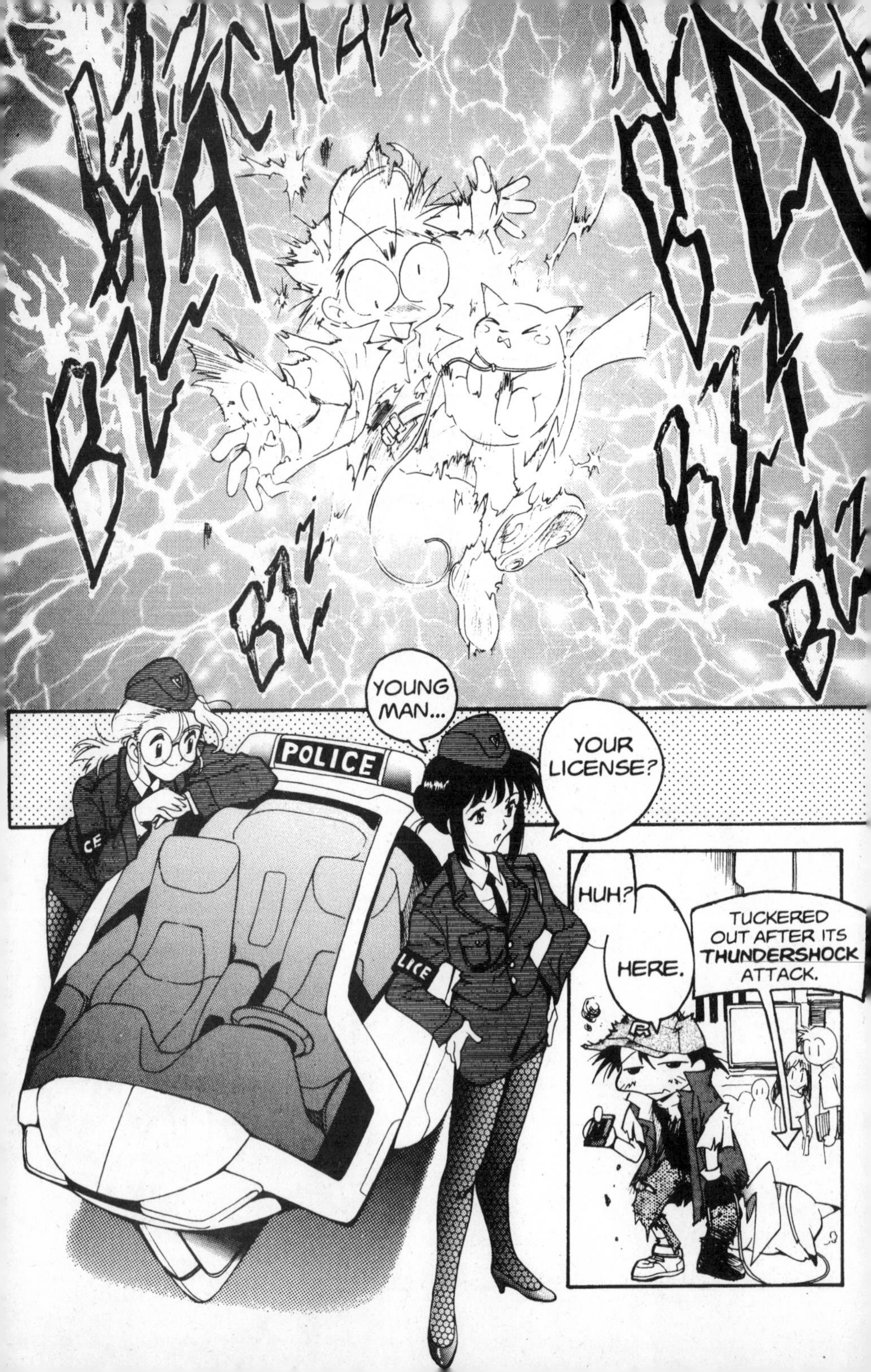
YOUNG MAN...
YOUR LICENSE?
HUH?
HERE.
TUCKERED OUT AFTER ITS **THUNDERSHOCK** ATTACK.

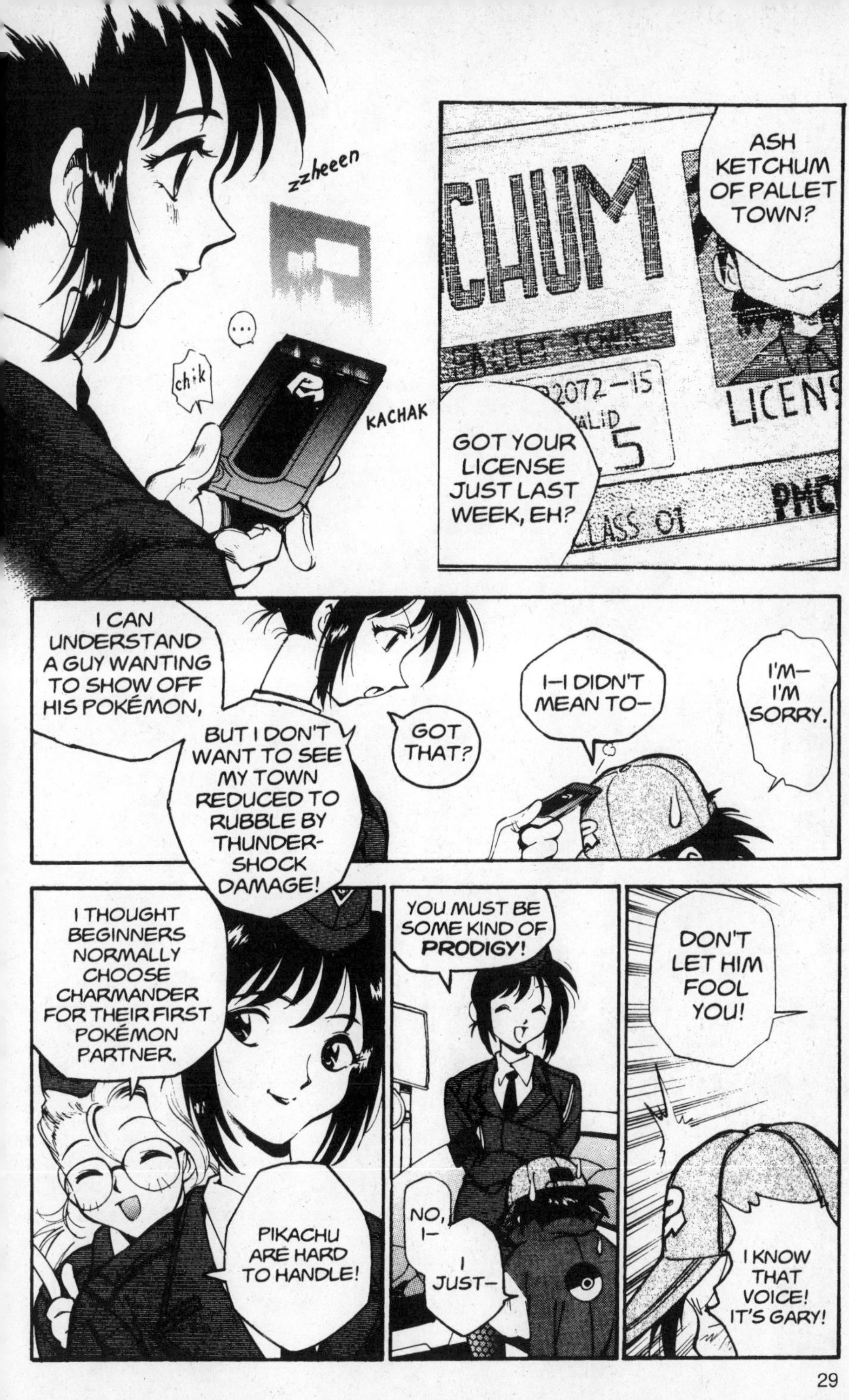

zzheeen
...
chik
KACHAK
ASH KETCHUM OF PALLET TOWN?
GOT YOUR LICENSE JUST LAST WEEK, EH?
I CAN UNDERSTAND A GUY WANTING TO SHOW OFF HIS POKÉMON,
BUT I DON'T WANT TO SEE MY TOWN REDUCED TO RUBBLE BY THUNDER-SHOCK DAMAGE!
GOT THAT?
I-I DIDN'T MEAN TO-
I'M- I'M SORRY.
I THOUGHT BEGINNERS NORMALLY CHOOSE CHARMANDER FOR THEIR FIRST POKÉMON PARTNER.
PIKACHU ARE HARD TO HANDLE!
YOU MUST BE SOME KIND OF **PRODIGY**!
NO, I-
I JUST-
DON'T LET HIM FOOL YOU!
I KNOW THAT VOICE! IT'S GARY!

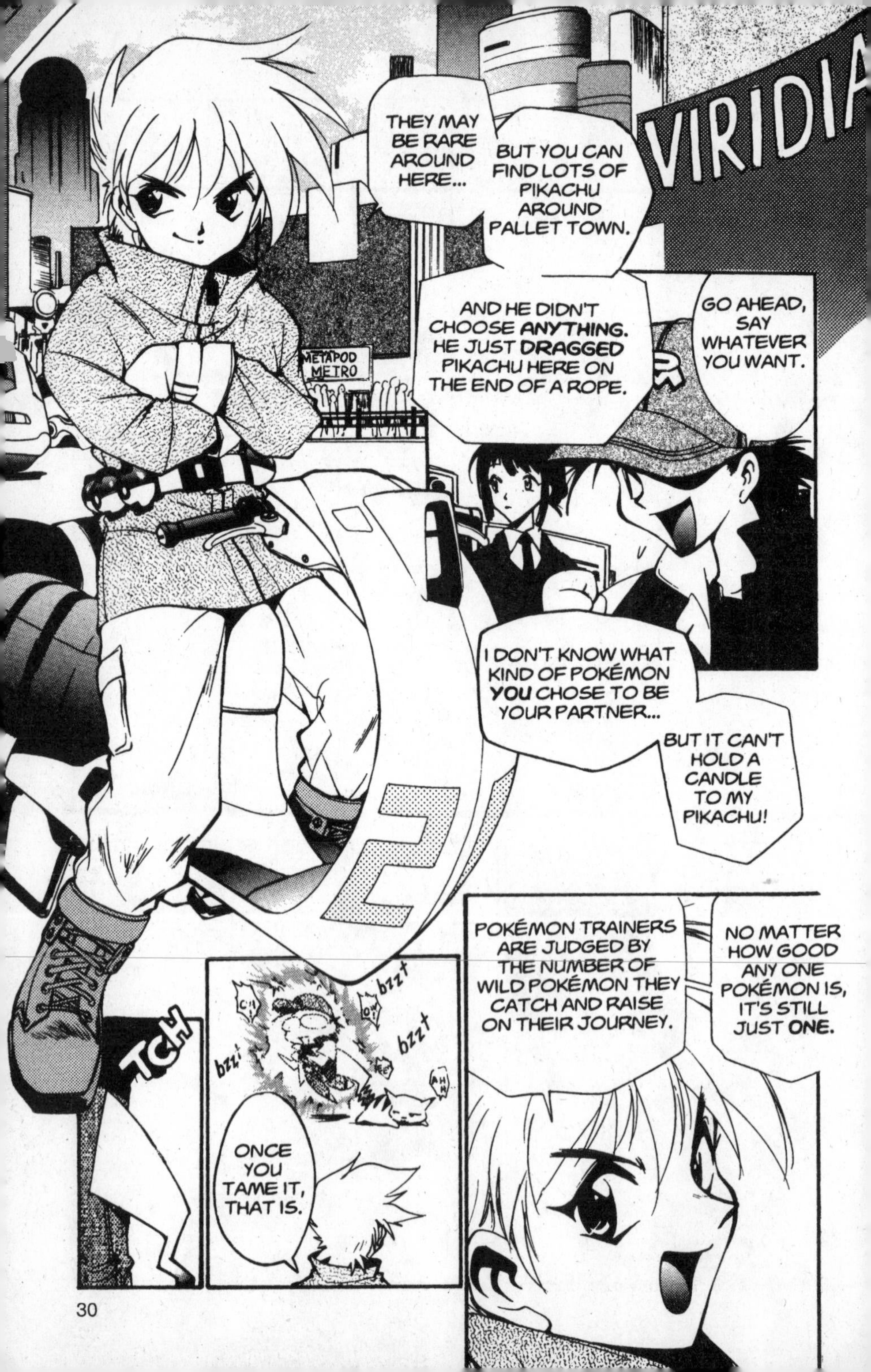
VIRIDIA
THEY MAY BE RARE AROUND HERE...
BUT YOU CAN FIND LOTS OF PIKACHU AROUND PALLET TOWN.
METAPOD METRO
AND HE DIDN'T CHOOSE **ANYTHING.** HE JUST **DRAGGED** PIKACHU HERE ON THE END OF A ROPE.
GO AHEAD, SAY WHATEVER YOU WANT.
I DON'T KNOW WHAT KIND OF POKÉMON **YOU** CHOSE TO BE YOUR PARTNER...
BUT IT CAN'T HOLD A CANDLE TO MY PIKACHU!
TCH
bzzt
bzzt
bzzt
ONCE YOU TAME IT, THAT IS.
POKÉMON TRAINERS ARE JUDGED BY THE NUMBER OF WILD POKÉMON THEY CATCH AND RAISE ON THEIR JOURNEY.
NO MATTER HOW GOOD ANY ONE POKÉMON IS, IT'S STILL JUST **ONE.**

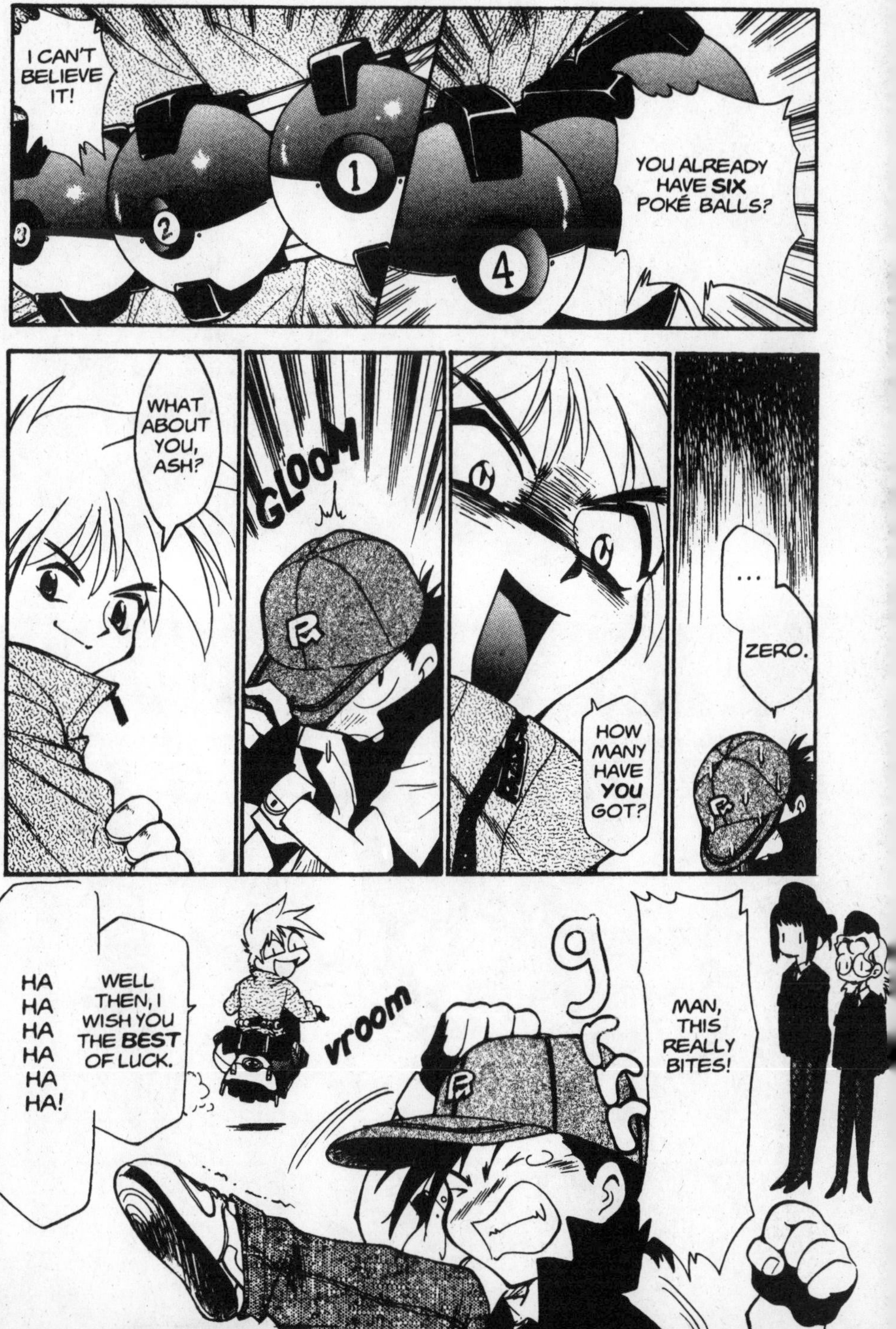
I CAN'T BELIEVE IT!
YOU ALREADY HAVE **SIX** POKÉ BALLS?
WHAT ABOUT YOU, ASH?
GLOOM
HOW MANY HAVE **YOU** GOT?
...
ZERO.
HA HA HA HA HA HA!
WELL THEN, I WISH YOU THE **BEST** OF LUCK.
vroom
MAN, THIS REALLY BITES!

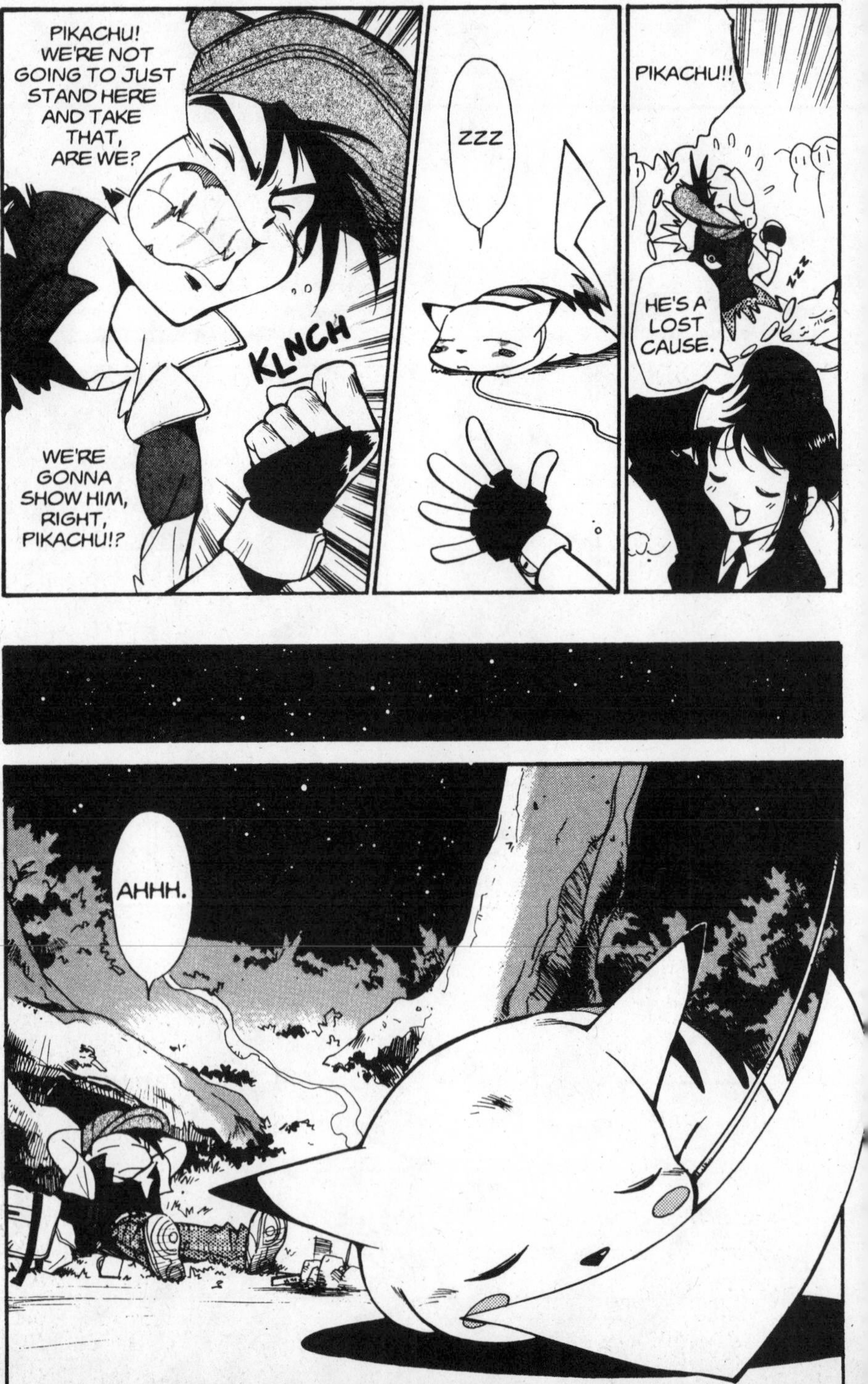
PIKACHU! WE'RE NOT GOING TO JUST STAND HERE AND TAKE THAT, ARE WE?
KLNCH
WE'RE GONNA SHOW HIM, RIGHT, PIKACHU!?
ZZZ
PIKACHU!!
ZZZ
HE'S A LOST CAUSE.
AHHH.

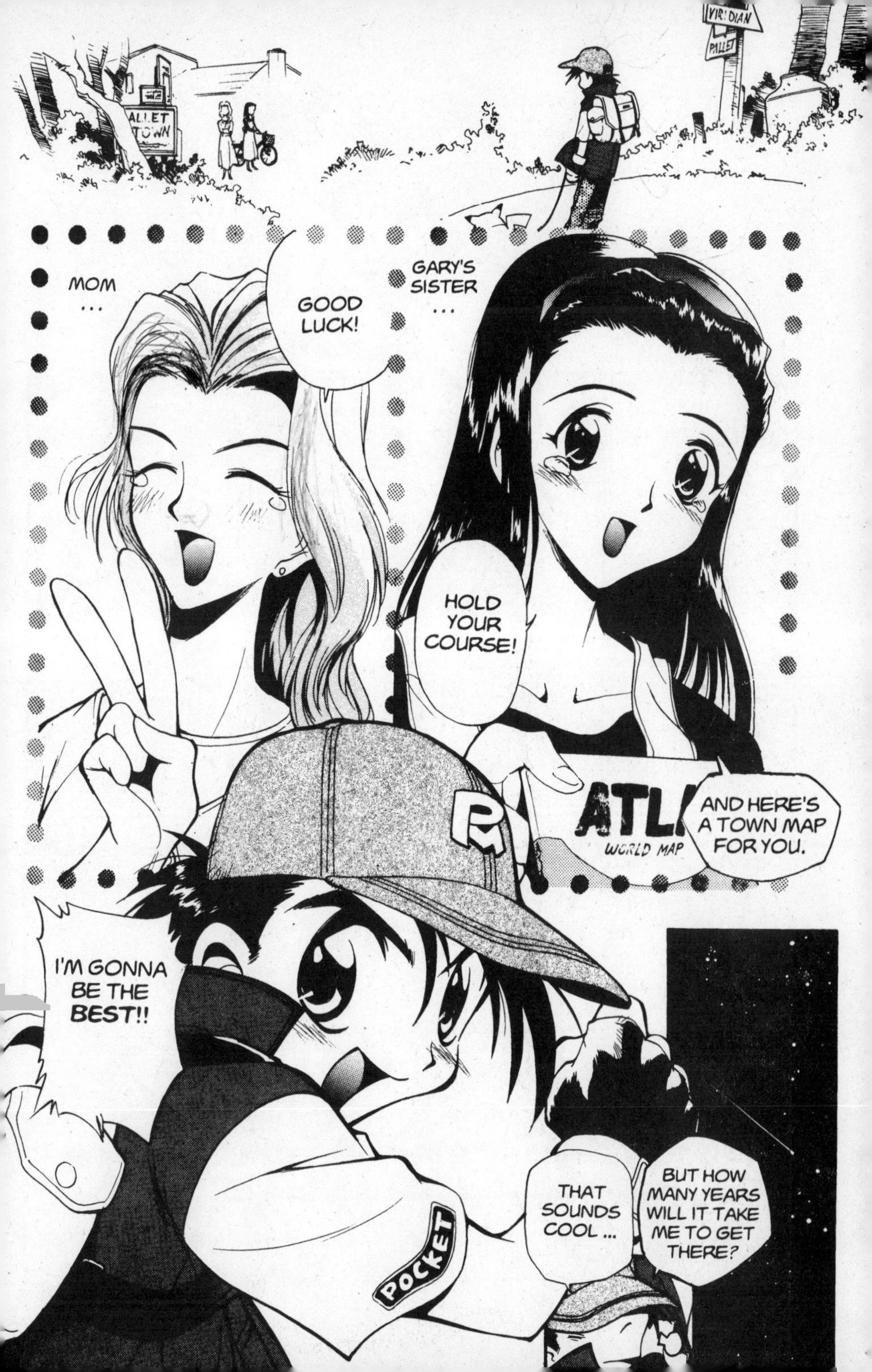
VIRIDIAN
PALLET
MOM ...
GOOD LUCK!
GARY'S SISTER ...
HOLD YOUR COURSE!
ATL
WORLD MAP
AND HERE'S A TOWN MAP FOR YOU.
I'M GONNA BE THE BEST!!
POCKET
THAT SOUNDS COOL ...
BUT HOW MANY YEARS WILL IT TAKE ME TO GET THERE?

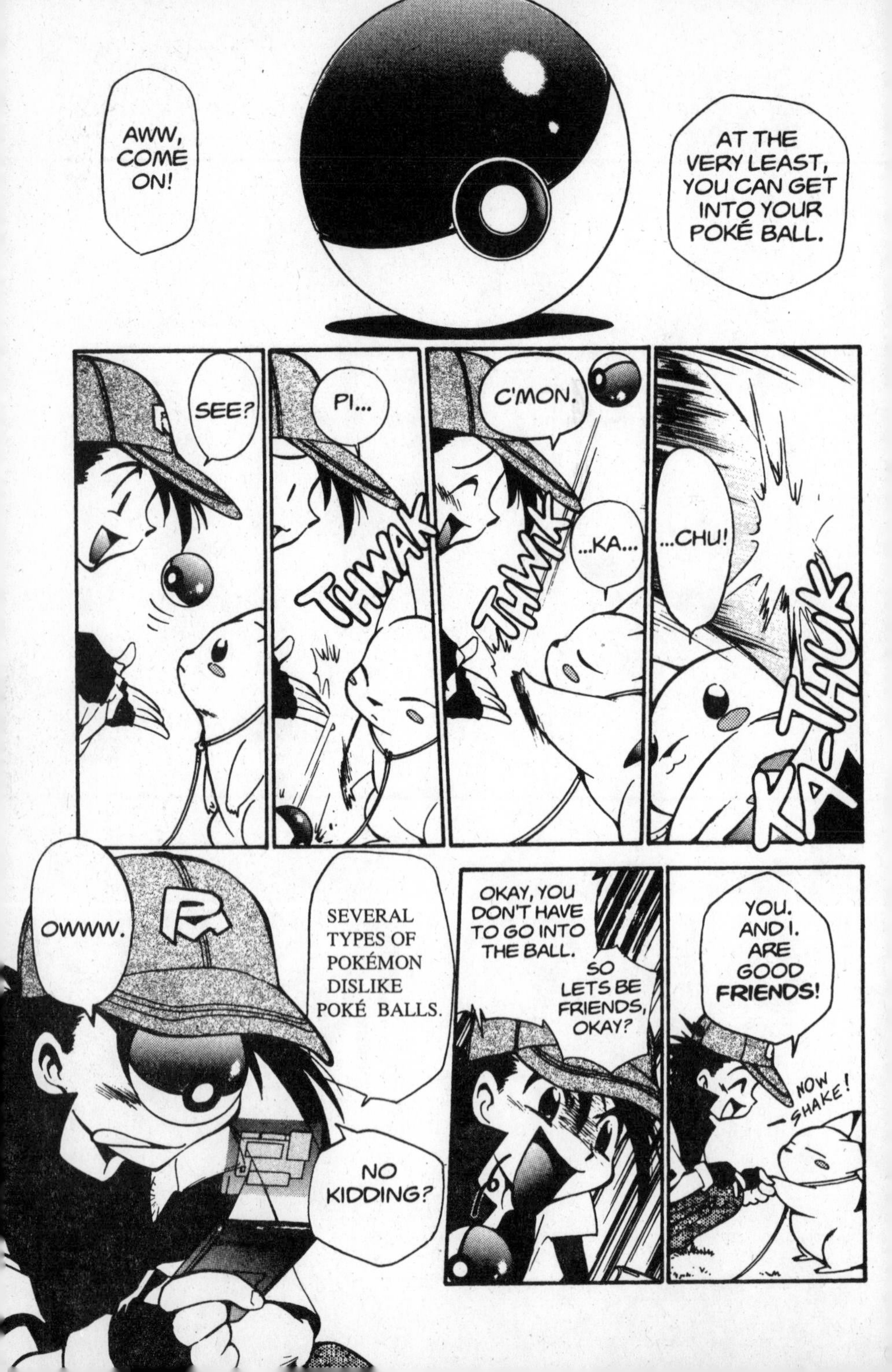
AWW, COME ON!
AT THE VERY LEAST, YOU CAN GET INTO YOUR POKÉ BALL.
SEE?
PI...
THWAK
C'MON.
THWAK
...KA...
...CHU!
KA-THUK
OWWW.
SEVERAL TYPES OF POKÉMON DISLIKE POKÉ BALLS.
NO KIDDING?
OKAY, YOU DON'T HAVE TO GO INTO THE BALL.
SO LETS BE FRIENDS, OKAY?
YOU. AND I. ARE GOOD FRIENDS!
NOW SHAKE!

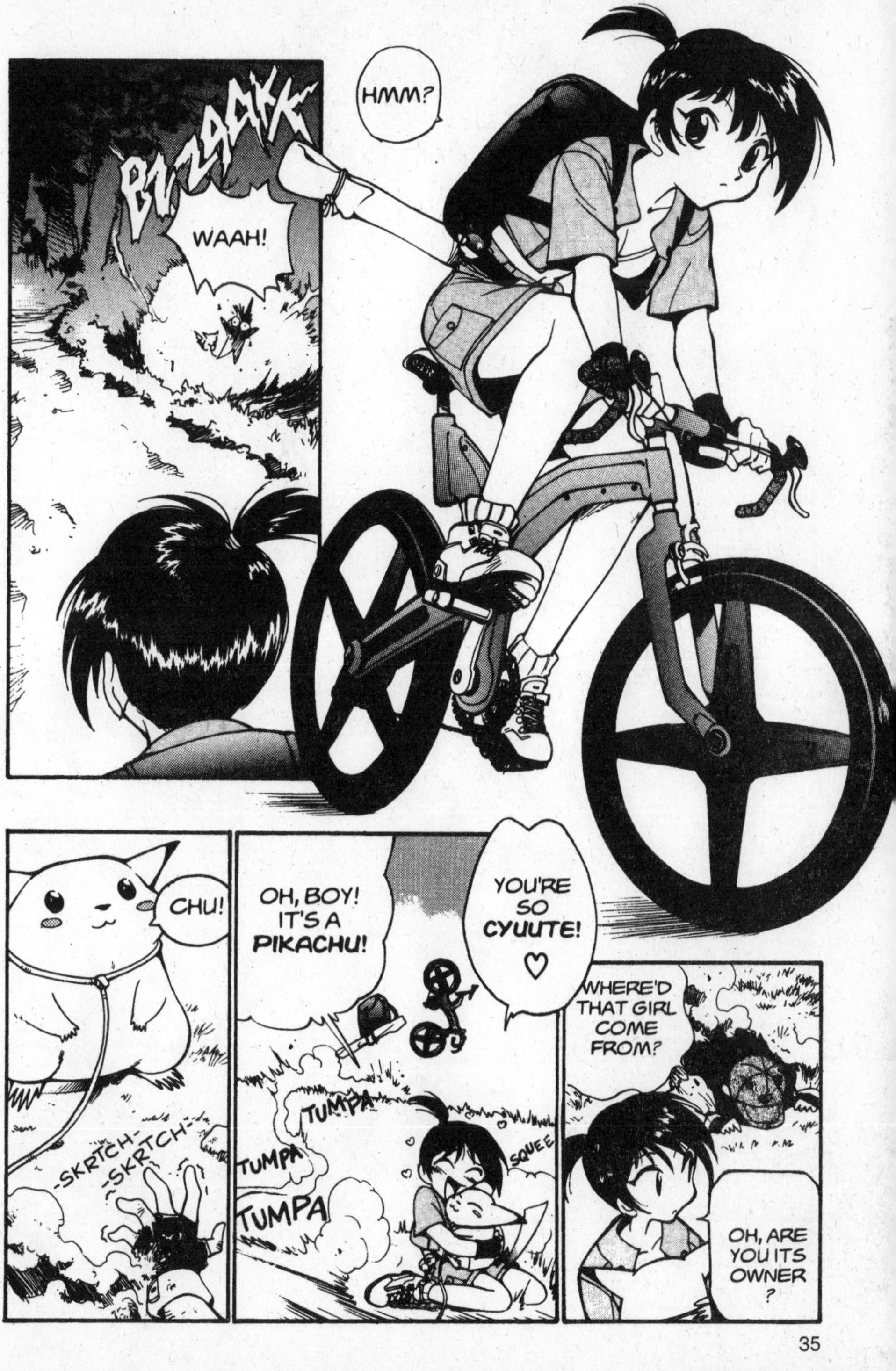
BRZAAK
WAAH!
HMM?
CHU!
-SKRTCH-
-SKRTCH-
OH, BOY! IT'S A PIKACHU!
YOU'RE SO CYUUTE! ♡
TUMPA
TUMPA
TUMPA
SQUEE
WHERE'D THAT GIRL COME FROM?
OH, ARE YOU ITS OWNER ?

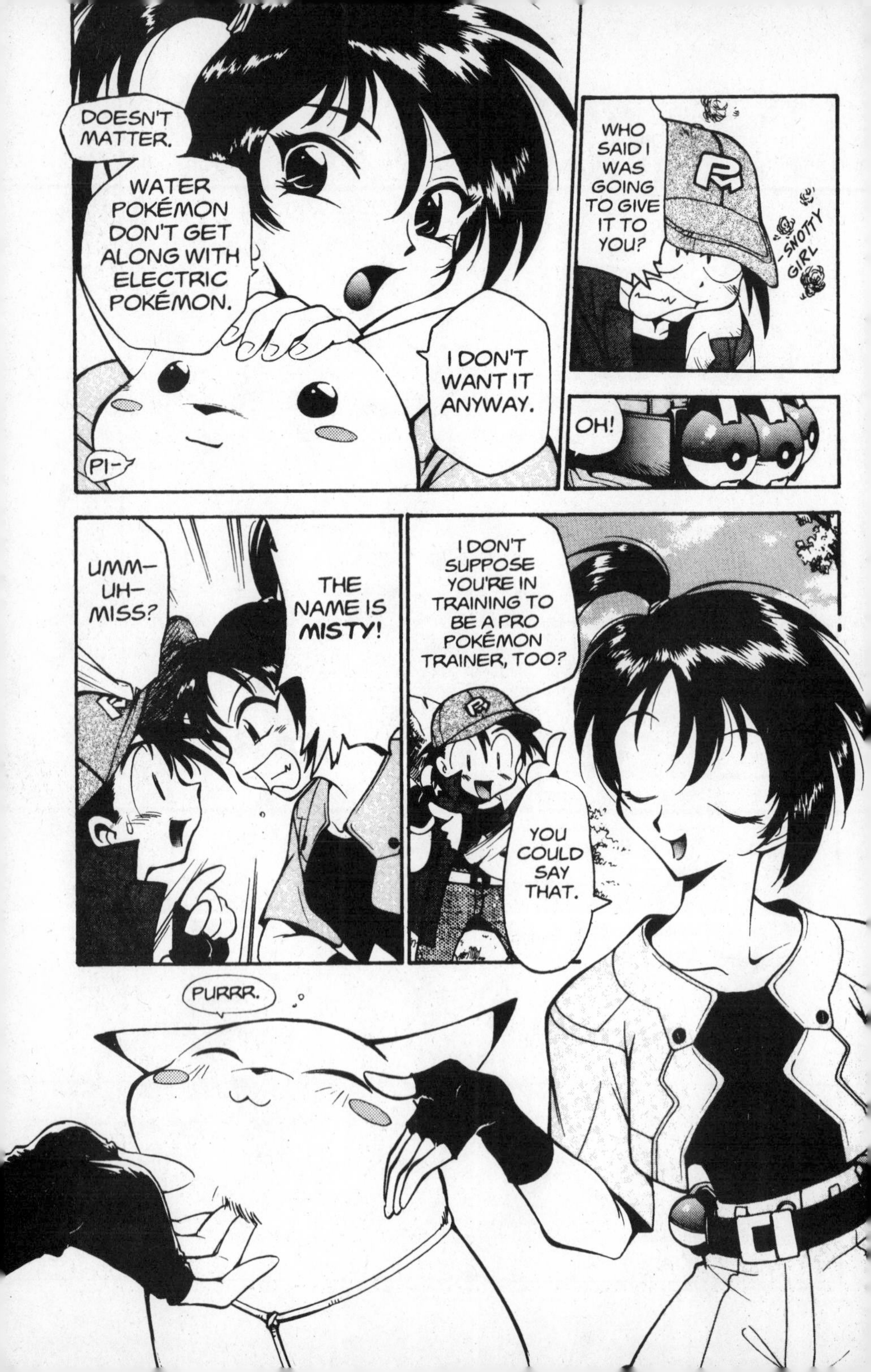
DOESN'T MATTER.
WATER POKÉMON DON'T GET ALONG WITH ELECTRIC POKÉMON.
I DON'T WANT IT ANYWAY.
PI-
WHO SAID I WAS GOING TO GIVE IT TO YOU?
-SNOTTY GIRL
OH!
UMM- UH- MISS?
THE NAME IS **MISTY**!
I DON'T SUPPOSE YOU'RE IN TRAINING TO BE A PRO POKÉMON TRAINER, TOO?
YOU COULD SAY THAT.
PURRR.

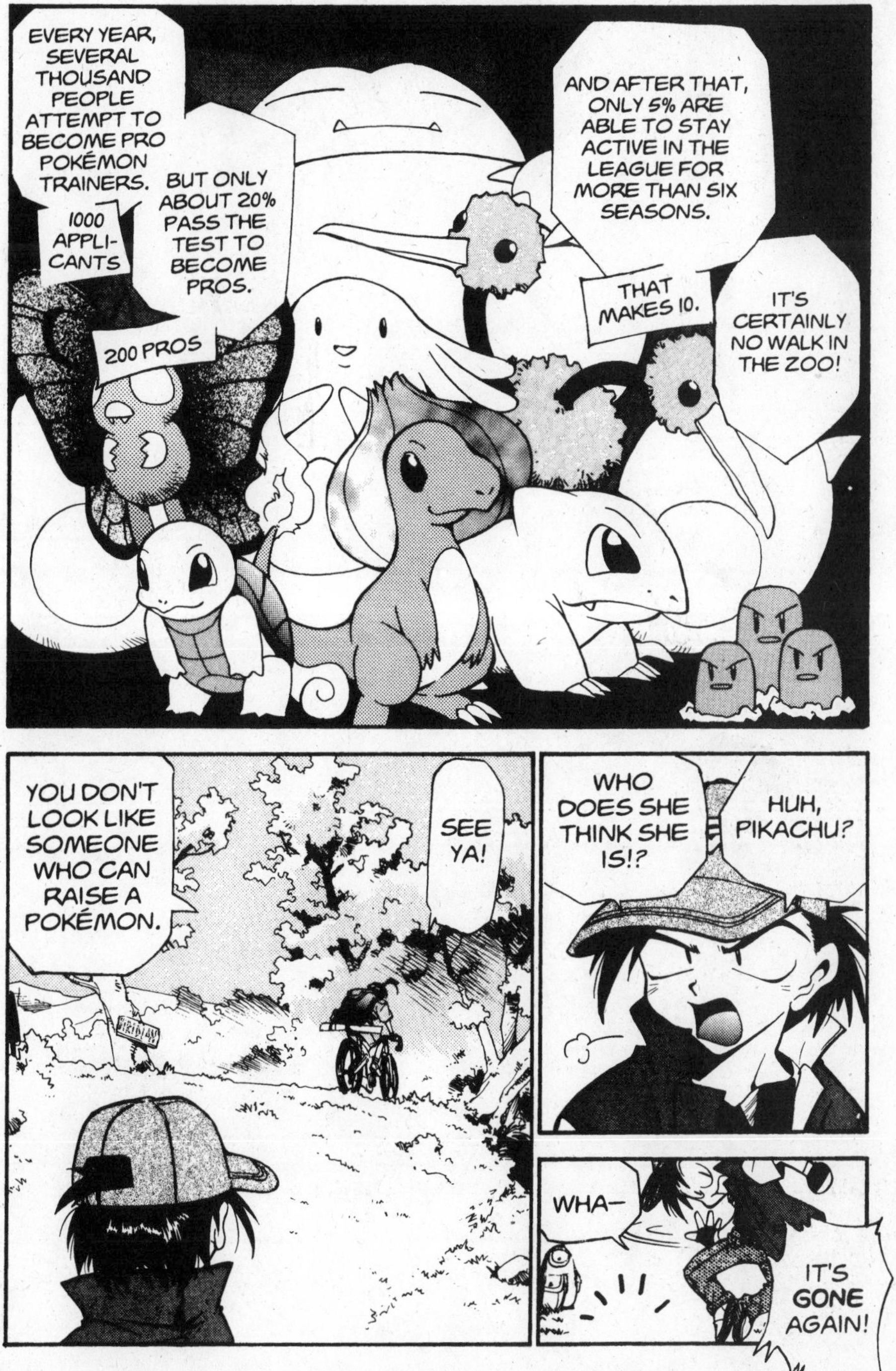
EVERY YEAR, SEVERAL THOUSAND PEOPLE ATTEMPT TO BECOME PRO POKÉMON TRAINERS.
1000 APPLI-CANTS
BUT ONLY ABOUT 20% PASS THE TEST TO BECOME PROS.
200 PROS
AND AFTER THAT, ONLY 5% ARE ABLE TO STAY ACTIVE IN THE LEAGUE FOR MORE THAN SIX SEASONS.
THAT MAKES 10.
IT'S CERTAINLY NO WALK IN THE ZOO!
YOU DON'T LOOK LIKE SOMEONE WHO CAN RAISE A POKÉMON.
SEE YA!
WHO DOES SHE THINK SHE IS!?
HUH, PIKACHU?
WHA-
IT'S GONE AGAIN!

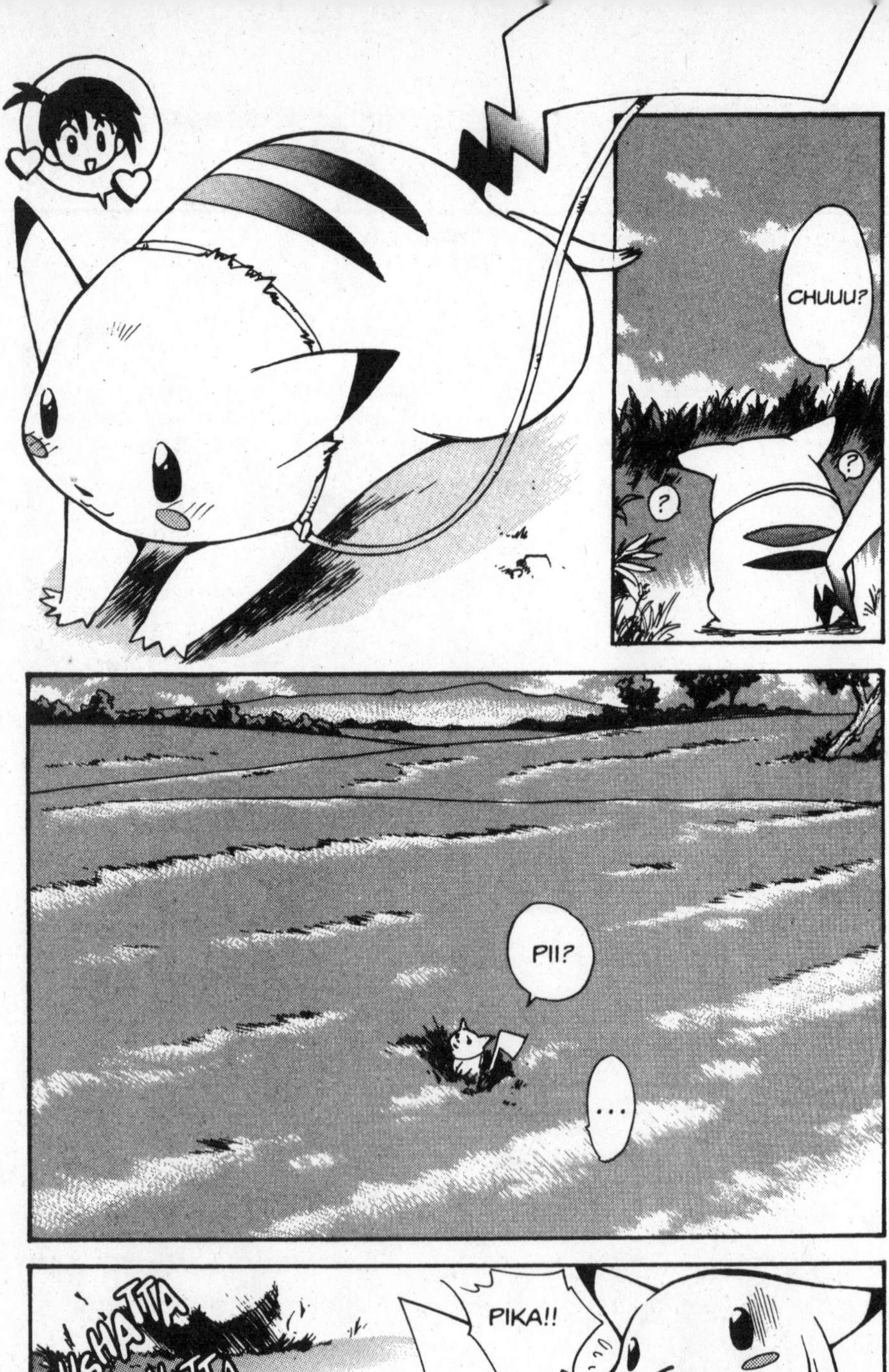

CHUUU?
PII?
...
KUSHATTA KUSHATTA
PIKA!!

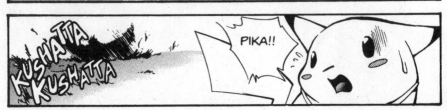

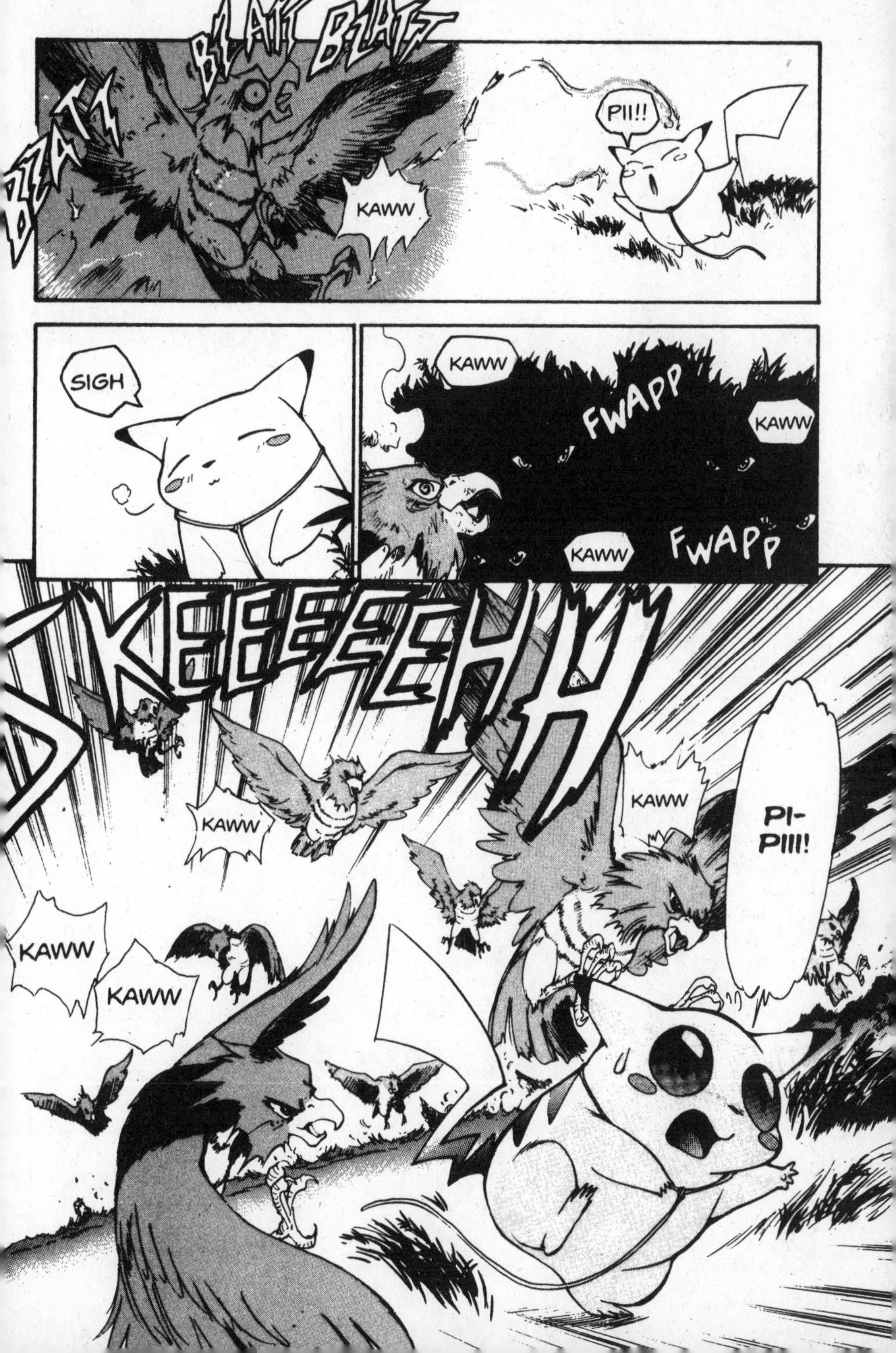
BZATT
BLATT BLATT
KAWW
PII!!
SIGH
KAWW
FWAPP
KAWW
KAWW
FWAPP
KEEEEEHH
KAWW
KAWW
PI-
PIII!
KAWW
KAWW

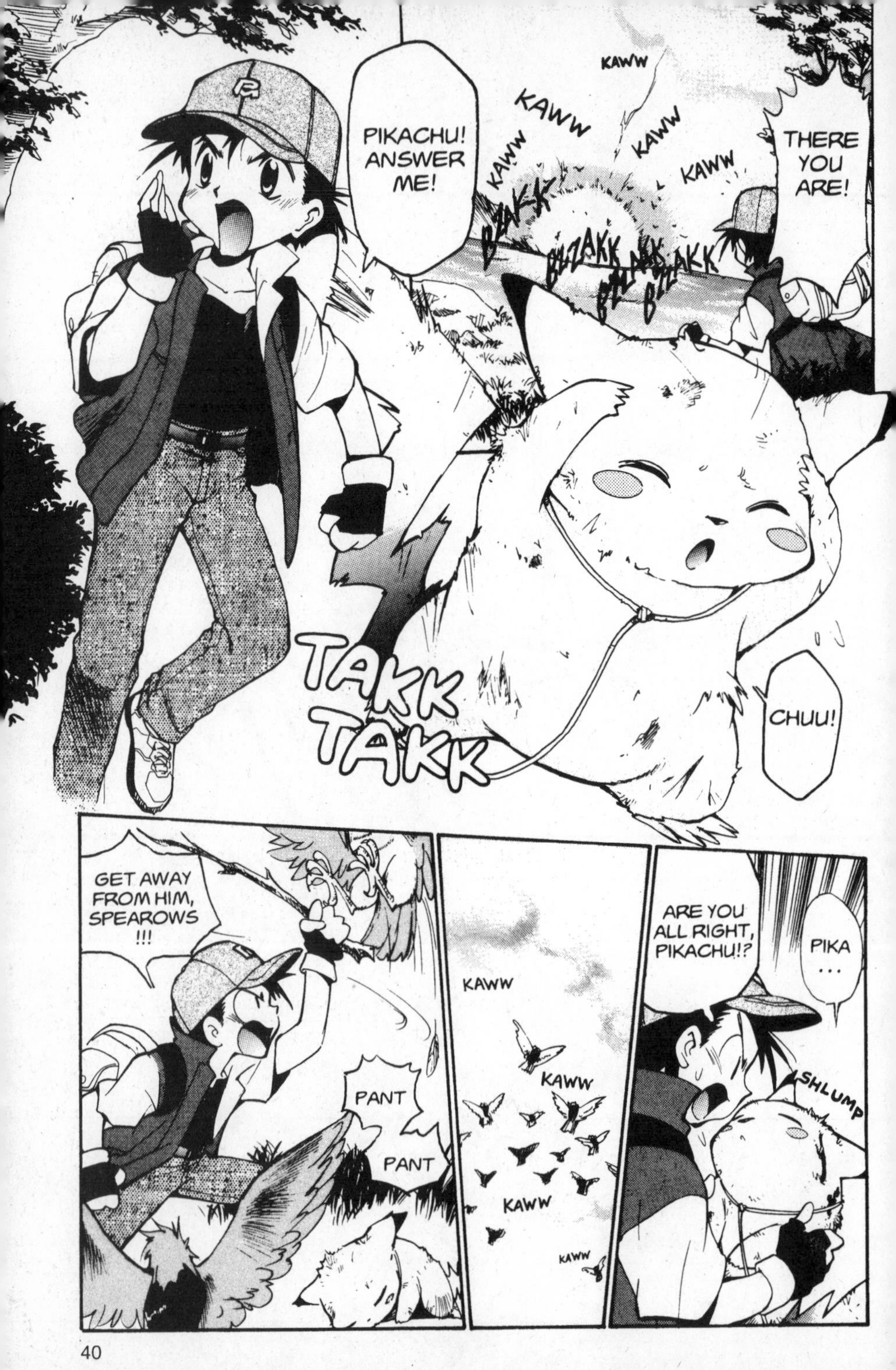
PIKACHU! ANSWER ME!
KAWW
KAWW
KAWW
KAWW
KAWW
THERE YOU ARE!
TAKK TAKK
CHUU!
GET AWAY FROM HIM, SPEAROWS !!!
PANT
PANT
KAWW
KAWW
KAWW
KAWW
ARE YOU ALL RIGHT, PIKACHU!?
PIKA . . .
SHLUMP

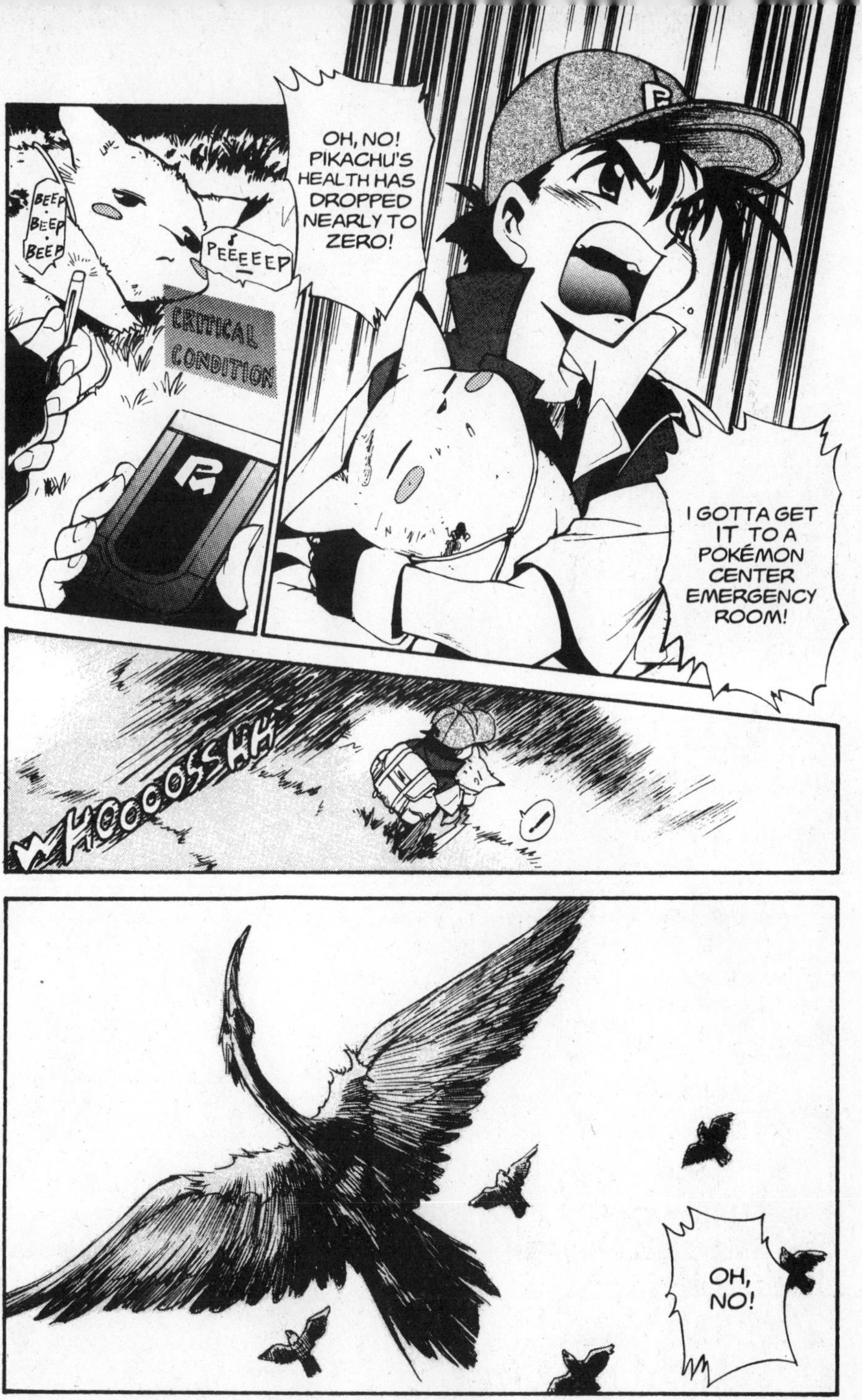
BEEP
BEEP
BEEP
PEEEEEP
CRITICAL CONDITION
OH, NO! PIKACHU'S HEALTH HAS DROPPED NEARLY TO ZERO!
I GOTTA GET IT TO A POKÉMON CENTER EMERGENCY ROOM!
WHOOOOSSHH
!
OH, NO!

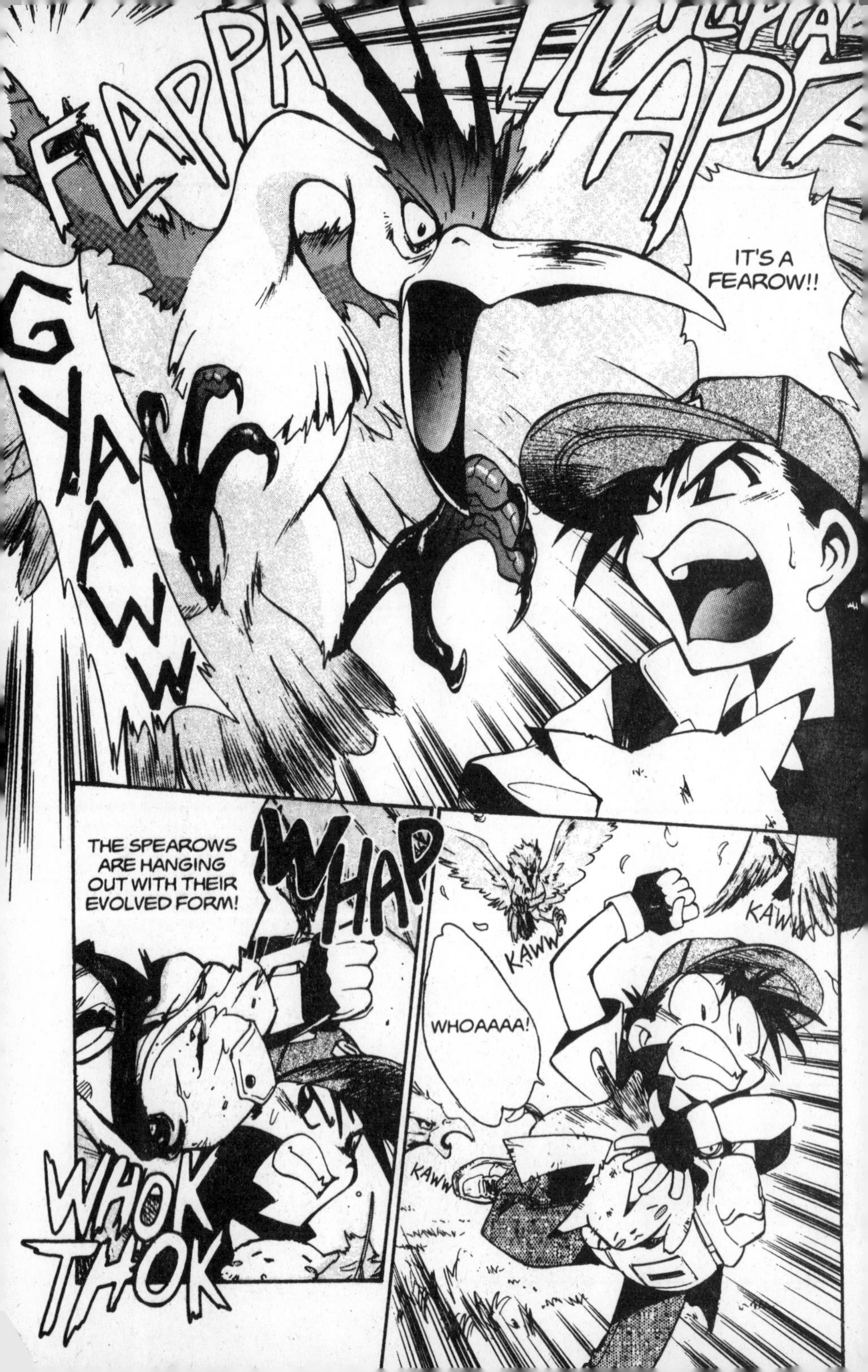
FLAPPA
FLAPPA
GYAAWW
IT'S A FEAROW!!
THE SPEAROWS ARE HANGING OUT WITH THEIR EVOLVED FORM!
WHAP
WHOK
THOK
KAWW
KAWW
WHOAAAA!
KAWW

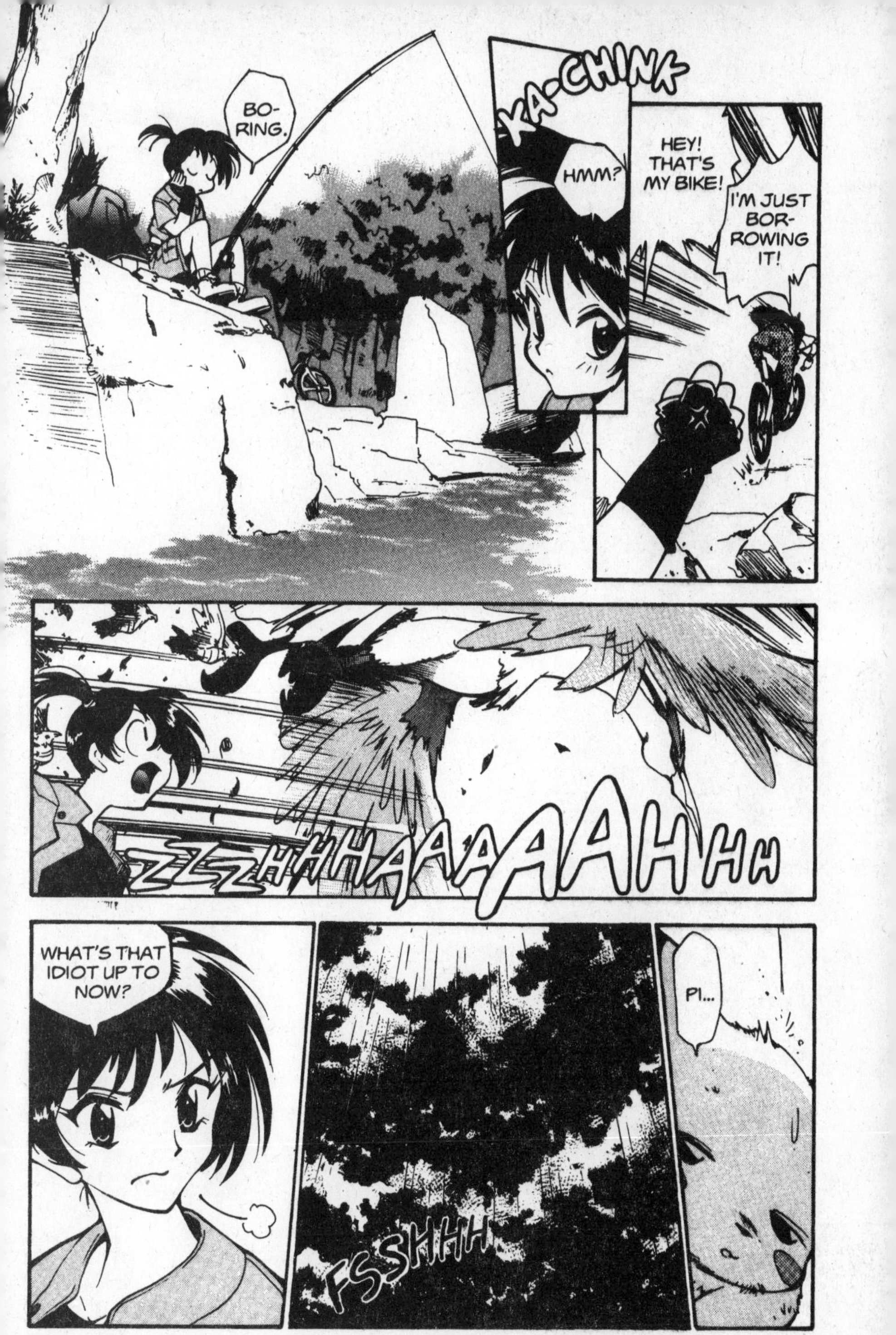
BO-RING.
KA-CHINK
HMM?
HEY! THAT'S MY BIKE!
I'M JUST BOR-ROWING IT!
ZZZHHHAAAAAHHH
WHAT'S THAT IDIOT UP TO NOW?
FSSHHH
PI...

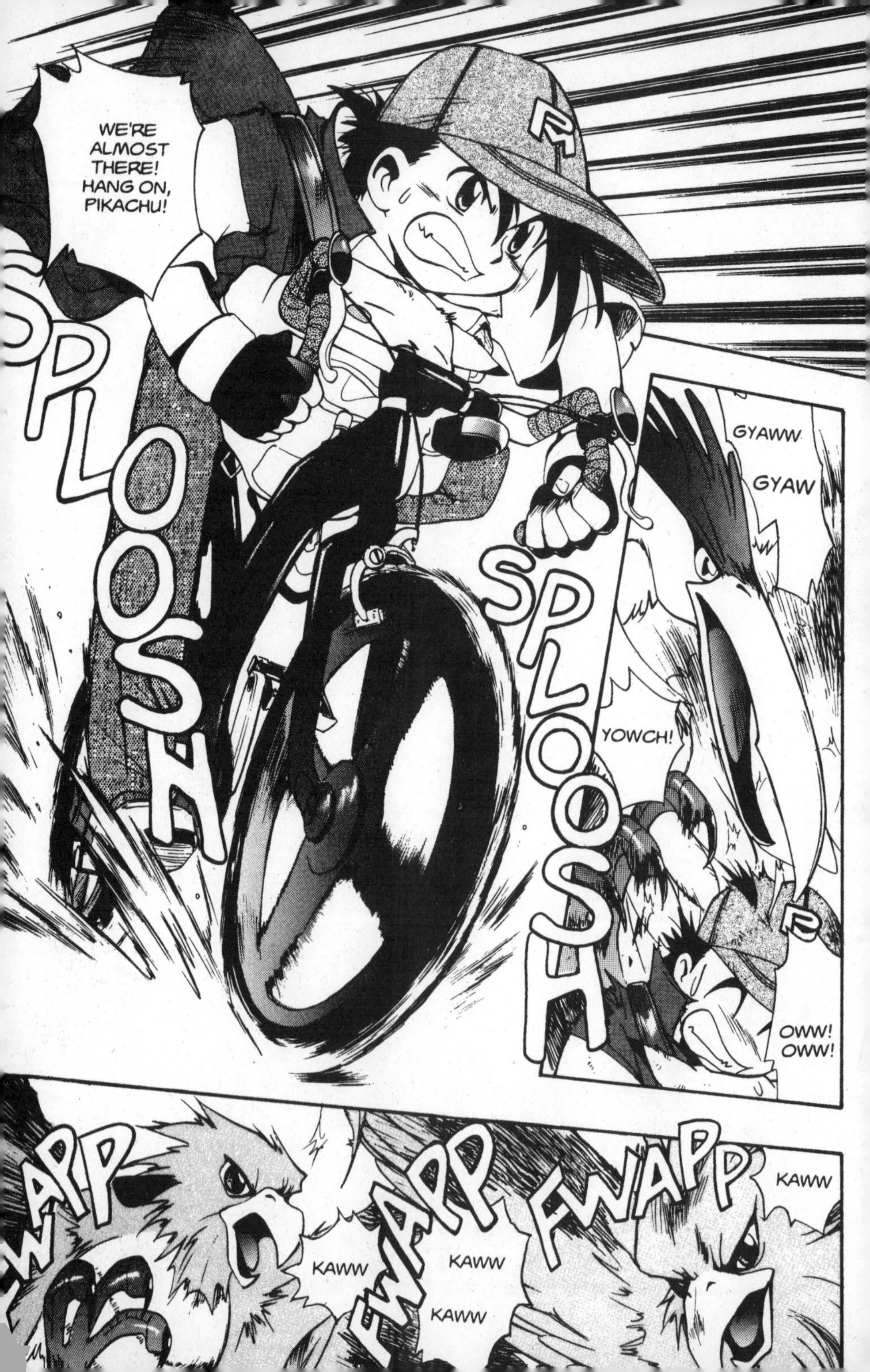
WE'RE ALMOST THERE! HANG ON, PIKACHU!
SPLOOSH
SPLOOSH
GYAWW
GYAW
YOWCH!
OWW! OWW!
WAPP
KAWW
FWAPP
KAWW
KAWW
FWAPP
KAWW

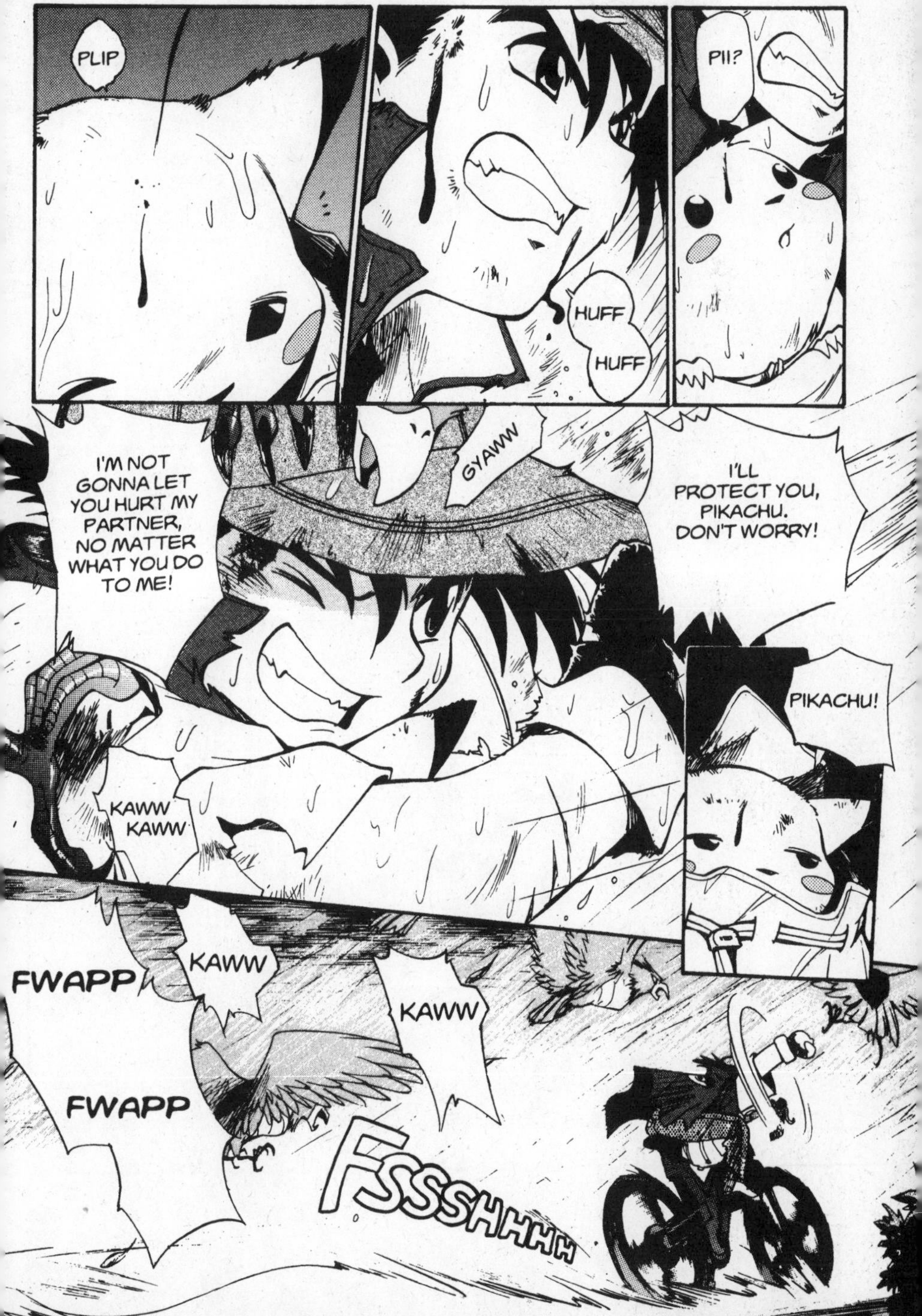
PLIP
HUFF
HUFF
PII?
I'M NOT GONNA LET YOU HURT MY PARTNER, NO MATTER WHAT YOU DO TO ME!
GYAWW
I'LL PROTECT YOU, PIKACHU. DON'T WORRY!
KAWW KAWW
PIKACHU!
FWAPP
KAWW
KAWW
FWAPP
FSSSHHHH

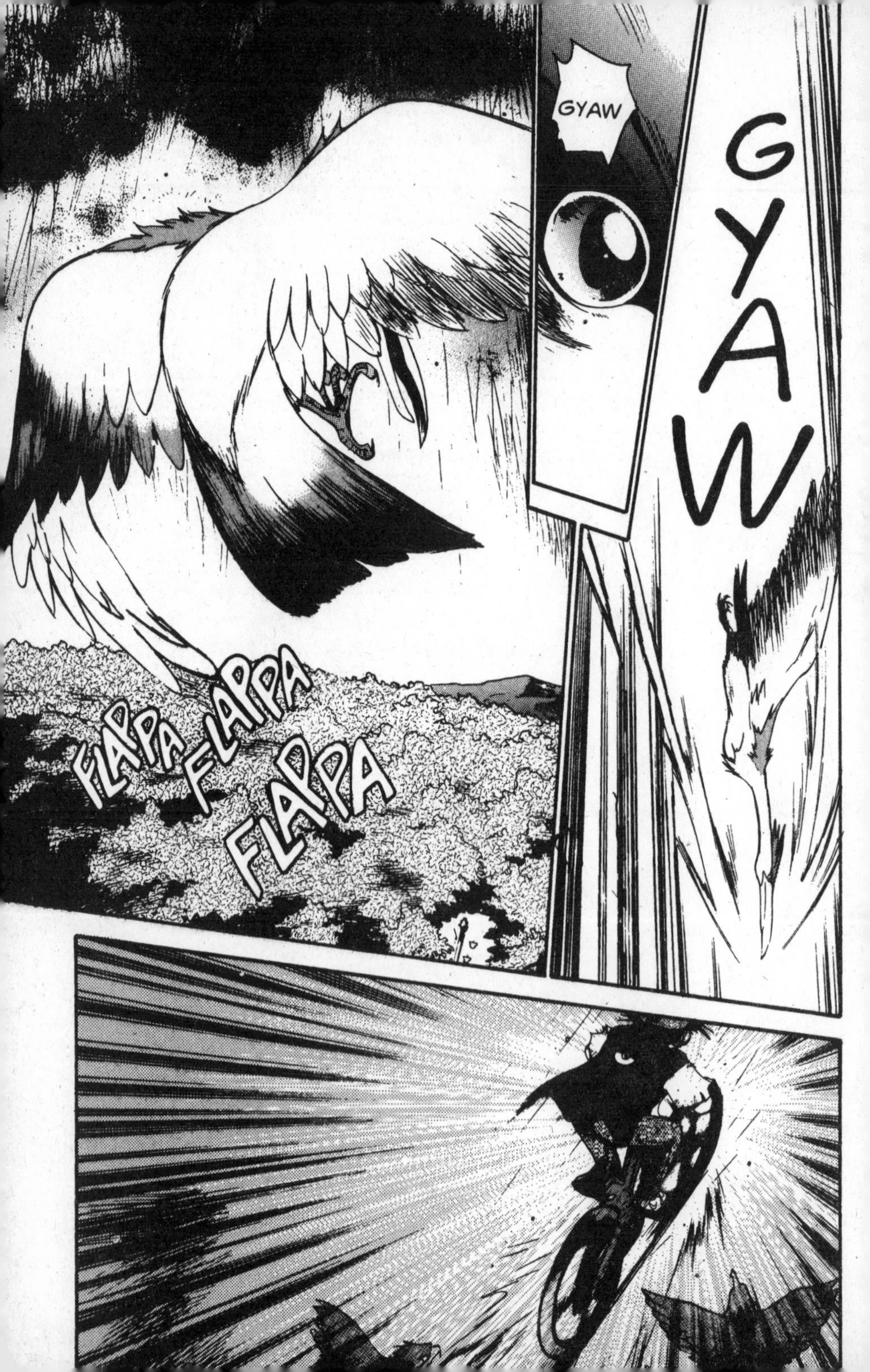
GYAW
GYAW
FLAPPA FLAPPA FLAPPA

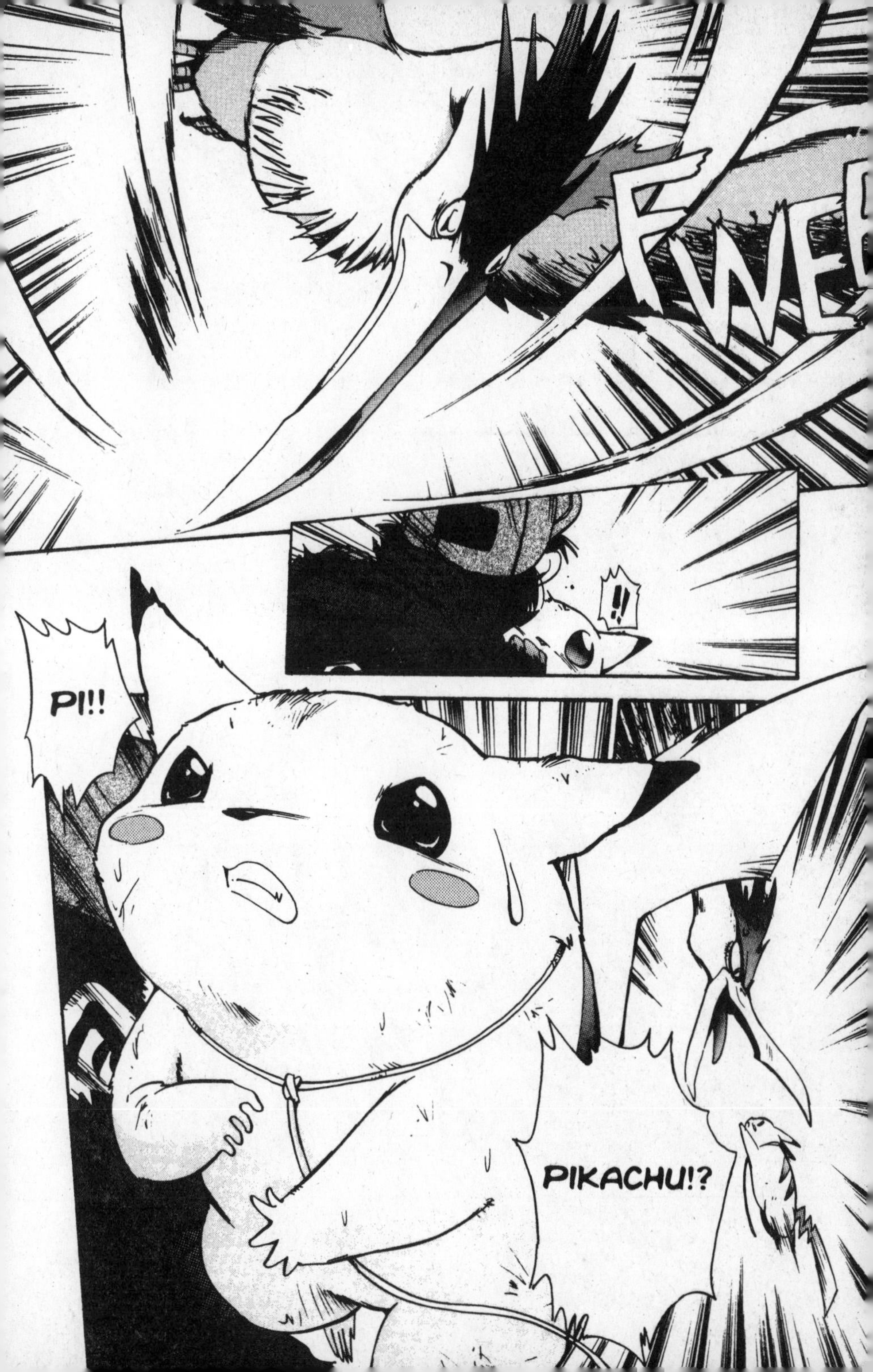
FWEE
!!
PI!!
PIKACHU!?

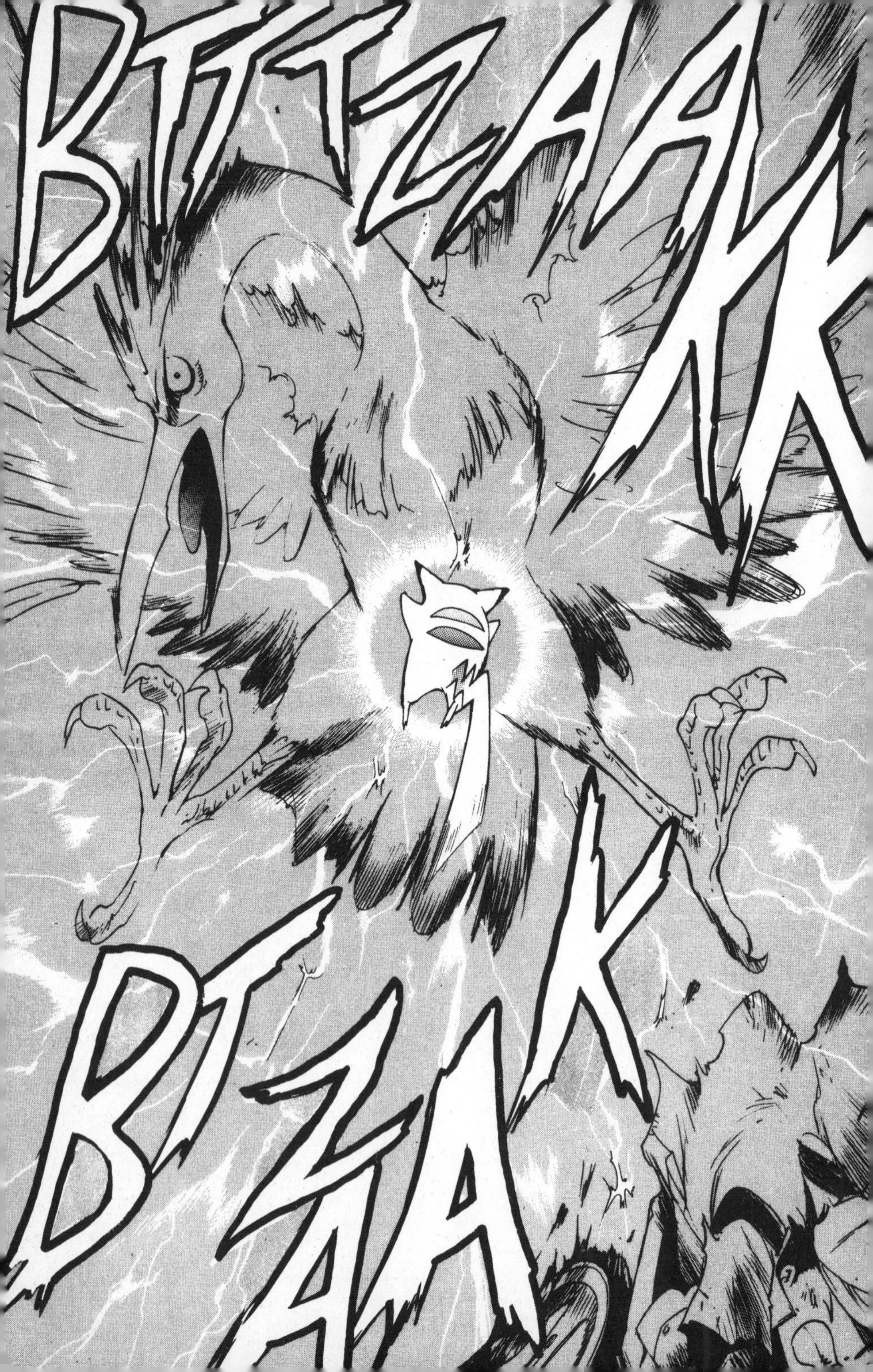
BTTZAAAK
BTZAAK

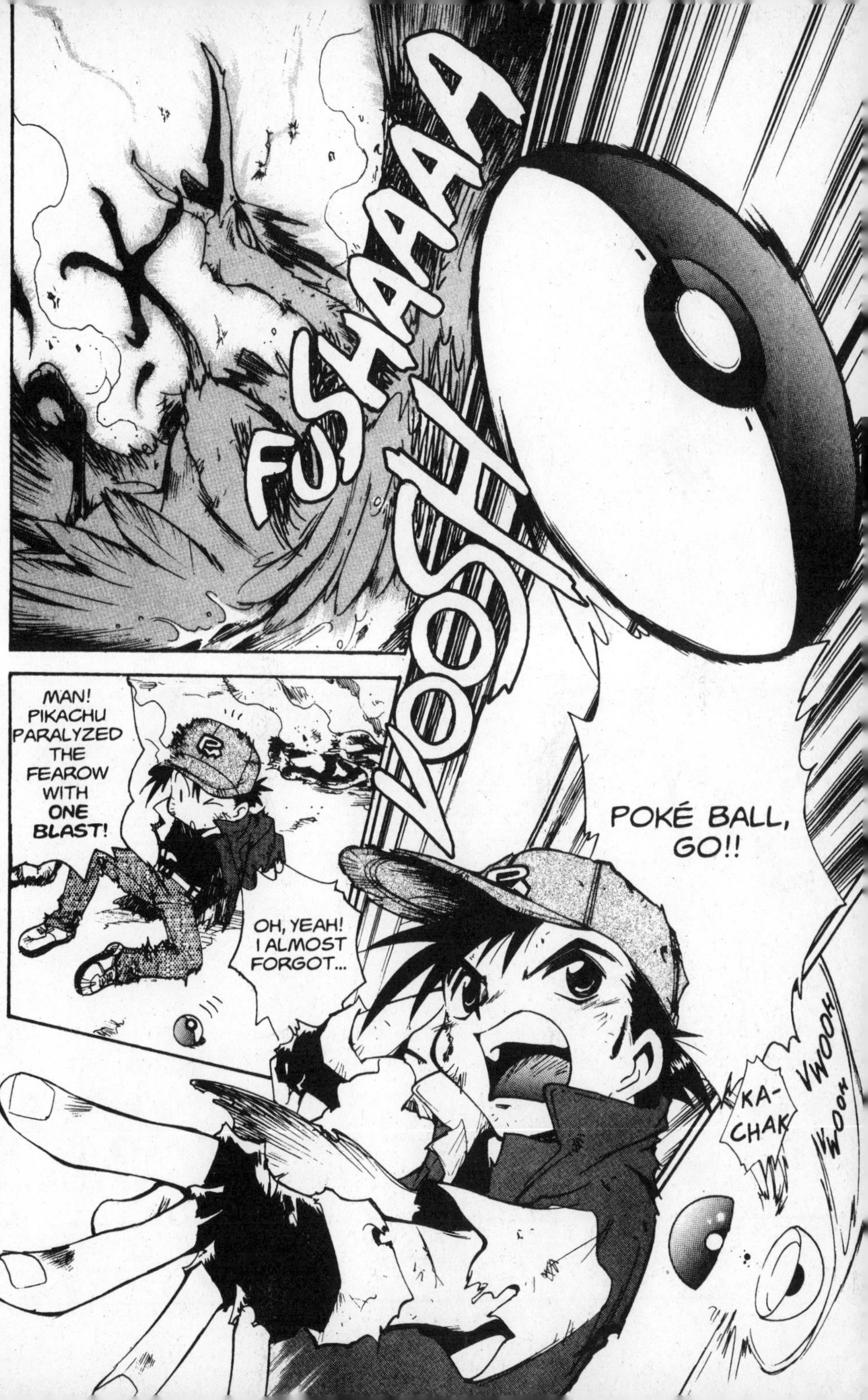
FUSHAAA
VWOOSH
MAN! PIKACHU PARALYZED THE FEAROW WITH ONE BLAST!
OH, YEAH! I ALMOST FORGOT...
POKÉ BALL, GO!!
KA-CHAK
VWOOH
WOOOH

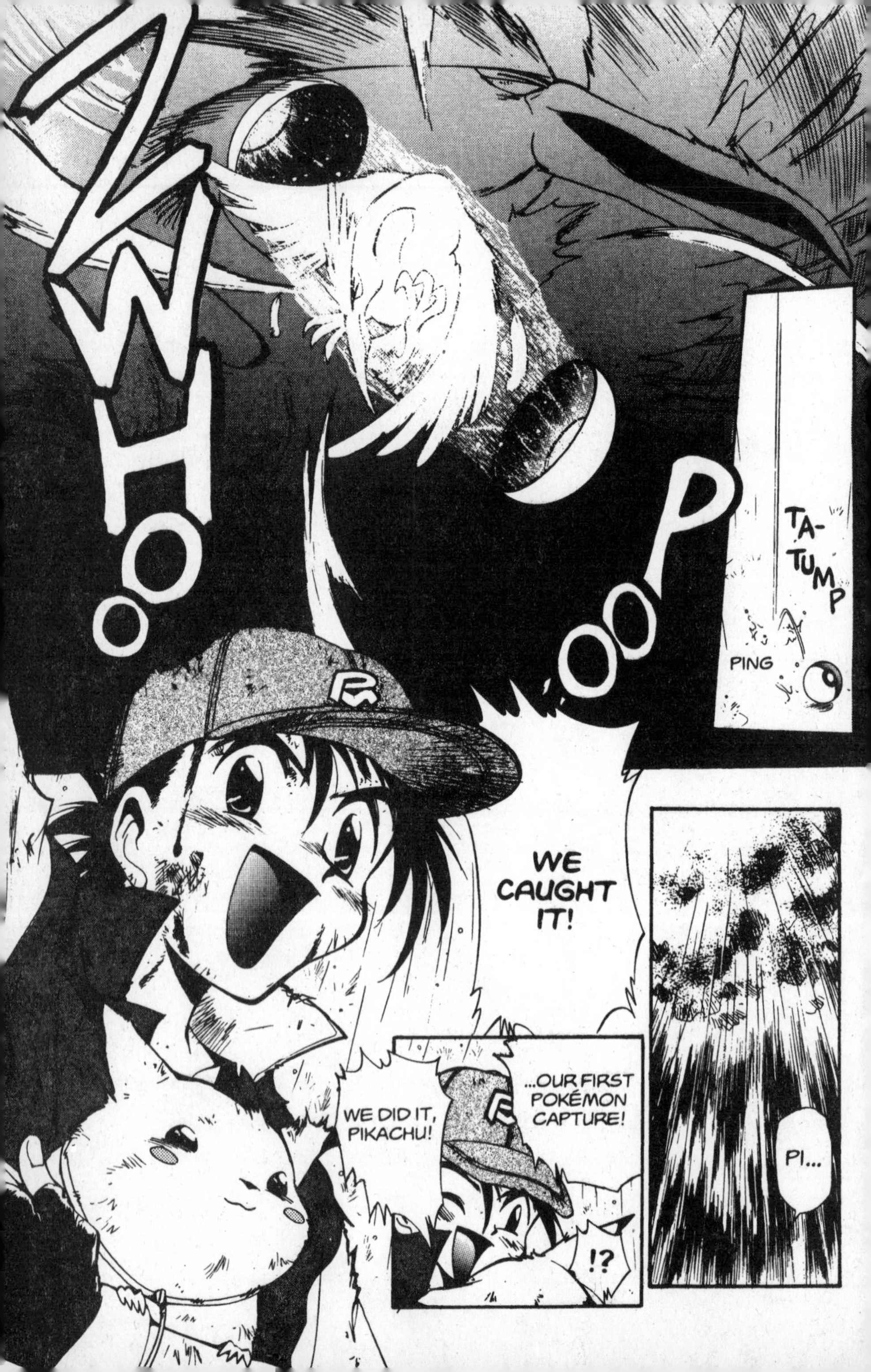
WHOOOOP!
TA-TUMP
PING
WE CAUGHT IT!
WE DID IT, PIKACHU!
...OUR FIRST POKÉMON CAPTURE!
!?
PI...

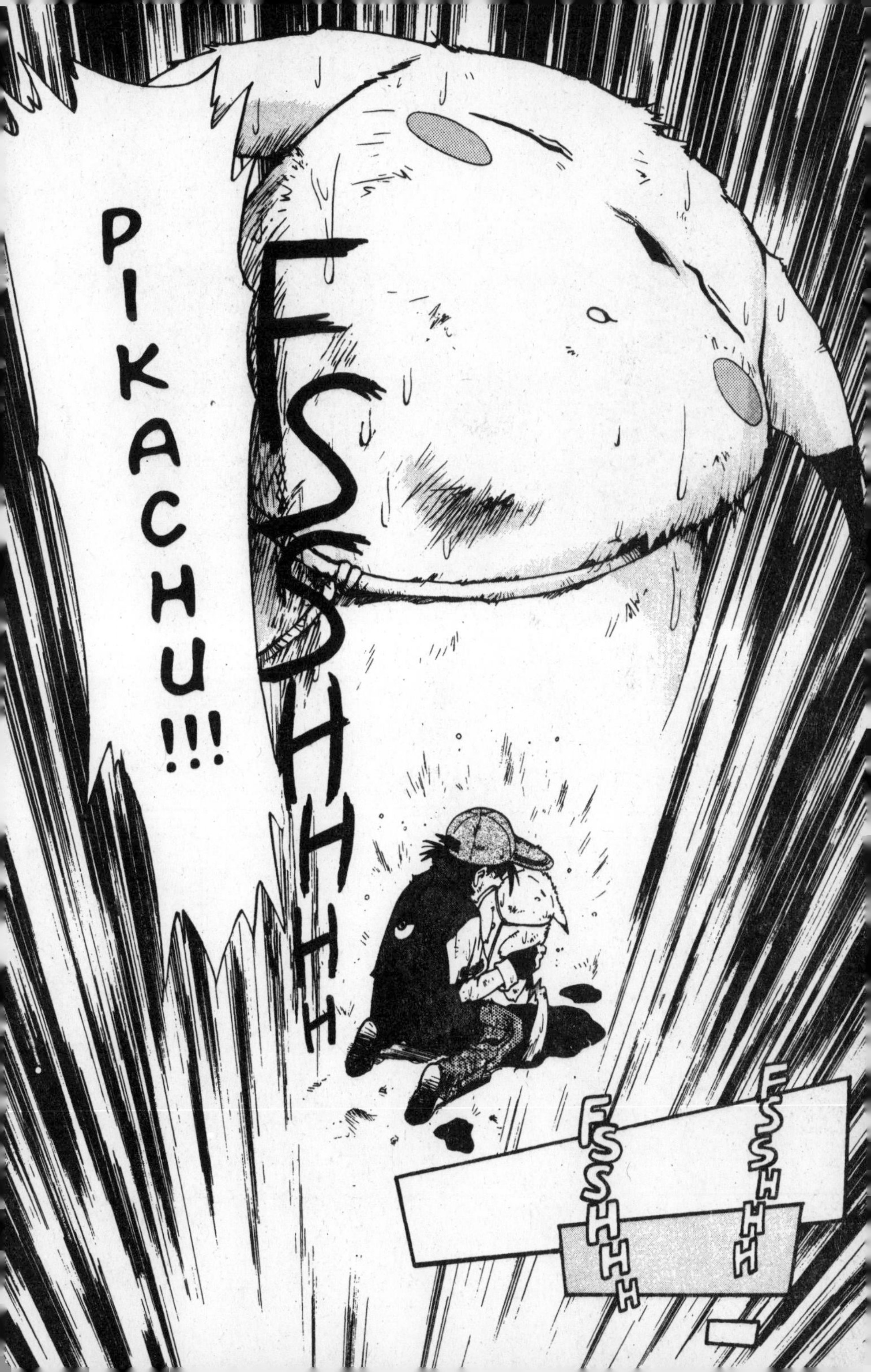
PIKACHU!!!
FSSHHHHH
FSSHHH
FSSHHH

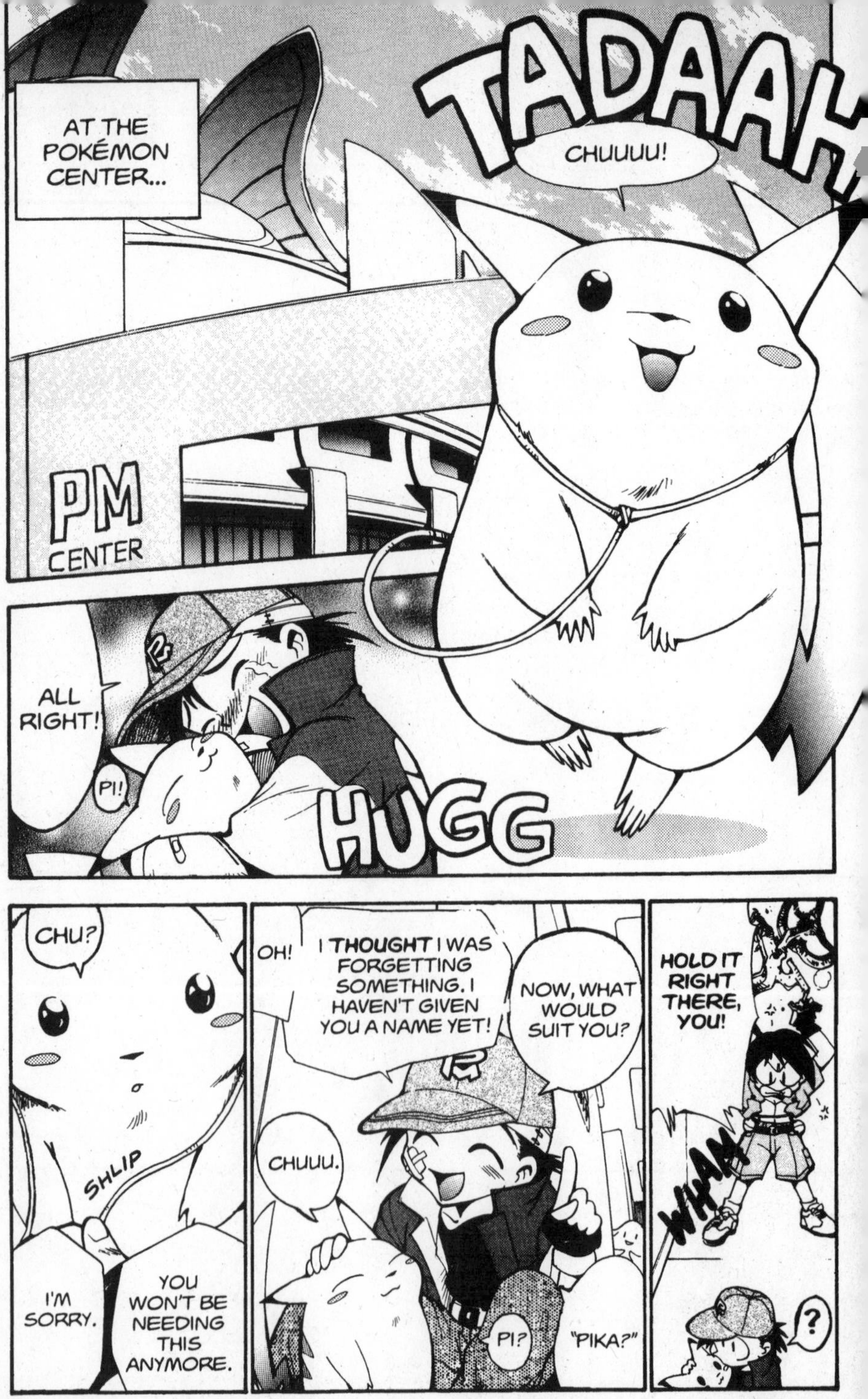
AT THE POKÉMON CENTER...
TADAAH
CHUUUU!
PM CENTER
ALL RIGHT!
PI!
HUGG
CHU?
SHLIP
I'M SORRY.
YOU WON'T BE NEEDING THIS ANYMORE.
OH!
I **THOUGHT** I WAS FORGETTING SOMETHING. I HAVEN'T GIVEN YOU A NAME YET!
NOW, WHAT WOULD SUIT YOU?
CHUUU.
PI?
"PIKA?"
HOLD IT RIGHT THERE, YOU!
WHAM
?

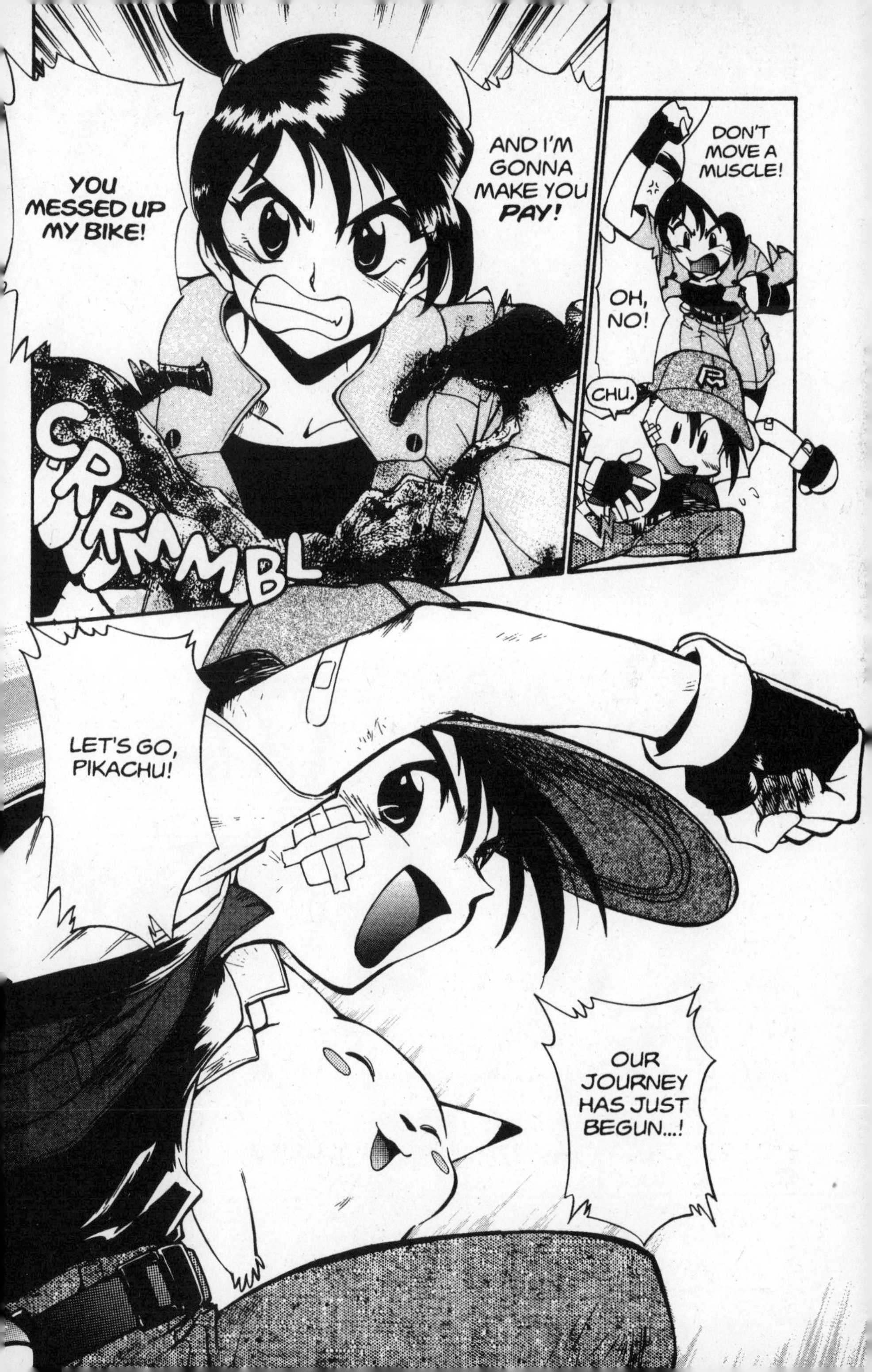
YOU MESSED UP MY BIKE!
AND I'M GONNA MAKE YOU PAY!
CRRMMBL
DON'T MOVE A MUSCLE!
OH, NO!
CHU.
LET'S GO, PIKACHU!
OUR JOURNEY HAS JUST BEGUN...!

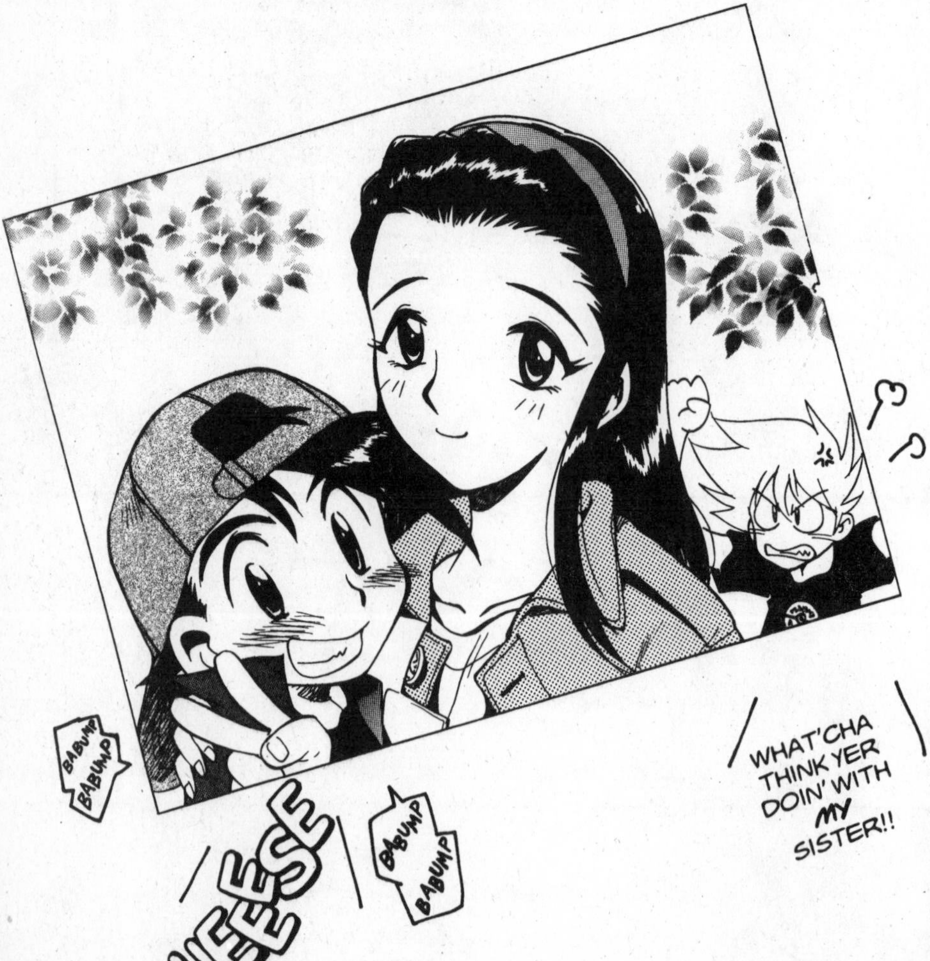
BABUMP BABUMP
CHEEESE
BABUMP BABUMP
WHAT'CHA THINK YER DOIN' WITH *MY* SISTER!!

CHAPTER 2
PLAY MISTY FOR ME

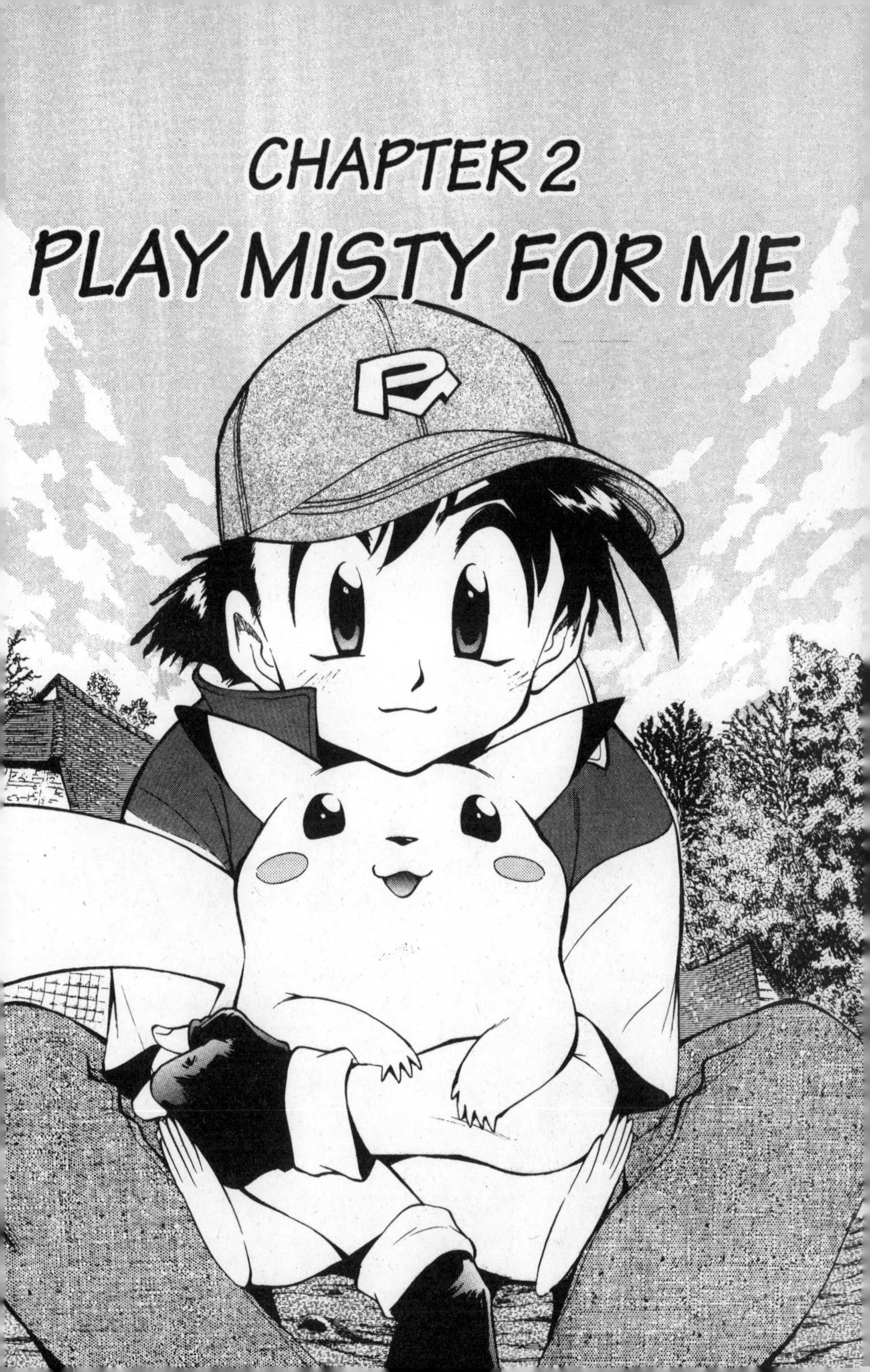

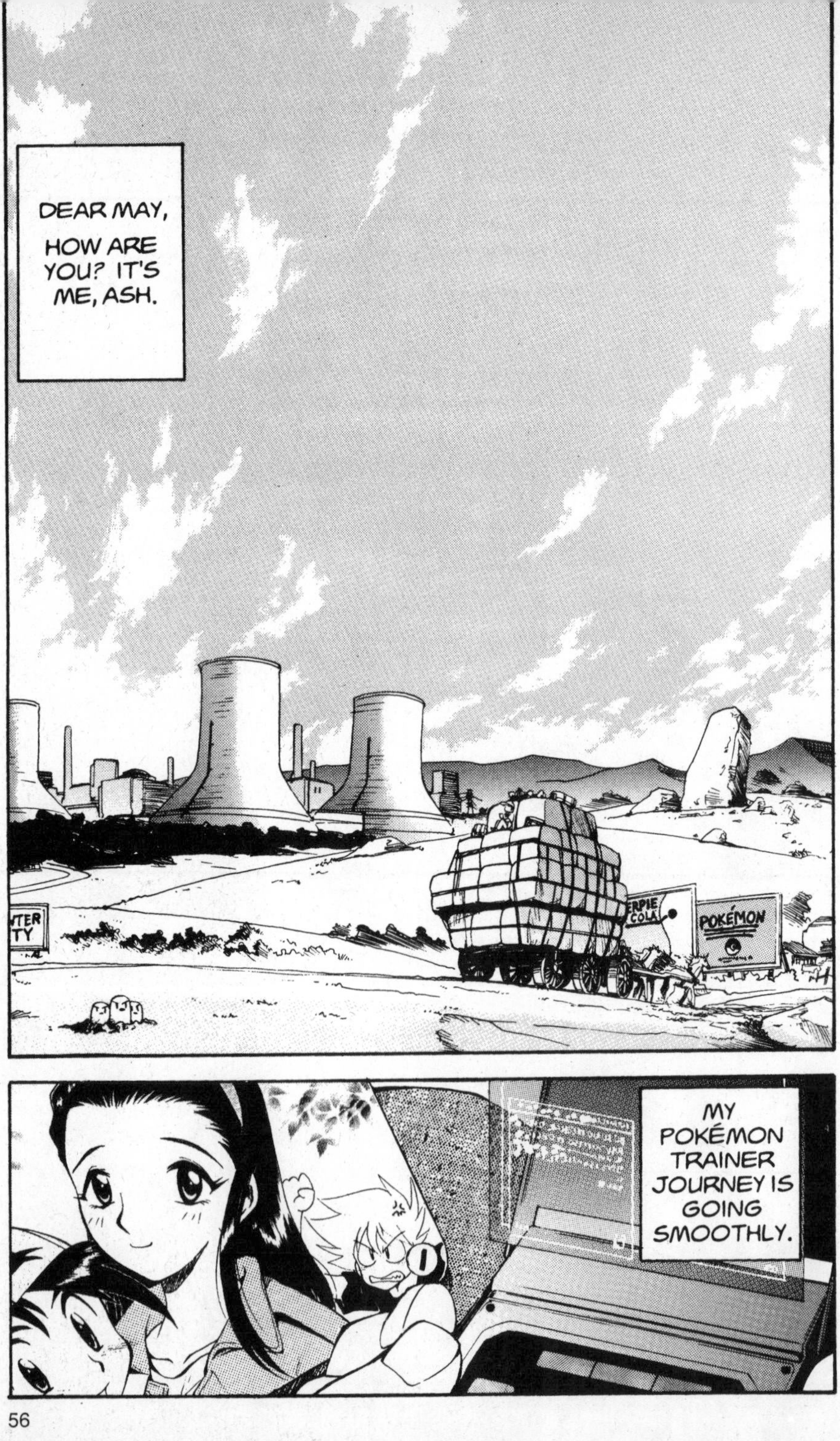
DEAR MAY,
HOW ARE YOU? IT'S ME, ASH.
POKÉMON
MY POKÉMON TRAINER JOURNEY IS GOING SMOOTHLY.

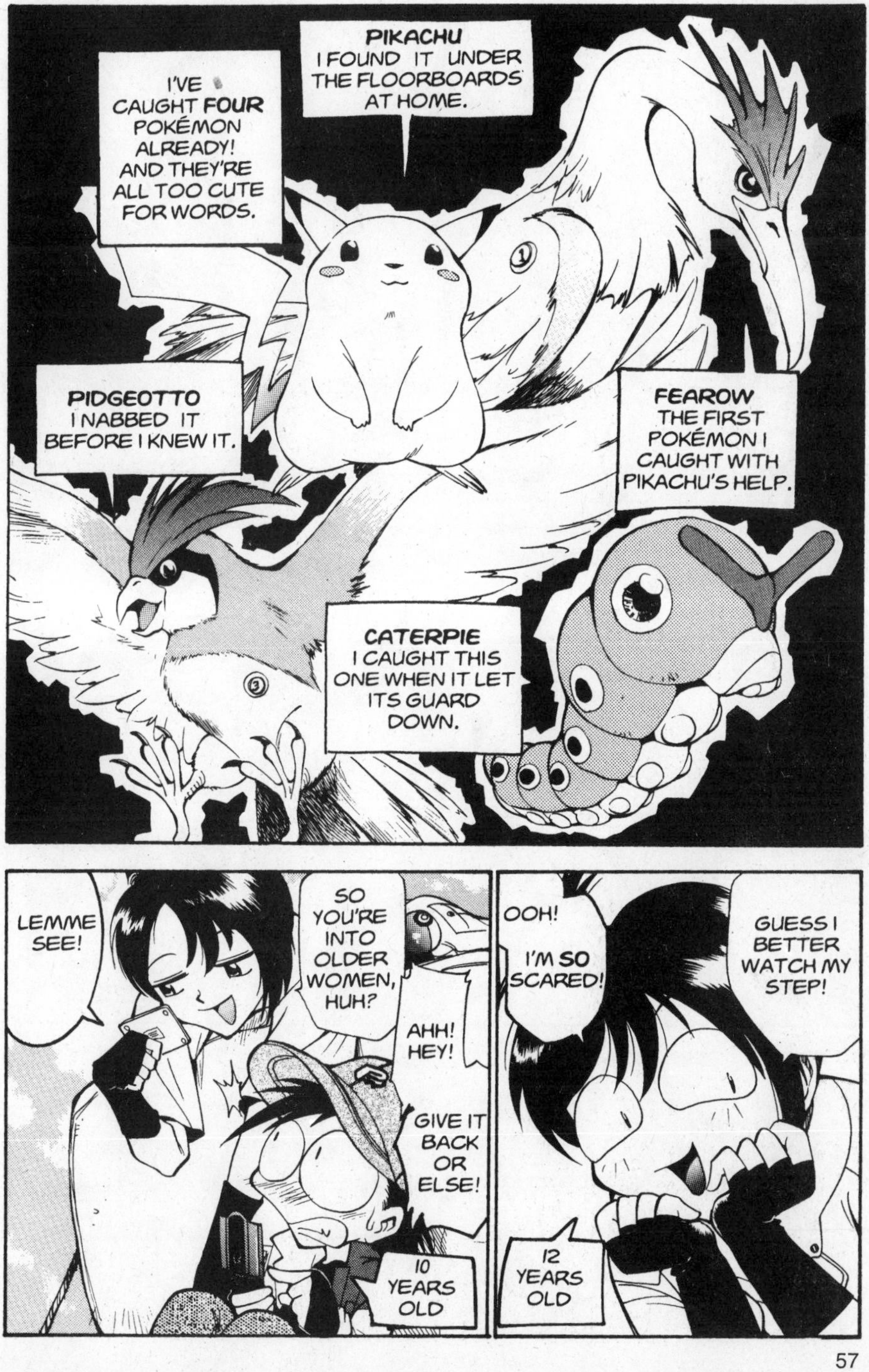
I'VE CAUGHT **FOUR** POKÉMON ALREADY! AND THEY'RE ALL TOO CUTE FOR WORDS.
PIKACHU I FOUND IT UNDER THE FLOORBOARDS AT HOME.
PIDGEOTTO I NABBED IT BEFORE I KNEW IT.
FEAROW THE FIRST POKÉMON I CAUGHT WITH PIKACHU'S HELP.
CATERPIE I CAUGHT THIS ONE WHEN IT LET ITS GUARD DOWN.
LEMME SEE!
SO YOU'RE INTO OLDER WOMEN, HUH?
AHH! HEY!
GIVE IT BACK OR ELSE!
10 YEARS OLD
OOH!
I'M **SO** SCARED!
GUESS I BETTER WATCH MY STEP!
12 YEARS OLD

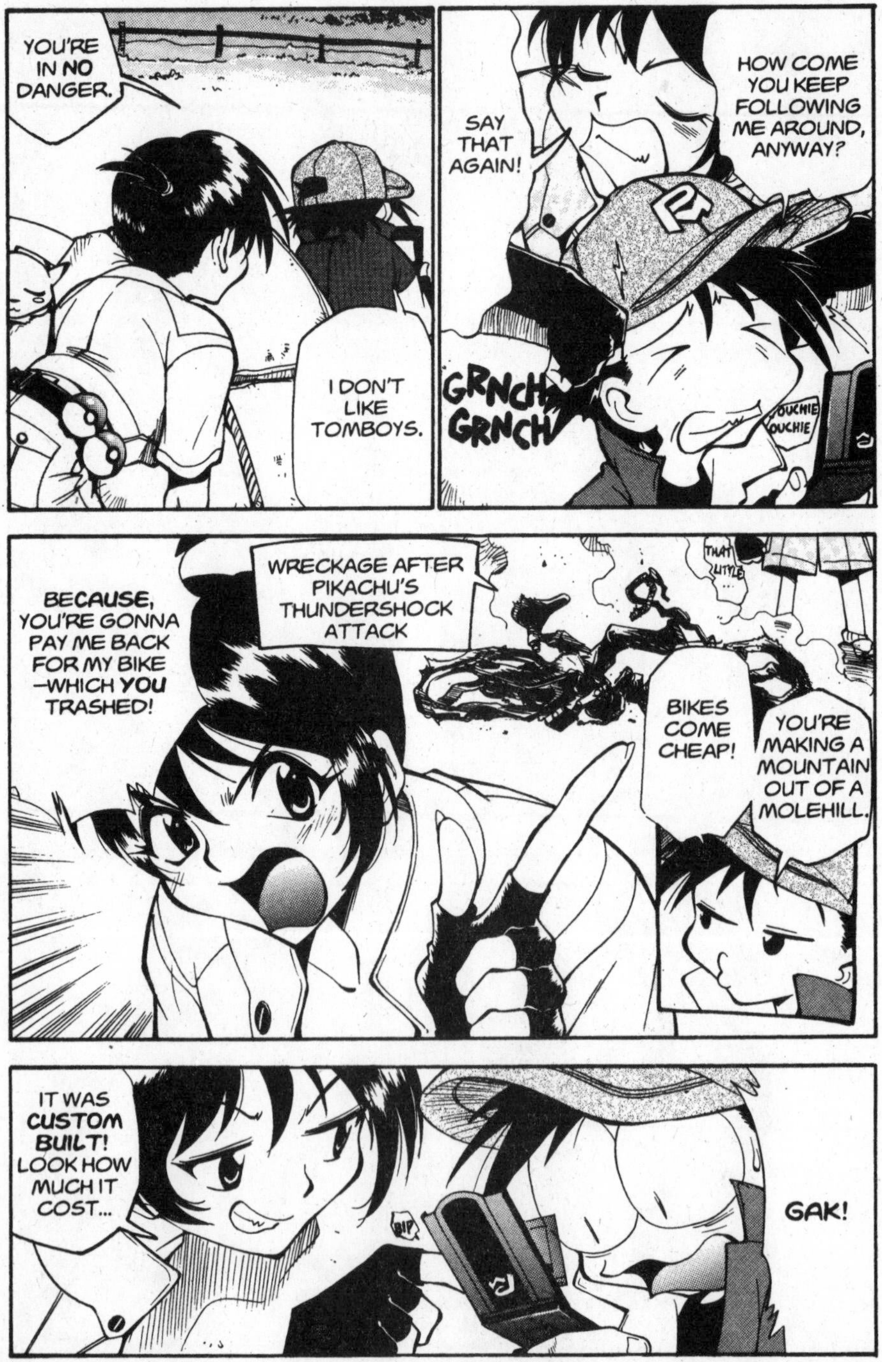
YOU'RE IN NO DANGER.
I DON'T LIKE TOMBOYS.
SAY THAT AGAIN!
HOW COME YOU KEEP FOLLOWING ME AROUND, ANYWAY?
GRNCH GRNCH
OUCHIE OUCHIE
BECAUSE, YOU'RE GONNA PAY ME BACK FOR MY BIKE —WHICH YOU TRASHED!
WRECKAGE AFTER PIKACHU'S THUNDERSHOCK ATTACK
THAT LITTLE ...
BIKES COME CHEAP!
YOU'RE MAKING A MOUNTAIN OUT OF A MOLEHILL.
IT WAS CUSTOM BUILT! LOOK HOW MUCH IT COST...
BIP
GAK!

10,000

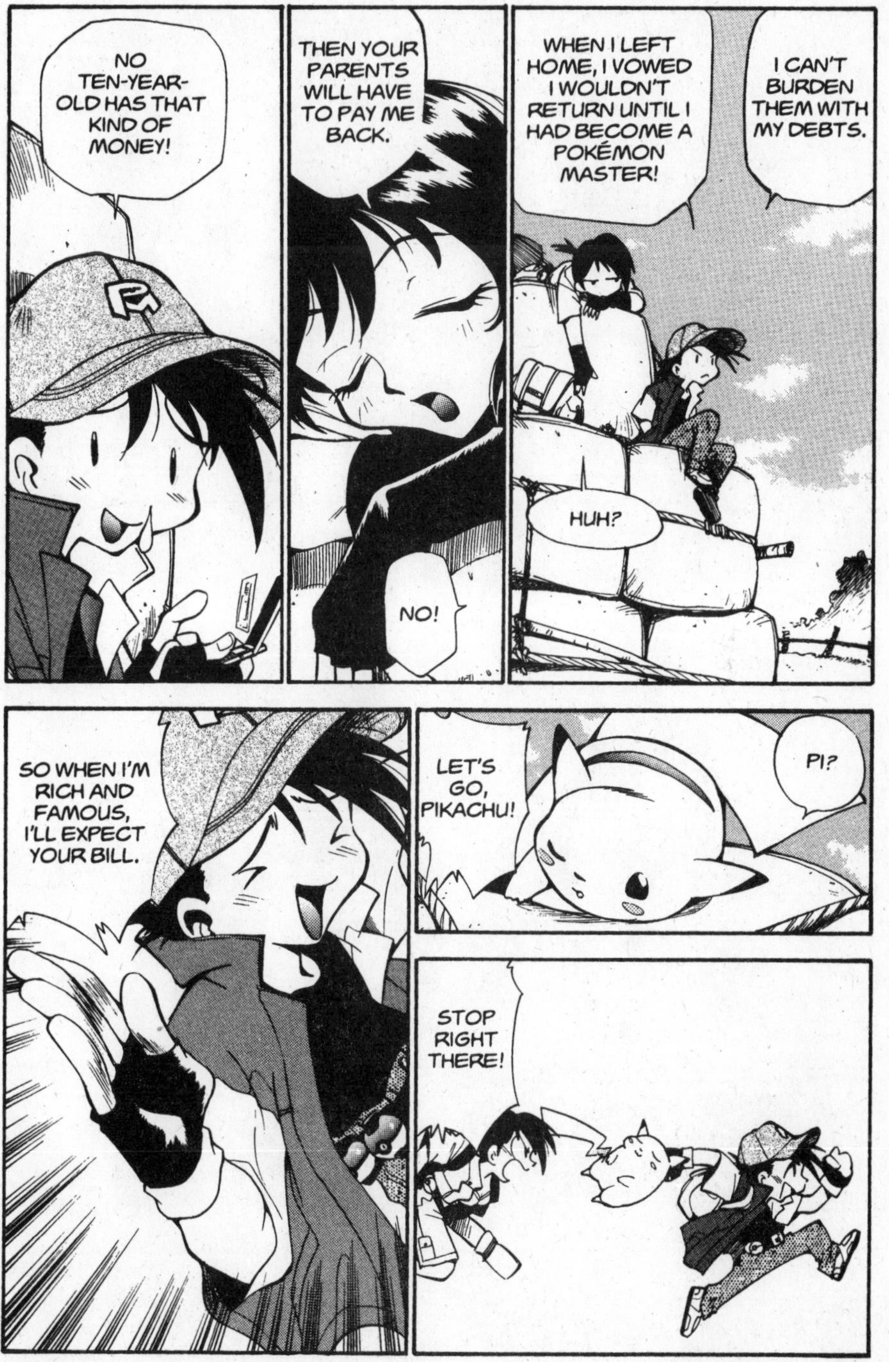
NO TEN-YEAR-OLD HAS THAT KIND OF MONEY!
THEN YOUR PARENTS WILL HAVE TO PAY ME BACK.
NO!
WHEN I LEFT HOME, I VOWED I WOULDN'T RETURN UNTIL I HAD BECOME A POKÉMON MASTER!
I CAN'T BURDEN THEM WITH MY DEBTS.
HUH?
SO WHEN I'M RICH AND FAMOUS, I'LL EXPECT YOUR BILL.
LET'S GO, PIKACHU!
PI?
STOP RIGHT THERE!

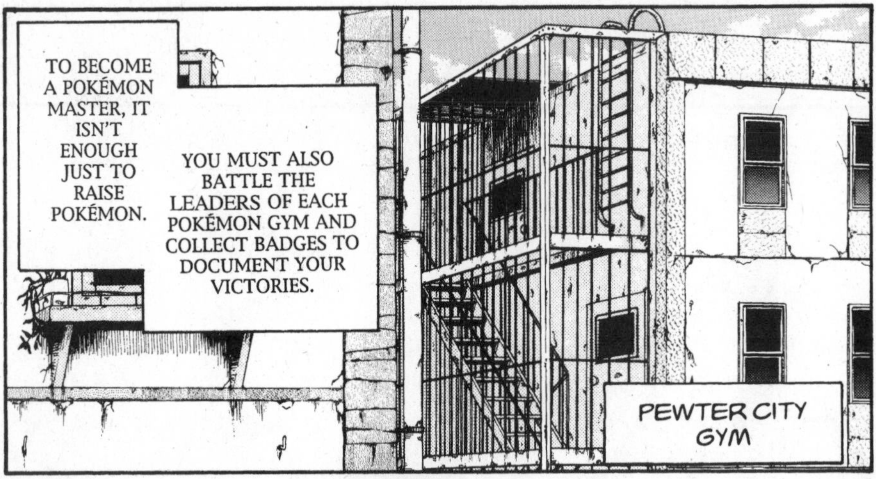
TO BECOME A POKÉMON MASTER, IT ISN'T ENOUGH JUST TO RAISE POKÉMON.
YOU MUST ALSO BATTLE THE LEADERS OF EACH POKÉMON GYM AND COLLECT BADGES TO DOCUMENT YOUR VICTORIES.
PEWTER CITY GYM

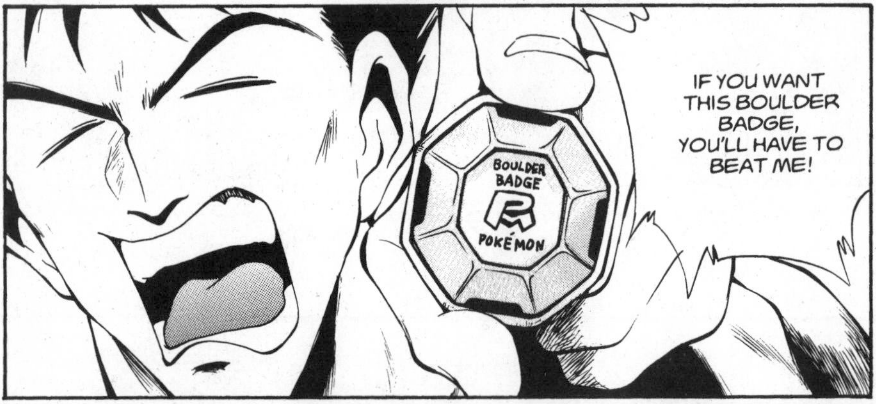
BOULDER BADGE
POKÉMON
IF YOU WANT THIS BOULDER BADGE, YOU'LL HAVE TO BEAT ME!

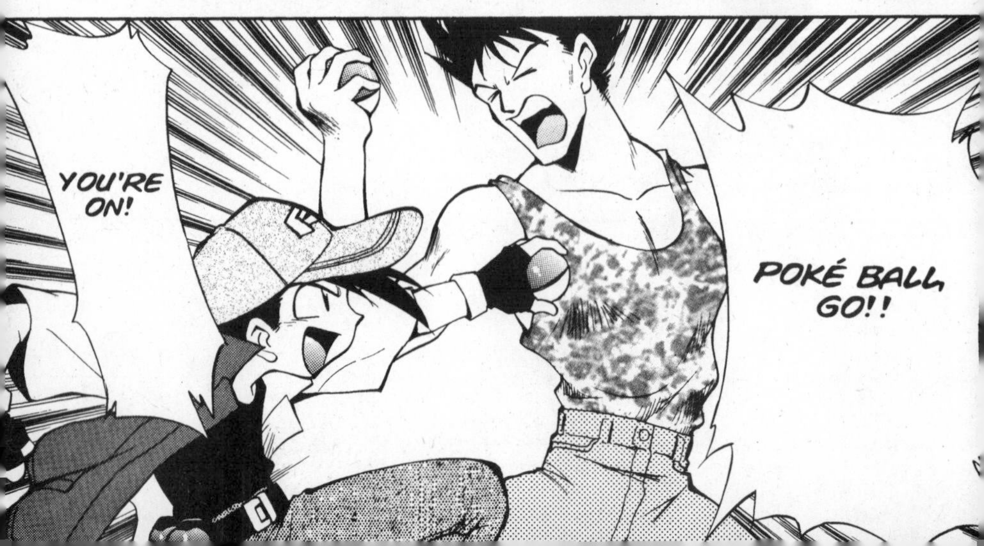
YOU'RE ON!
POKÉ BALL GO!!

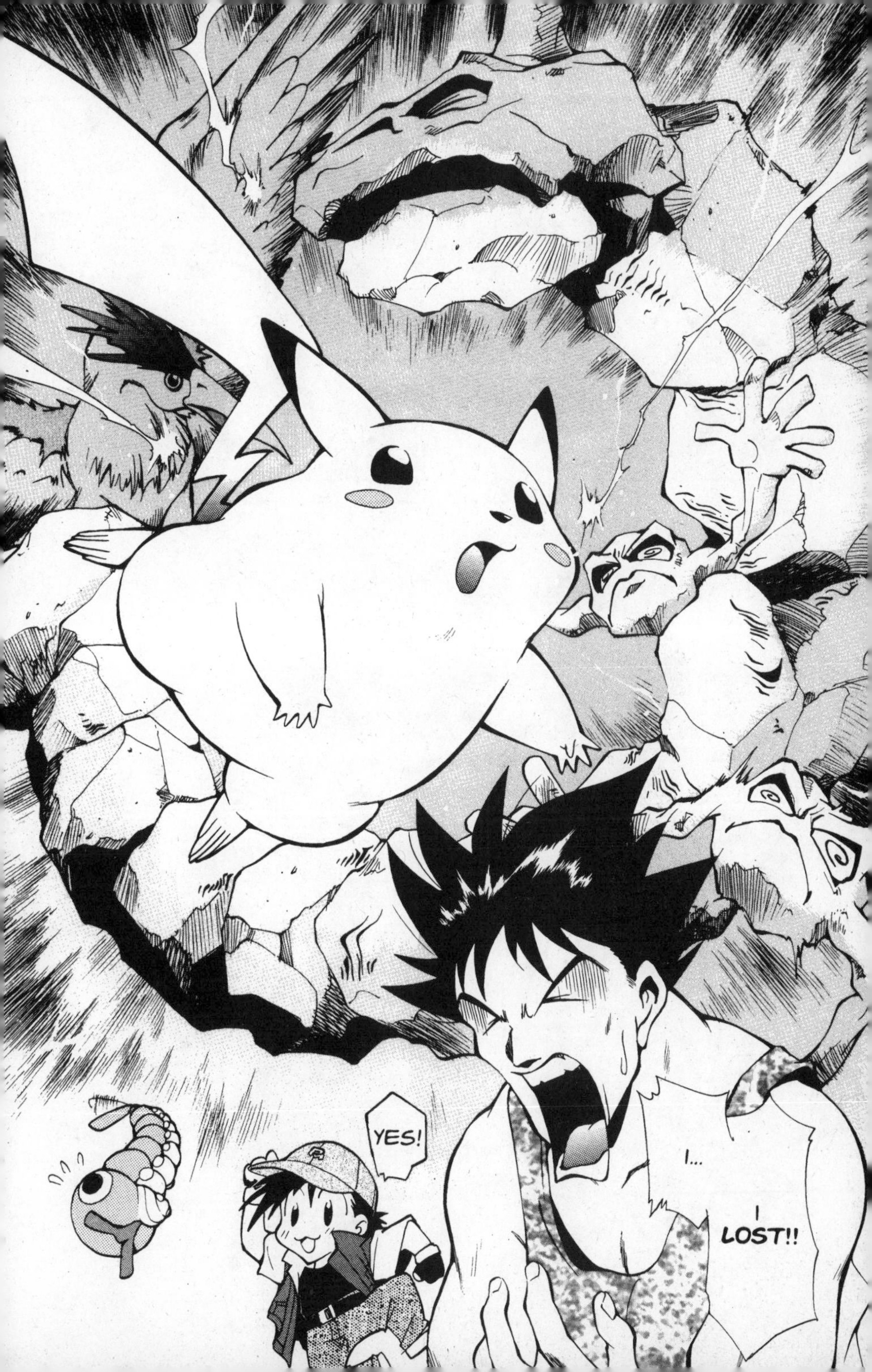
I...
I LOST!!
YES!

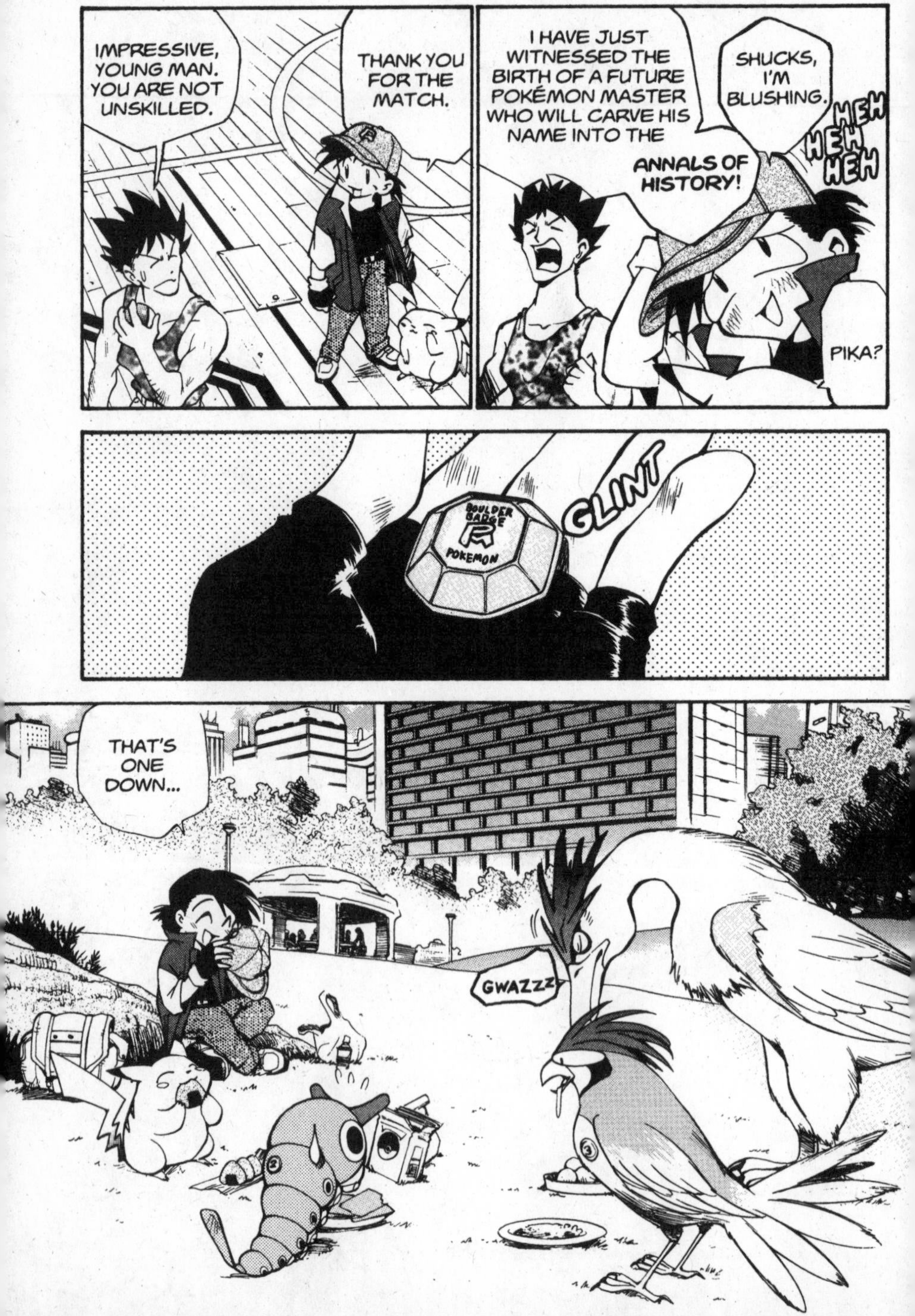
IMPRESSIVE, YOUNG MAN. YOU ARE NOT UNSKILLED.
THANK YOU FOR THE MATCH.
I HAVE JUST WITNESSED THE BIRTH OF A FUTURE POKÉMON MASTER WHO WILL CARVE HIS NAME INTO THE
ANNALS OF HISTORY!
SHUCKS, I'M BLUSHING.
HEH HEH HEH
PIKA?
BOULDER BADGE
POKEMON
GLINT
THAT'S ONE DOWN...
GWAZZZ

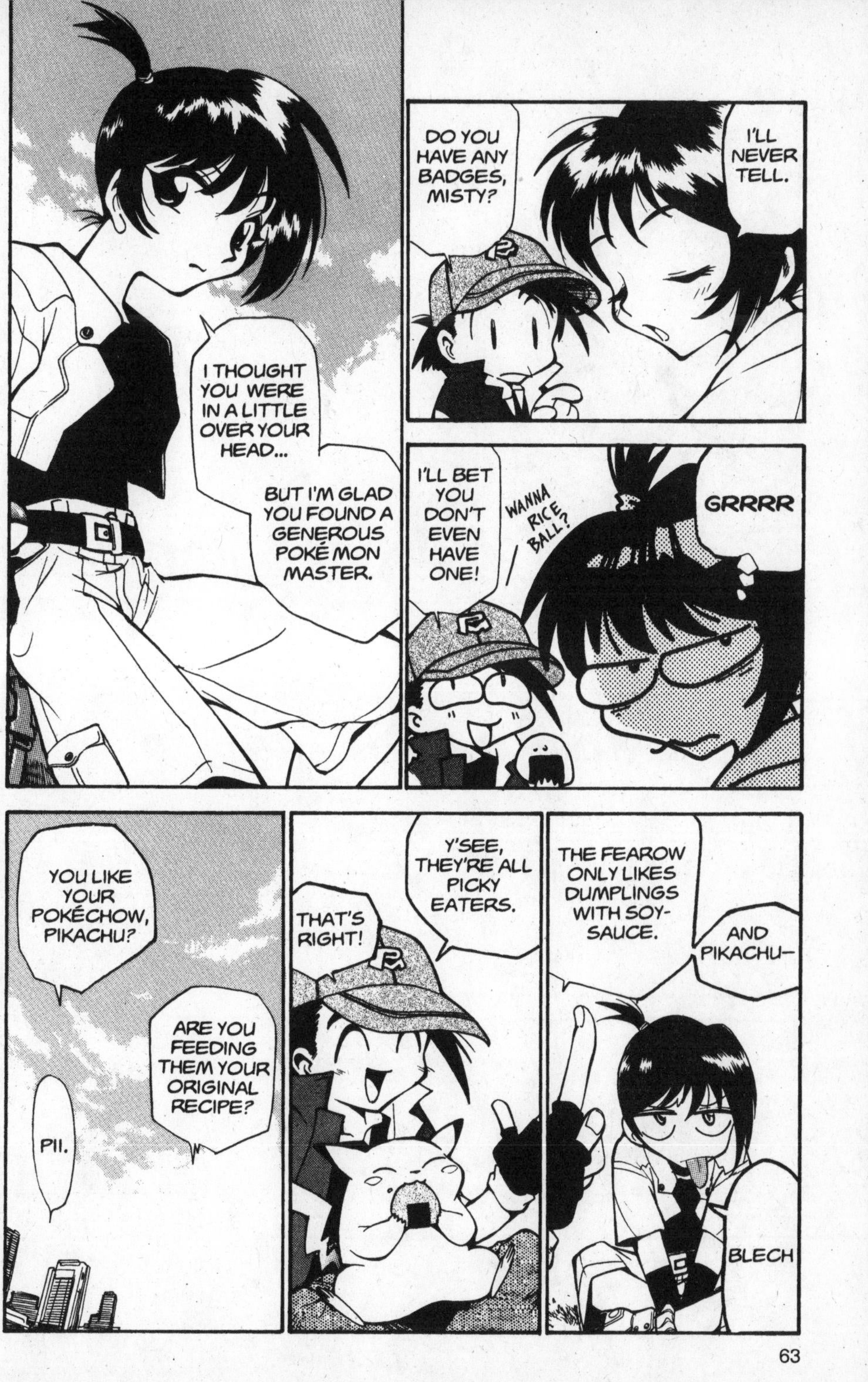
I THOUGHT YOU WERE IN A LITTLE OVER YOUR HEAD...
BUT I'M GLAD YOU FOUND A GENEROUS POKÉMON MASTER.
DO YOU HAVE ANY BADGES, MISTY?
I'LL NEVER TELL.
I'LL BET YOU DON'T EVEN HAVE ONE!
WANNA RICE BALL?
GRRRR
YOU LIKE YOUR POKÉCHOW, PIKACHU?
ARE YOU FEEDING THEM YOUR ORIGINAL RECIPE?
PII.
Y'SEE, THEY'RE ALL PICKY EATERS.
THAT'S RIGHT!
THE FEAROW ONLY LIKES DUMPLINGS WITH SOY-SAUCE.
AND PIKACHU—
BLECH

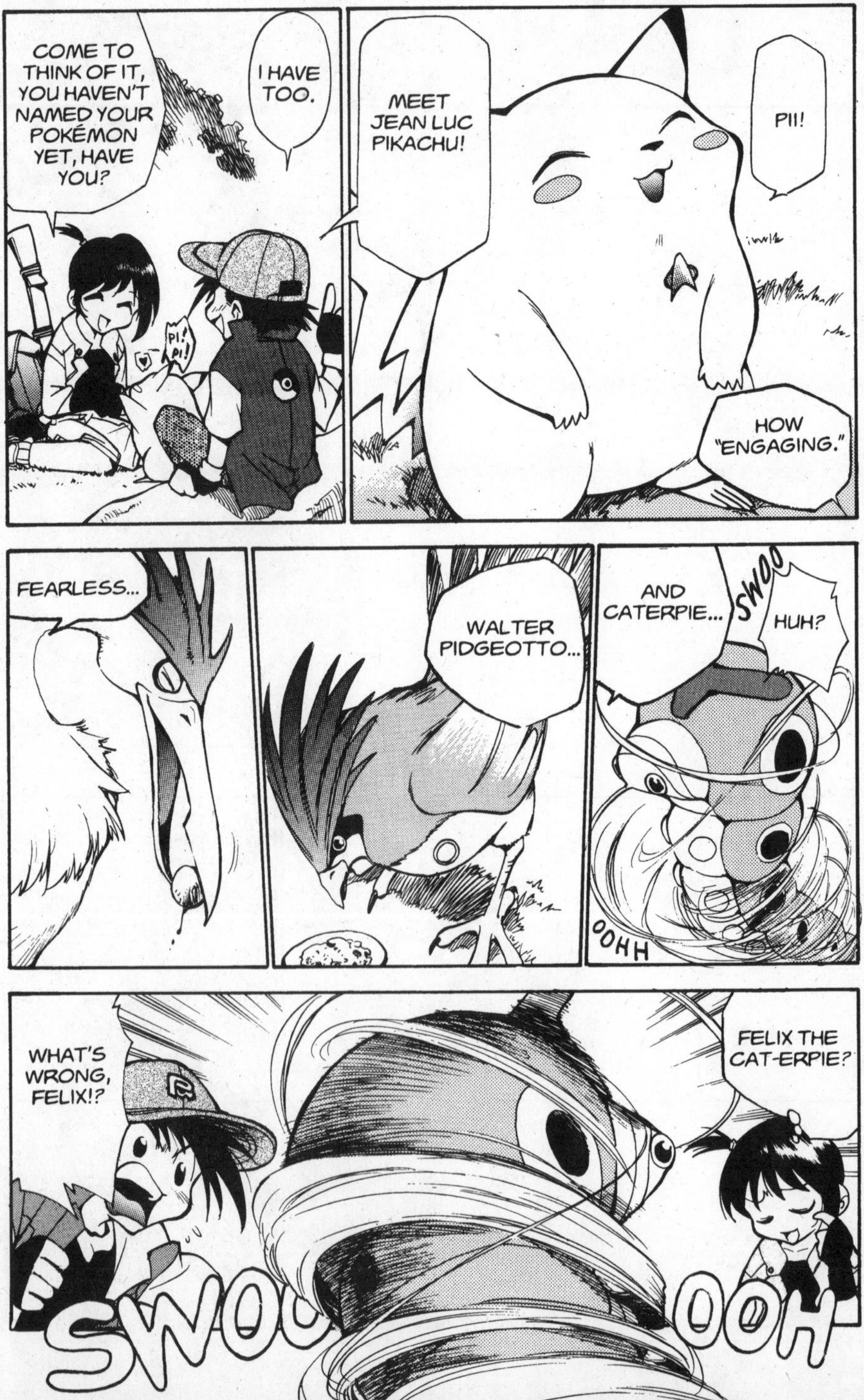
COME TO THINK OF IT, YOU HAVEN'T NAMED YOUR POKÉMON YET, HAVE YOU?
I HAVE TOO.
PI! PI!
MEET JEAN LUC PIKACHU!
PII!
HOW "ENGAGING."
FEARLESS...
WALTER PIDGEOTTO...
AND CATERPIE...
SWOOOHH
HUH?
WHAT'S WRONG, FELIX!?
FELIX THE CAT-ERPIE?
SWOOOOOH

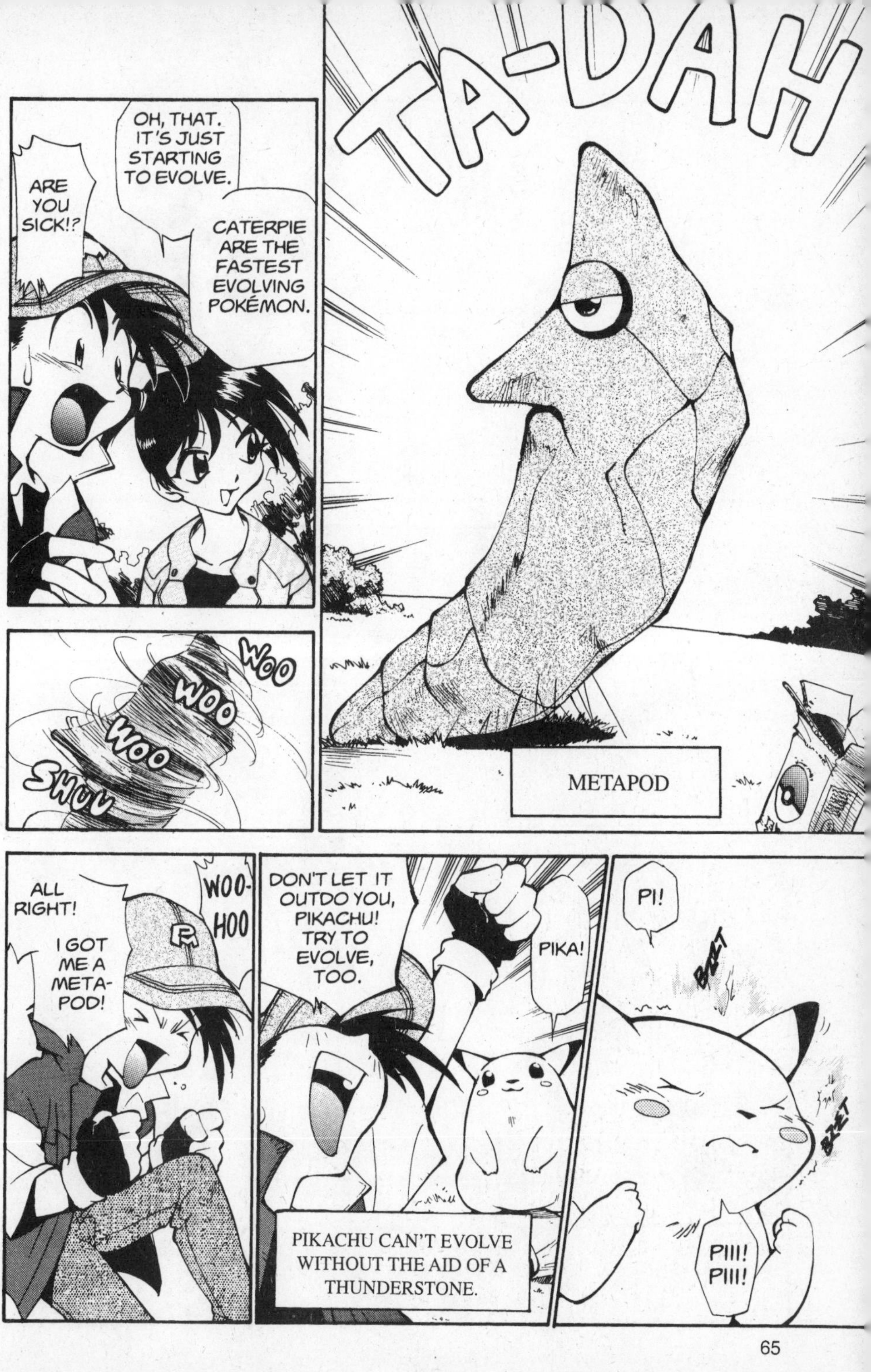
ARE YOU SICK!?
OH, THAT. IT'S JUST STARTING TO EVOLVE.
CATERPIE ARE THE FASTEST EVOLVING POKÉMON.
WOO
WOO
WOO
SHUU
TA-DAH
METAPOD
ALL RIGHT!
WOO-HOO
I GOT ME A META-POD!
DON'T LET IT OUTDO YOU, PIKACHU! TRY TO EVOLVE, TOO.
PIKA!
PIKACHU CAN'T EVOLVE WITHOUT THE AID OF A THUNDERSTONE.
PI!
BZZT
BZZT
PIII! PIII!

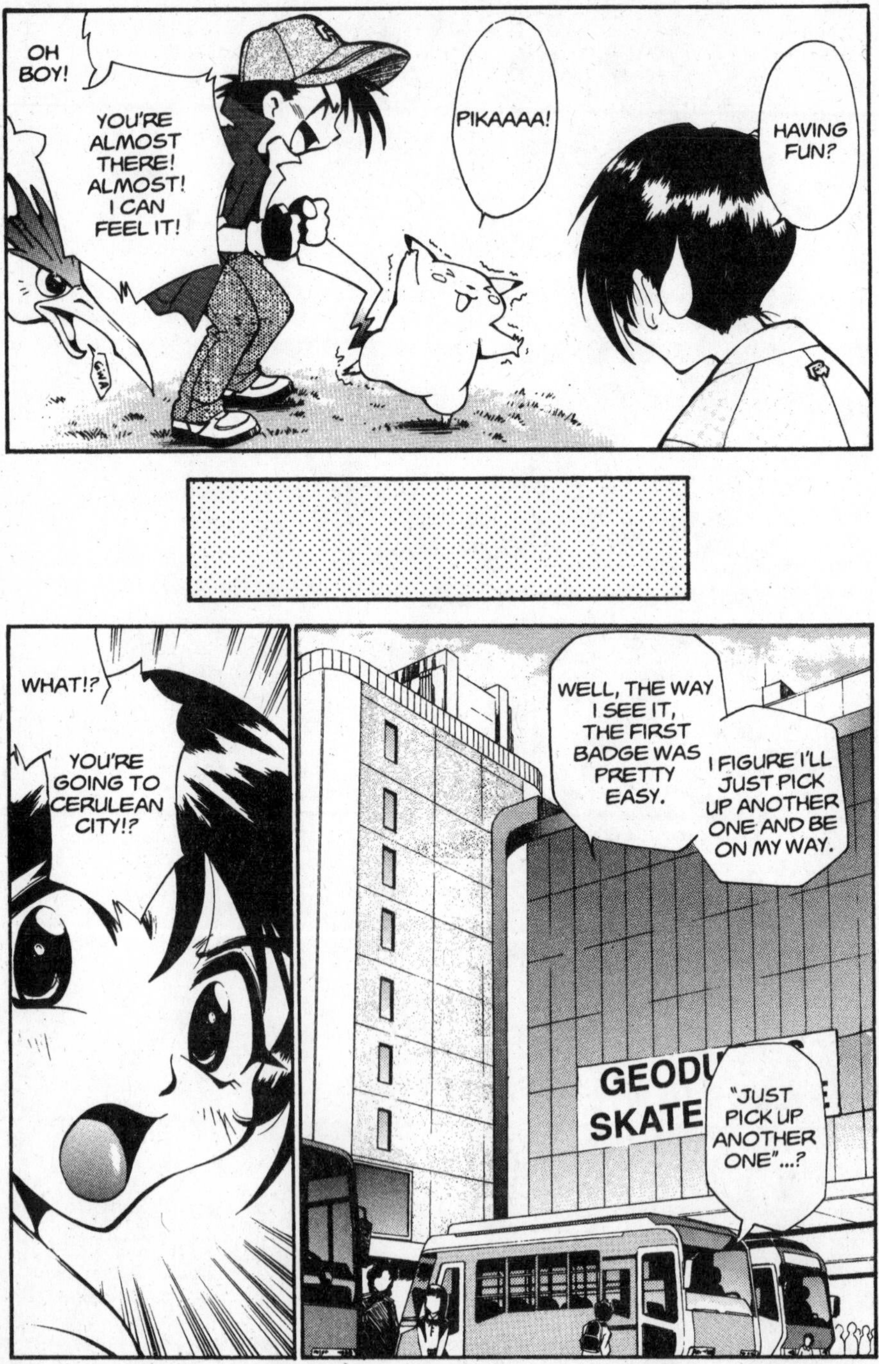
OH BOY!
YOU'RE ALMOST THERE! ALMOST! I CAN FEEL IT!
PIKAAAA!
HAVING FUN?
WHAT!?
YOU'RE GOING TO CERULEAN CITY!?
WELL, THE WAY I SEE IT, THE FIRST BADGE WAS PRETTY EASY.
I FIGURE I'LL JUST PICK UP ANOTHER ONE AND BE ON MY WAY.
GEODU
SKATE
"JUST PICK UP ANOTHER ONE"...?

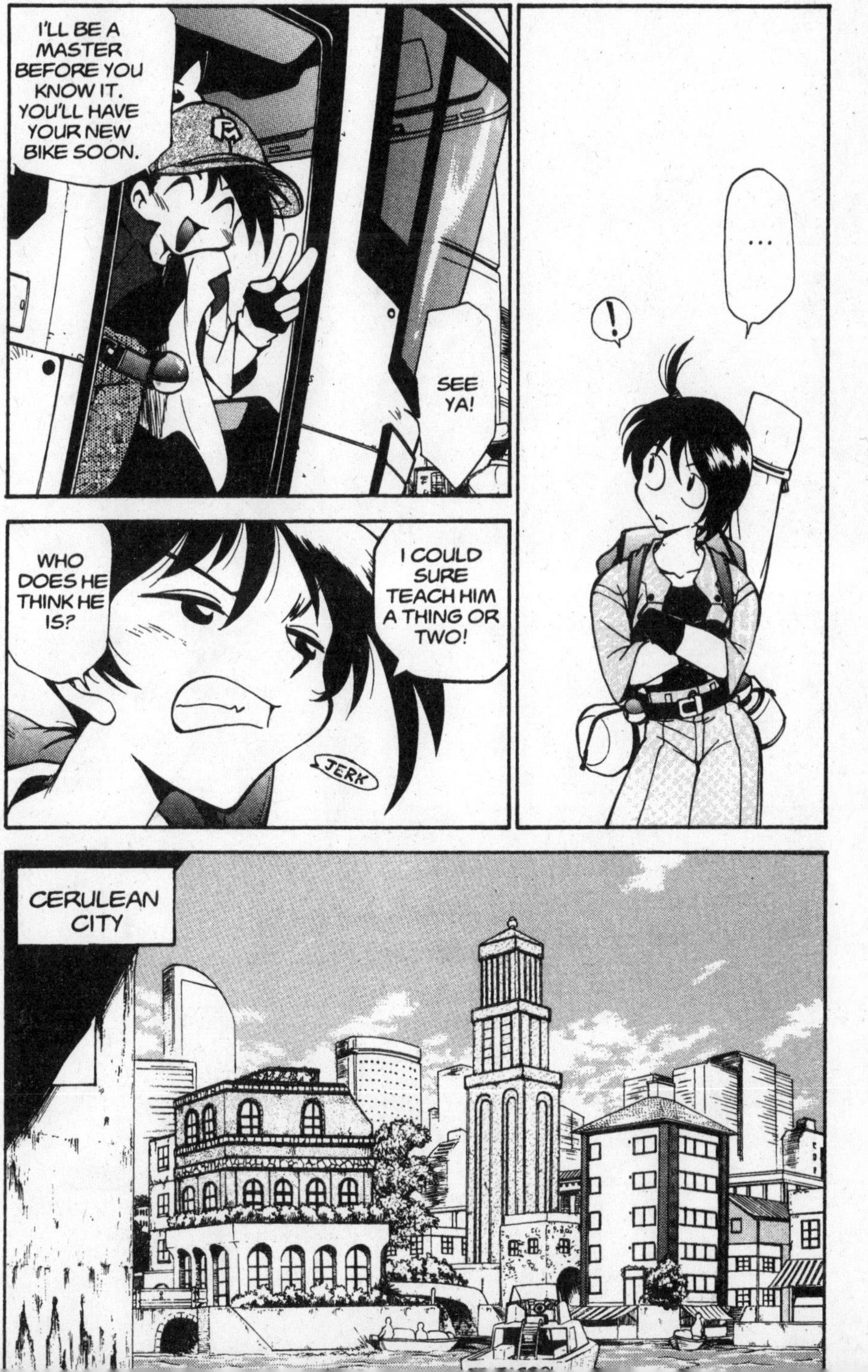
I'LL BE A MASTER BEFORE YOU KNOW IT. YOU'LL HAVE YOUR NEW BIKE SOON.
SEE YA!
WHO DOES HE THINK HE IS?
I COULD SURE TEACH HIM A THING OR TWO!
JERK
!
...
CERULEAN CITY

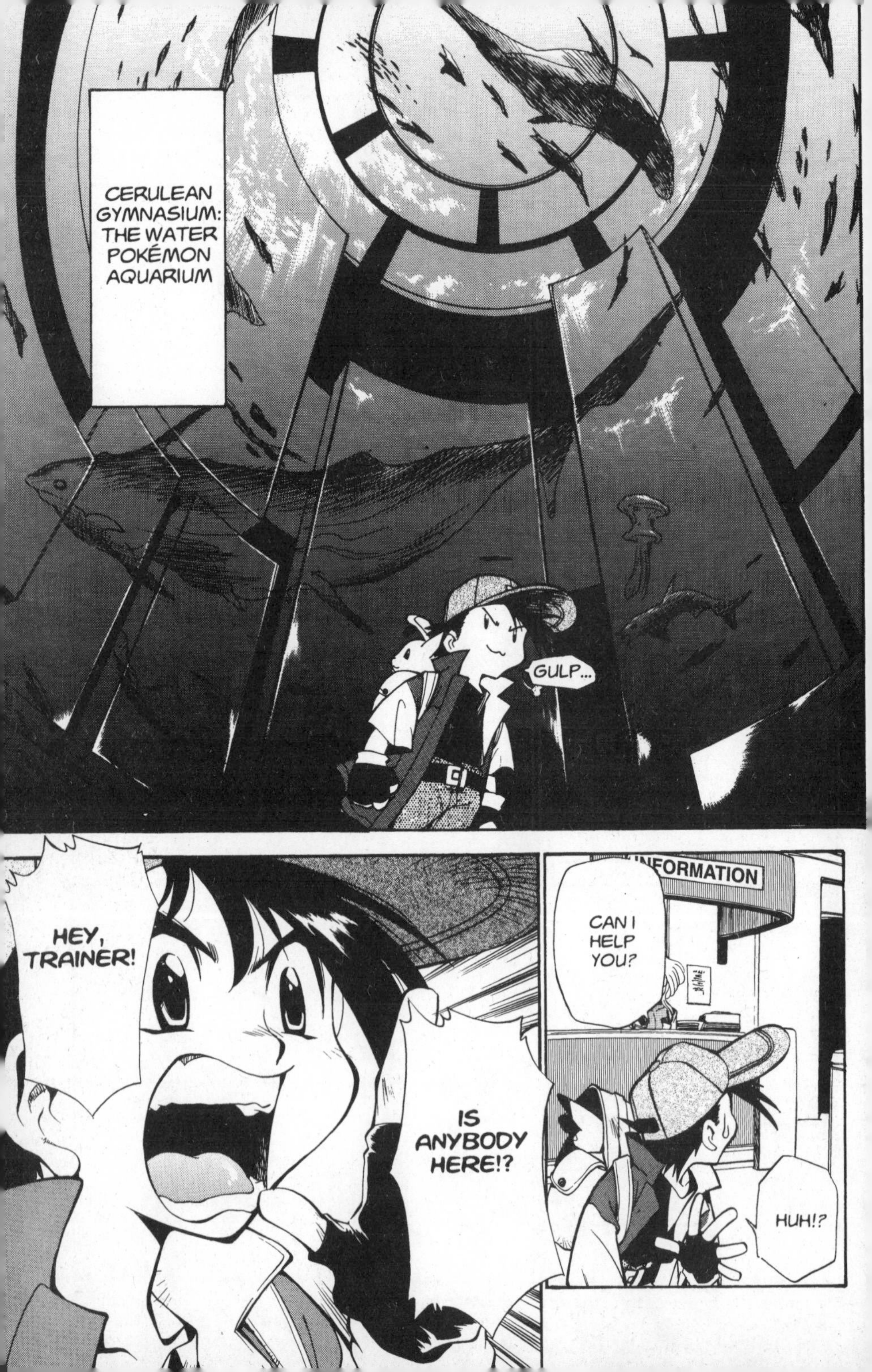
CERULEAN GYMNASIUM: THE WATER POKÉMON AQUARIUM
GULP...
HEY, TRAINER!
IS ANYBODY HERE!?
INFORMATION
CAN I HELP YOU?
HUH!?

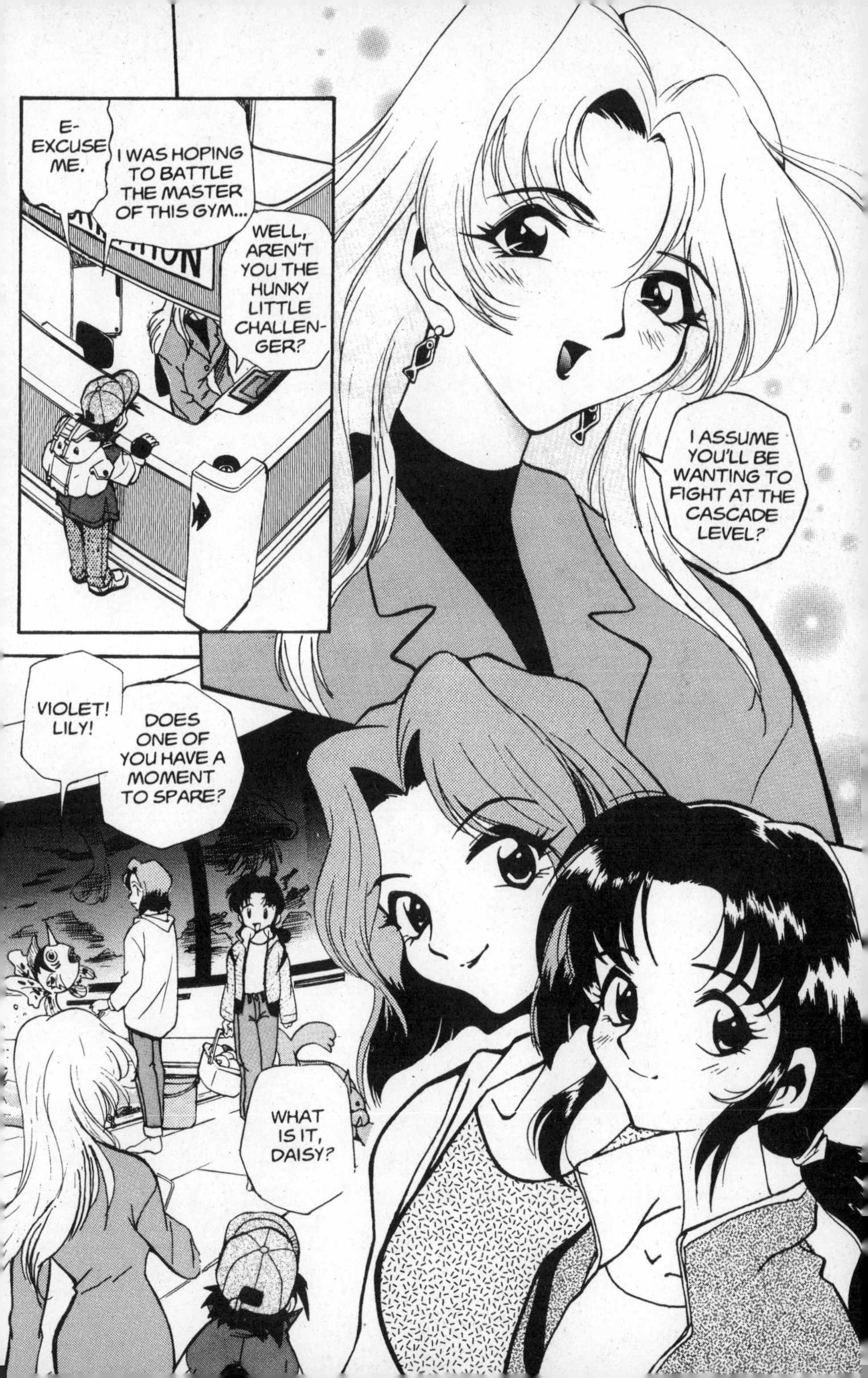
E-EXCUSE ME.
I WAS HOPING TO BATTLE THE MASTER OF THIS GYM...
WELL, AREN'T YOU THE HUNKY LITTLE CHALLENGER?
I ASSUME YOU'LL BE WANTING TO FIGHT AT THE CASCADE LEVEL?
VIOLET! LILY!
DOES ONE OF YOU HAVE A MOMENT TO SPARE?
WHAT IS IT, DAISY?

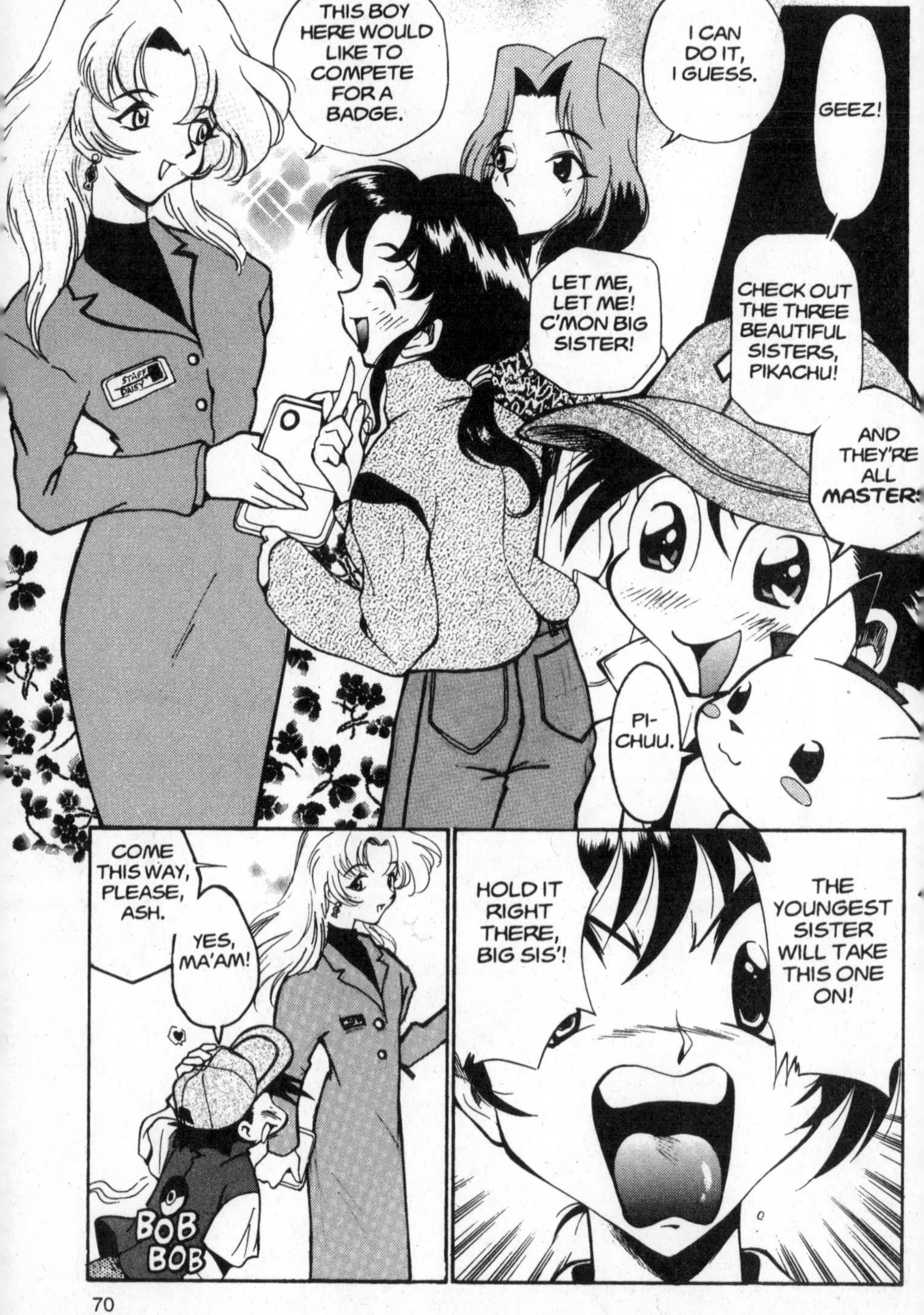
THIS BOY HERE WOULD LIKE TO COMPETE FOR A BADGE.
STAFF DAISY
I CAN DO IT, I GUESS.
GEEZ!
LET ME, LET ME! C'MON BIG SISTER!
CHECK OUT THE THREE BEAUTIFUL SISTERS, PIKACHU!
AND THEY'RE ALL MASTERS
PI-CHUU.
COME THIS WAY, PLEASE, ASH.
YES, MA'AM!
BOB BOB
HOLD IT RIGHT THERE, BIG SIS'!
THE YOUNGEST SISTER WILL TAKE THIS ONE ON!

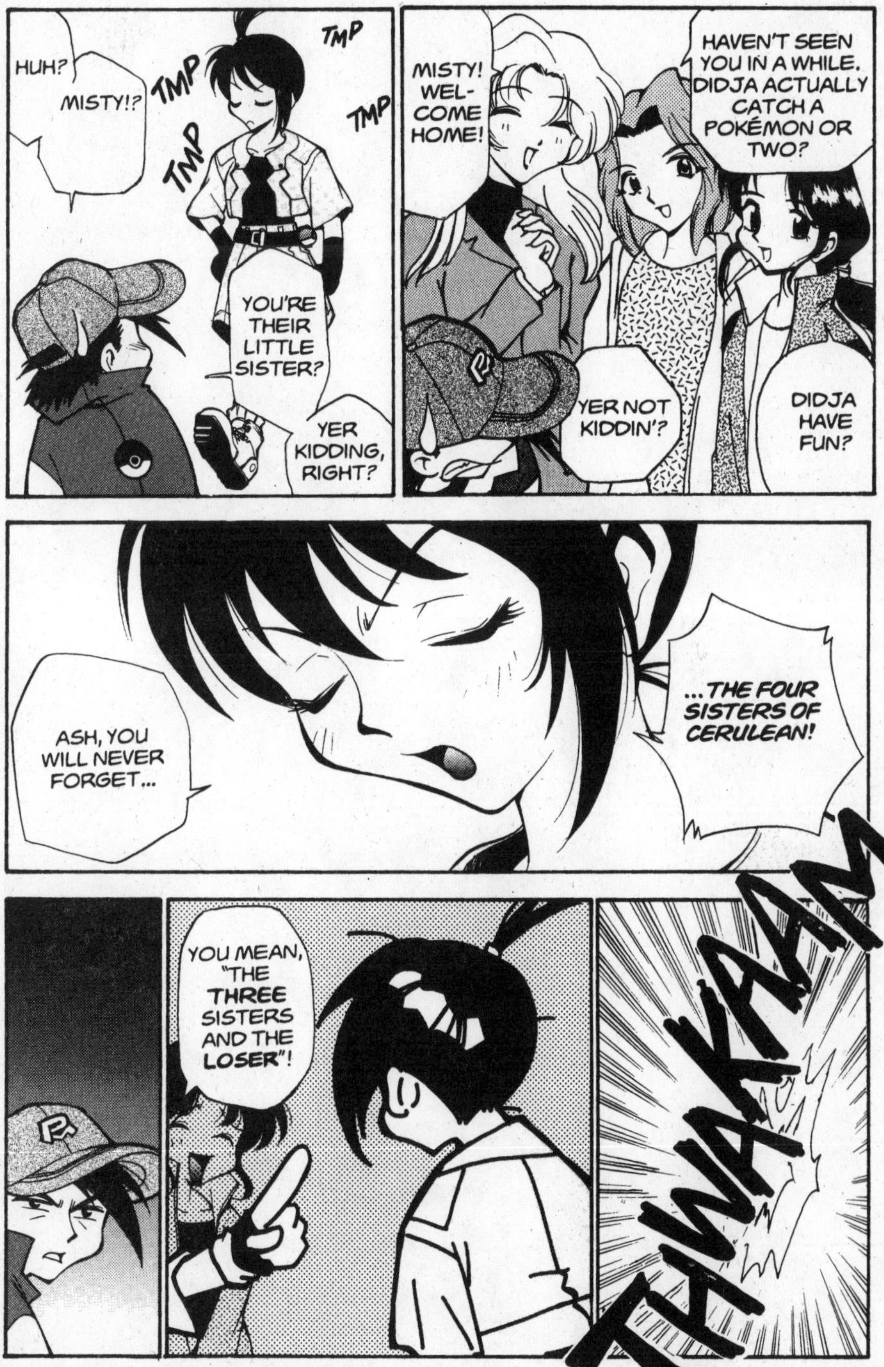
HUH?
MISTY!?
TMP
TMP
TMP
TMP
YOU'RE THEIR LITTLE SISTER?
YER KIDDING, RIGHT?
MISTY! WEL-COME HOME!
HAVEN'T SEEN YOU IN A WHILE. DIDJA ACTUALLY CATCH A POKÉMON OR TWO?
YER NOT KIDDIN'?
DIDJA HAVE FUN?
ASH, YOU WILL NEVER FORGET...
...THE FOUR SISTERS OF CERULEAN!
YOU MEAN, "THE THREE SISTERS AND THE LOSER"!
THWAKAM

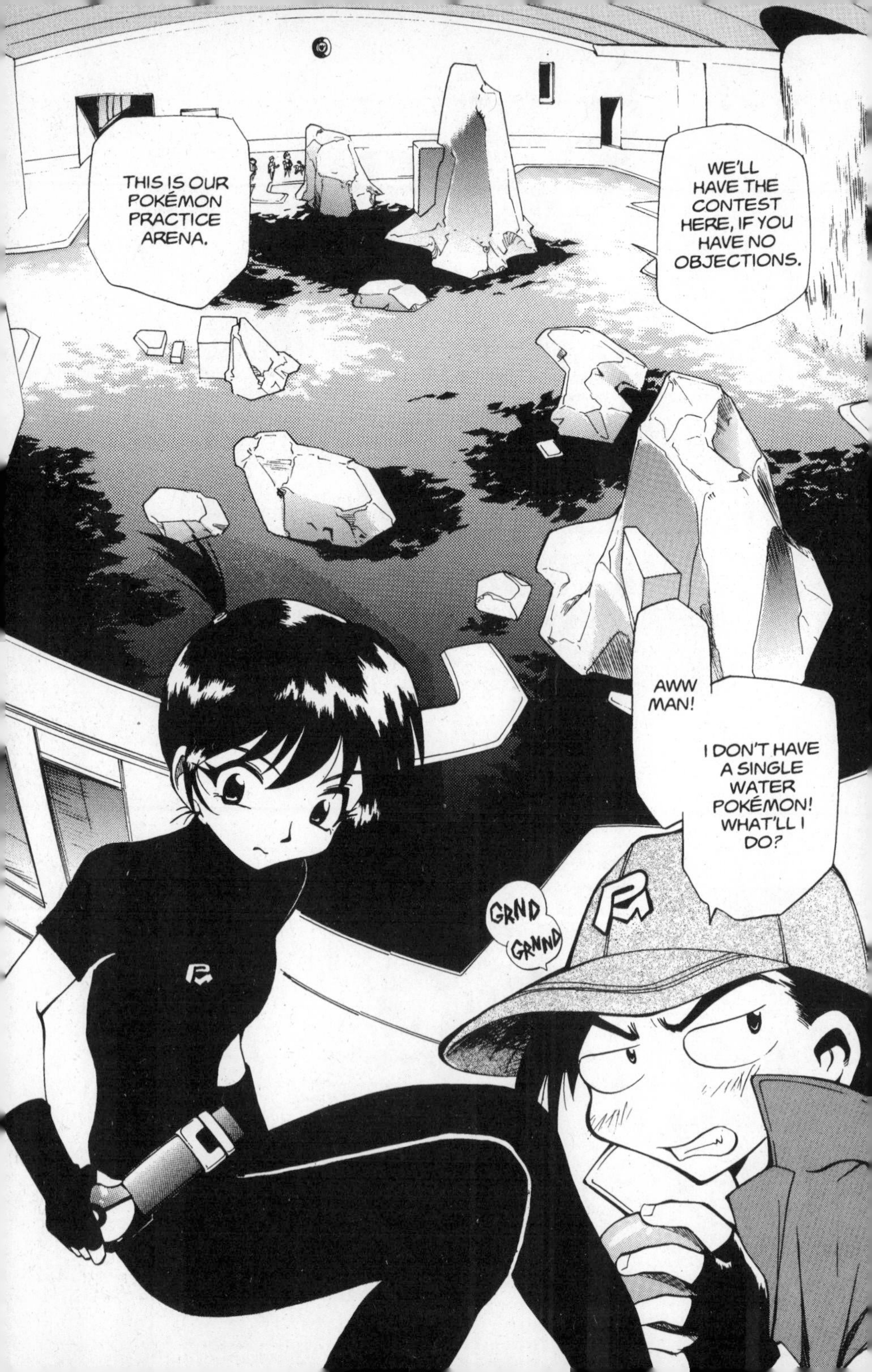
THIS IS OUR POKÉMON PRACTICE ARENA.
WE'LL HAVE THE CONTEST HERE, IF YOU HAVE NO OBJECTIONS.
AWW MAN!
I DON'T HAVE A SINGLE WATER POKÉMON! WHAT'LL I DO?
GRND GRNND

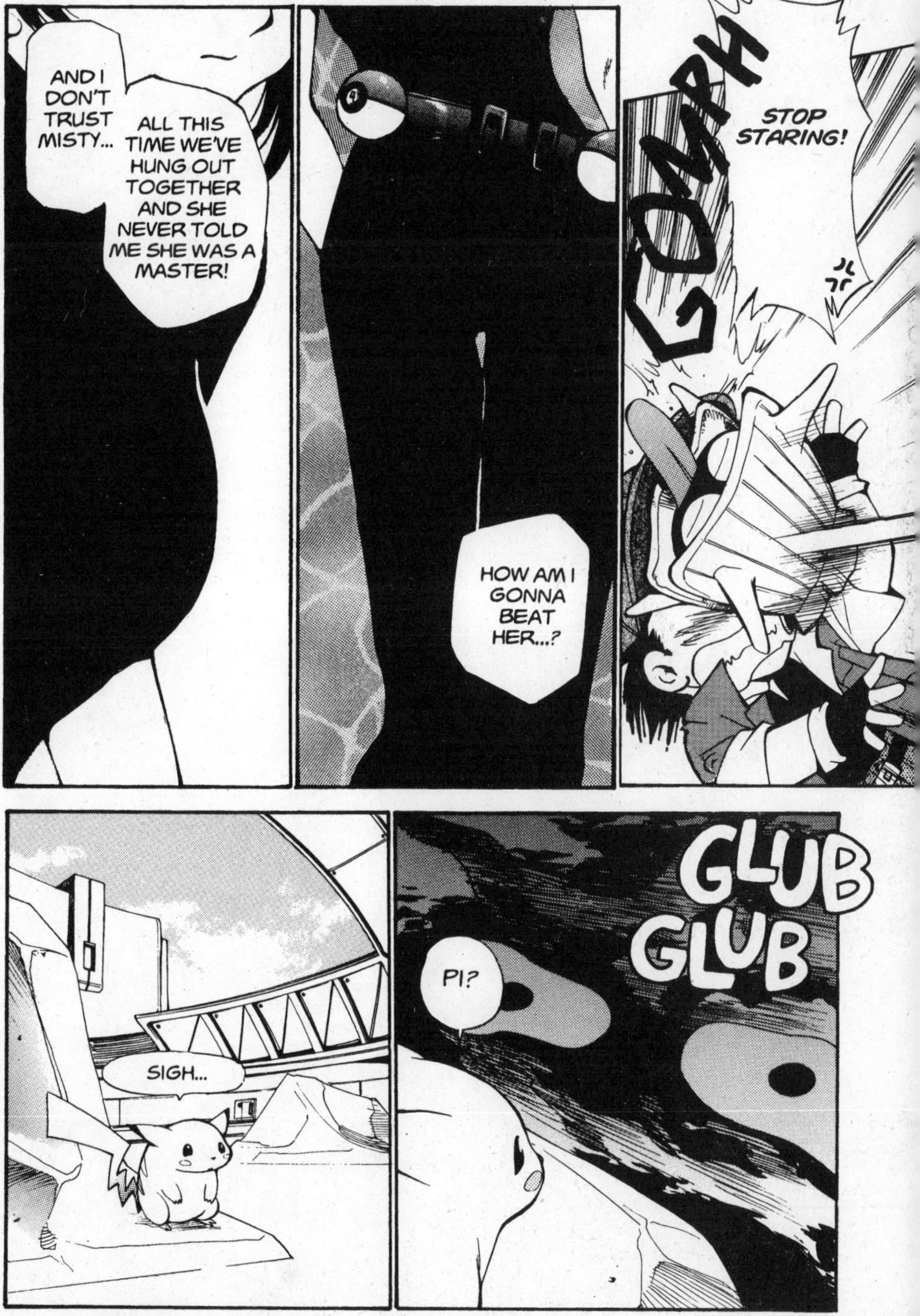

AND I DON'T TRUST MISTY...
ALL THIS TIME WE'VE HUNG OUT TOGETHER AND SHE NEVER TOLD ME SHE WAS A MASTER!
HOW AM I GONNA BEAT HER...?
GOMPH
STOP STARING!
SIGH...
GLUB GLUB
PI?

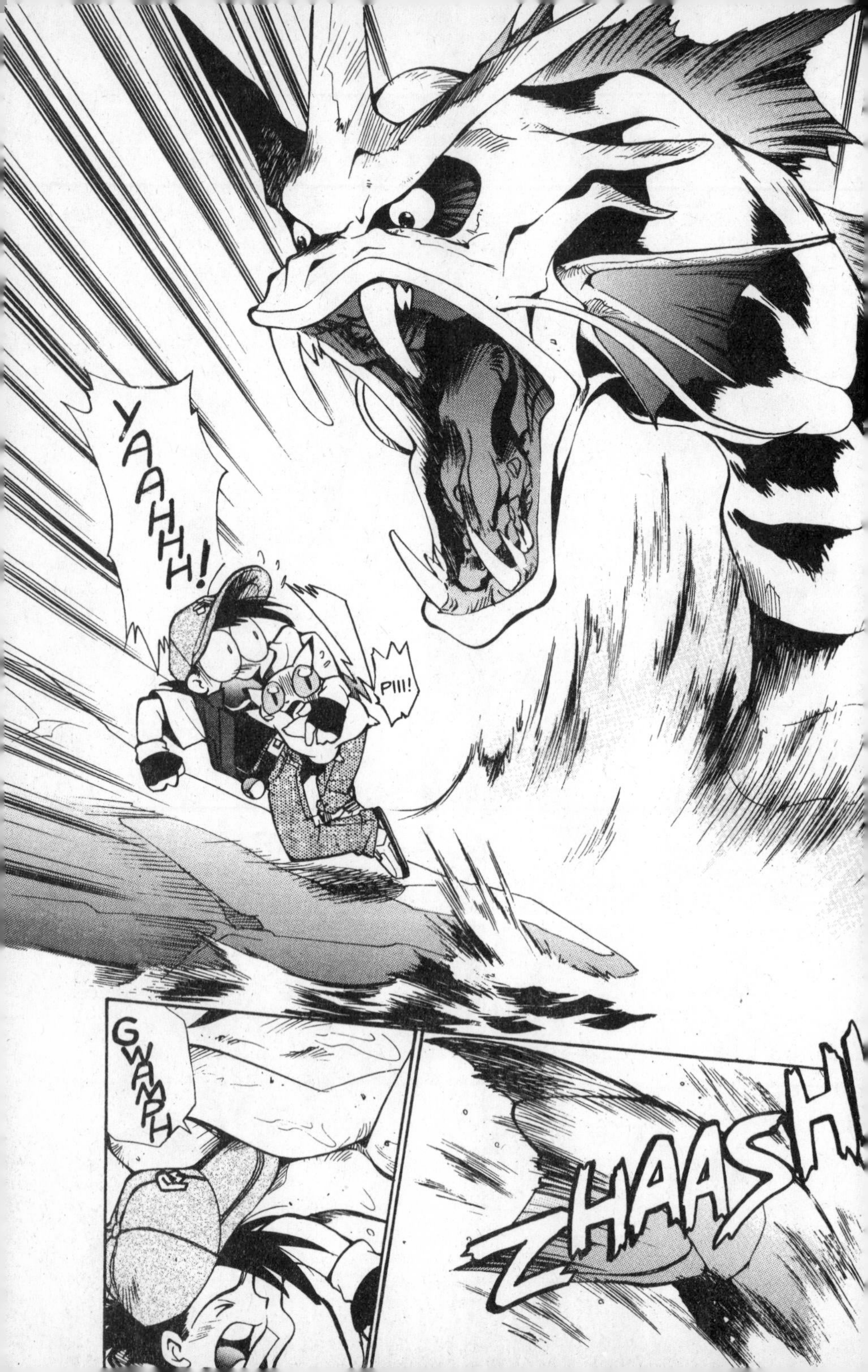
YAAHHH!
PIII!
GWAMPH
ZHAASH!

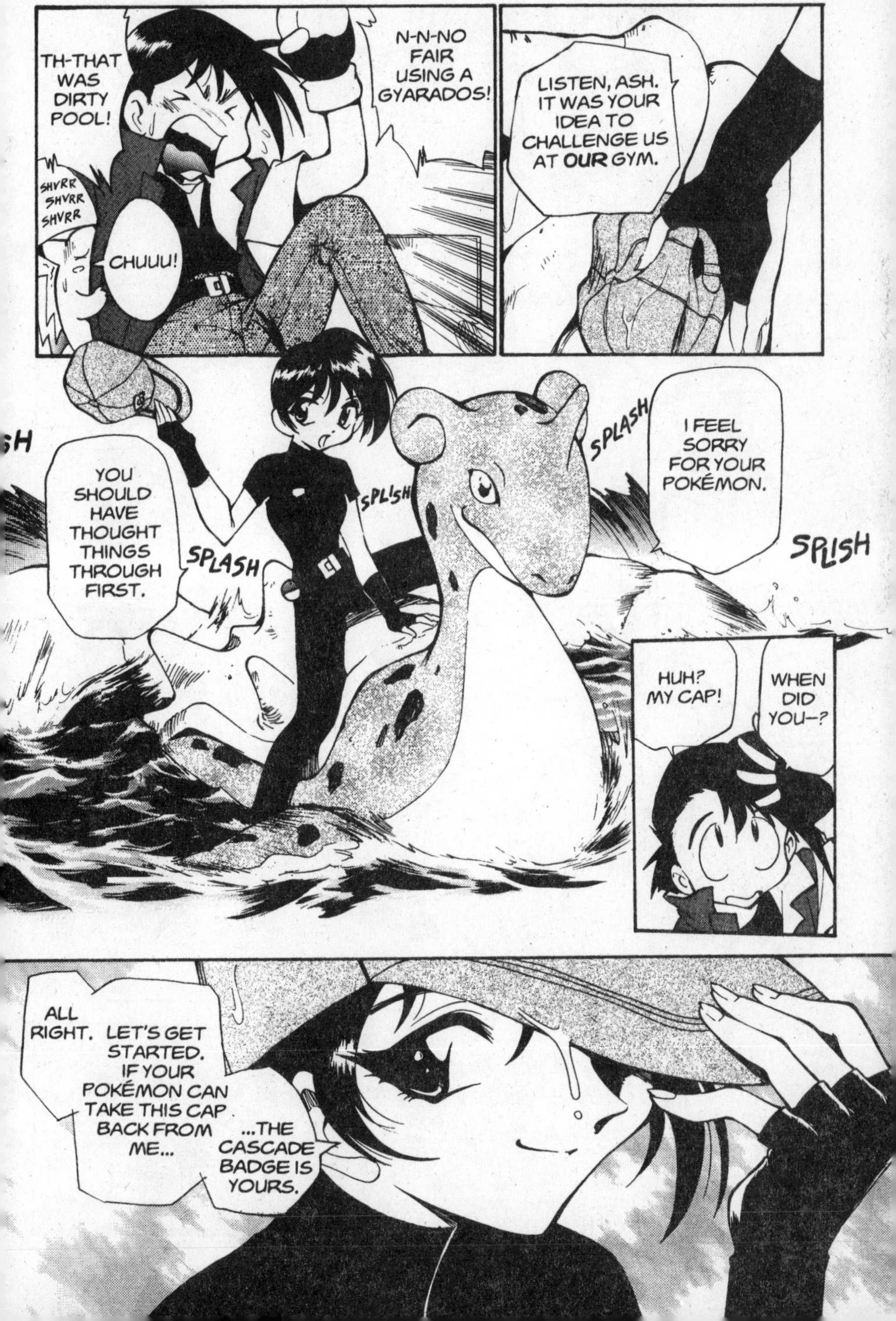
TH-THAT WAS DIRTY POOL!
N-N-NO FAIR USING A GYARADOS!
SHVRR SHVRR SHVRR
CHUUU!
LISTEN, ASH. IT WAS YOUR IDEA TO CHALLENGE US AT OUR GYM.
YOU SHOULD HAVE THOUGHT THINGS THROUGH FIRST.
SPLASH
SPLISH
SPLASH
I FEEL SORRY FOR YOUR POKÉMON.
SPLISH
HUH? MY CAP!
WHEN DID YOU–?
ALL RIGHT.
LET'S GET STARTED. IF YOUR POKÉMON CAN TAKE THIS CAP BACK FROM ME...
...THE CASCADE BADGE IS YOURS.

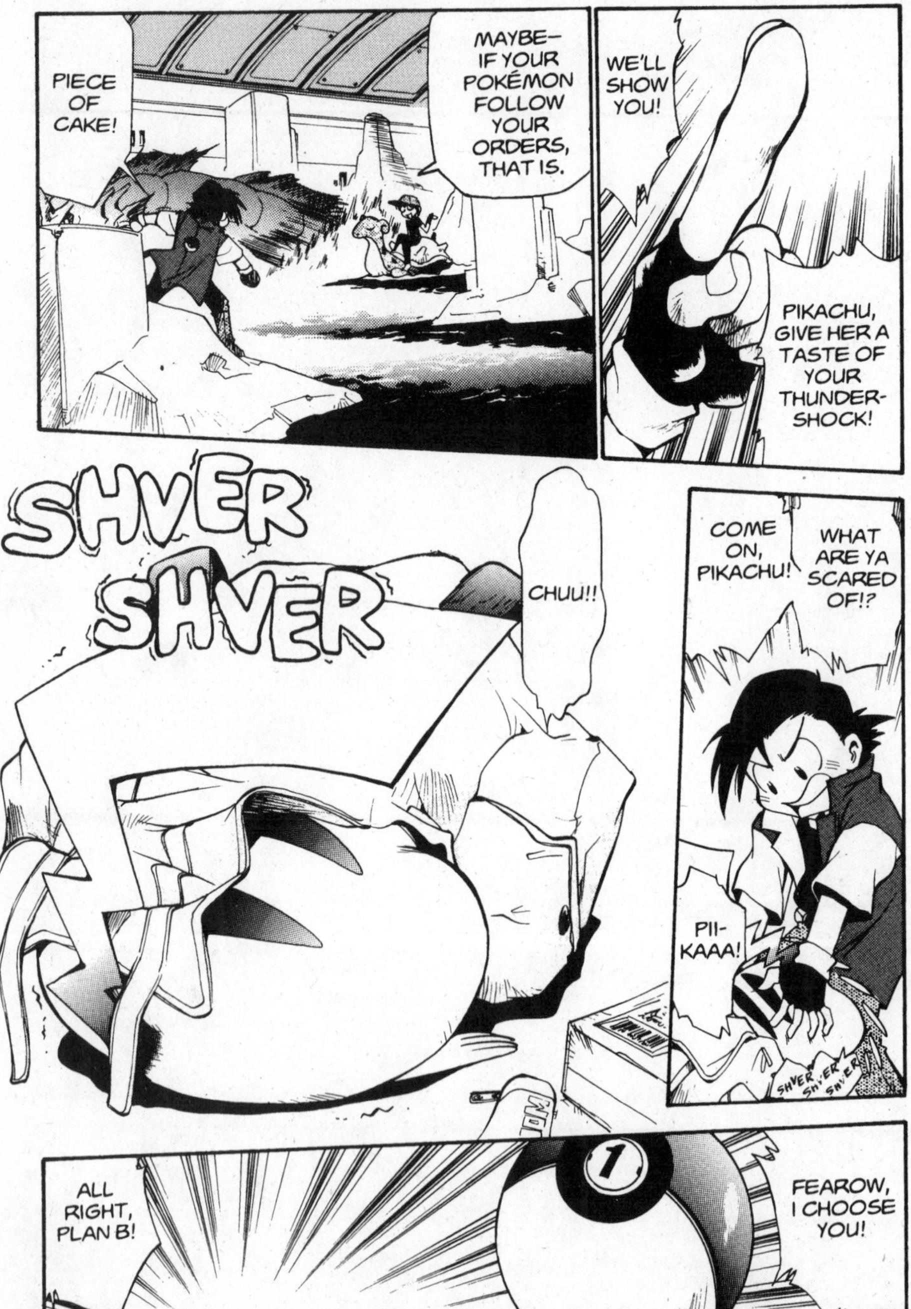
PIECE OF CAKE!
MAYBE— IF YOUR POKÉMON FOLLOW YOUR ORDERS, THAT IS.
WE'LL SHOW YOU!
PIKACHU, GIVE HER A TASTE OF YOUR THUNDER-SHOCK!
SHVER SHVER
CHUU!!
COME ON, PIKACHU!
WHAT ARE YA SCARED OF!?
PII-KAAA!
SHVER SHVER SHVER
ALL RIGHT, PLAN B!
FEAROW, I CHOOSE YOU!

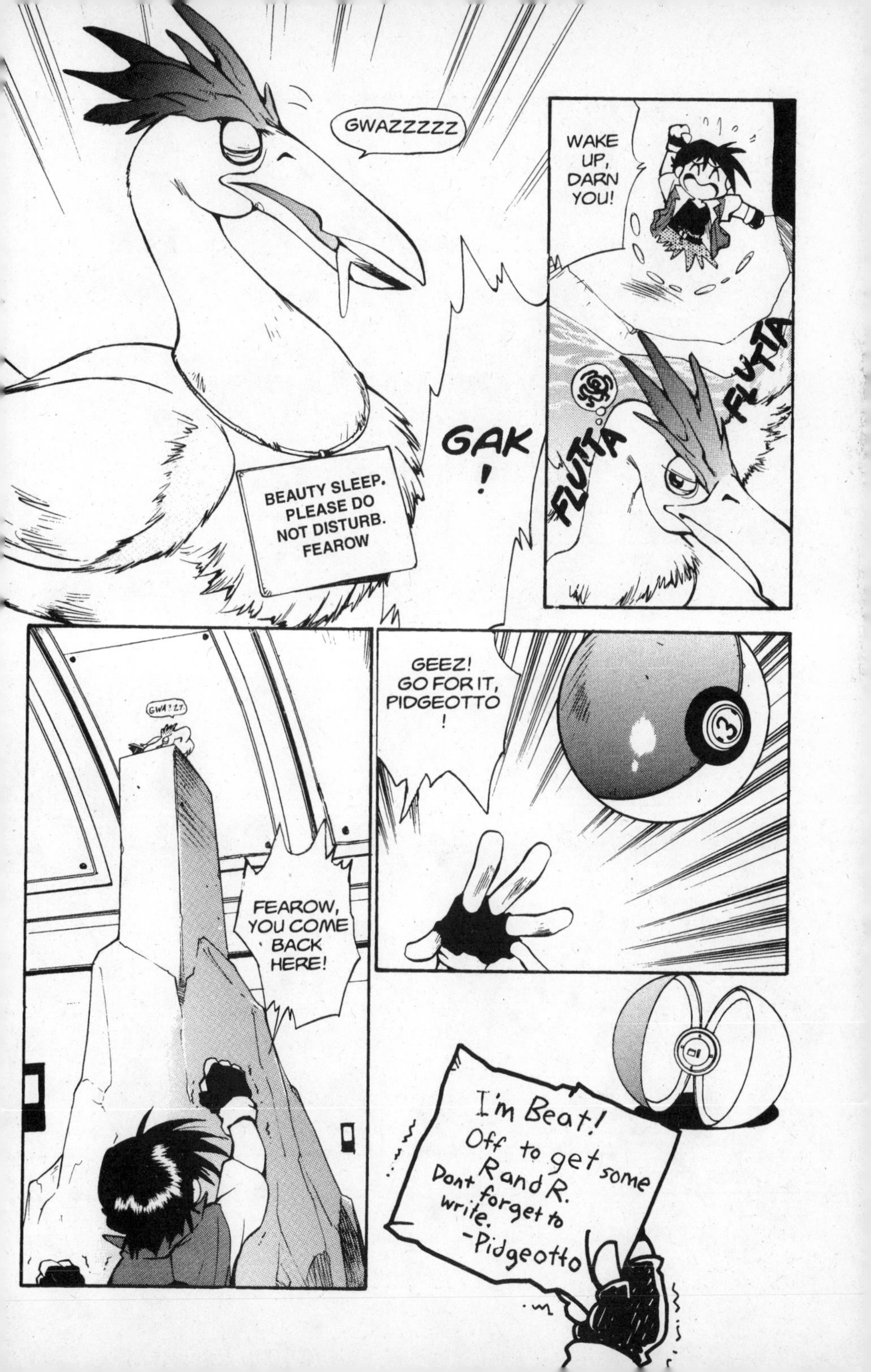
GWAZZZZZ
BEAUTY SLEEP. PLEASE DO NOT DISTURB. FEAROW
GAK!
WAKE UP, DARN YOU!
FLUTTA FLUTTA
GWAZZZ
FEAROW, YOU COME BACK HERE!
GEEZ! GO FOR IT, PIDGEOTTO!
I'm Beat! Off to get some R and R. Dont forget to write. -Pidgeotto

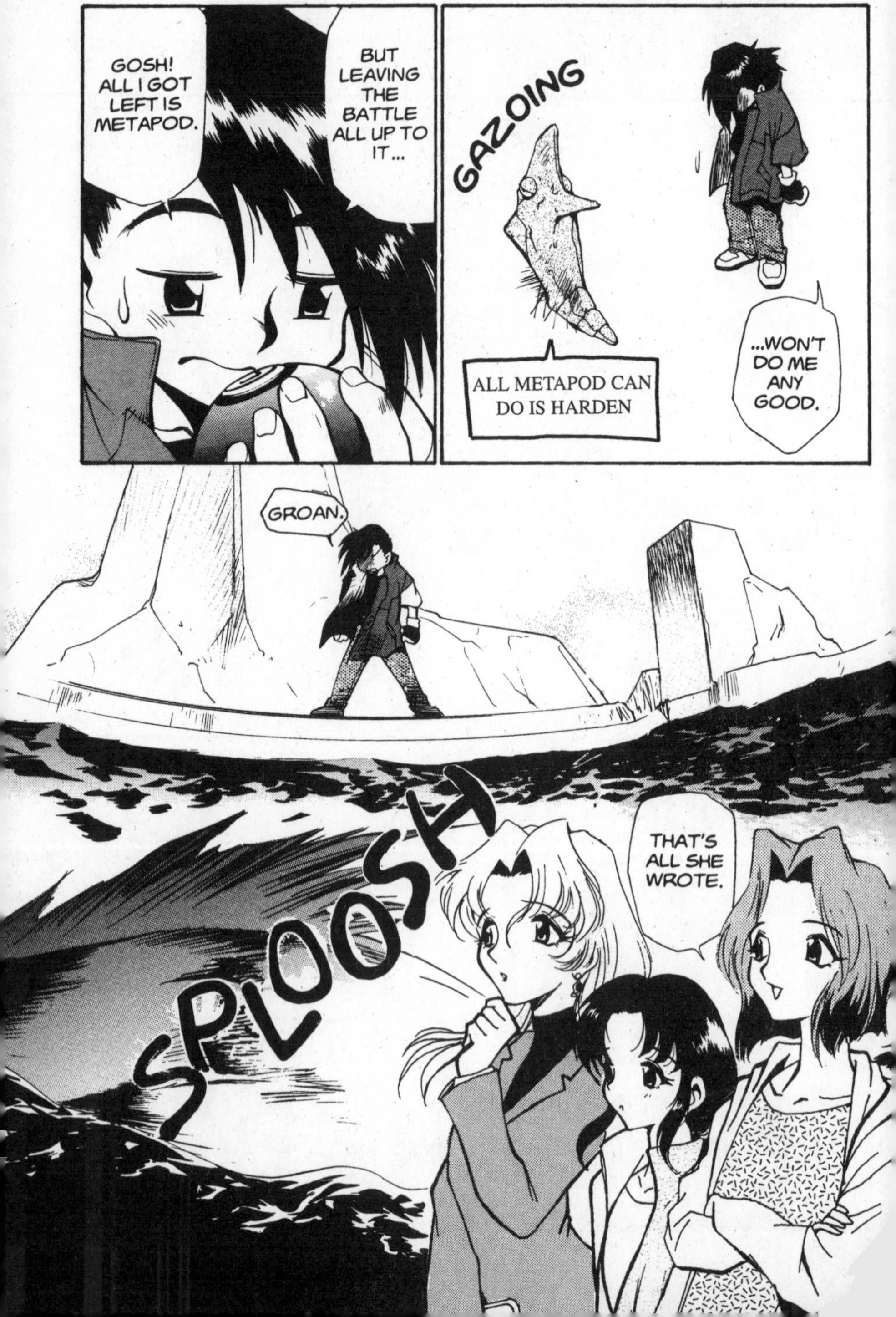

GOSH! ALL I GOT LEFT IS METAPOD.
BUT LEAVING THE BATTLE ALL UP TO IT...
GAZOING
ALL METAPOD CAN DO IS HARDEN
...WON'T DO ME ANY GOOD.
GROAN.
SPLOOSH
THAT'S ALL SHE WROTE.

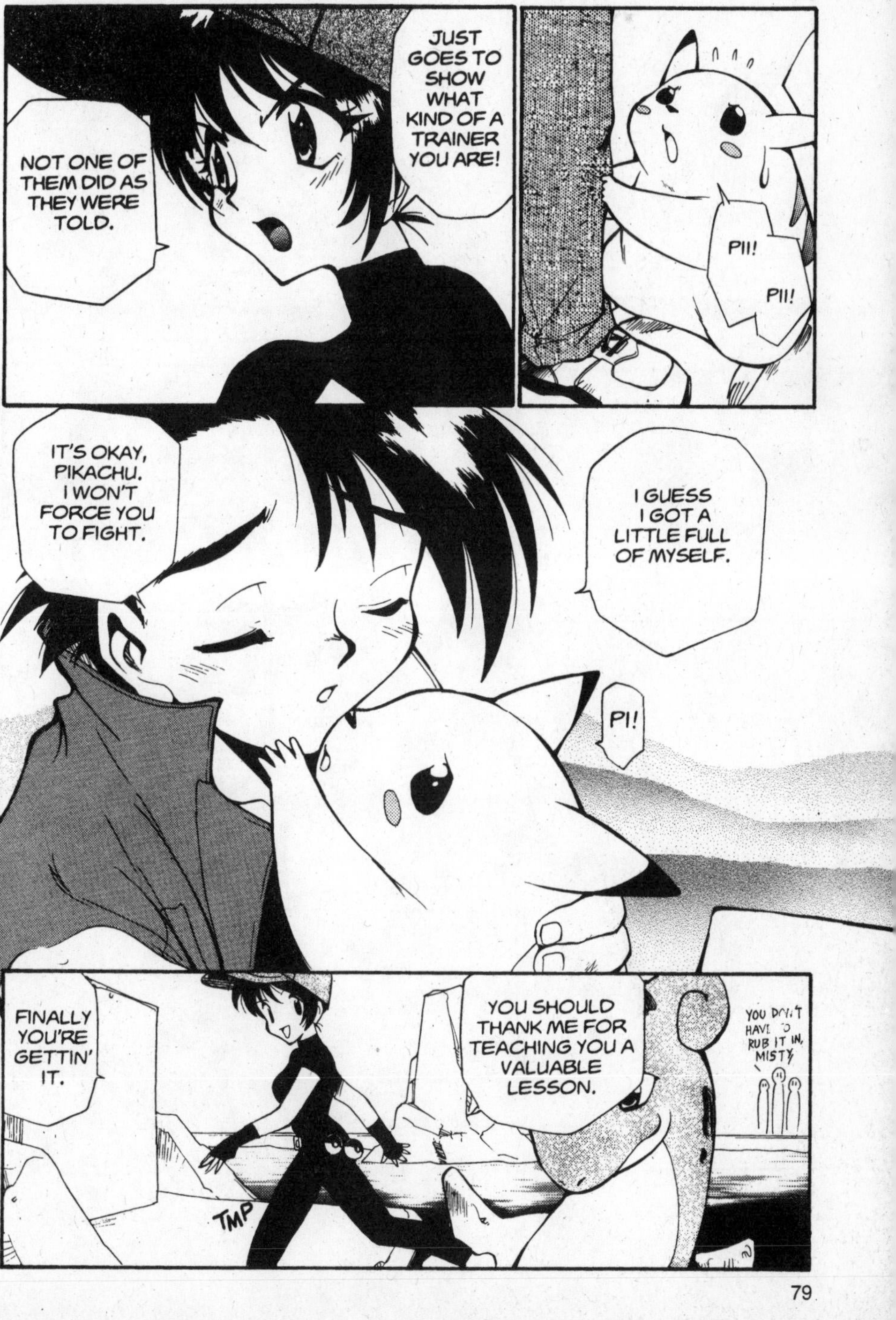
NOT ONE OF THEM DID AS THEY WERE TOLD.
JUST GOES TO SHOW WHAT KIND OF A TRAINER YOU ARE!
PII!
PII!
IT'S OKAY, PIKACHU. I WON'T FORCE YOU TO FIGHT.
I GUESS I GOT A LITTLE FULL OF MYSELF.
PI!
FINALLY YOU'RE GETTIN' IT.
YOU SHOULD THANK ME FOR TEACHING YOU A VALUABLE LESSON.
YOU DON'T HAVE TO RUB IT IN, MISTY
TMP

GYARADOS HERE EVOLVED FROM MY FIRST POKÉMON, A MAGIKARP THAT I CAUGHT AND RAISED.

IT'LL EVEN FOLLOW INSTRUCTIONS AS SPECIFIC AS "GO GET THAT GUY'S HAT."

BUT YOU JUST PET AND PLAY WITH YOUR POKÉMON LIKE THEY'RE TOYS!

HOW CAN YOU GAIN YOUR POKÉMONS' CONFIDENCE THAT WAY!?

BLAH BLAH BLAH

BOO HOO

BLAH BLAH

OH MY GAWD. MISTY'S STARTED ONE OF HER LECTURES.

SHE'LL GO ON FOR HOURS.

EH?

L-LOOK AT META-POD!

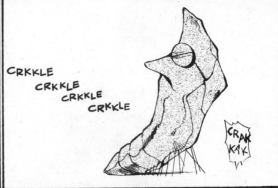

CRKKLE CRKKLE CRKKLE CRKKLE

CRAK KAK

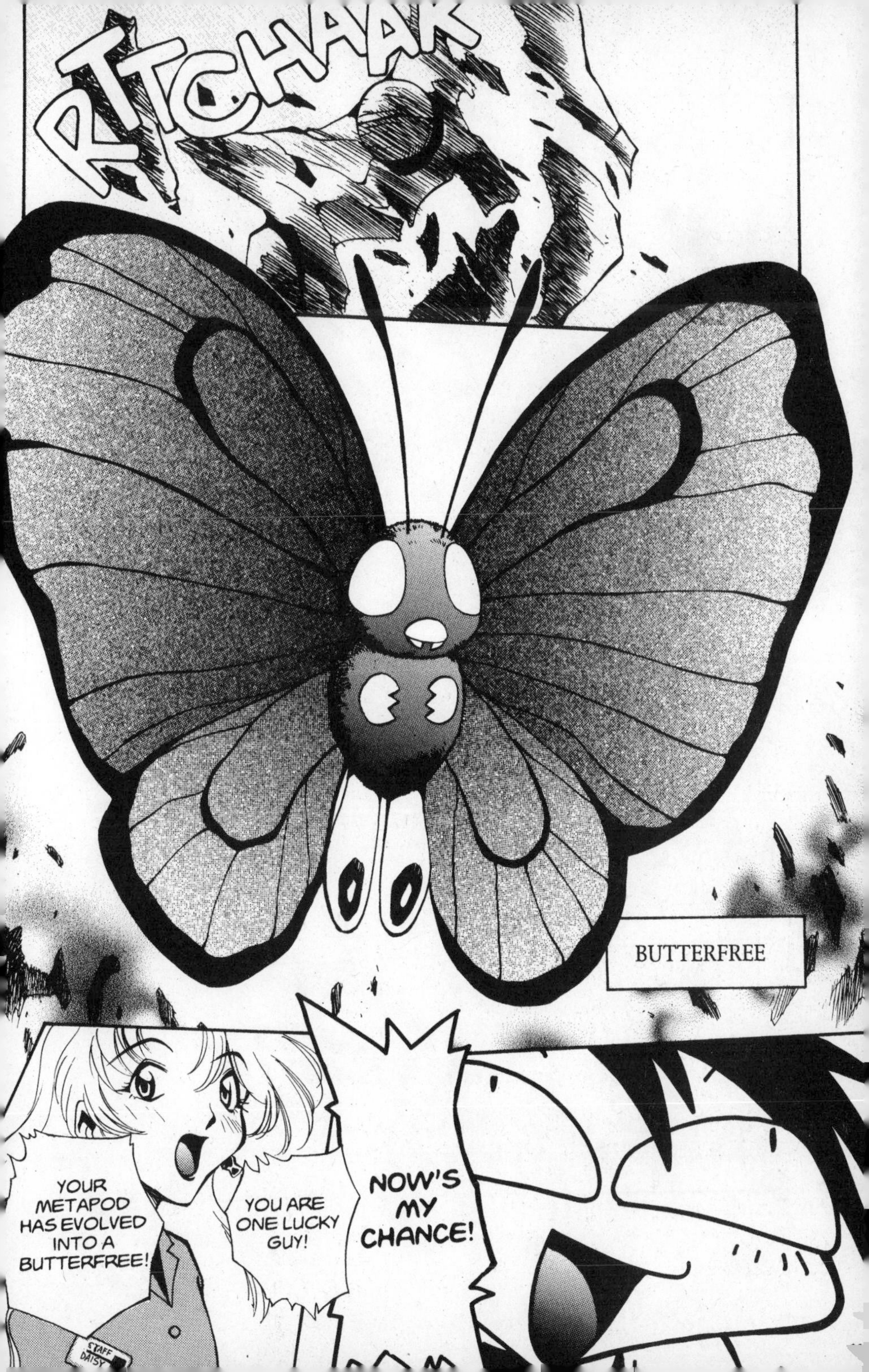

RITCHAAK
BUTTERFREE
YOUR METAPOD HAS EVOLVED INTO A BUTTERFREE!
YOU ARE ONE LUCKY GUY!
NOW'S MY CHANCE!
STAFF DAISY

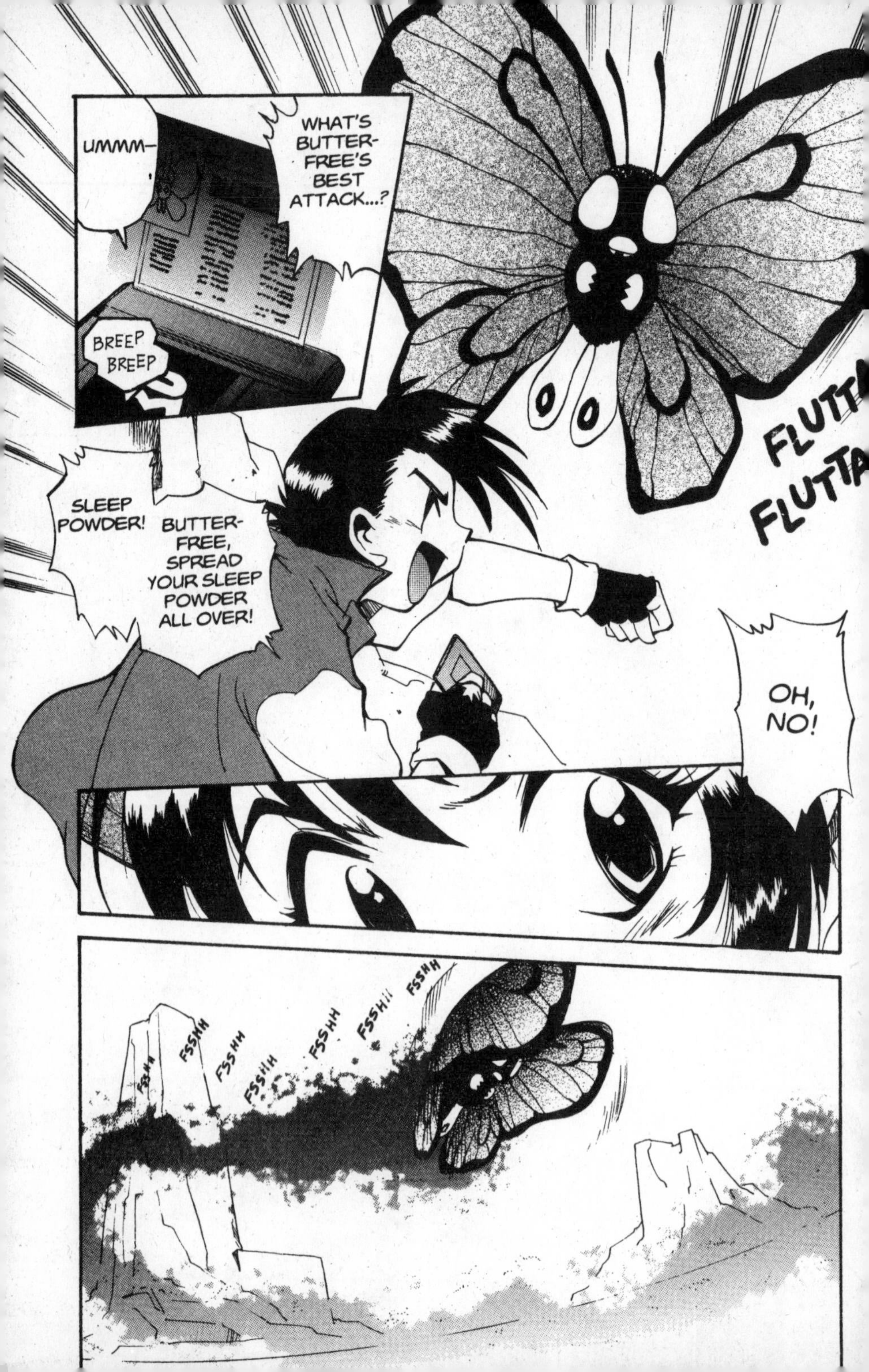
UMMM-
WHAT'S BUTTER-FREE'S BEST ATTACK...?
BREEP BREEP
FLUTTA FLUTTA
SLEEP POWDER!
BUTTER-FREE, SPREAD YOUR SLEEP POWDER ALL OVER!
OH, NO!
FSSHH
FSSHH
FSSHH
FSSHH
FSSHH
FSSHH
FSSHH

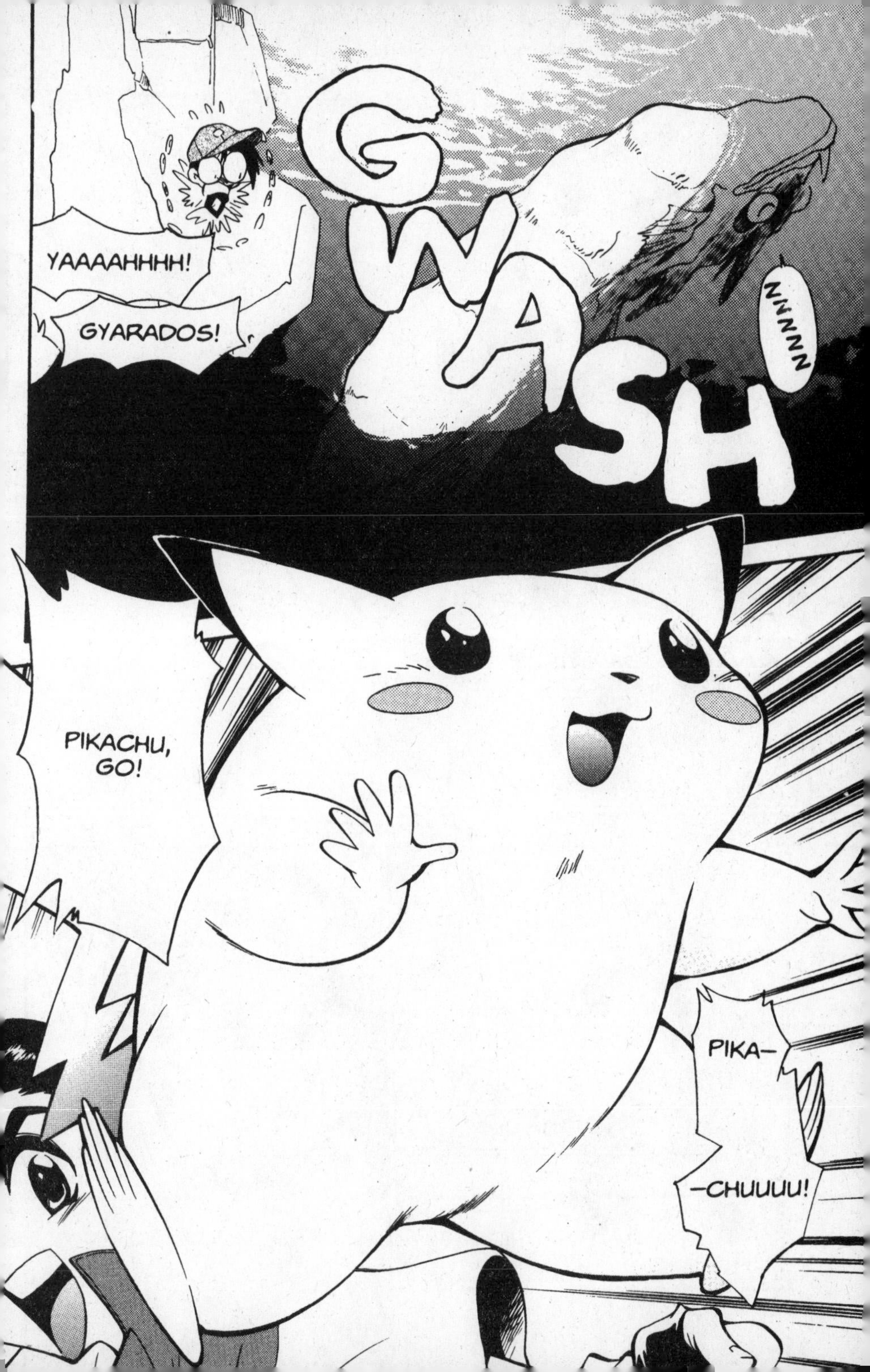
YAAAAHHHH!
GYARADOS!
GWASH
NNNNN
PIKACHU, GO!
PIKA–
–CHUUUU!

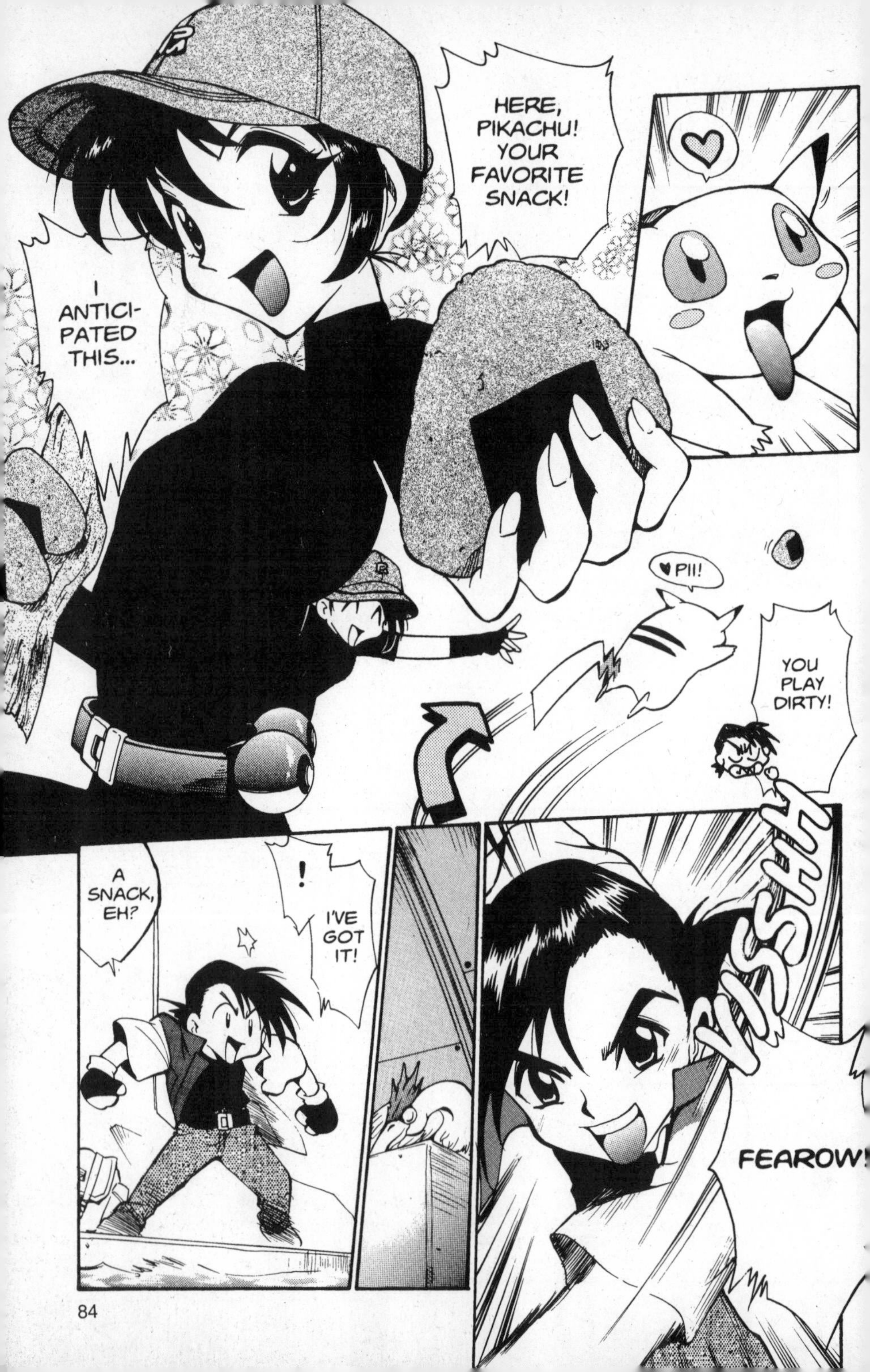
I ANTICI-PATED THIS...
HERE, PIKACHU! YOUR FAVORITE SNACK!
♥
♥ PII!
YOU PLAY DIRTY!
A SNACK, EH?
!
I'VE GOT IT!
FEAROW!

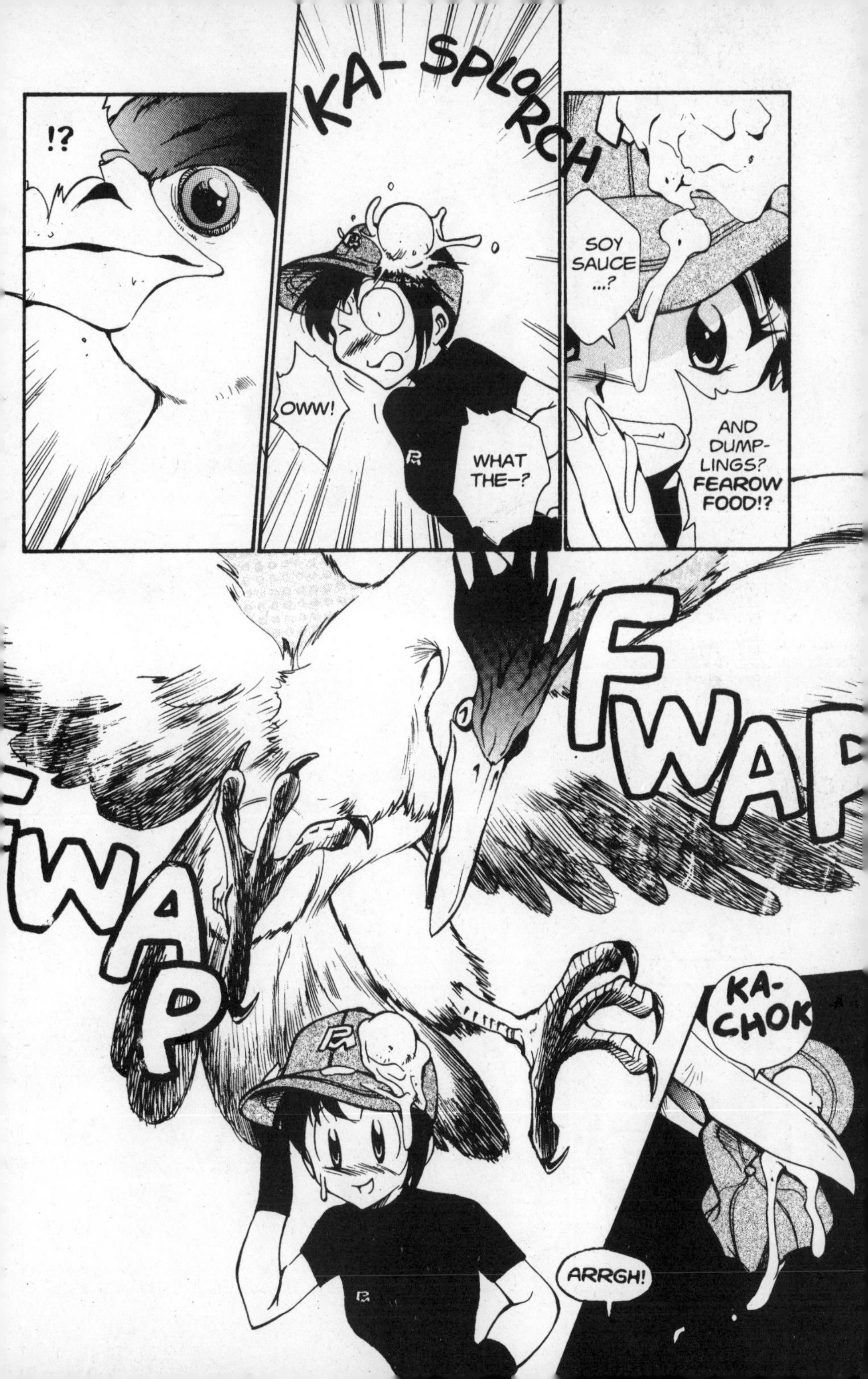
!?
KA-SPLORCH
OWW!
WHAT THE–?
SOY SAUCE ...?
AND DUMP-LINGS? FEAROW FOOD!?
FWAP
FWAP
KA-CHOK
ARRGH!

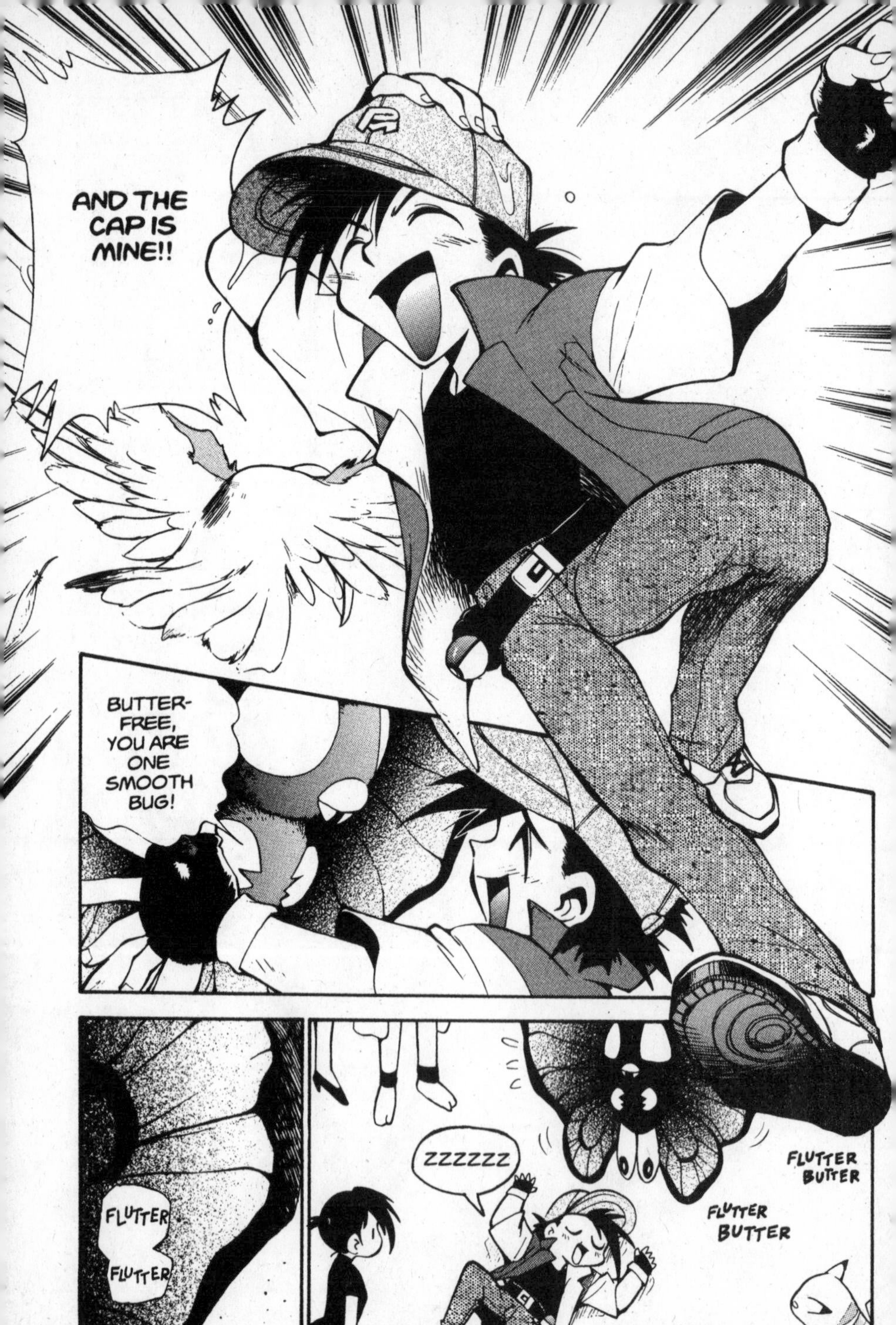
AND THE CAP IS MINE!!
BUTTER-FREE, YOU ARE ONE SMOOTH BUG!
FLUTTER
FLUTTER
ZZZZZZ
FLUTTER BUTTER
FLUTTER BUTTER

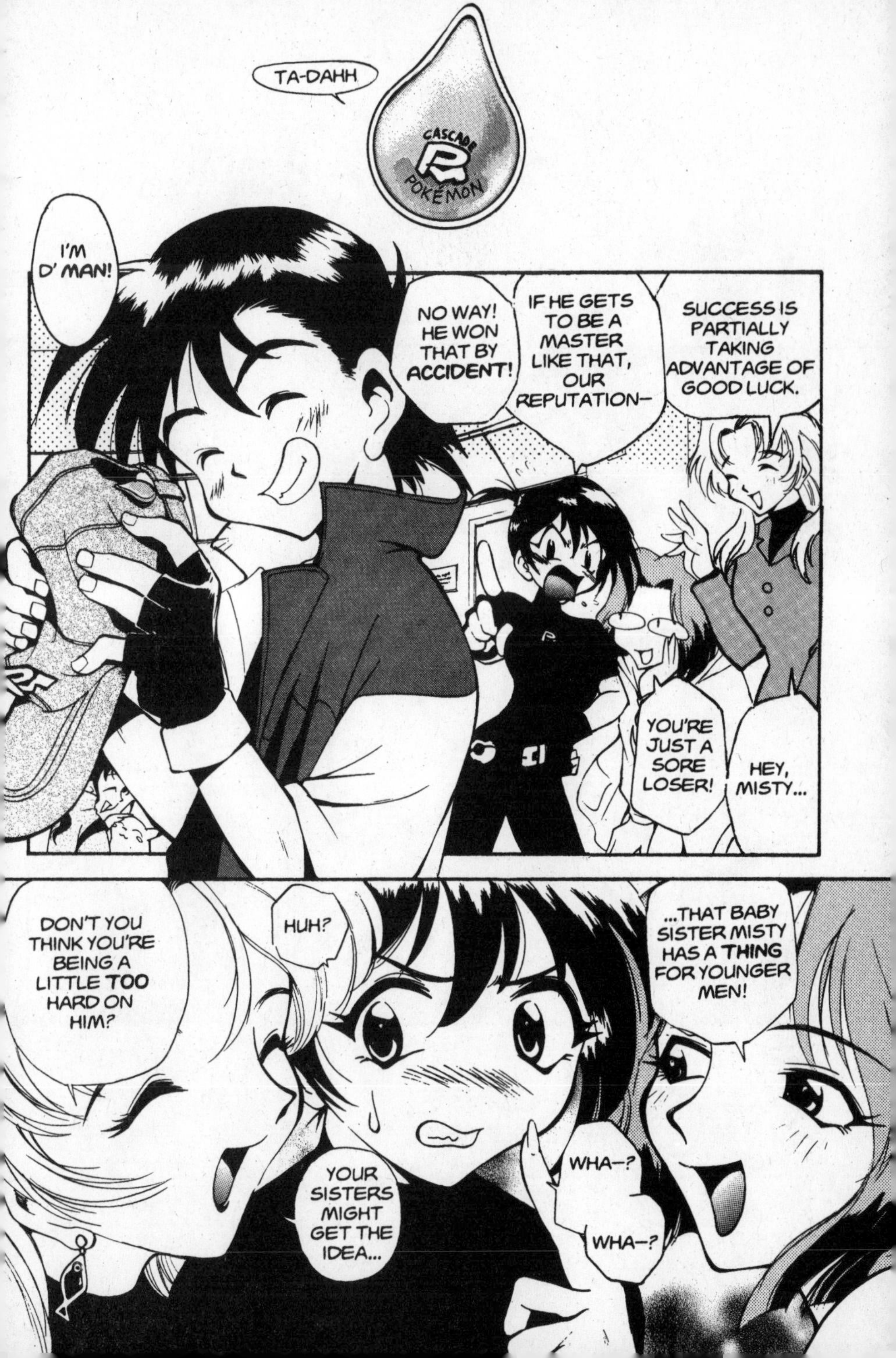
TA-DAHH
CASCADE
POKÉMON
I'M D' MAN!
NO WAY! HE WON THAT BY ACCIDENT!
IF HE GETS TO BE A MASTER LIKE THAT, OUR REPUTATION–
SUCCESS IS PARTIALLY TAKING ADVANTAGE OF GOOD LUCK.
YOU'RE JUST A SORE LOSER!
HEY, MISTY...
DON'T YOU THINK YOU'RE BEING A LITTLE TOO HARD ON HIM?
HUH?
...THAT BABY SISTER MISTY HAS A THING FOR YOUNGER MEN!
YOUR SISTERS MIGHT GET THE IDEA...
WHA–?
WHA–?

OHHH NOOoo
WAAAH! I'M SO SCARED!
NO BOY IS SAFE AROUND A GIRL LIKE YOU!
ARE YOU OUT OF YOUR MIND!?
YARGG
WAMMBA
WAMMBA
WAMMBA
COME ON. WE'VE GOT WORK TO DO.
THEY MAKE A CUTE COUPLE.
PII?

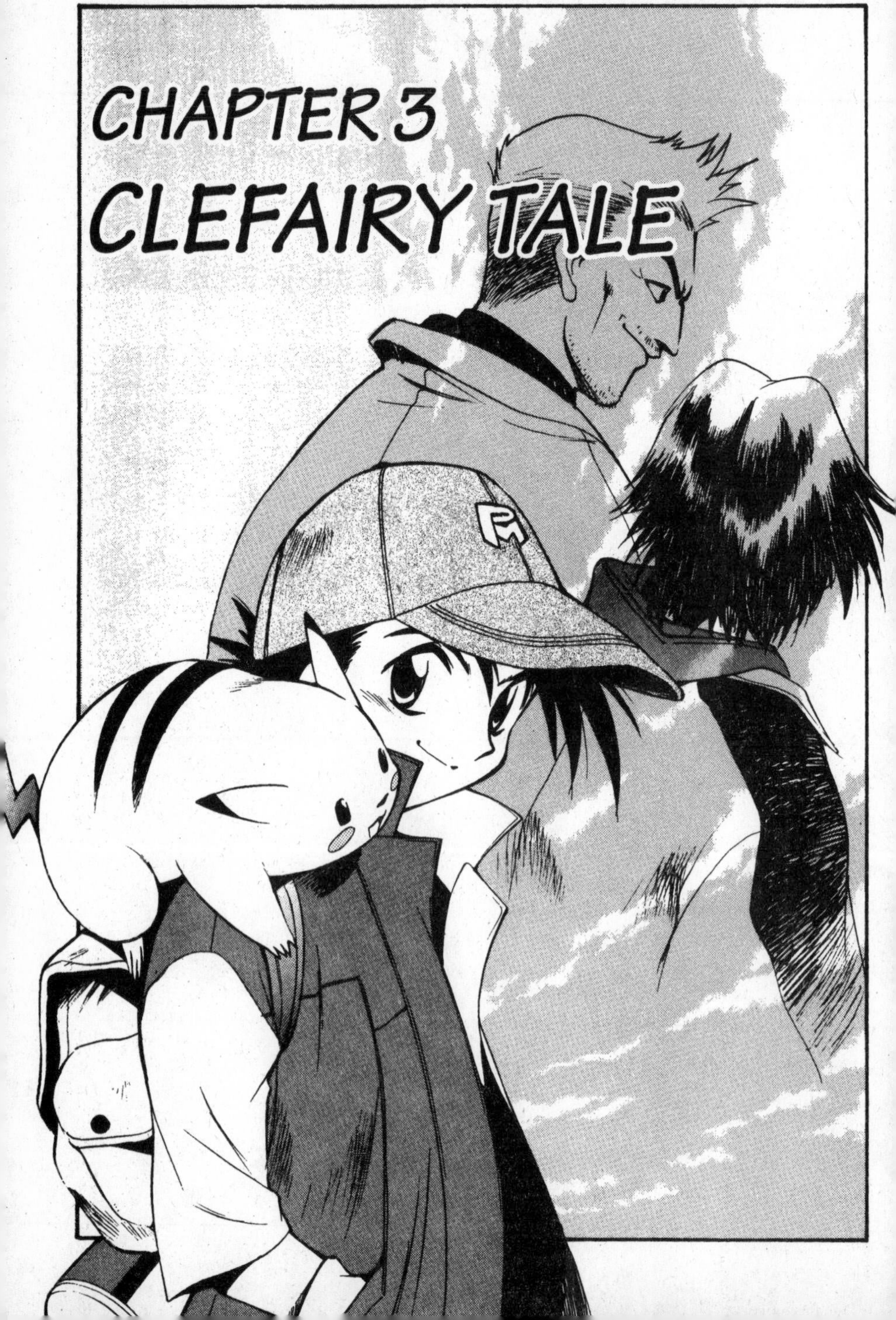
CHAPTER 3
CLEFAIRY TALE

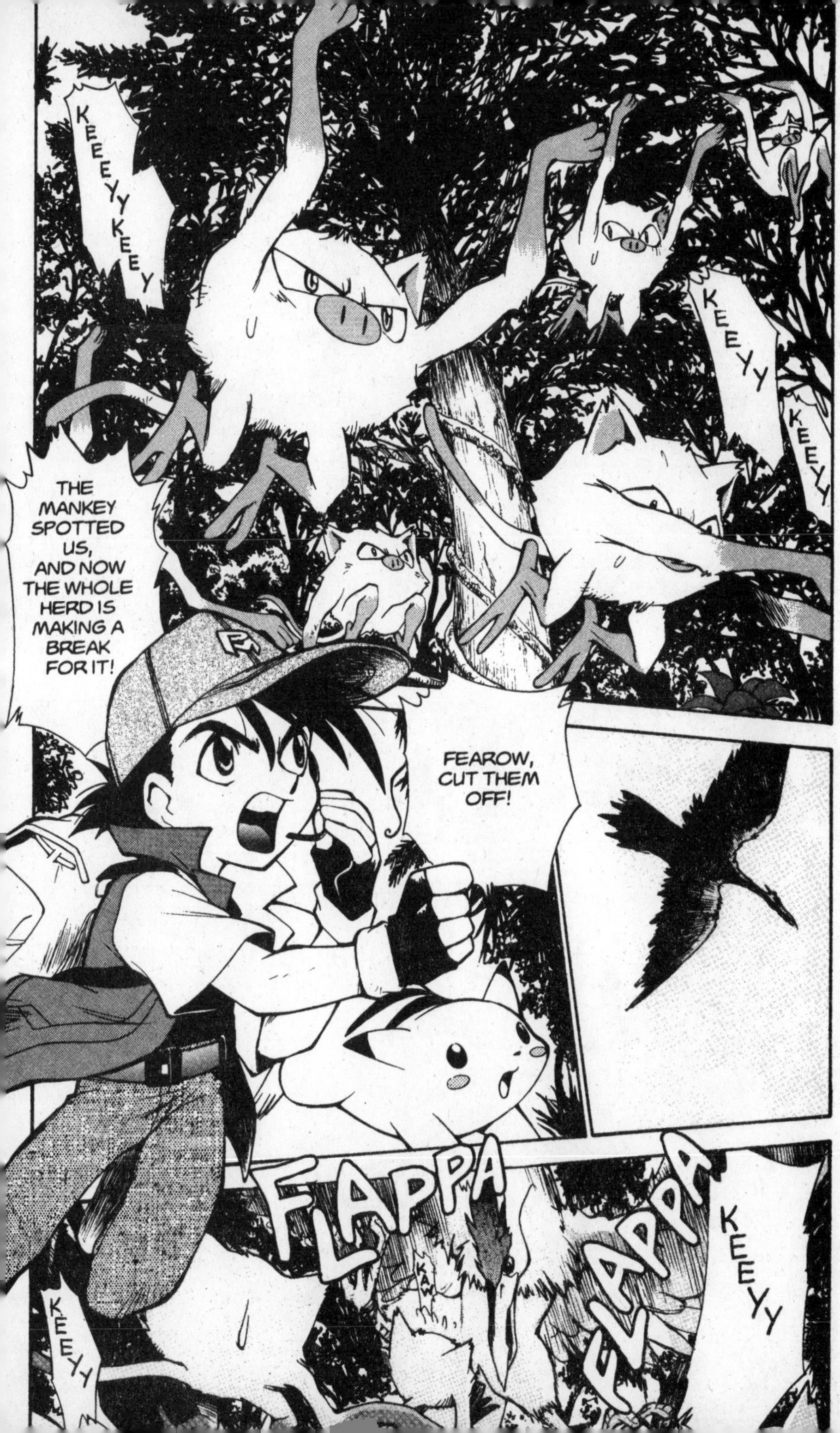
KEEEYYKEEY
THE MANKEY SPOTTED US, AND NOW THE WHOLE HERD IS MAKING A BREAK FOR IT!
KEEYY
KEEYY
FEAROW, CUT THEM OFF!
KEEYY
FLAPPA
KAW
FLAPPA
KEEYY

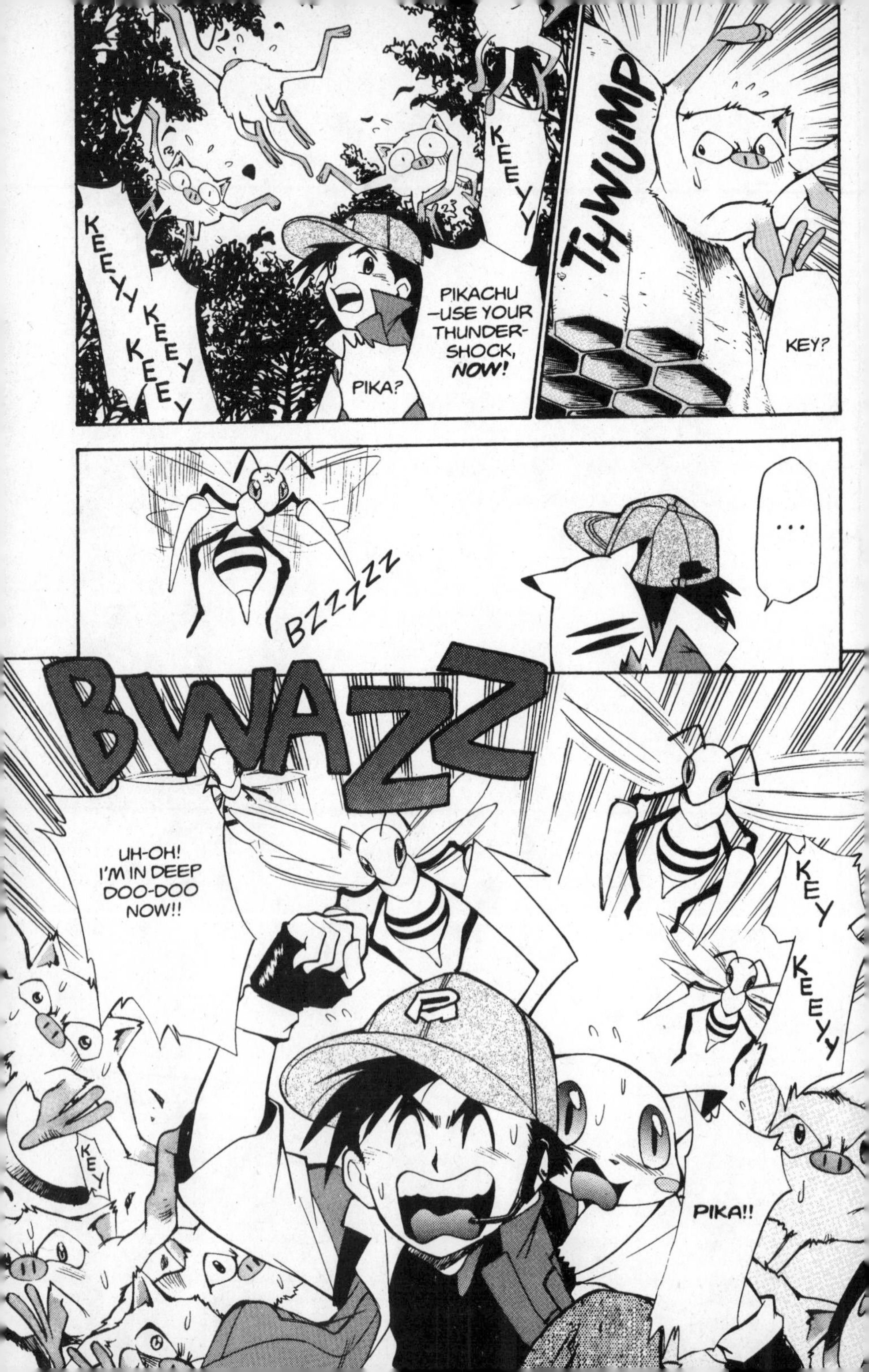
KEEYY
KEEYY
KEEYY KEEEY KEEEY
PIKACHU —USE YOUR THUNDER-SHOCK, NOW!
PIKA?
THWUMP
KEY?
BZZZZZ
...
BWAZZ
UH-OH! I'M IN DEEP DOO-DOO NOW!!
KEY KEEYY
KEY
PIKA!!

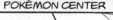
POKÉMON CENTER

YOU'RE KIDDING! ARE YOU TELLING ME MY LEVEL HASN'T GONE UP AT ALL?

I'M NOT EVEN AT THUNDER LEVEL?

YOUR TRAINER'S EXPERIENCE HAS NOTHING TO DO WITH YOUR LEVEL. IT DOESN'T GO UP JUST BECAUSE YOU CAUGHT SOME MORE POKÉMON.

YOU SEE...

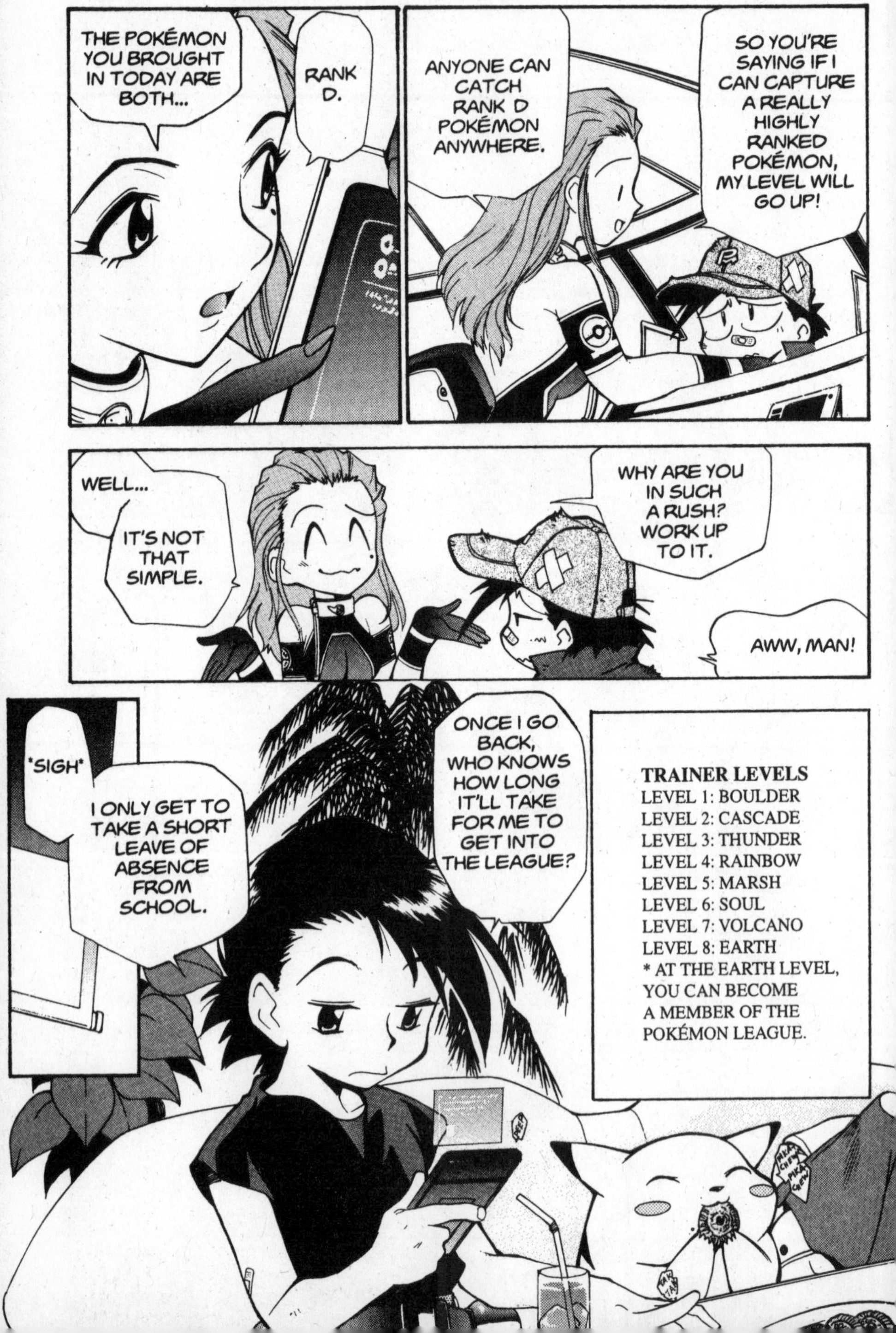

THE POKÉMON YOU BROUGHT IN TODAY ARE BOTH...
RANK D.
ANYONE CAN CATCH RANK D POKÉMON ANYWHERE.
SO YOU'RE SAYING IF I CAN CAPTURE A REALLY HIGHLY RANKED POKÉMON, MY LEVEL WILL GO UP!
WELL...
IT'S NOT THAT SIMPLE.
WHY ARE YOU IN SUCH A RUSH? WORK UP TO IT.
AWW, MAN!
SIGH
I ONLY GET TO TAKE A SHORT LEAVE OF ABSENCE FROM SCHOOL.
ONCE I GO BACK, WHO KNOWS HOW LONG IT'LL TAKE FOR ME TO GET INTO THE LEAGUE?
TRAINER LEVELS
LEVEL 1: BOULDER
LEVEL 2: CASCADE
LEVEL 3: THUNDER
LEVEL 4: RAINBOW
LEVEL 5: MARSH
LEVEL 6: SOUL
LEVEL 7: VOLCANO
LEVEL 8: EARTH
* AT THE EARTH LEVEL, YOU CAN BECOME A MEMBER OF THE POKÉMON LEAGUE.

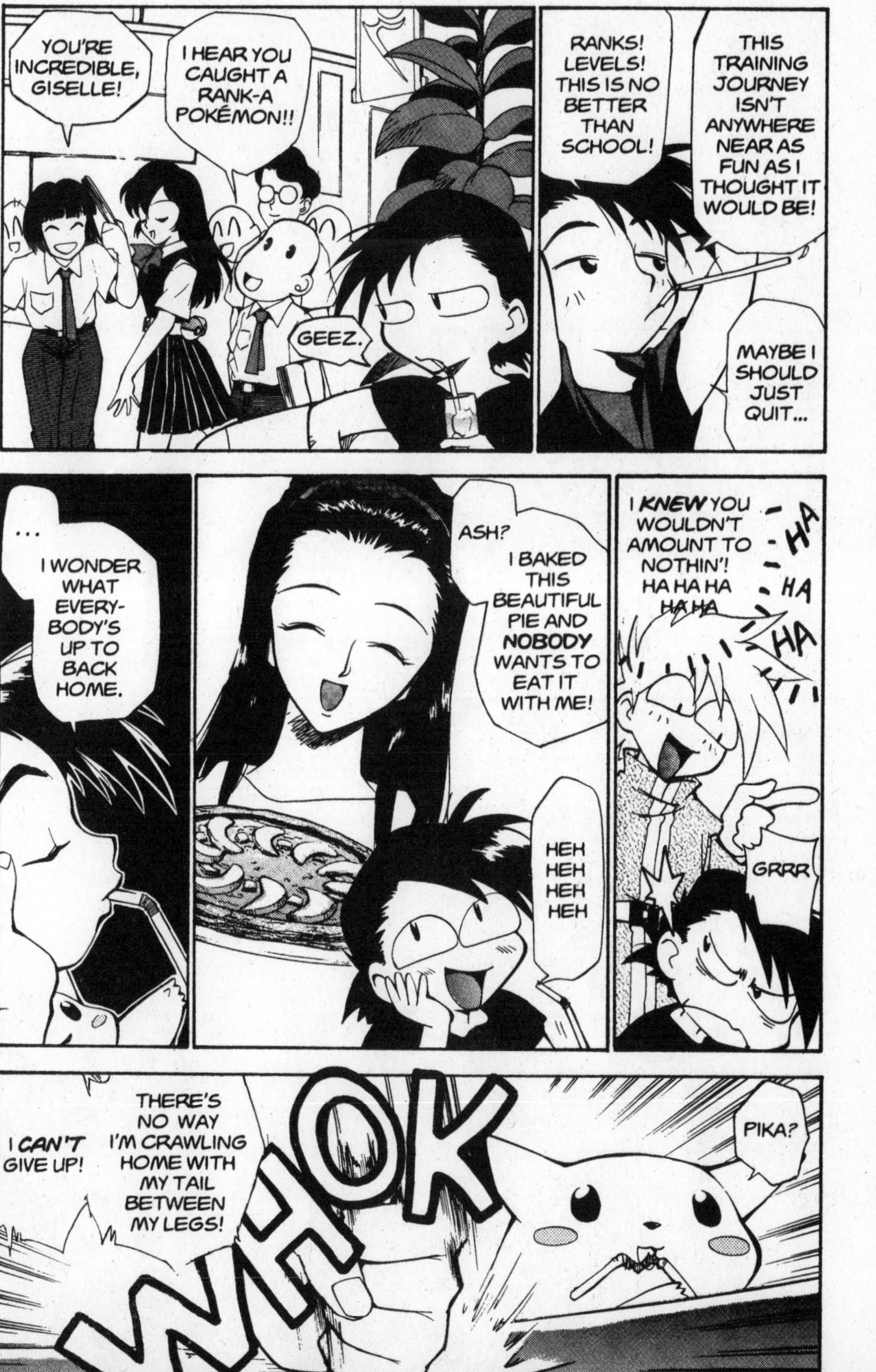
YOU'RE INCREDIBLE, GISELLE!
I HEAR YOU CAUGHT A RANK-A POKÉMON!!
GEEZ.
RANKS! LEVELS! THIS IS NO BETTER THAN SCHOOL!
THIS TRAINING JOURNEY ISN'T ANYWHERE NEAR AS FUN AS I THOUGHT IT WOULD BE!
MAYBE I SHOULD JUST QUIT...
...
I WONDER WHAT EVERY-BODY'S UP TO BACK HOME.
ASH?
I BAKED THIS BEAUTIFUL PIE AND **NOBODY** WANTS TO EAT IT WITH ME!
HEH HEH HEH HEH
I ***KNEW*** YOU WOULDN'T AMOUNT TO NOTHIN'! HA HA HA HA HA
HA HA HA
GRRR
I ***CAN'T*** GIVE UP!
THERE'S NO WAY I'M CRAWLING HOME WITH MY TAIL BETWEEN MY LEGS!
WHOK
PIKA?

BUT I'M GONNA NEED TO LEARN A LOT MORE TO BEAT GARY!

SECRET STUFF...

THINGS NOBODY ELSE KNOWS.

SECRET POKÉMON MAP SOLD HERE! *NOBODY ELSE* KNOWS HOW TO CAPTURE THESE HIGH-RANKING POKÉMON!

NOW THAT SOUNDS MIGHTY FISHY.

PIKA.

BYOYOINNG

KACHING

BUT HOW CAN I RESIST!?

HEH HEH

87TH POKÉM... CREAT... CUP CON...

MAKE YERSELF AT HOME, YOUNG 'UN!

THIS ISN'T JUST MIGHTY FISHY, IT'S **SUPER** FISHY!

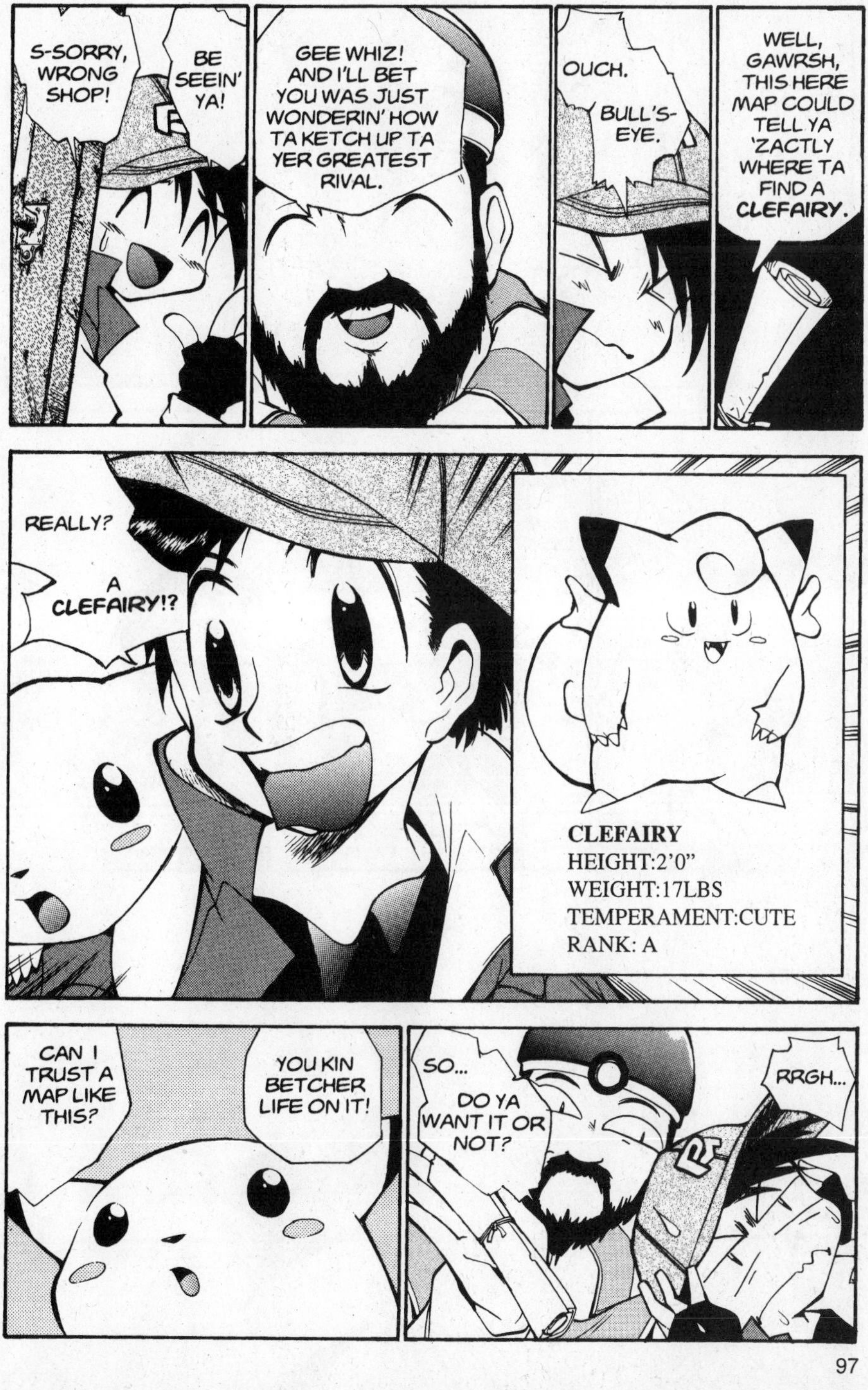
S-SORRY, WRONG SHOP!
BE SEEIN' YA!
GEE WHIZ! AND I'LL BET YOU WAS JUST WONDERIN' HOW TA KETCH UP TA YER GREATEST RIVAL.
OUCH.
BULL'S-EYE.
WELL, GAWRSH, THIS HERE MAP COULD TELL YA 'ZACTLY WHERE TA FIND A CLEFAIRY.
REALLY?
A CLEFAIRY!?
CLEFAIRY
HEIGHT:2'0"
WEIGHT:17LBS
TEMPERAMENT:CUTE
RANK: A
CAN I TRUST A MAP LIKE THIS?
YOU KIN BETCHER LIFE ON IT!
SO...
DO YA WANT IT OR NOT?
RRGH...

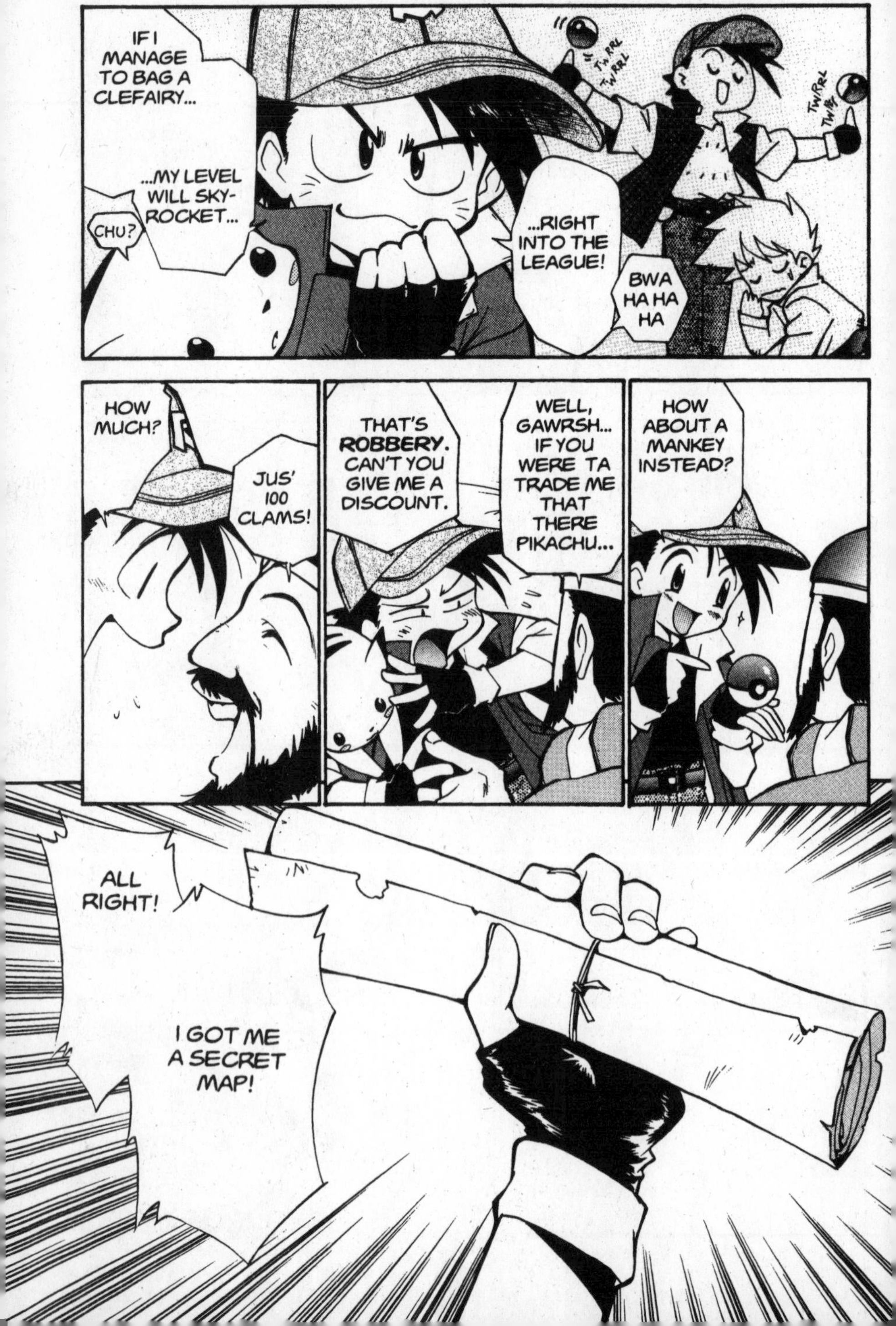

IF I MANAGE TO BAG A CLEFAIRY...
...MY LEVEL WILL SKY-ROCKET...
CHU?
...RIGHT INTO THE LEAGUE!
TWIRRL TWIRRL
TWIRRL TWIRRL
BWA HA HA HA HA
HOW MUCH?
JUS' 100 CLAMS!
THAT'S **ROBBERY**. CAN'T YOU GIVE ME A DISCOUNT.
WELL, GAWRSH... IF YOU WERE TA TRADE ME THAT THERE PIKACHU...
HOW ABOUT A MANKEY INSTEAD?
ALL RIGHT!
I GOT ME A SECRET MAP!

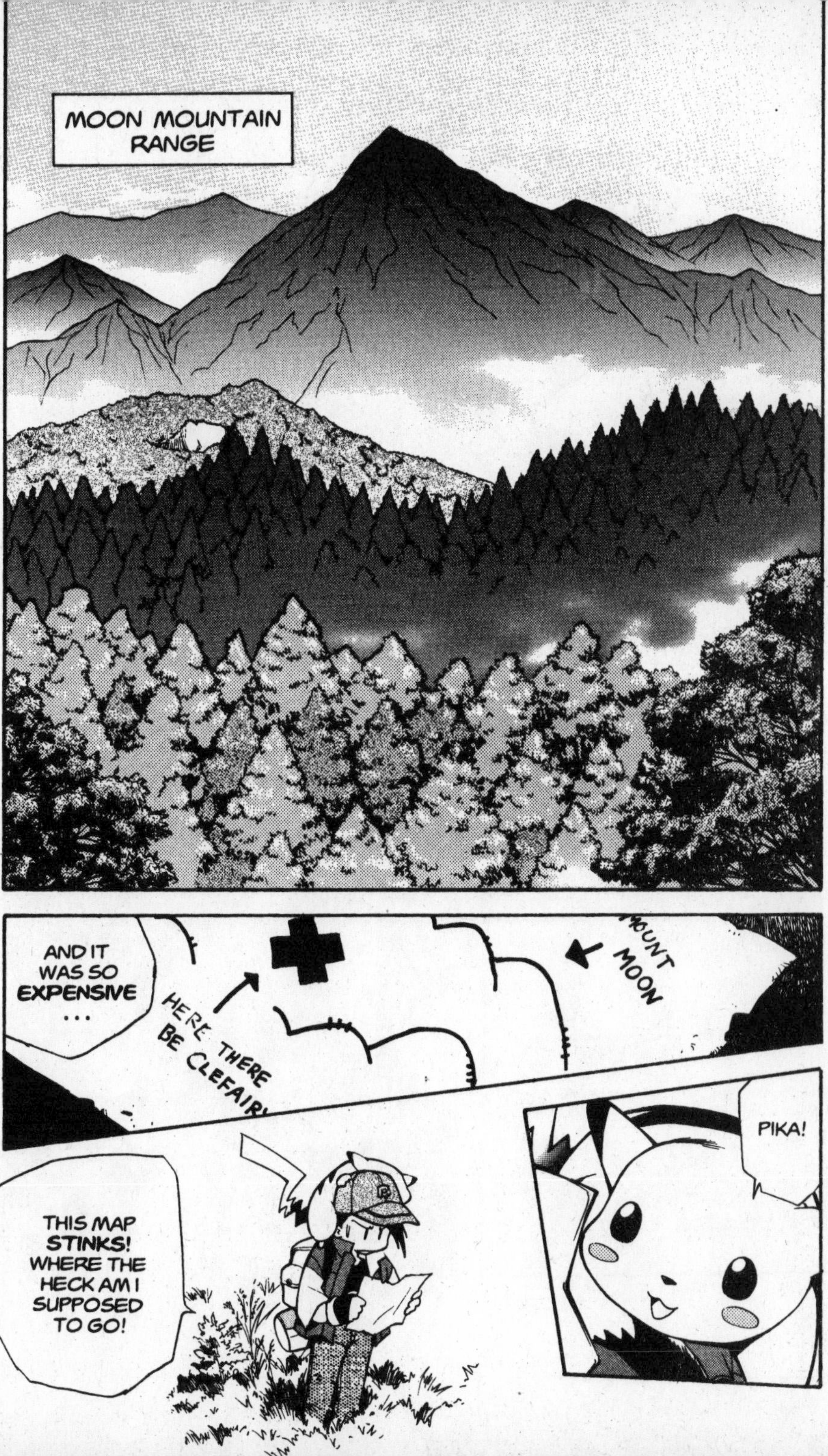
MOON MOUNTAIN RANGE
AND IT WAS SO EXPENSIVE ...
HERE THERE BE CLEFAIR
MOUNT MOON
THIS MAP STINKS! WHERE THE HECK AM I SUPPOSED TO GO!
PIKA!

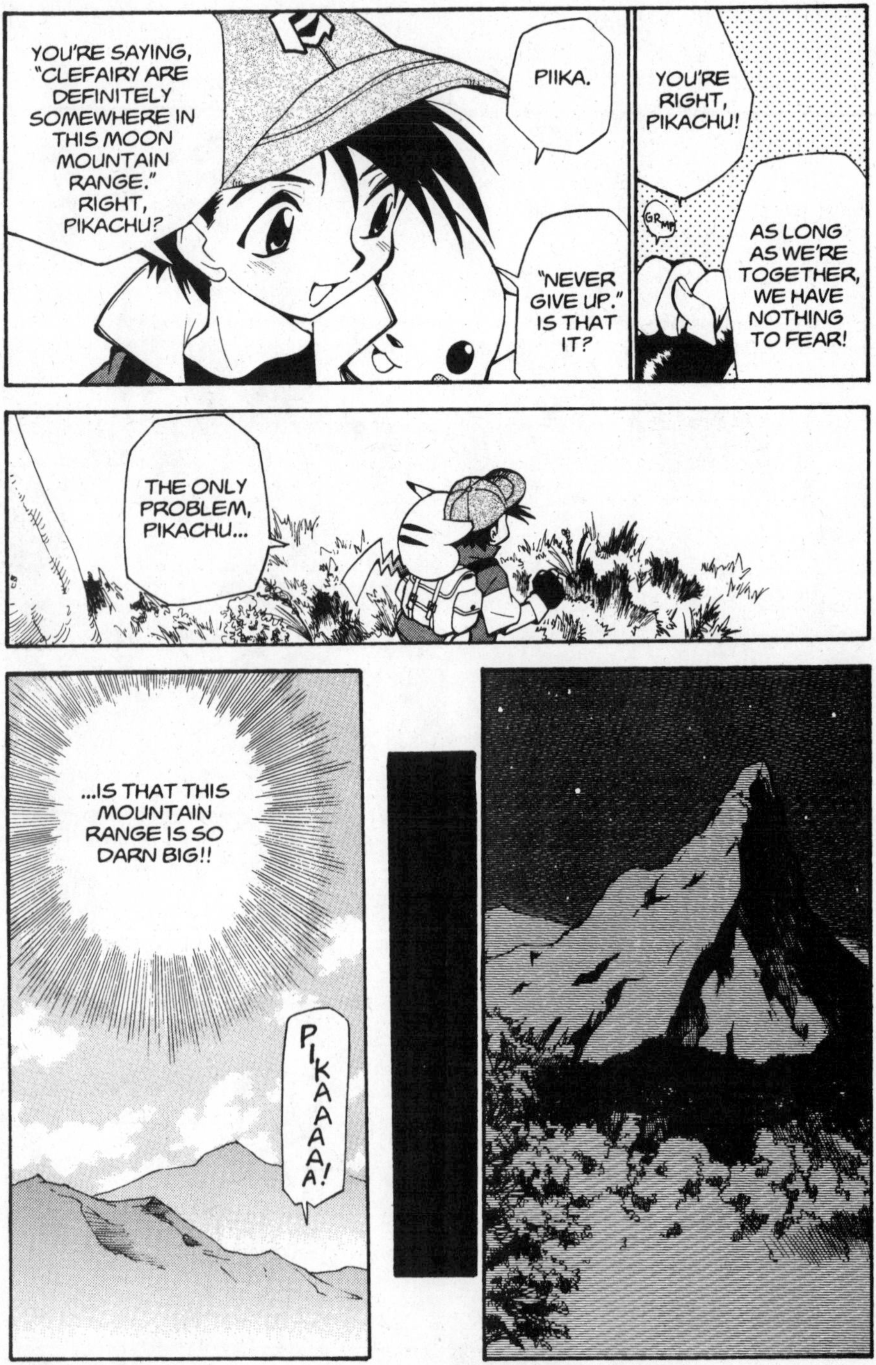
YOU'RE SAYING, "CLEFAIRY ARE DEFINITELY SOMEWHERE IN THIS MOON MOUNTAIN RANGE." RIGHT, PIKACHU?
PIIKA.
"NEVER GIVE UP." IS THAT IT?
YOU'RE RIGHT, PIKACHU!
GRMP
AS LONG AS WE'RE TOGETHER, WE HAVE NOTHING TO FEAR!
THE ONLY PROBLEM, PIKACHU...
...IS THAT THIS MOUNTAIN RANGE IS SO DARN BIG!!
PIKAAAAAA!

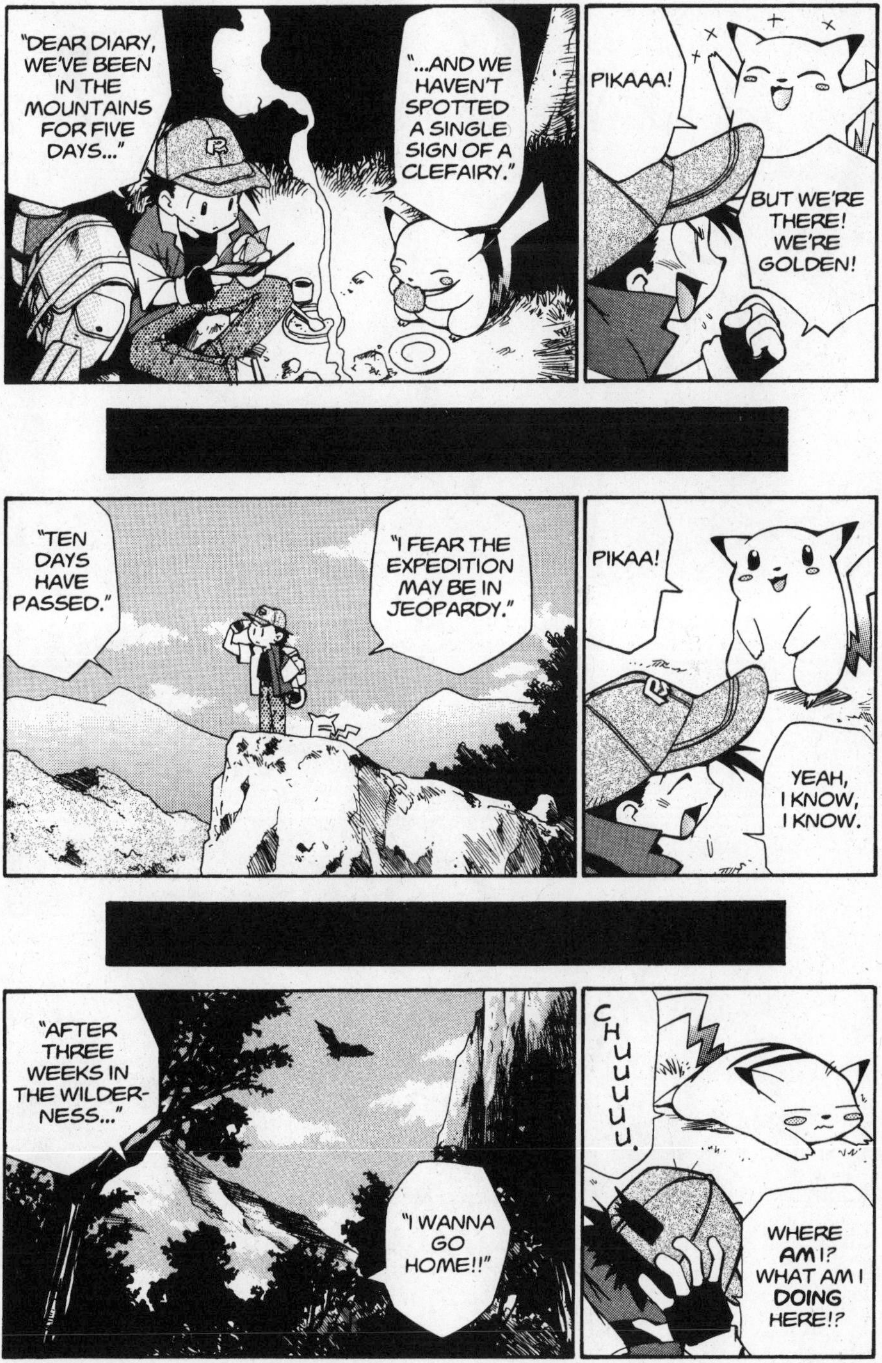
"DEAR DIARY, WE'VE BEEN IN THE MOUNTAINS FOR FIVE DAYS..."
"...AND WE HAVEN'T SPOTTED A SINGLE SIGN OF A CLEFAIRY."
PIKAAA!
BUT WE'RE THERE! WE'RE GOLDEN!
"TEN DAYS HAVE PASSED."
"I FEAR THE EXPEDITION MAY BE IN JEOPARDY."
PIKAA!
YEAH, I KNOW, I KNOW.
"AFTER THREE WEEKS IN THE WILDER-NESS..."
"I WANNA GO HOME!!"
CHUUUUU.
WHERE AM I!? WHAT AM I DOING HERE!?

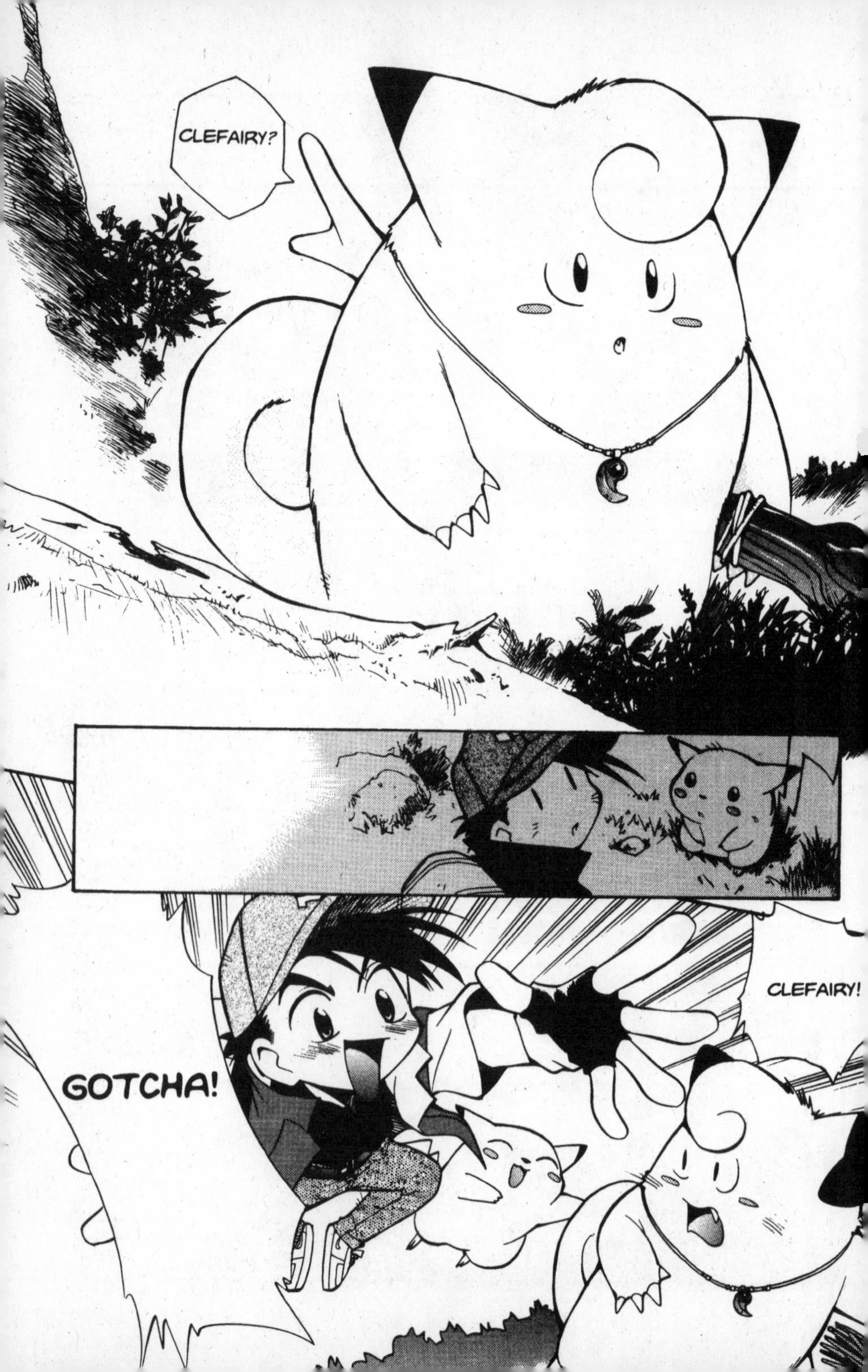
CLEFAIRY?
CLEFAIRY!
GOTCHA!

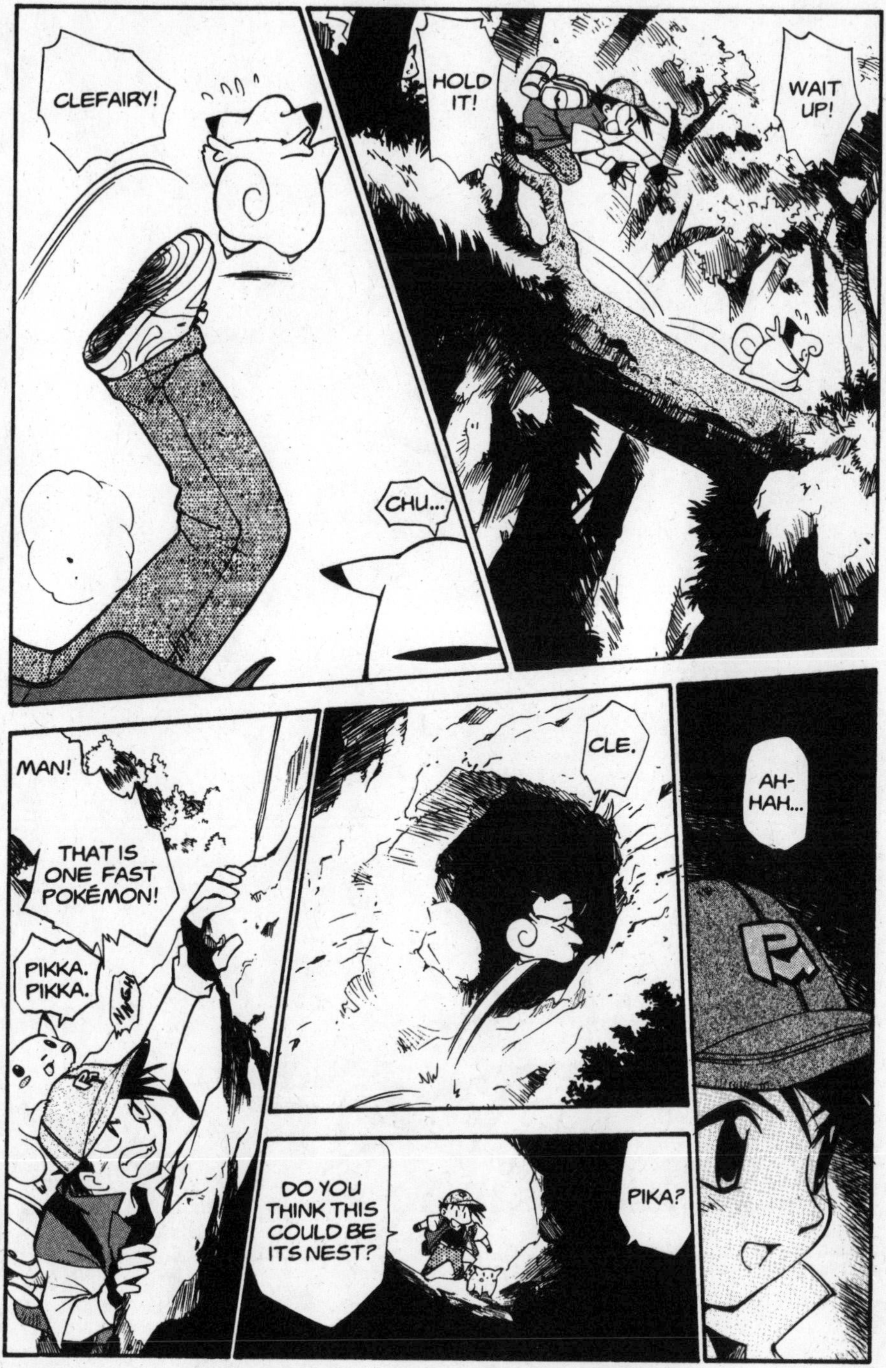
CLEFAIRY!
CHU...
HOLD IT!
WAIT UP!
MAN!
THAT IS ONE FAST POKéMON!
PIKKA. PIKKA.
CLE.
DO YOU THINK THIS COULD BE ITS NEST?
PIKA?
AH-HAH...

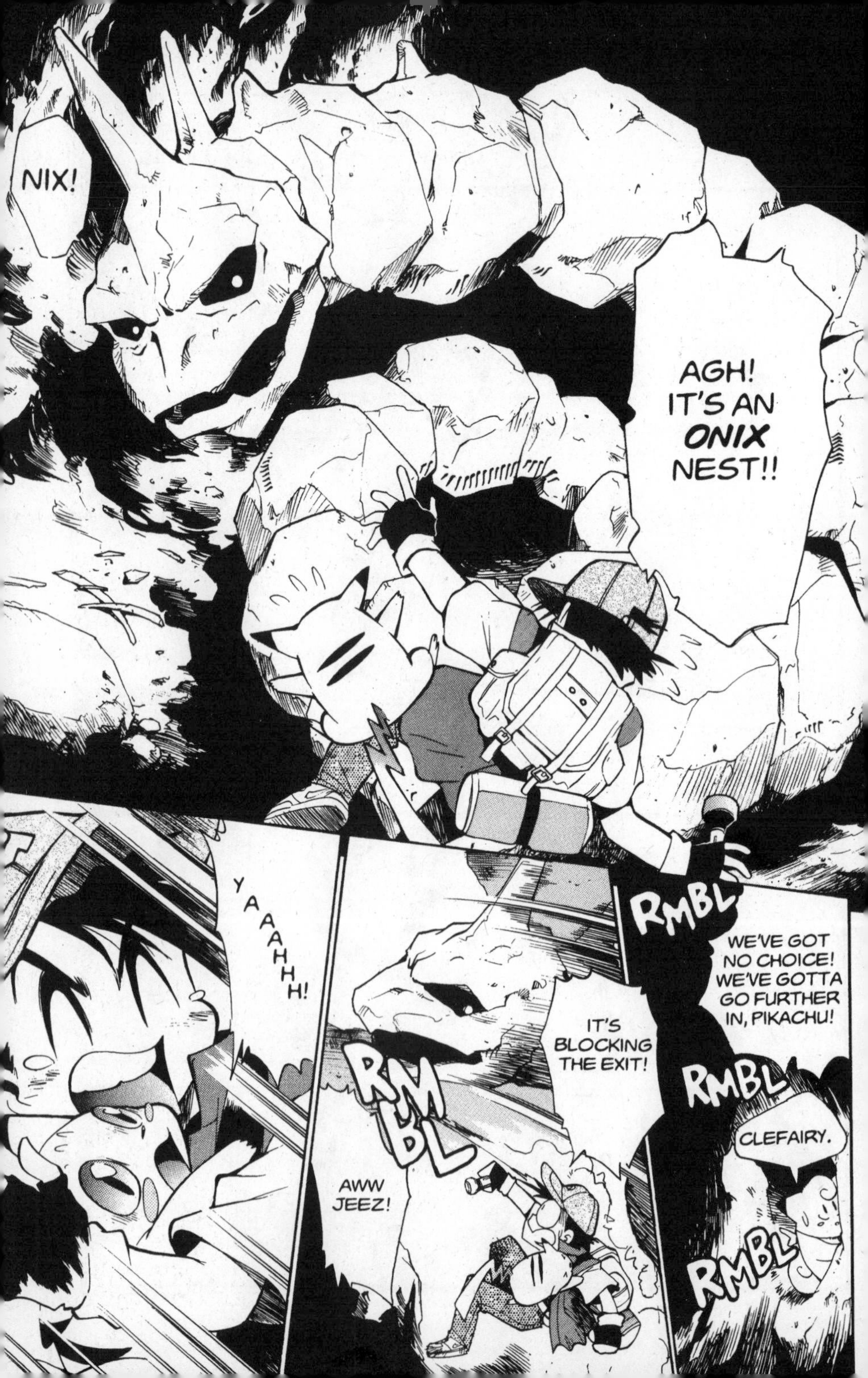
NIX!
AGH! IT'S AN ONIX NEST!!
YAAAHHH!
RMBL
WE'VE GOT NO CHOICE! WE'VE GOTTA GO FURTHER IN, PIKACHU!
IT'S BLOCKING THE EXIT!
RMBL
RMBL
AWW JEEZ!
CLEFAIRY.
RMBL

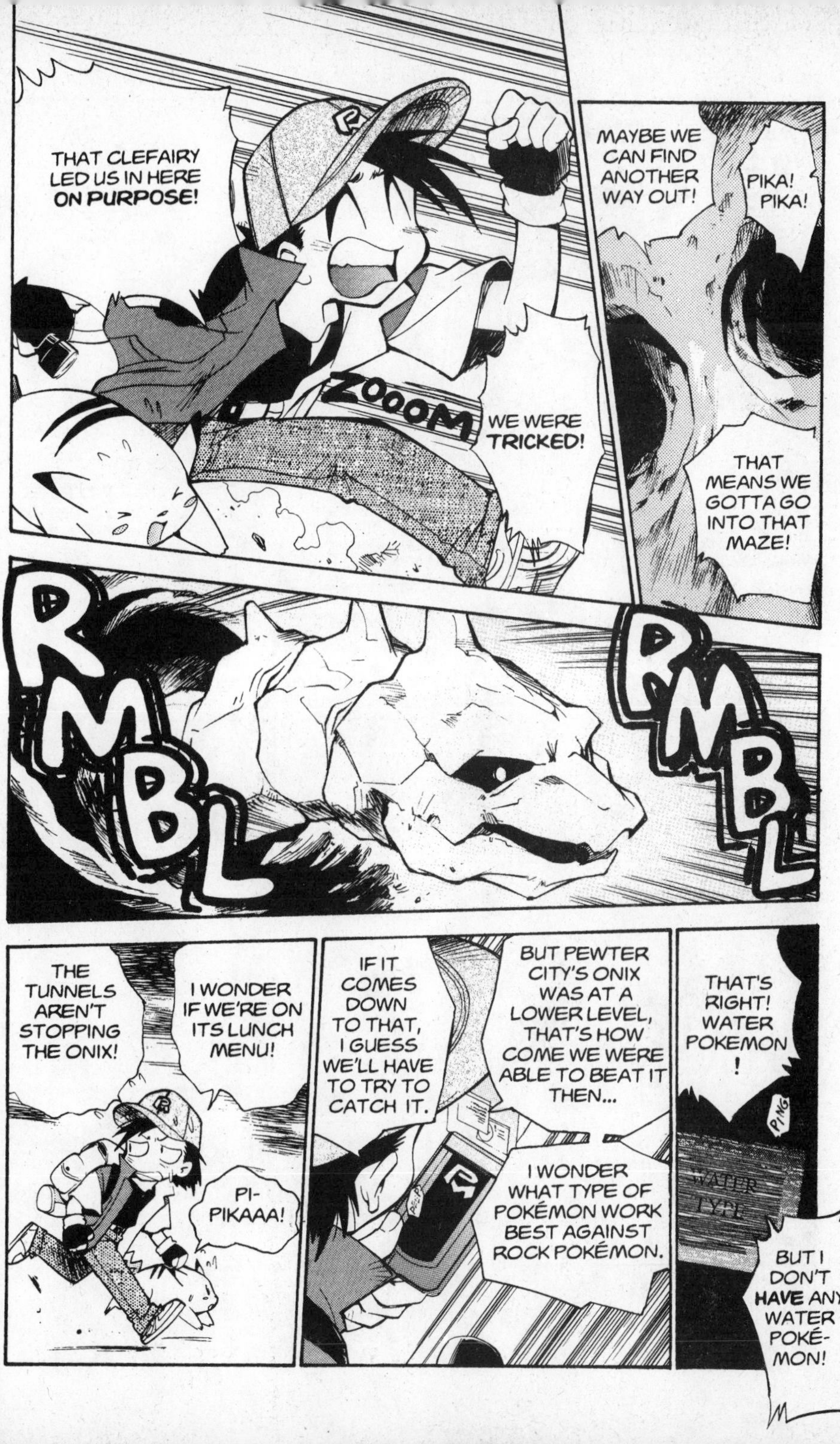
THAT CLEFAIRY LED US IN HERE ON PURPOSE!
ZOOOM
WE WERE TRICKED!
MAYBE WE CAN FIND ANOTHER WAY OUT!
PIKA! PIKA!
THAT MEANS WE GOTTA GO INTO THAT MAZE!
RMBL
RMBL
THE TUNNELS AREN'T STOPPING THE ONIX!
I WONDER IF WE'RE ON ITS LUNCH MENU!
PI-PIKAAA!
IF IT COMES DOWN TO THAT, I GUESS WE'LL HAVE TO TRY TO CATCH IT.
BUT PEWTER CITY'S ONIX WAS AT A LOWER LEVEL, THAT'S HOW COME WE WERE ABLE TO BEAT IT THEN...
I WONDER WHAT TYPE OF POKÉMON WORK BEST AGAINST ROCK POKÉMON.
THAT'S RIGHT! WATER POKEMON!
PING
WATER TYPE
BUT I DON'T HAVE ANY WATER POKÉMON!

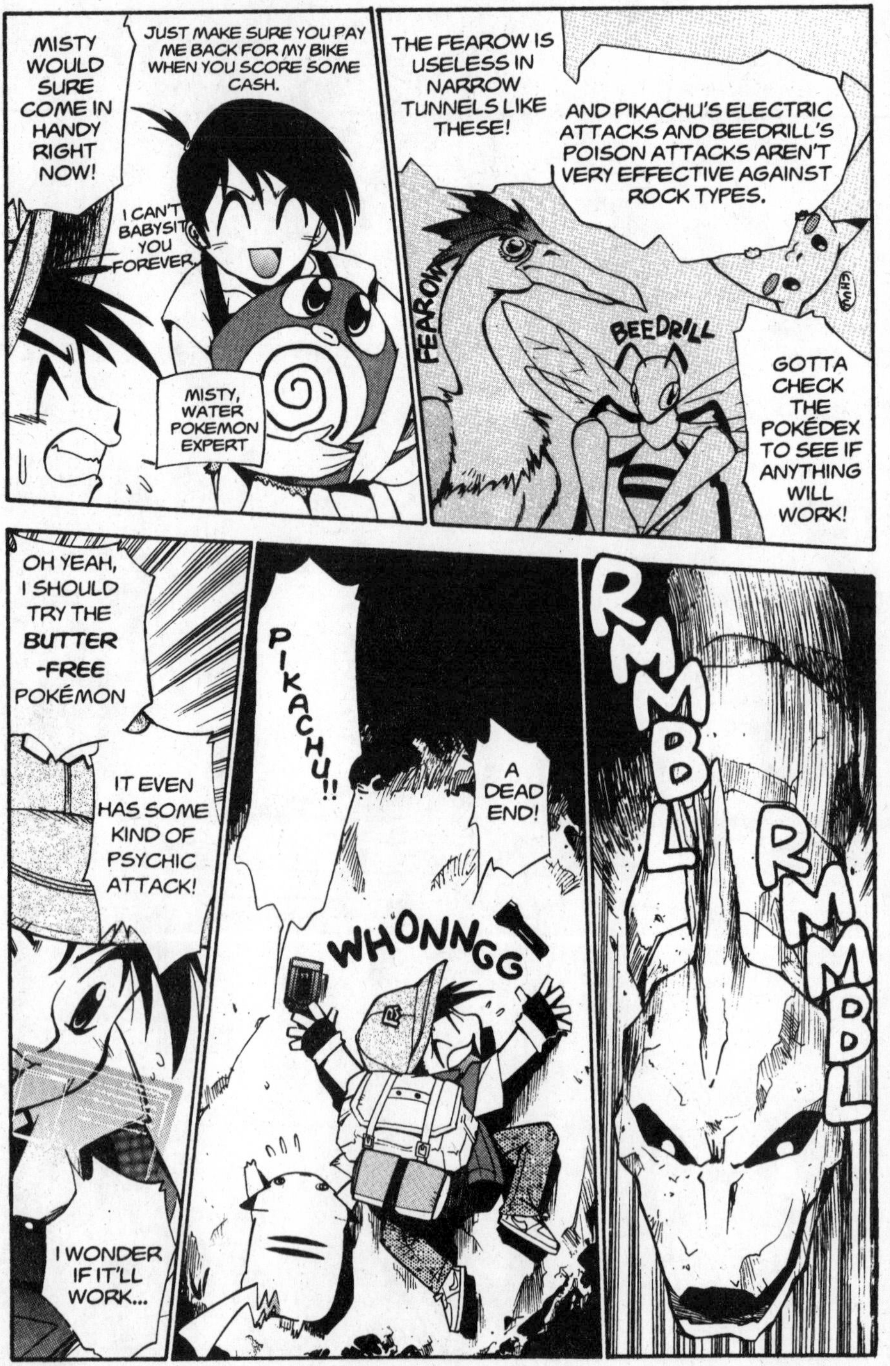

MISTY WOULD SURE COME IN HANDY RIGHT NOW!
JUST MAKE SURE YOU PAY ME BACK FOR MY BIKE WHEN YOU SCORE SOME CASH.
I CAN'T BABYSIT YOU FOREVER.
MISTY, WATER POKEMON EXPERT
THE FEAROW IS USELESS IN NARROW TUNNELS LIKE THESE!
AND PIKACHU'S ELECTRIC ATTACKS AND BEEDRILL'S POISON ATTACKS AREN'T VERY EFFECTIVE AGAINST ROCK TYPES.
FEAROW
BEEDRILL
CHU
GOTTA CHECK THE POKÉDEX TO SEE IF ANYTHING WILL WORK!
OH YEAH, I SHOULD TRY THE **BUTTER-FREE** POKÉMON
IT EVEN HAS SOME KIND OF PSYCHIC ATTACK!
I WONDER IF IT'LL WORK...
PIKACHU!!
A DEAD END!
WHONNGG
RMMBL
RMMBL

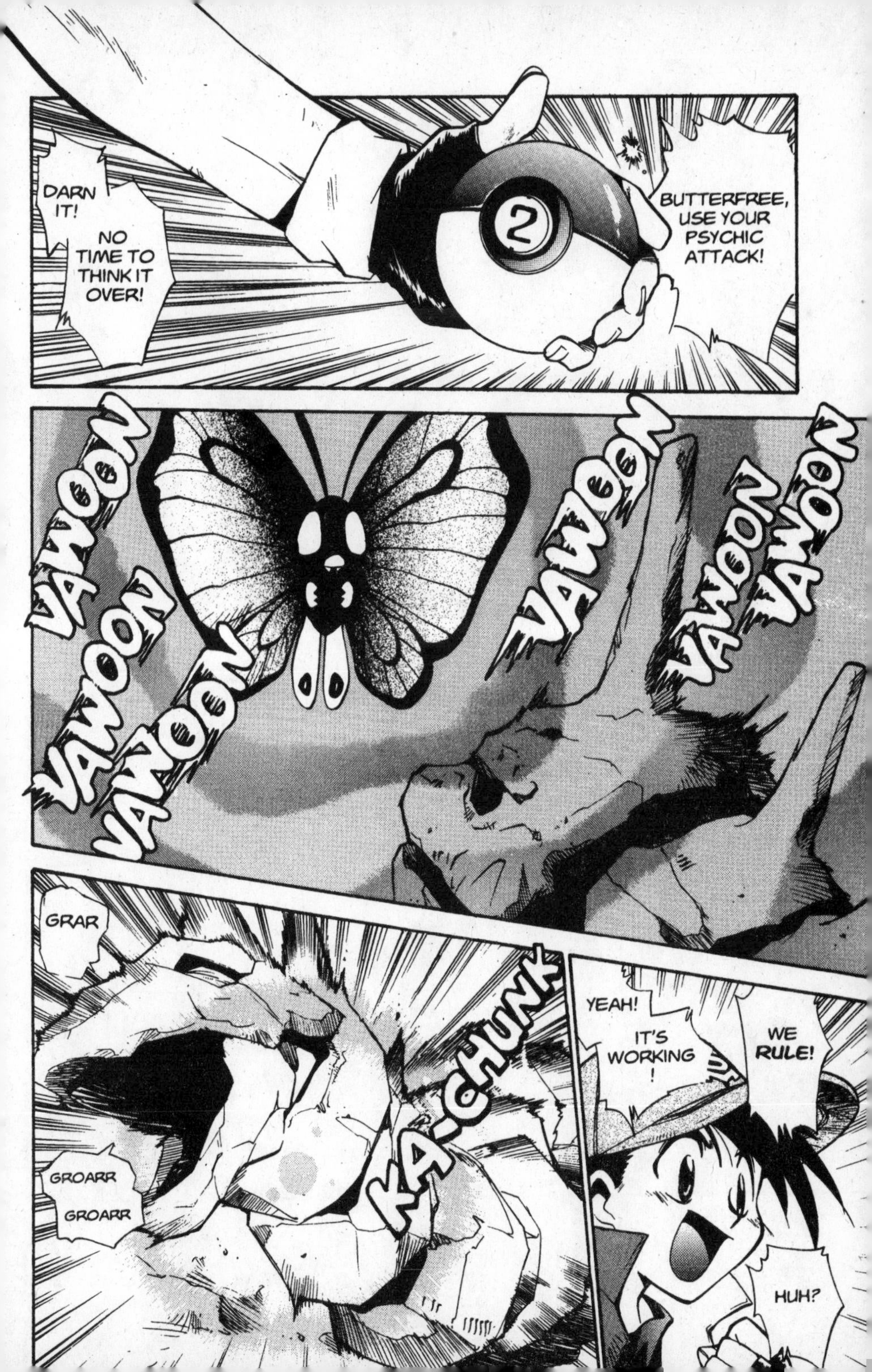
DARN IT!
NO TIME TO THINK IT OVER!
BUTTERFREE, USE YOUR PSYCHIC ATTACK!
VAWOON
VAWOON
VAWOON
VAWOON
VAWOON
VAWOON
VAWOON
GRAR
KA-CHUNK
GROARR
GROARR
YEAH!
IT'S WORKING!
WE RULE!
HUH?

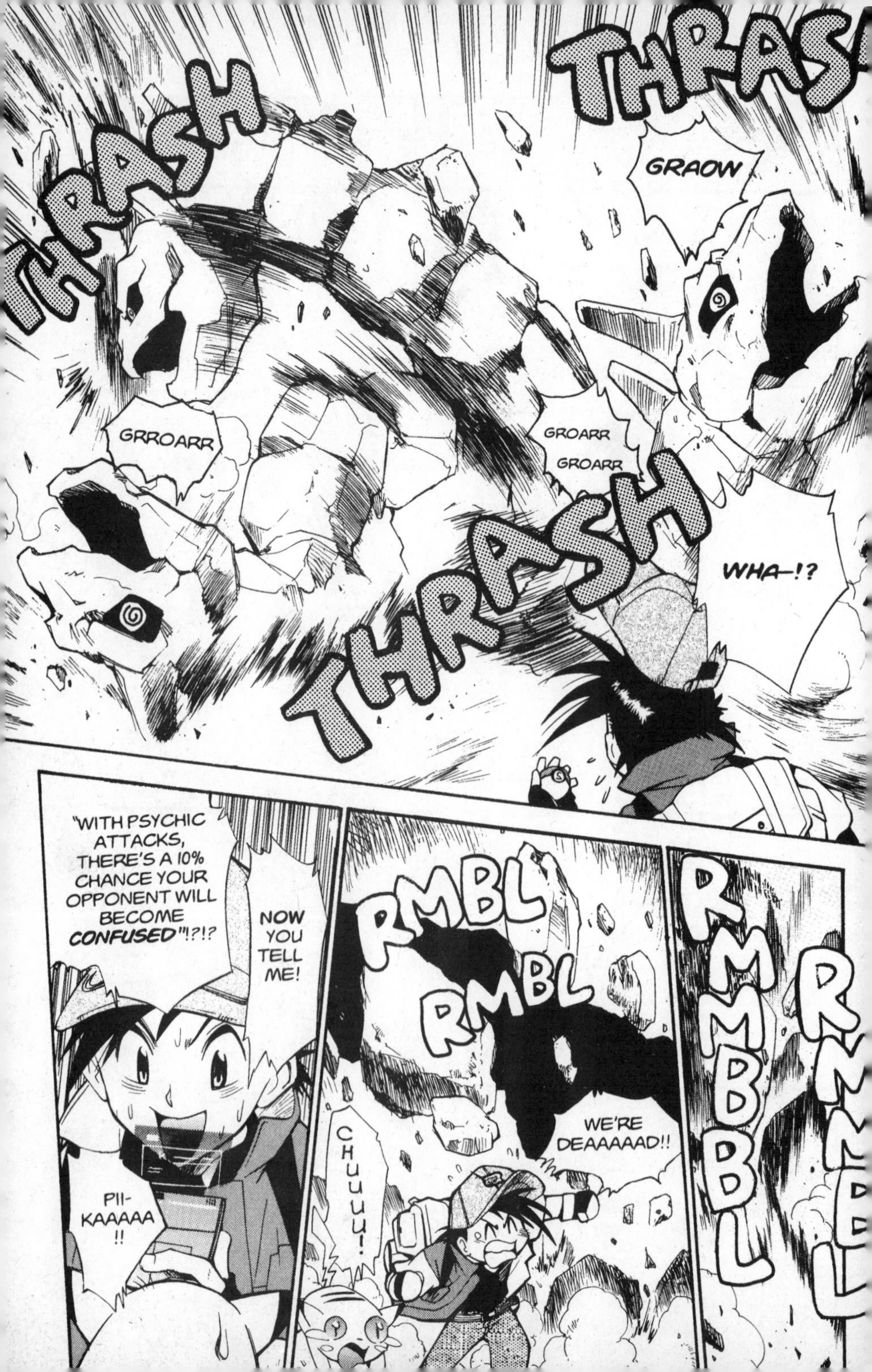
THRASH
THRAS
GRAOW
GRRROARR
GROARR
GROARR
THRASH
WHA-!?
"WITH PSYCHIC ATTACKS, THERE'S A 10% CHANCE YOUR OPPONENT WILL BECOME CONFUSED"!?!?
NOW YOU TELL ME!
PII-KAAAAAA!!
RMBL
RMBL
CHUUUU!
WE'RE DEAAAAAD!!
RMMBBL

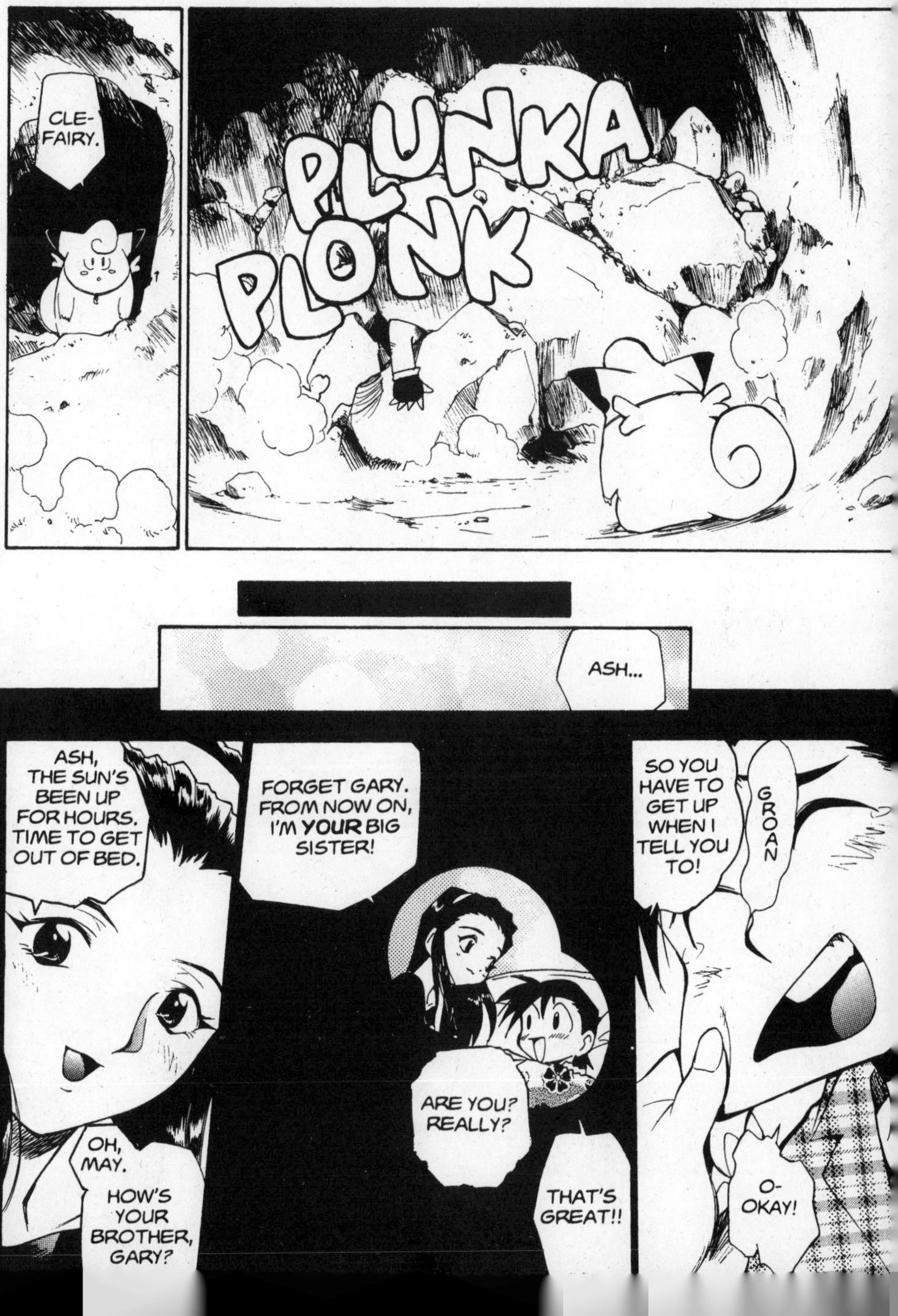
CLE-FAIRY.
PLUNKA
PLONK
ASH...
ASH, THE SUN'S BEEN UP FOR HOURS. TIME TO GET OUT OF BED.
OH, MAY.
HOW'S YOUR BROTHER, GARY?
FORGET GARY. FROM NOW ON, I'M **YOUR** BIG SISTER!
ARE YOU? REALLY?
THAT'S GREAT!!
SO YOU HAVE TO GET UP WHEN I TELL YOU TO!
GROAN
O-OKAY!

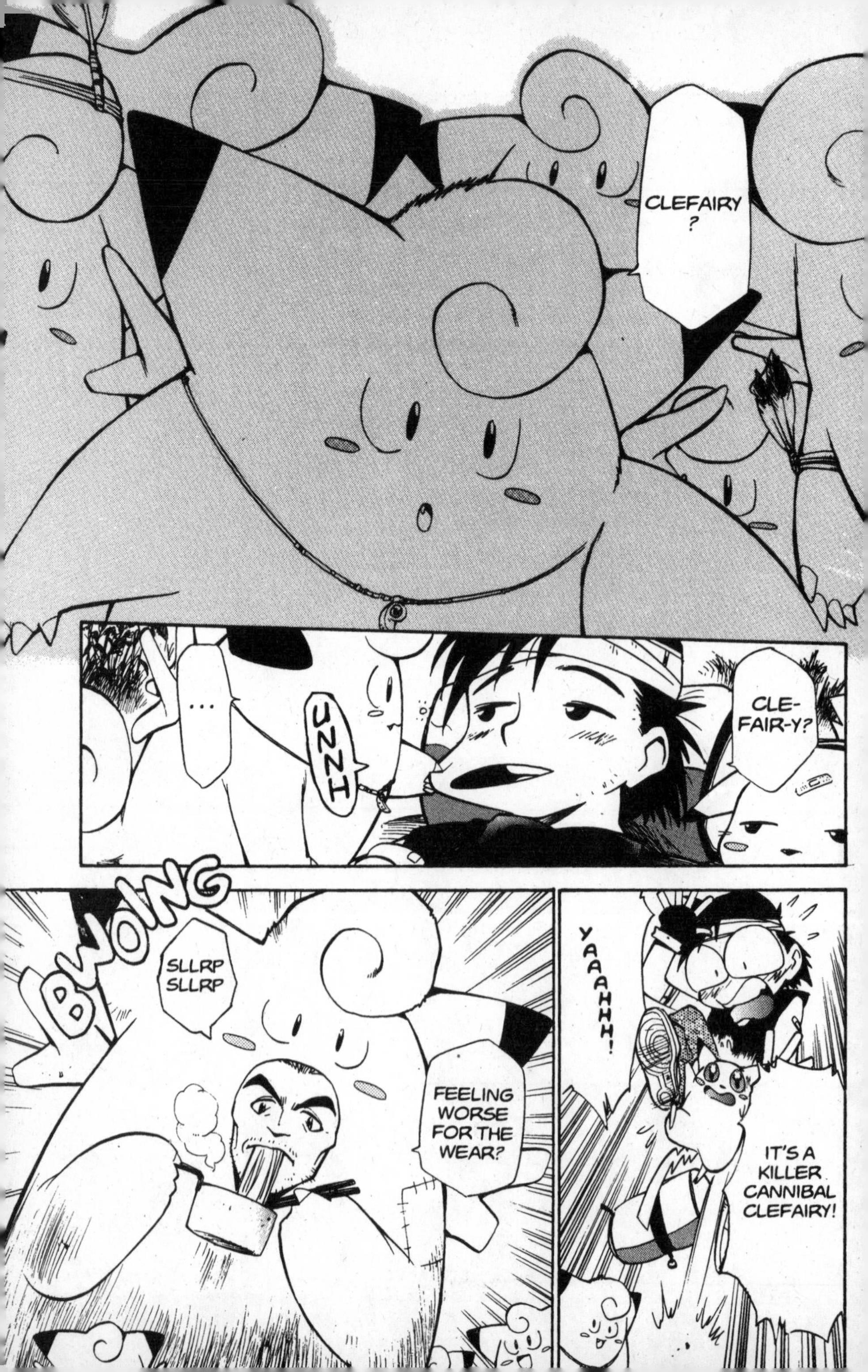
CLEFAIRY ?
...
UNNH
CLE- FAIR-Y?
BWOING
SLLRP SLLRP
FEELING WORSE FOR THE WEAR?
YAAAHHH!
IT'S A KILLER CANNIBAL CLEFAIRY!

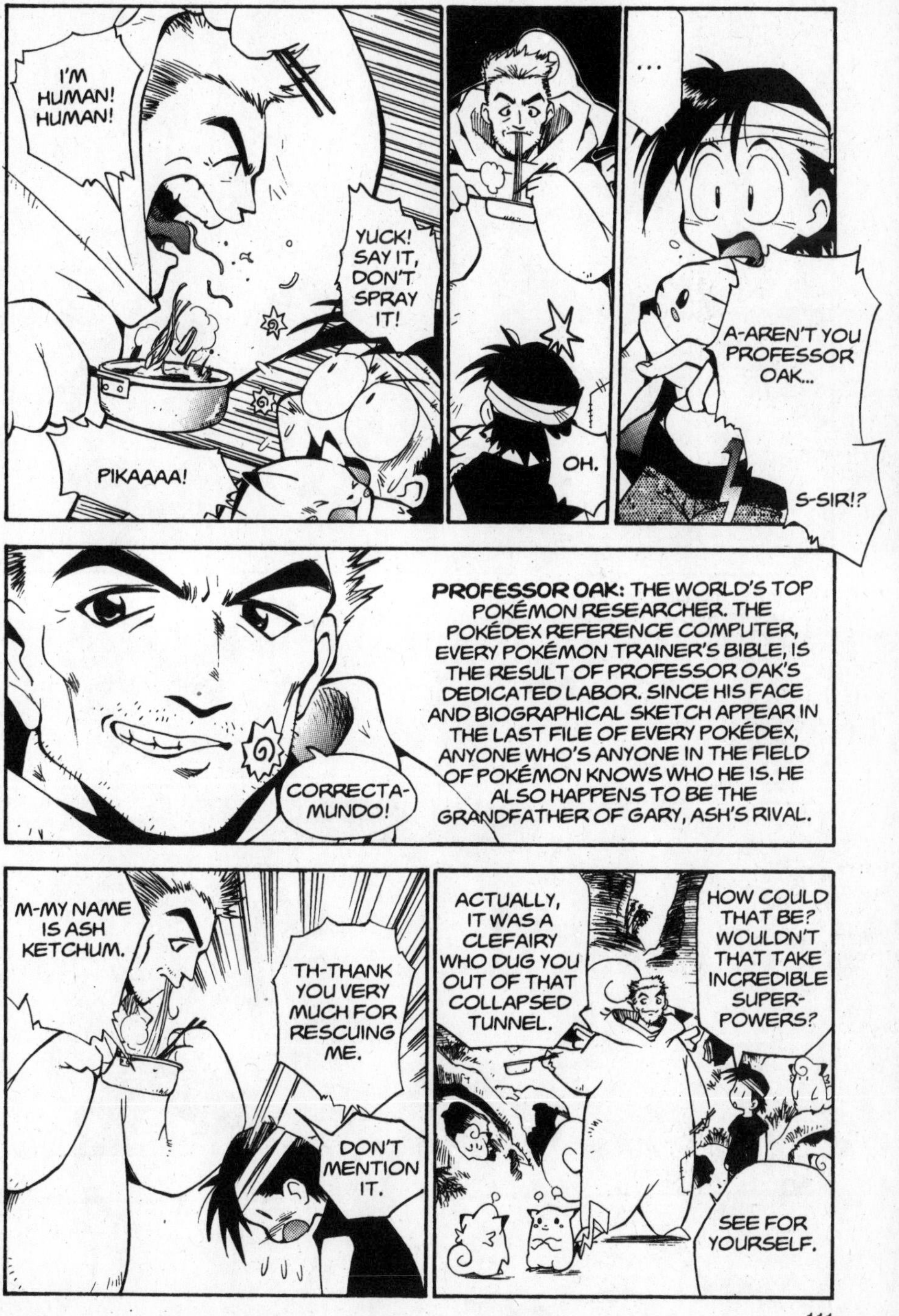

I'M HUMAN! HUMAN!
YUCK! SAY IT, DON'T SPRAY IT!
PIKAAAA!
OH.
...
A-AREN'T YOU PROFESSOR OAK...
S-SIR!?
PROFESSOR OAK: THE WORLD'S TOP POKÉMON RESEARCHER. THE POKÉDEX REFERENCE COMPUTER, EVERY POKÉMON TRAINER'S BIBLE, IS THE RESULT OF PROFESSOR OAK'S DEDICATED LABOR. SINCE HIS FACE AND BIOGRAPHICAL SKETCH APPEAR IN THE LAST FILE OF EVERY POKÉDEX, ANYONE WHO'S ANYONE IN THE FIELD OF POKÉMON KNOWS WHO HE IS. HE ALSO HAPPENS TO BE THE GRANDFATHER OF GARY, ASH'S RIVAL.
CORRECTA-MUNDO!
M-MY NAME IS ASH KETCHUM.
TH-THANK YOU VERY MUCH FOR RESCUING ME.
DON'T MENTION IT.
ACTUALLY, IT WAS A CLEFAIRY WHO DUG YOU OUT OF THAT COLLAPSED TUNNEL.
HOW COULD THAT BE? WOULDN'T THAT TAKE INCREDIBLE SUPER-POWERS?
SEE FOR YOURSELF.

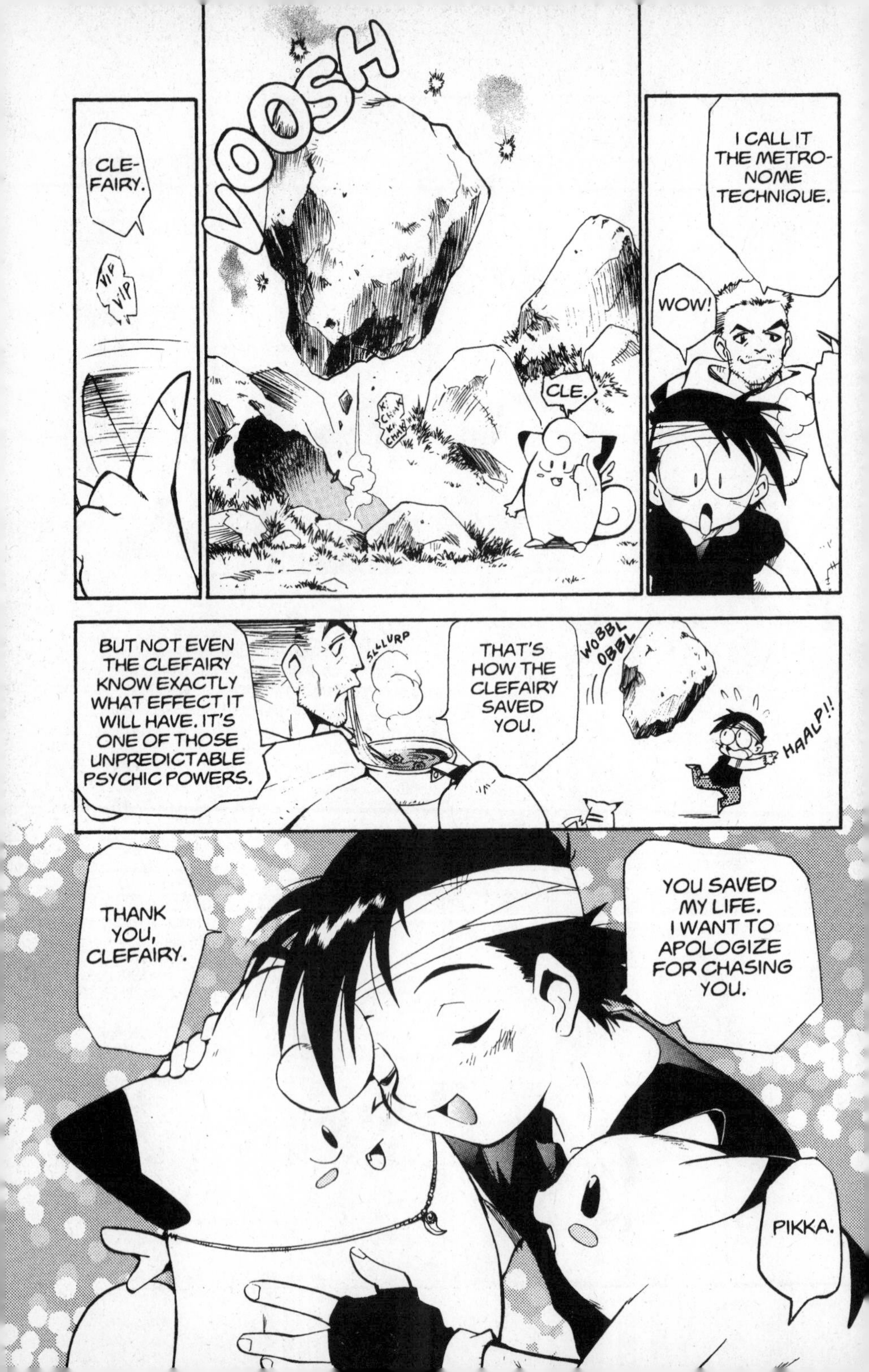
CLE-FAIRY.
VIP VIP
VOOSH
CLE.
I CALL IT THE METRO-NOME TECHNIQUE.
WOW!
BUT NOT EVEN THE CLEFAIRY KNOW EXACTLY WHAT EFFECT IT WILL HAVE. IT'S ONE OF THOSE UNPREDICTABLE PSYCHIC POWERS.
SLLLURP
THAT'S HOW THE CLEFAIRY SAVED YOU.
WOBBL OBBL
HAALP!!
THANK YOU, CLEFAIRY.
YOU SAVED MY LIFE. I WANT TO APOLOGIZE FOR CHASING YOU.
PIKKA.

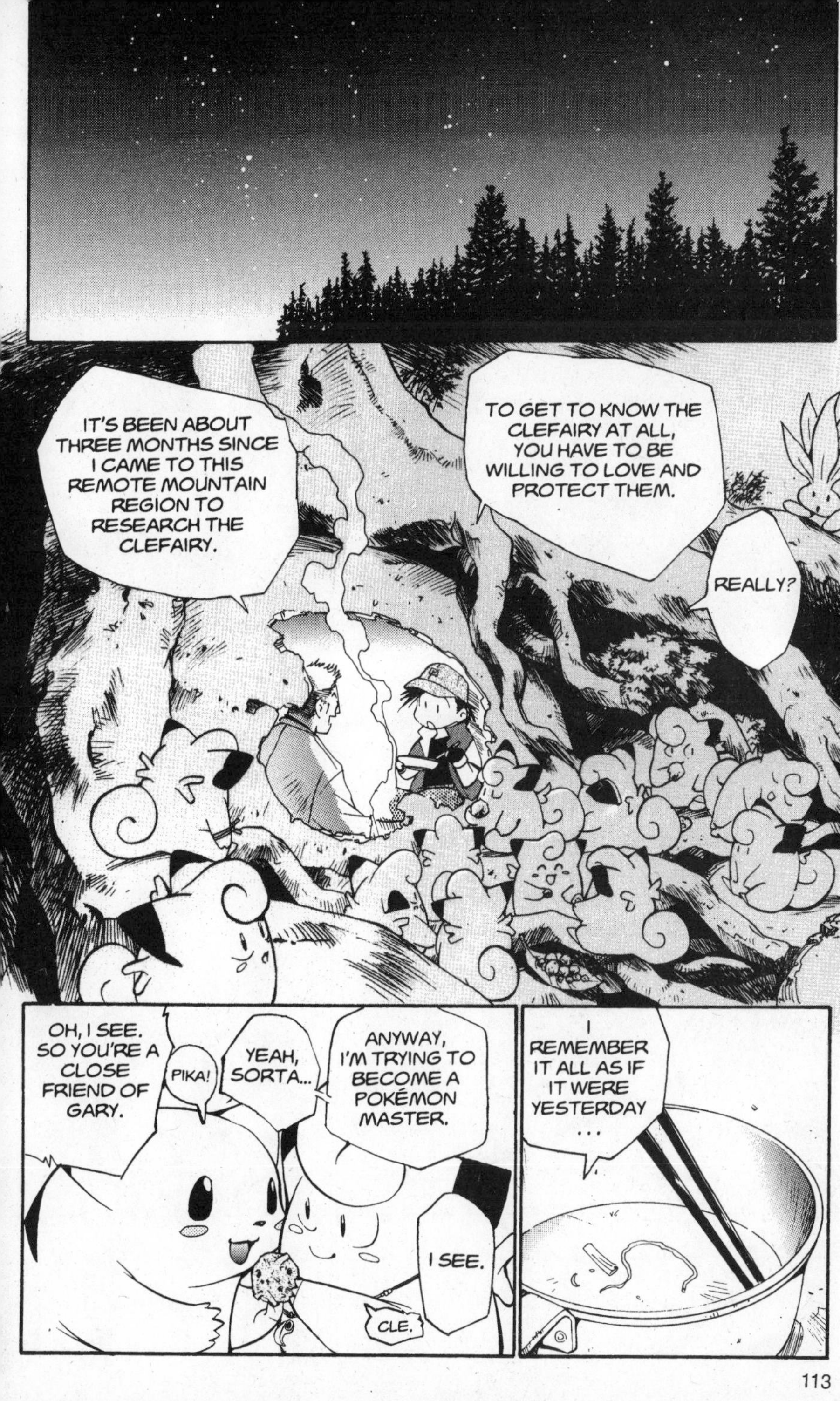
IT'S BEEN ABOUT THREE MONTHS SINCE I CAME TO THIS REMOTE MOUNTAIN REGION TO RESEARCH THE CLEFAIRY.
TO GET TO KNOW THE CLEFAIRY AT ALL, YOU HAVE TO BE WILLING TO LOVE AND PROTECT THEM.
REALLY?
OH, I SEE. SO YOU'RE A CLOSE FRIEND OF GARY.
PIKA!
YEAH, SORTA...
ANYWAY, I'M TRYING TO BECOME A POKÉMON MASTER.
I SEE.
CLE.
I REMEMBER IT ALL AS IF IT WERE YESTERDAY ...

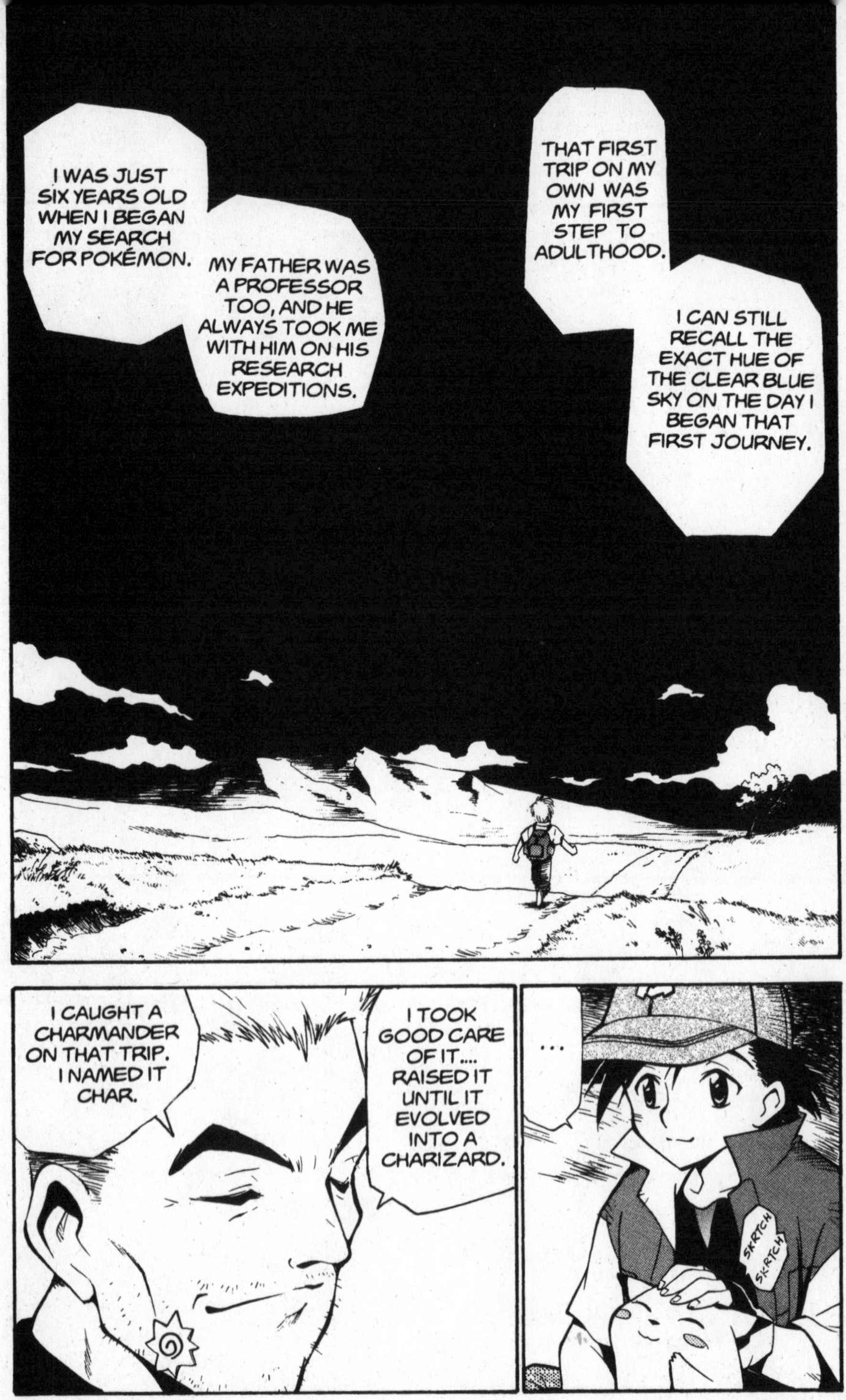
I WAS JUST SIX YEARS OLD WHEN I BEGAN MY SEARCH FOR POKÉMON.
MY FATHER WAS A PROFESSOR TOO, AND HE ALWAYS TOOK ME WITH HIM ON HIS RESEARCH EXPEDITIONS.
THAT FIRST TRIP ON MY OWN WAS MY FIRST STEP TO ADULTHOOD.
I CAN STILL RECALL THE EXACT HUE OF THE CLEAR BLUE SKY ON THE DAY I BEGAN THAT FIRST JOURNEY.
I CAUGHT A CHARMANDER ON THAT TRIP. I NAMED IT CHAR.
I TOOK GOOD CARE OF IT.... RAISED IT UNTIL IT EVOLVED INTO A CHARIZARD.
...
SKRTCH
SKRTCH

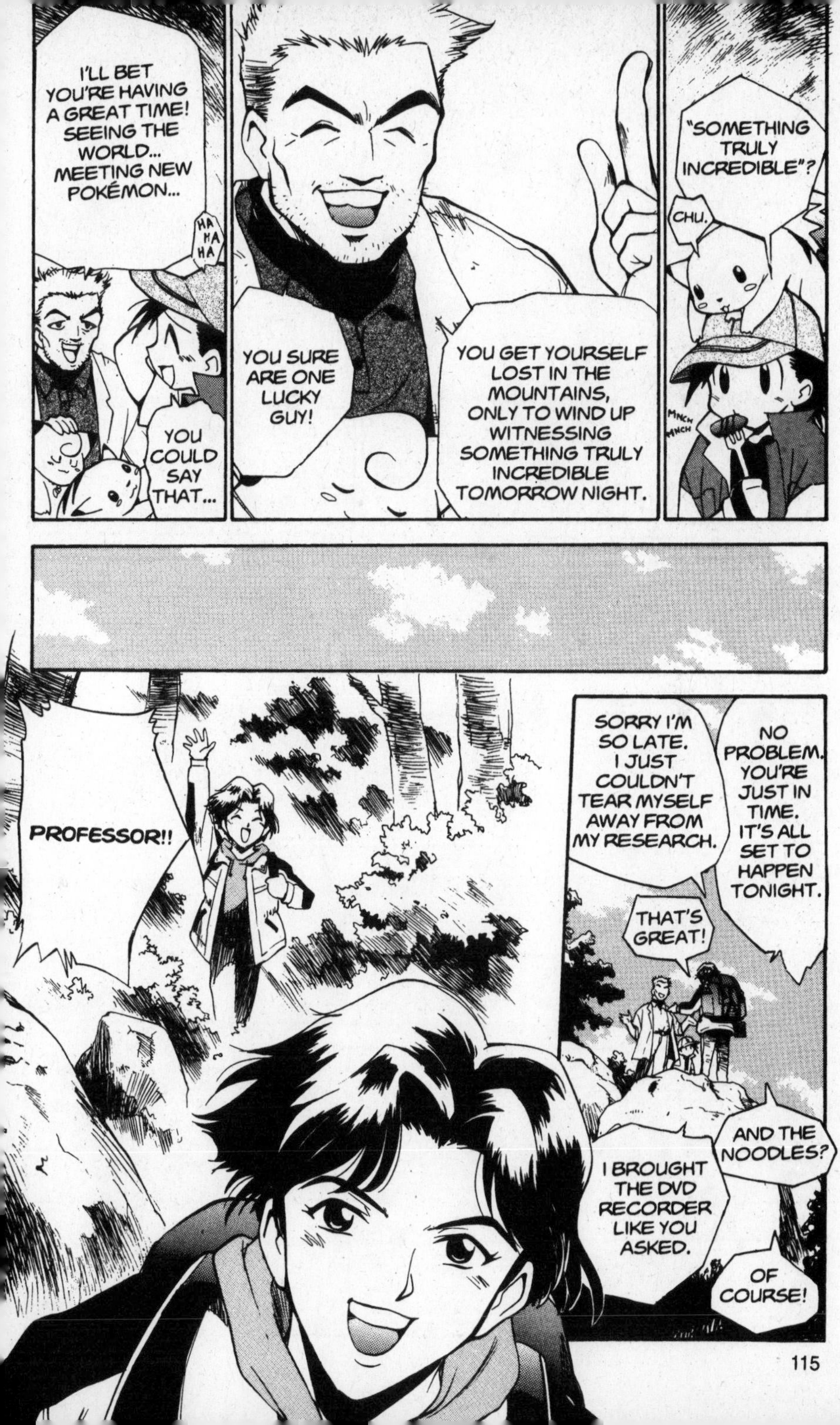
I'LL BET YOU'RE HAVING A GREAT TIME! SEEING THE WORLD... MEETING NEW POKÉMON...
HA HA HA
YOU COULD SAY THAT...
YOU SURE ARE ONE LUCKY GUY!
YOU GET YOURSELF LOST IN THE MOUNTAINS, ONLY TO WIND UP WITNESSING SOMETHING TRULY INCREDIBLE TOMORROW NIGHT.
"SOMETHING TRULY INCREDIBLE"?
CHU.
MNCH MNCH
PROFESSOR!!
SORRY I'M SO LATE. I JUST COULDN'T TEAR MYSELF AWAY FROM MY RESEARCH.
NO PROBLEM. YOU'RE JUST IN TIME. IT'S ALL SET TO HAPPEN TONIGHT.
THAT'S GREAT!
I BROUGHT THE DVD RECORDER LIKE YOU ASKED.
AND THE NOODLES?
OF COURSE!

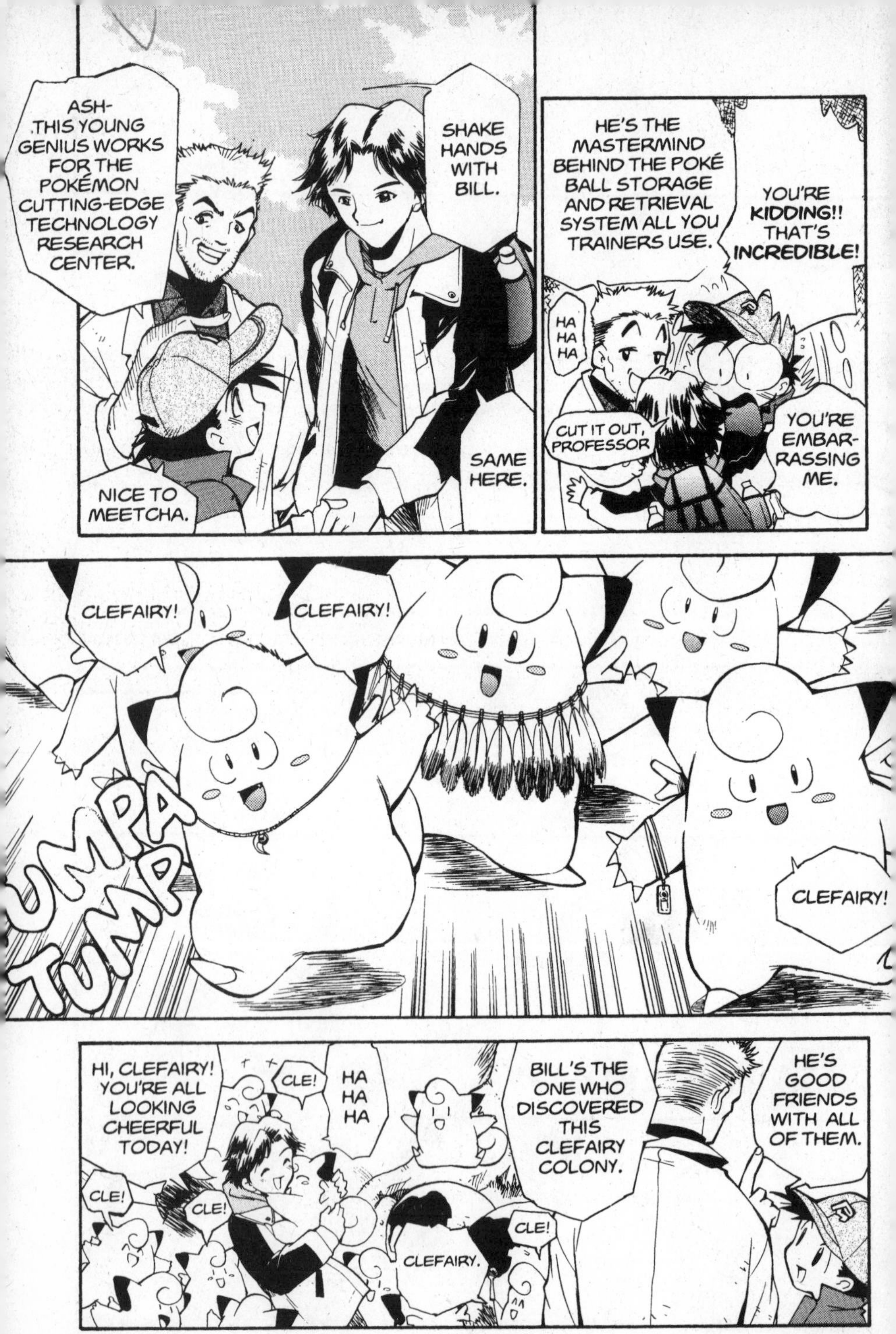
ASH- THIS YOUNG GENIUS WORKS FOR THE POKÉMON CUTTING-EDGE TECHNOLOGY RESEARCH CENTER.
SHAKE HANDS WITH BILL.
SAME HERE.
NICE TO MEETCHA.
HE'S THE MASTERMIND BEHIND THE POKÉ BALL STORAGE AND RETRIEVAL SYSTEM ALL YOU TRAINERS USE.
YOU'RE KIDDING!! THAT'S INCREDIBLE!
HA HA HA
CUT IT OUT, PROFESSOR
YOU'RE EMBARRASSING ME.
CLEFAIRY!
CLEFAIRY!
UMPA TUMP
CLEFAIRY!
HI, CLEFAIRY! YOU'RE ALL LOOKING CHEERFUL TODAY!
CLE!
HA HA HA
BILL'S THE ONE WHO DISCOVERED THIS CLEFAIRY COLONY.
HE'S GOOD FRIENDS WITH ALL OF THEM.
CLE!
CLE!
CLE!
CLEFAIRY.

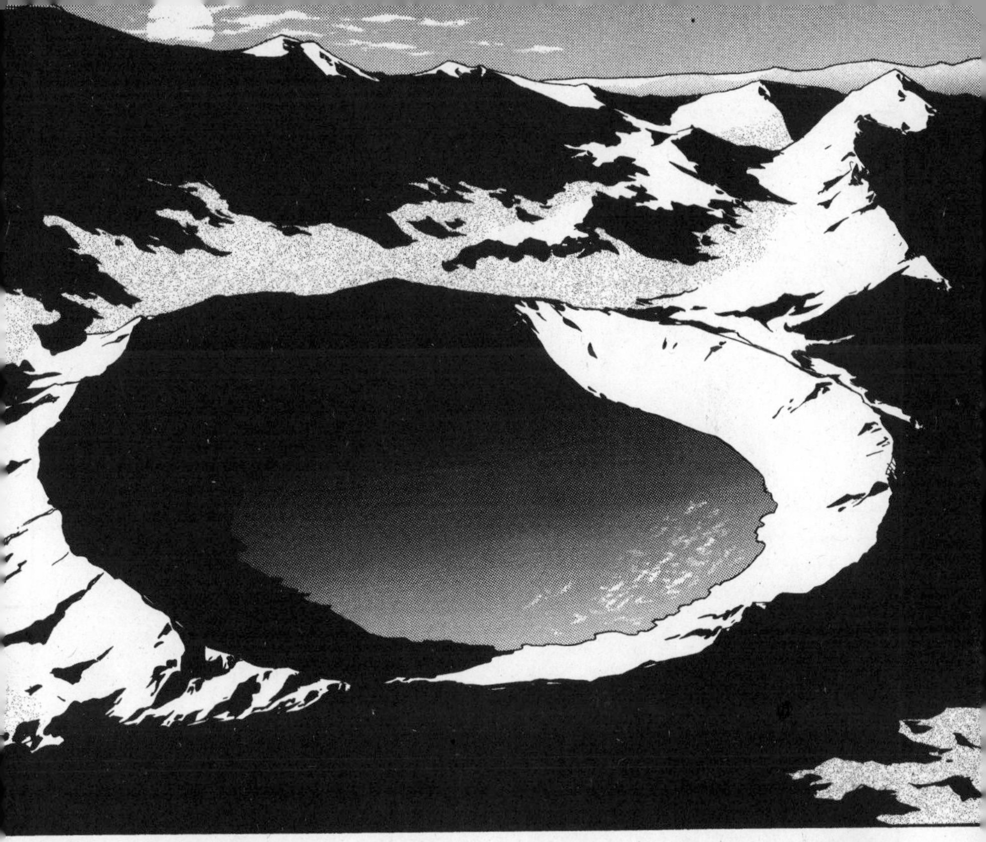

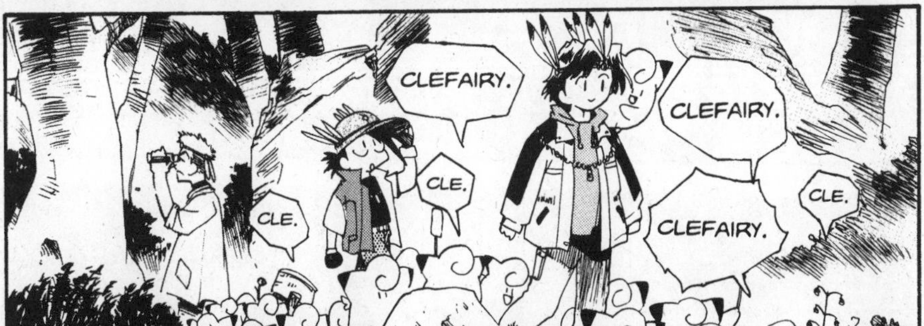

CLEFAIRY.
CLEFAIRY.
CLE.
CLE.
CLE.
CLEFAIRY.

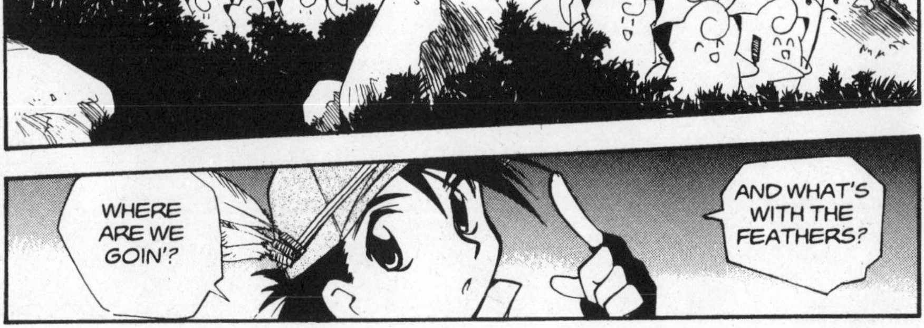

WHERE ARE WE GOIN'?
AND WHAT'S WITH THE FEATHERS?

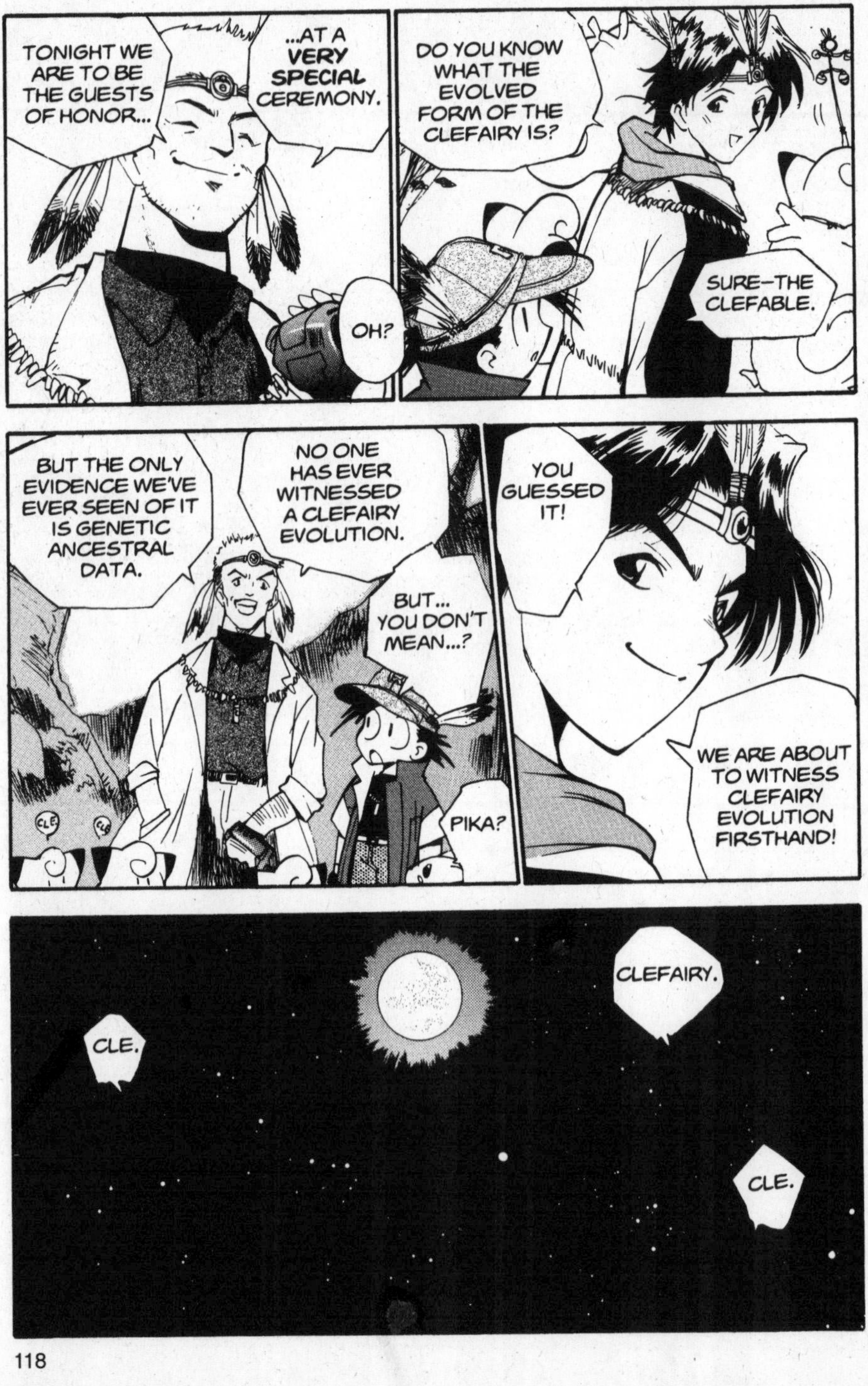

TONIGHT WE ARE TO BE THE GUESTS OF HONOR...
...AT A **VERY SPECIAL** CEREMONY.
DO YOU KNOW WHAT THE EVOLVED FORM OF THE CLEFAIRY IS?
OH?
SURE—THE CLEFABLE.
BUT THE ONLY EVIDENCE WE'VE EVER SEEN OF IT IS GENETIC ANCESTRAL DATA.
NO ONE HAS EVER WITNESSED A CLEFAIRY EVOLUTION.
BUT... YOU DON'T MEAN...?
CLE
CLE
PIKA?
YOU GUESSED IT!
WE ARE ABOUT TO WITNESS CLEFAIRY EVOLUTION FIRSTHAND!
CLE.
CLEFAIRY.
CLE.

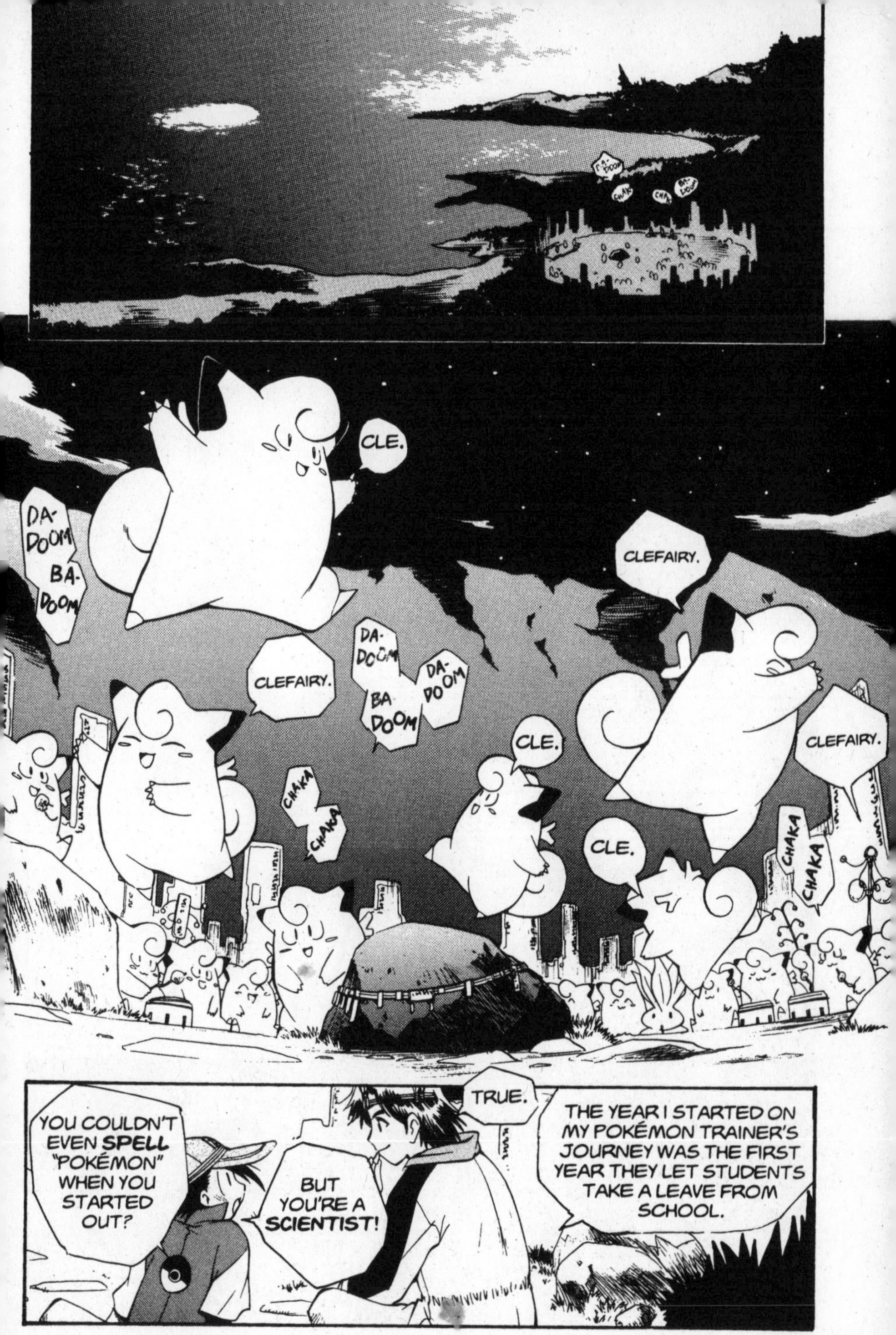
CLE.
DA-DOOM BA-DOOM
CLEFAIRY.
DA-DOOM
CLEFAIRY.
DA-DOOM BA-DOOM
CLE.
CLEFAIRY.
CHAKA CHAKA
CLE.
CHAKA CHAKA
YOU COULDN'T EVEN **SPELL** "POKÉMON" WHEN YOU STARTED OUT?
BUT YOU'RE A **SCIENTIST!**
TRUE.
THE YEAR I STARTED ON MY POKÉMON TRAINER'S JOURNEY WAS THE FIRST YEAR THEY LET STUDENTS TAKE A LEAVE FROM SCHOOL.

BACK THEN, I REALLY HATED SCHOOL. I WAS WILLING TO DO ANYTHING TO GET OUT OF GOING TO CLASSES.

BUT AS I SHARED ADVENTURES WITH MY POKÉMON, I BEGAN TO DEVELOP FEELINGS FOR THEM.

HAVE YOU EVER SEEN A VENUSAUR BLOOM?

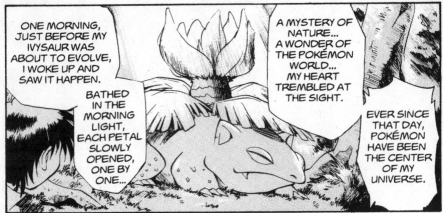

ONE MORNING, JUST BEFORE MY IVYSAUR WAS ABOUT TO EVOLVE, I WOKE UP AND SAW IT HAPPEN.

BATHED IN THE MORNING LIGHT, EACH PETAL SLOWLY OPENED, ONE BY ONE...

A MYSTERY OF NATURE... A WONDER OF THE POKÉMON WORLD... MY HEART TREMBLED AT THE SIGHT.

EVER SINCE THAT DAY, POKÉMON HAVE BEEN THE CENTER OF MY UNIVERSE.

BA-DOOM

CHAKA
CHAKA
CHA
CHAKA
CHAKA

ALL RIGHT! THE CEREMONY IS BEGINNING!

OH.

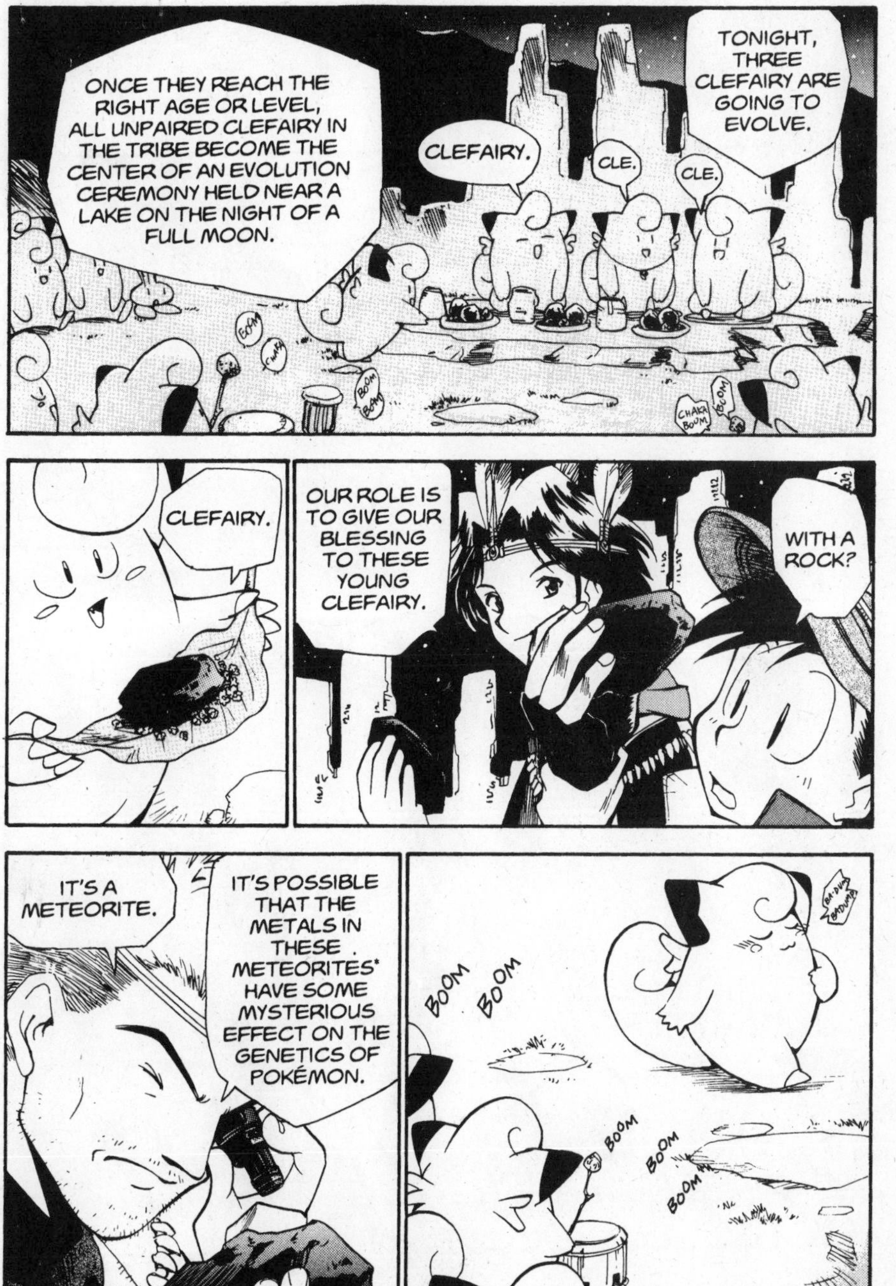
ONCE THEY REACH THE RIGHT AGE OR LEVEL, ALL UNPAIRED CLEFAIRY IN THE TRIBE BECOME THE CENTER OF AN EVOLUTION CEREMONY HELD NEAR A LAKE ON THE NIGHT OF A FULL MOON.
CLEFAIRY.
CLE.
CLE.
TONIGHT, THREE CLEFAIRY ARE GOING TO EVOLVE.
CLEFAIRY.
OUR ROLE IS TO GIVE OUR BLESSING TO THESE YOUNG CLEFAIRY.
WITH A ROCK?
IT'S A METEORITE.
IT'S POSSIBLE THAT THE METALS IN THESE METEORITES* HAVE SOME MYSTERIOUS EFFECT ON THE GENETICS OF POKÉMON.
*NICKEL IS A MAJOR COMPONENT OF METEORITES.
BOOM BOOM
BOOM BOOM BOOM

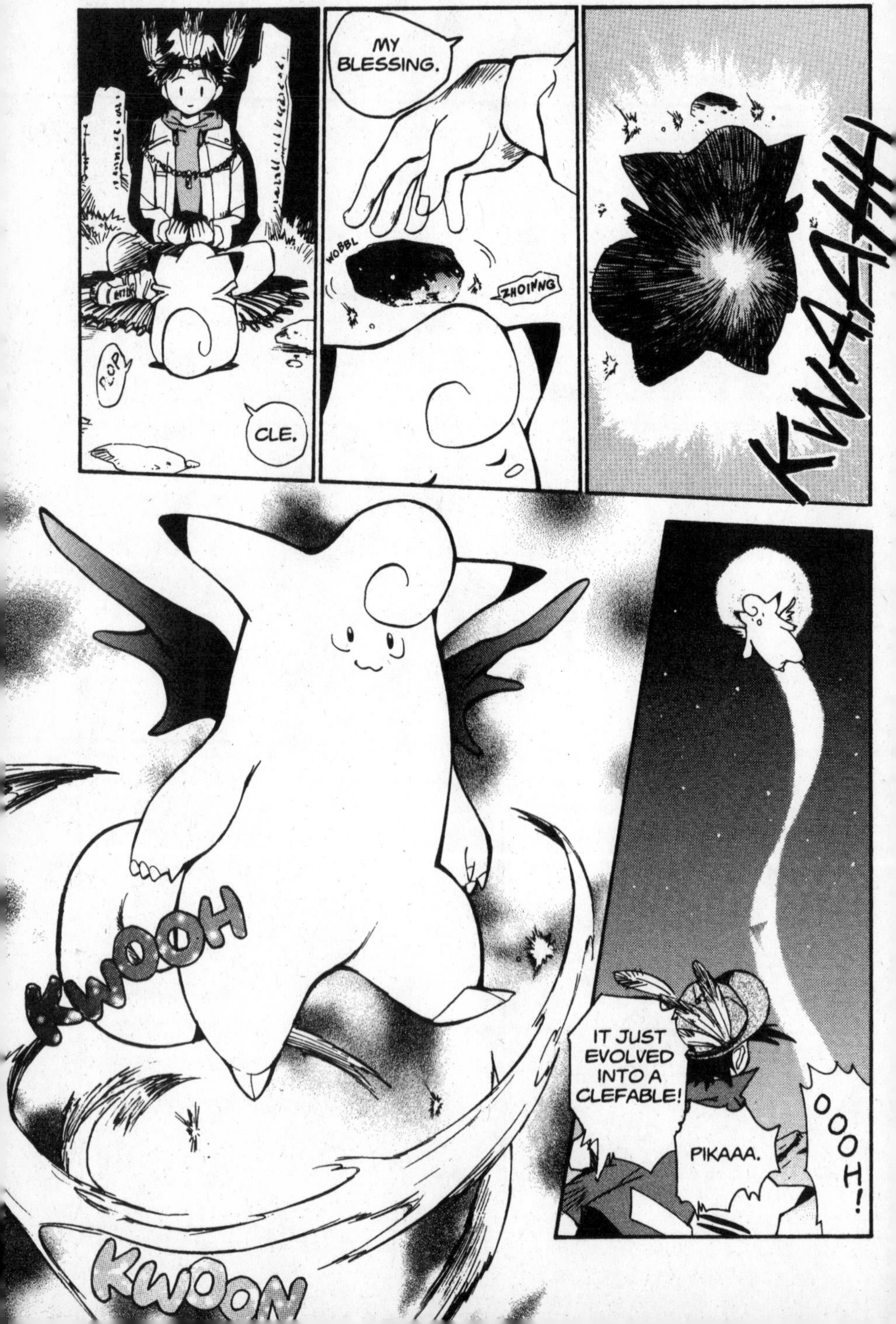
POP
CLE.
MY BLESSING.
WOBBL
ZHOINNG
KWAAHH
KWOOH
KWOON
IT JUST EVOLVED INTO A CLEFABLE!
PIKAAA.
OOOOH!

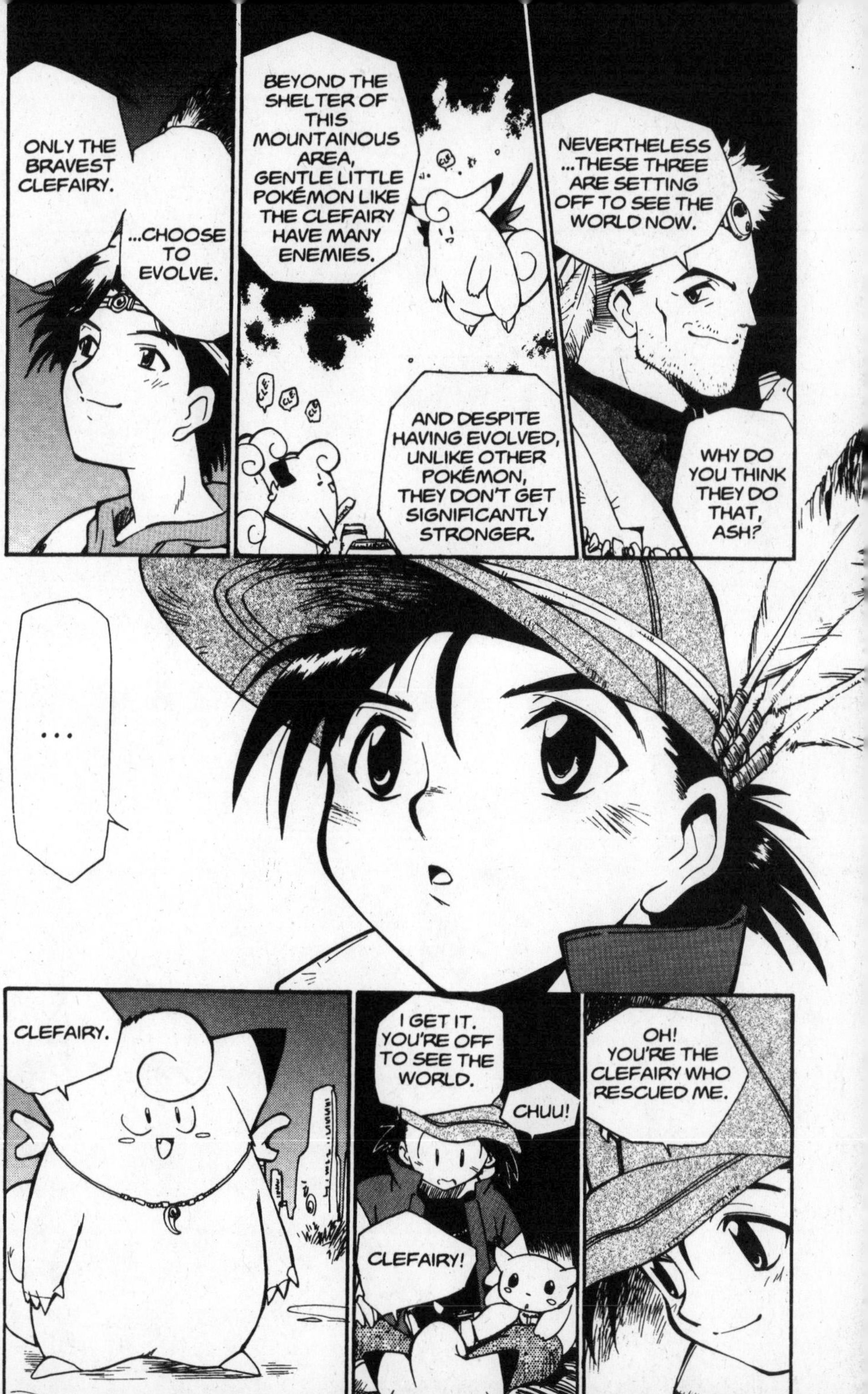
ONLY THE BRAVEST CLEFAIRY.
...CHOOSE TO EVOLVE.
BEYOND THE SHELTER OF THIS MOUNTAINOUS AREA, GENTLE LITTLE POKÉMON LIKE THE CLEFAIRY HAVE MANY ENEMIES.
CLE
CLE
CLE
CLE
AND DESPITE HAVING EVOLVED, UNLIKE OTHER POKÉMON, THEY DON'T GET SIGNIFICANTLY STRONGER.
NEVERTHELESS ...THESE THREE ARE SETTING OFF TO SEE THE WORLD NOW.
WHY DO YOU THINK THEY DO THAT, ASH?
...
CLEFAIRY.
I GET IT. YOU'RE OFF TO SEE THE WORLD.
CHUU!
CLEFAIRY!
OH! YOU'RE THE CLEFAIRY WHO RESCUED ME.

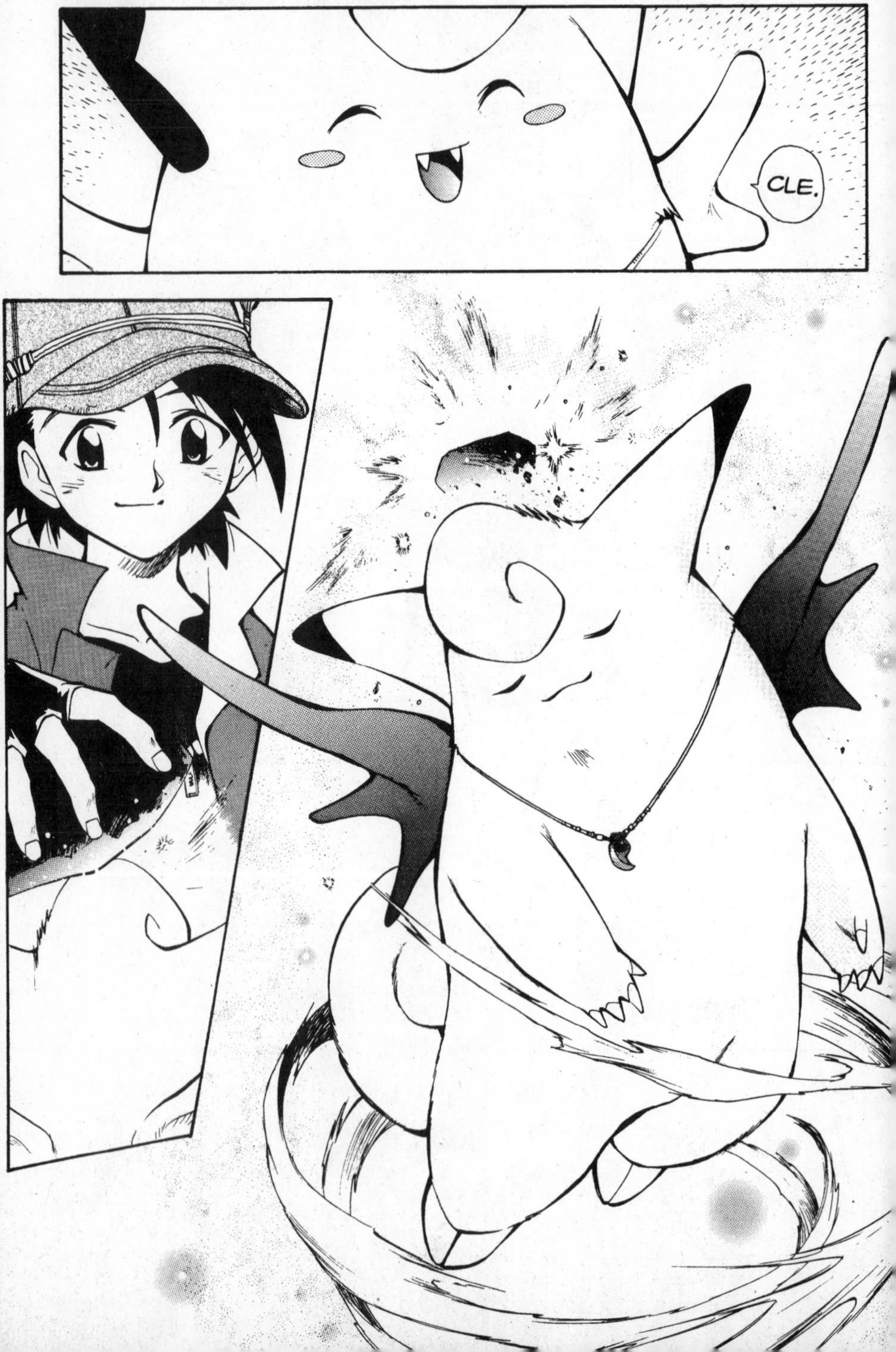
CLE.

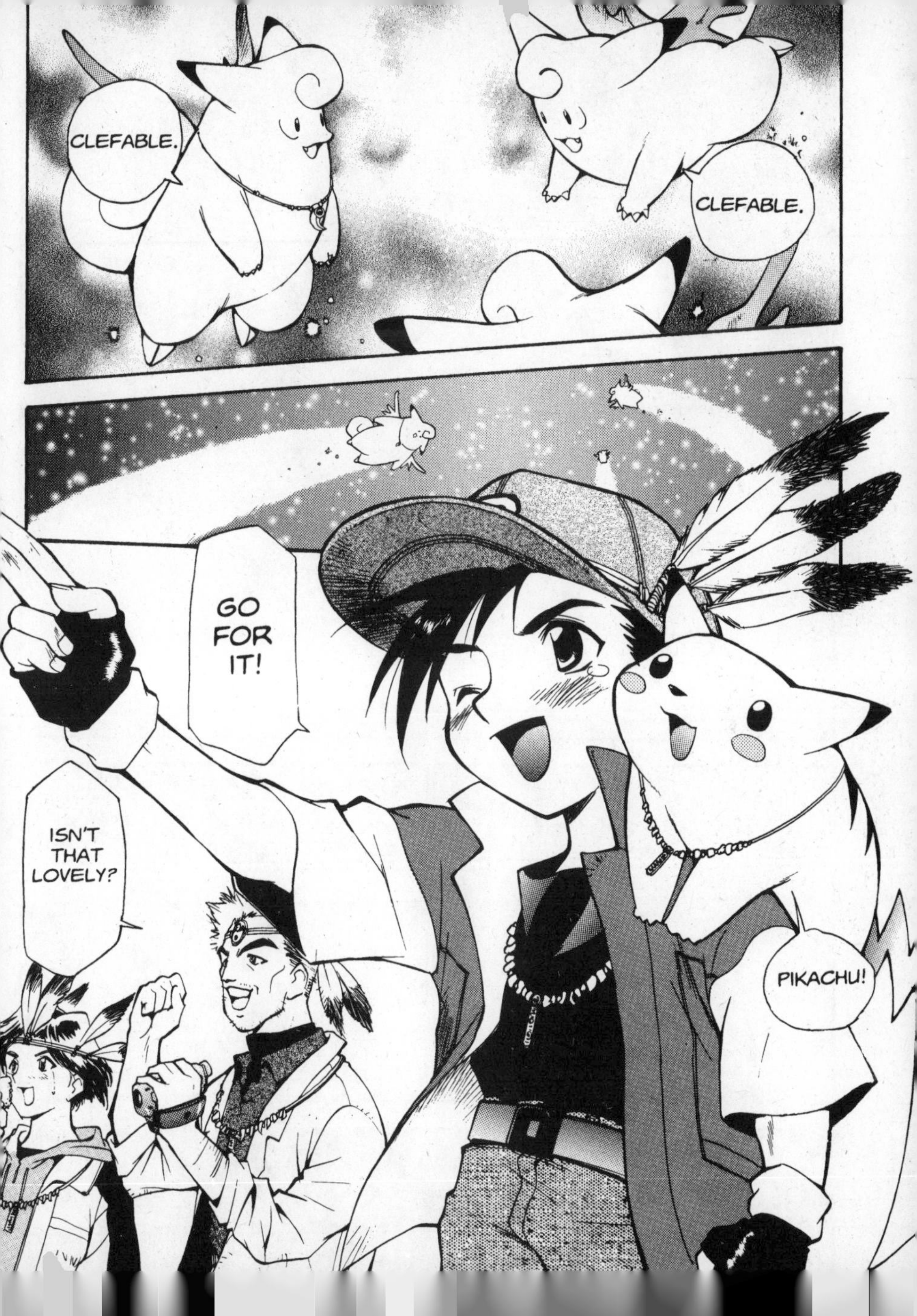
CLEFABLE.
CLEFABLE.
GO FOR IT!
ISN'T THAT LOVELY?
PIKACHU!

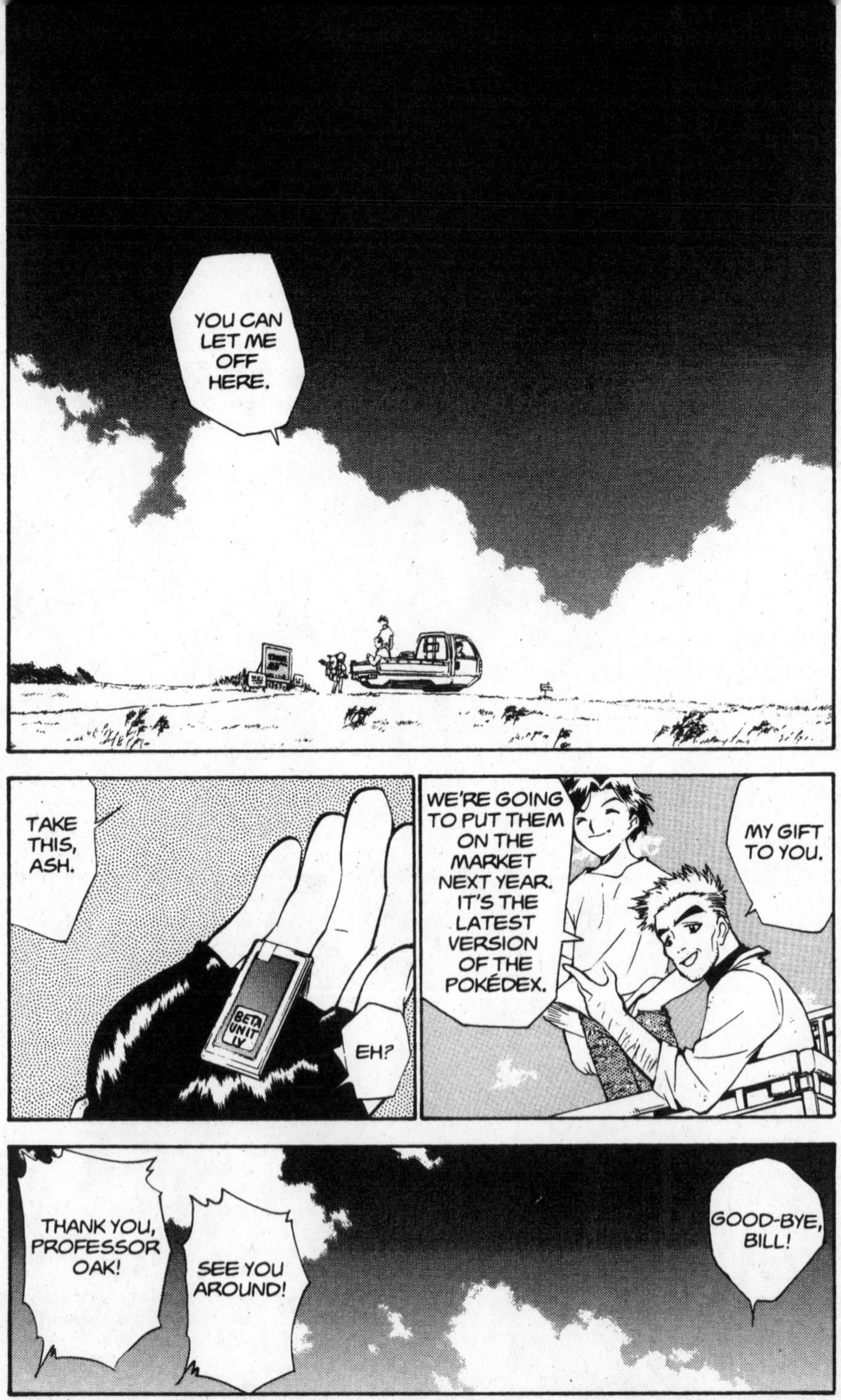
YOU CAN LET ME OFF HERE.
TAKE THIS, ASH.
BETA UNIT IV
EH?
WE'RE GOING TO PUT THEM ON THE MARKET NEXT YEAR. IT'S THE LATEST VERSION OF THE POKÉDEX.
MY GIFT TO YOU.
THANK YOU, PROFESSOR OAK!
SEE YOU AROUND!
GOOD-BYE, BILL!

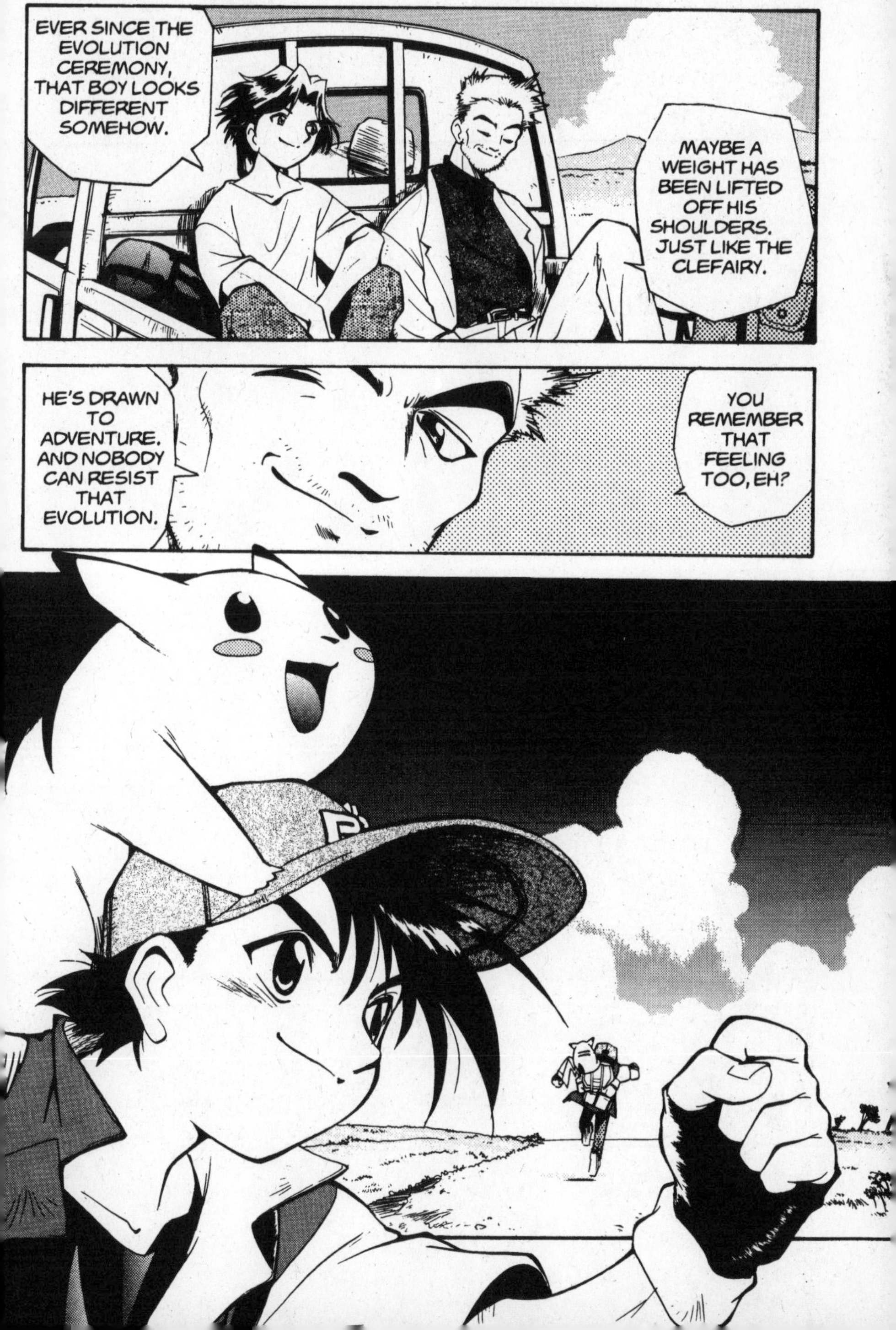
EVER SINCE THE EVOLUTION CEREMONY, THAT BOY LOOKS DIFFERENT SOMEHOW.
MAYBE A WEIGHT HAS BEEN LIFTED OFF HIS SHOULDERS. JUST LIKE THE CLEFAIRY.
HE'S DRAWN TO ADVENTURE. AND NOBODY CAN RESIST THAT EVOLUTION.
YOU REMEMBER THAT FEELING TOO, EH?

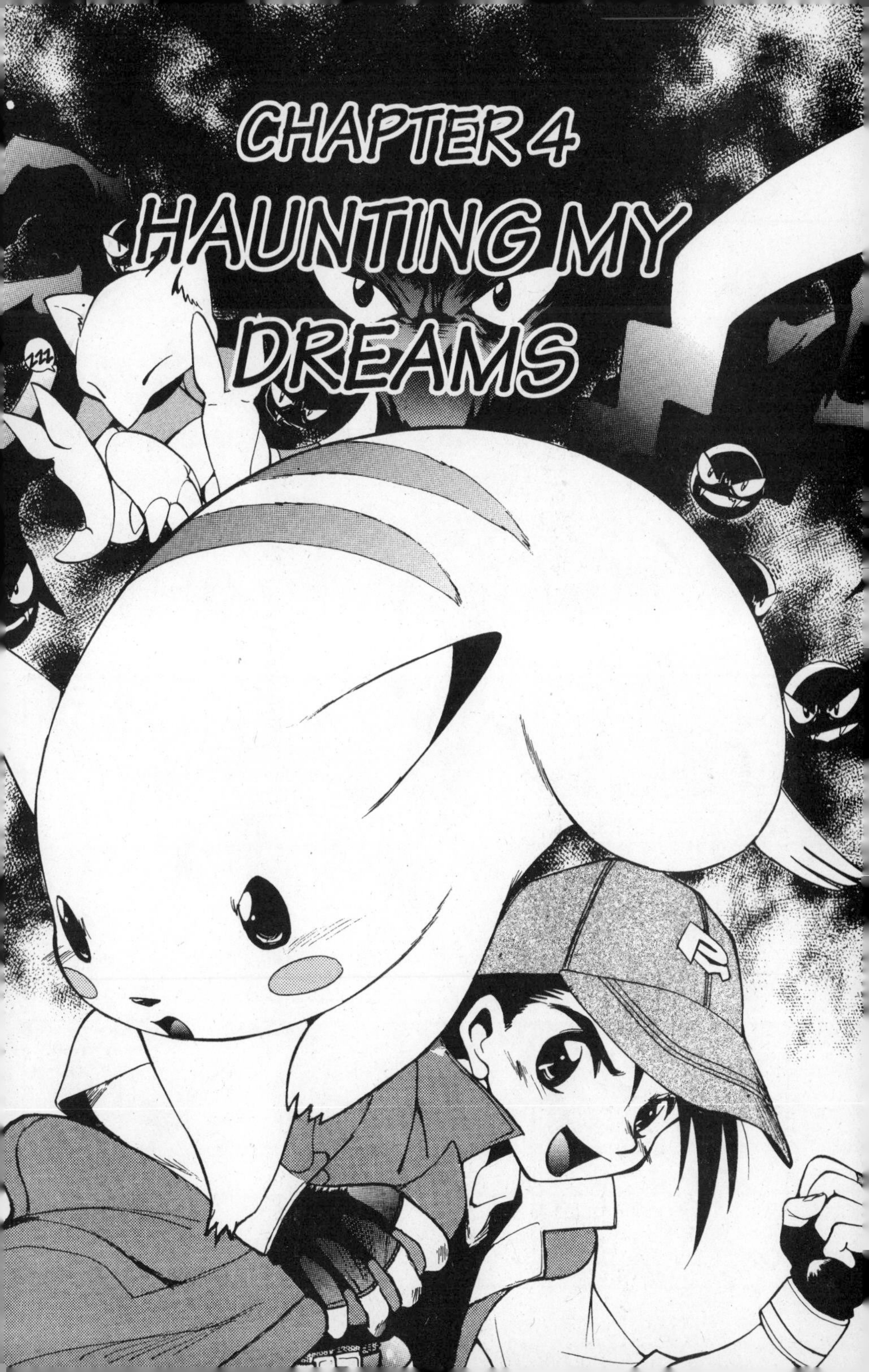
CHAPTER 4
HAUNTING MY DREAMS

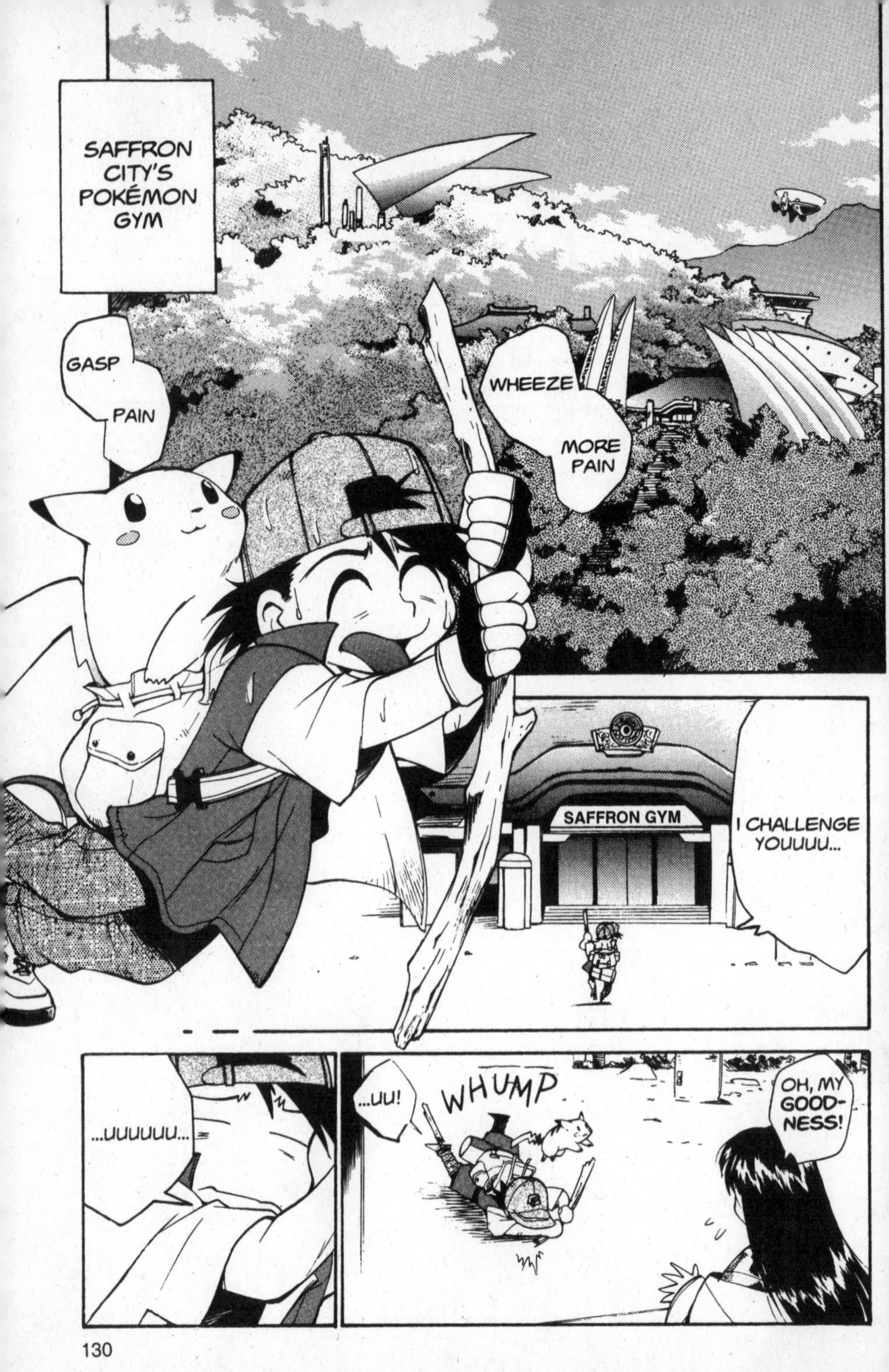
SAFFRON CITY'S POKÉMON GYM
GASP
PAIN
WHEEZE
MORE PAIN
SAFFRON GYM
I CHALLENGE YOUUUU...
...UUUUUU...
...UU!
WHUMP
OH, MY GOOD-NESS!

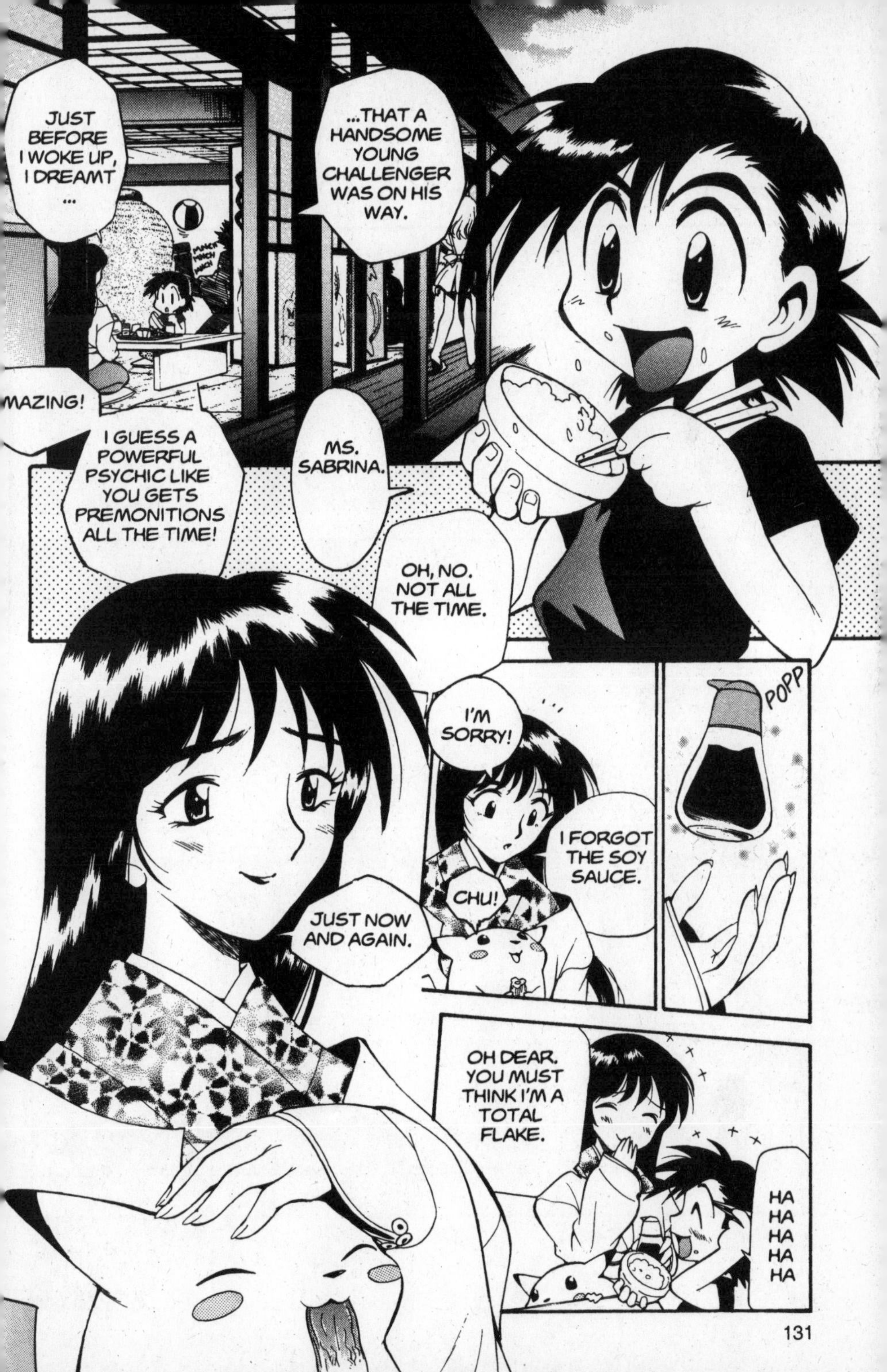

JUST BEFORE I WOKE UP, I DREAMT ...
...THAT A HANDSOME YOUNG CHALLENGER WAS ON HIS WAY.
MAZING!
I GUESS A POWERFUL PSYCHIC LIKE YOU GETS PREMONITIONS ALL THE TIME!
MS. SABRINA.
OH, NO. NOT ALL THE TIME.
JUST NOW AND AGAIN.
I'M SORRY!
I FORGOT THE SOY SAUCE.
CHU!
POPP
OH DEAR. YOU MUST THINK I'M A TOTAL FLAKE.
HA HA HA HA HA

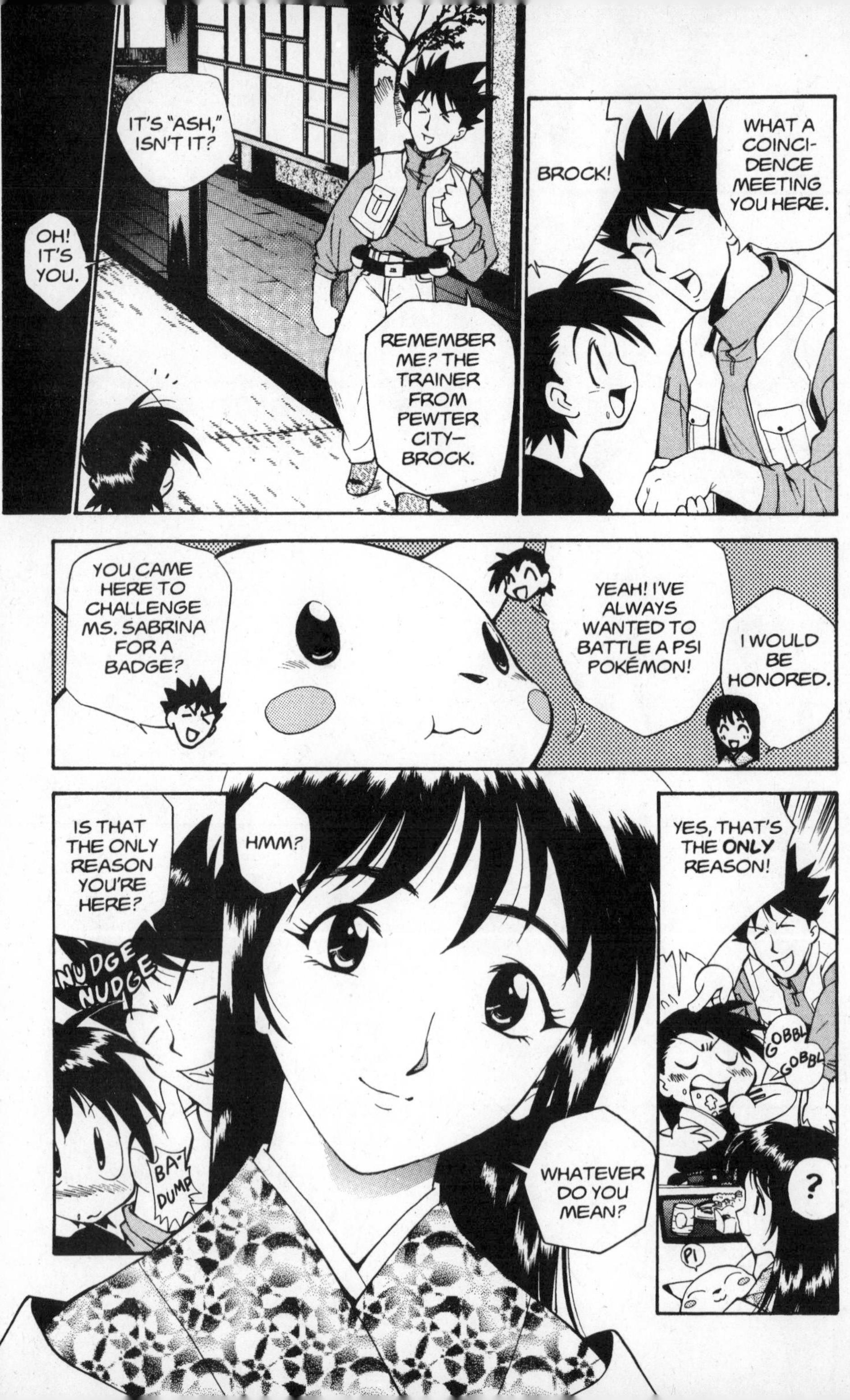
IT'S "ASH," ISN'T IT?
OH! IT'S YOU.
REMEMBER ME? THE TRAINER FROM PEWTER CITY—BROCK.
BROCK!
WHAT A COINCIDENCE MEETING YOU HERE.
YOU CAME HERE TO CHALLENGE MS. SABRINA FOR A BADGE?
YEAH! I'VE ALWAYS WANTED TO BATTLE A PSI POKÉMON!
I WOULD BE HONORED.
IS THAT THE ONLY REASON YOU'RE HERE?
HMM?
NUDGE NUDGE
BA-DUMP
WHATEVER DO YOU MEAN?
YES, THAT'S THE **ONLY** REASON!
GOBBL GOBBL
?
PI

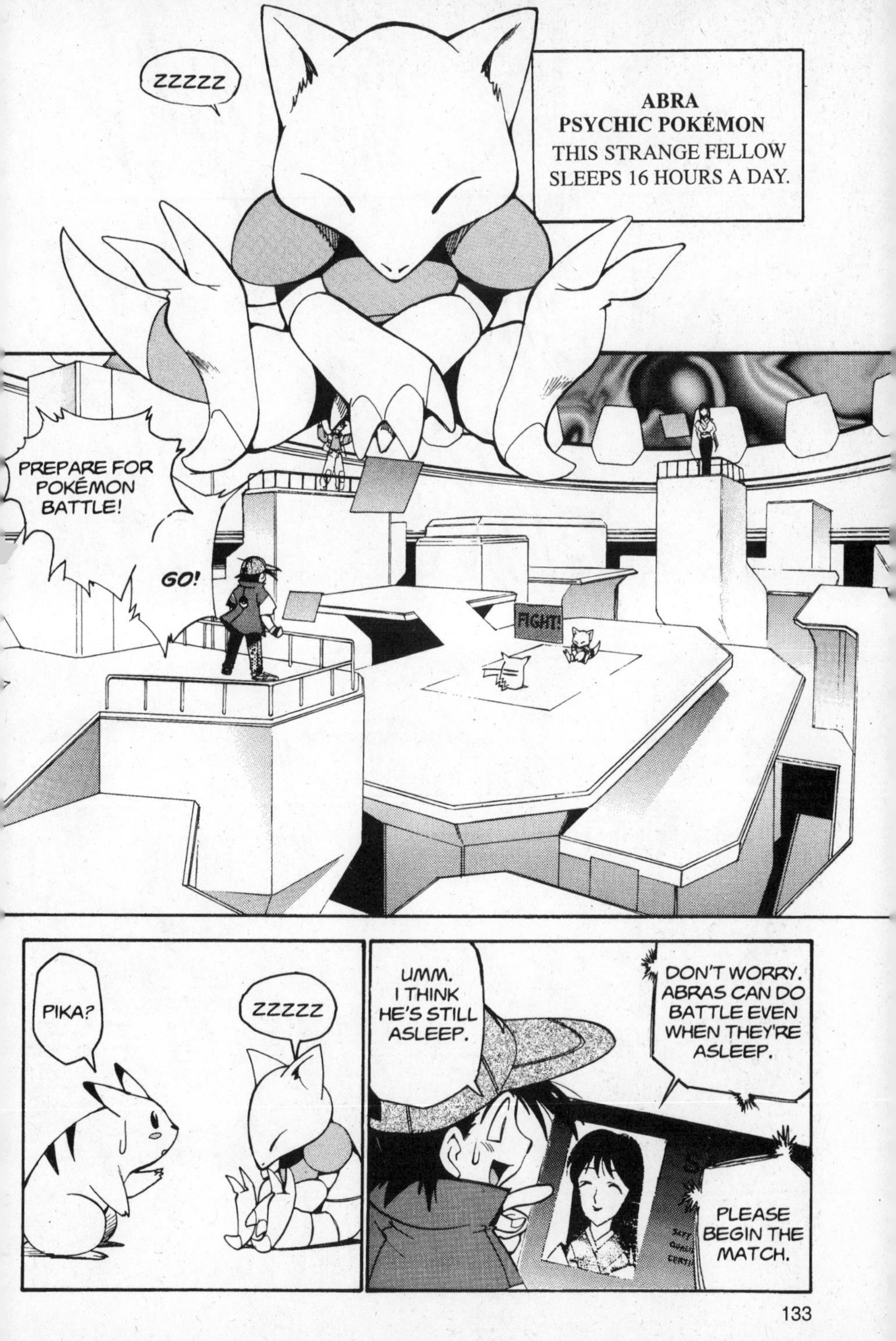
ZZZZZ
ABRA
PSYCHIC POKÉMON
THIS STRANGE FELLOW SLEEPS 16 HOURS A DAY.
PREPARE FOR POKÉMON BATTLE!
GO!
FIGHT!
PIKA?
ZZZZZ
UMM. I THINK HE'S STILL ASLEEP.
DON'T WORRY. ABRAS CAN DO BATTLE EVEN WHEN THEY'RE ASLEEP.
PLEASE BEGIN THE MATCH.

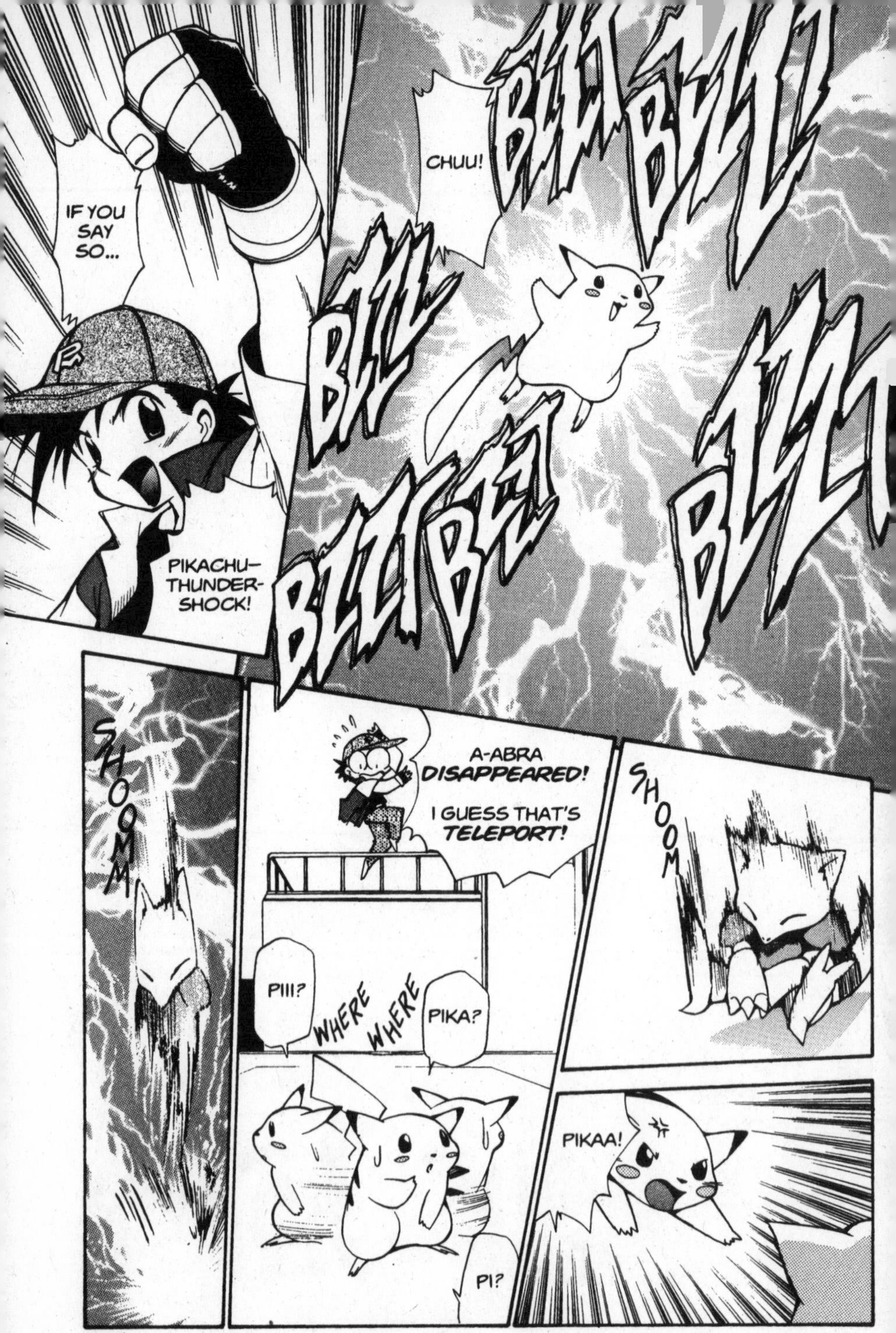
IF YOU SAY SO...
PIKACHU— THUNDER-SHOCK!
CHUU!
SHOOMM
A-ABRA DISAPPEARED!
I GUESS THAT'S TELEPORT!
PIII?
WHERE
WHERE
PIKA?
PI?
SHOOM
PIKAA!

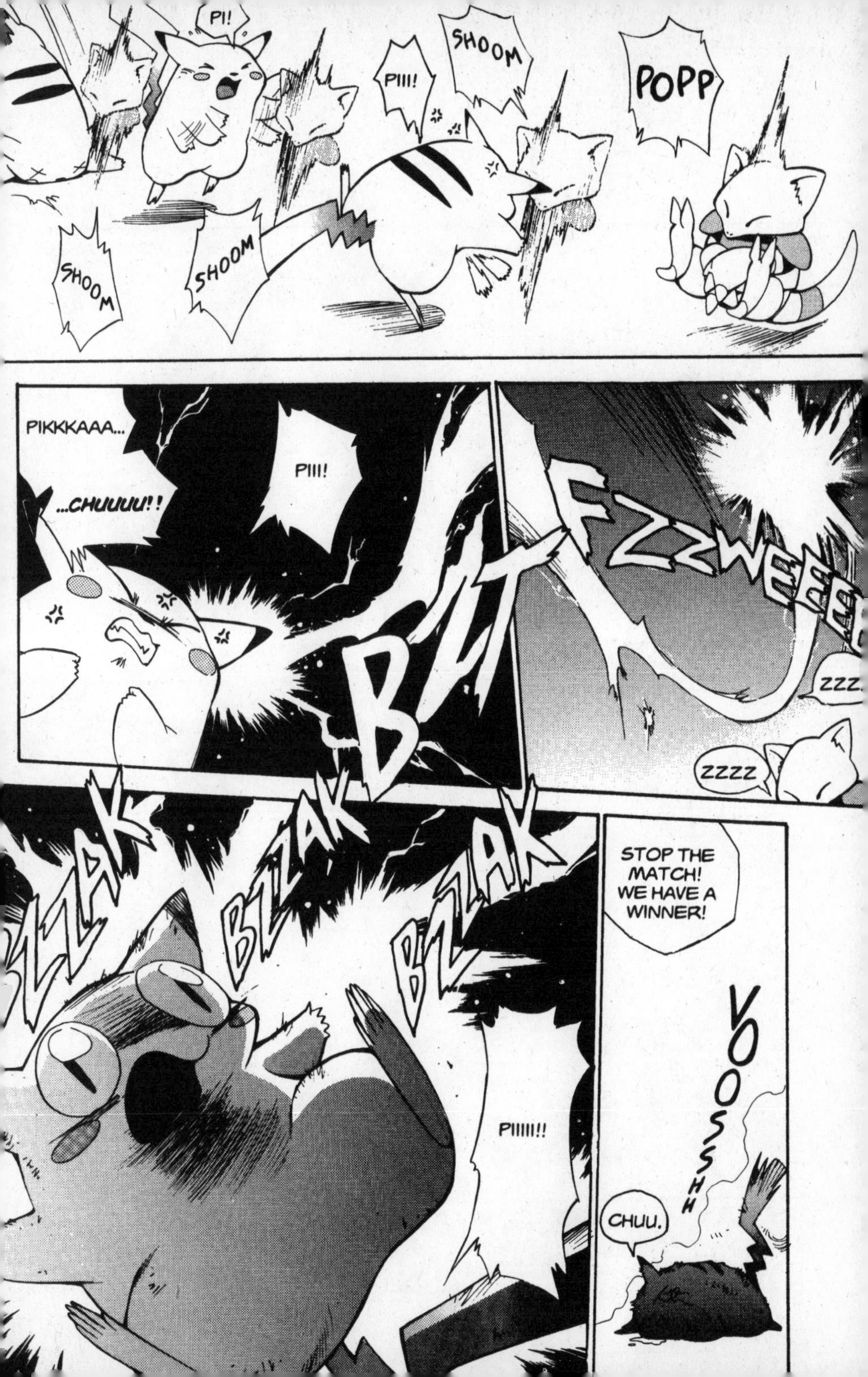
PI!
SHOOM
SHOOM
PIII!
SHOOM
POPP
PIKKKAAA...
...CHUUUU!!
PIII!
BLT
FZZWEEE
ZZZ.
ZZZZ
BZZAK
BZZAK
BZZAK
PIIIII!!
STOP THE MATCH! WE HAVE A WINNER!
VOOSSHH
CHUU.

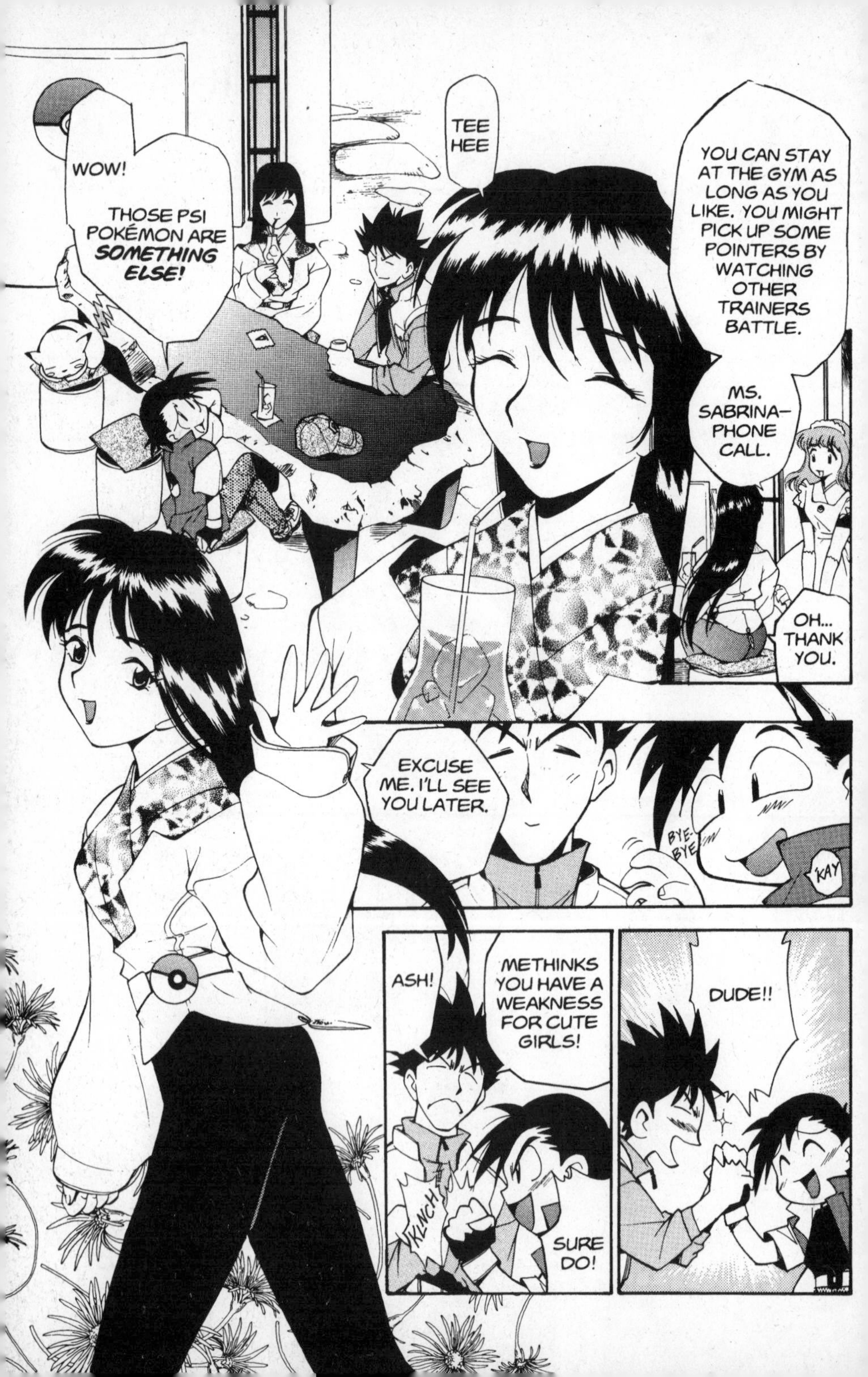
WOW!
THOSE PSI POKéMON ARE SOMETHING ELSE!
TEE HEE
YOU CAN STAY AT THE GYM AS LONG AS YOU LIKE. YOU MIGHT PICK UP SOME POINTERS BY WATCHING OTHER TRAINERS BATTLE.
MS. SABRINA—PHONE CALL.
OH... THANK YOU.
EXCUSE ME. I'LL SEE YOU LATER.
BYE-BYE
'KAY
ASH!
METHINKS YOU HAVE A WEAKNESS FOR CUTE GIRLS!
KLNCH
SURE DO!
DUDE!!

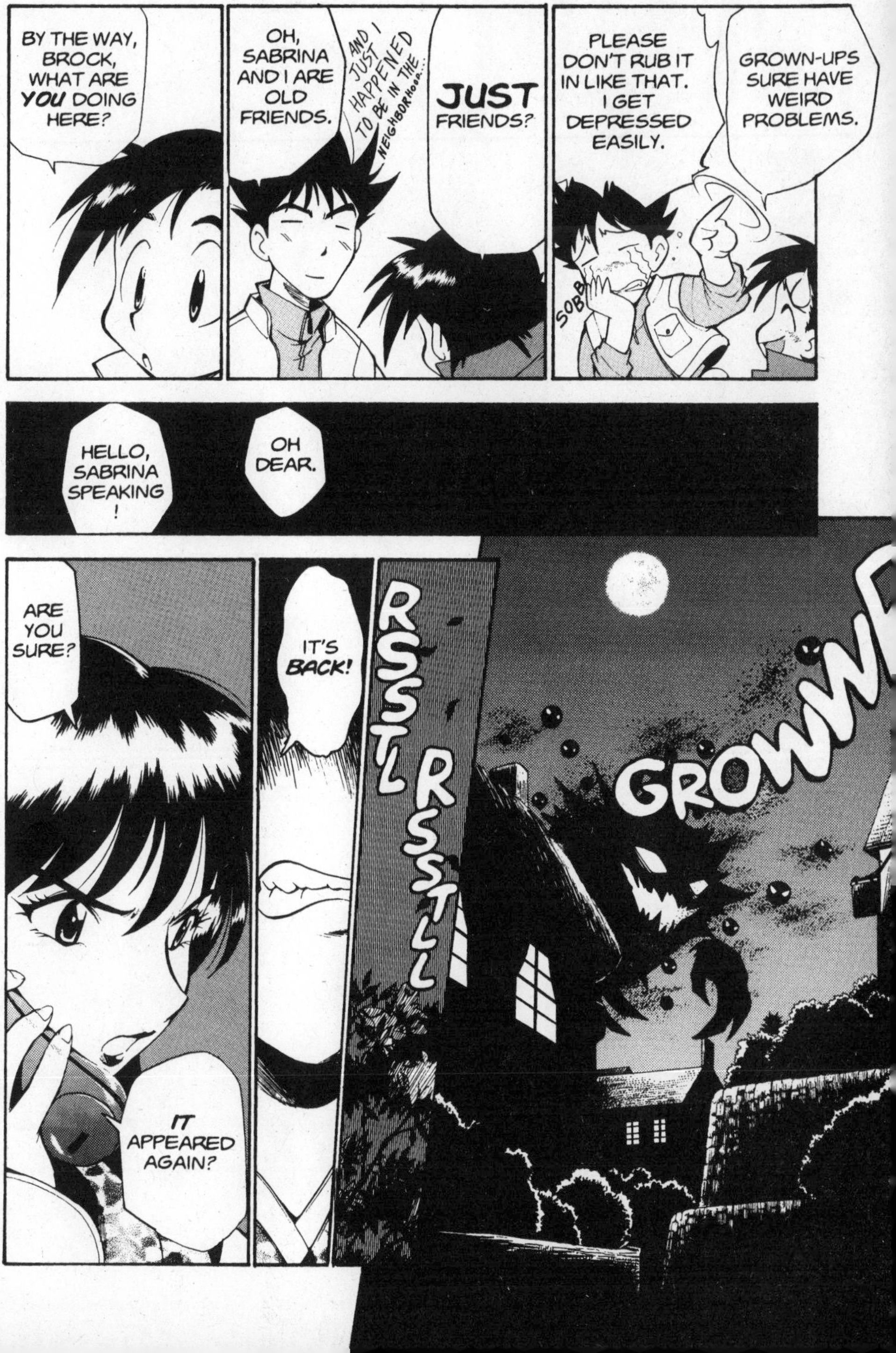
BY THE WAY, BROCK, WHAT ARE YOU DOING HERE?
OH, SABRINA AND I ARE OLD FRIENDS.
AND I JUST HAPPENED TO BE IN THE NEIGHBORHOOD...
JUST FRIENDS?
PLEASE DON'T RUB IT IN LIKE THAT. I GET DEPRESSED EASILY.
SOB
GROWN-UPS SURE HAVE WEIRD PROBLEMS.
HELLO, SABRINA SPEAKING!
OH DEAR.
ARE YOU SURE?
IT APPEARED AGAIN?
IT'S BACK!
RSSTL
RSSTLL
GROWW

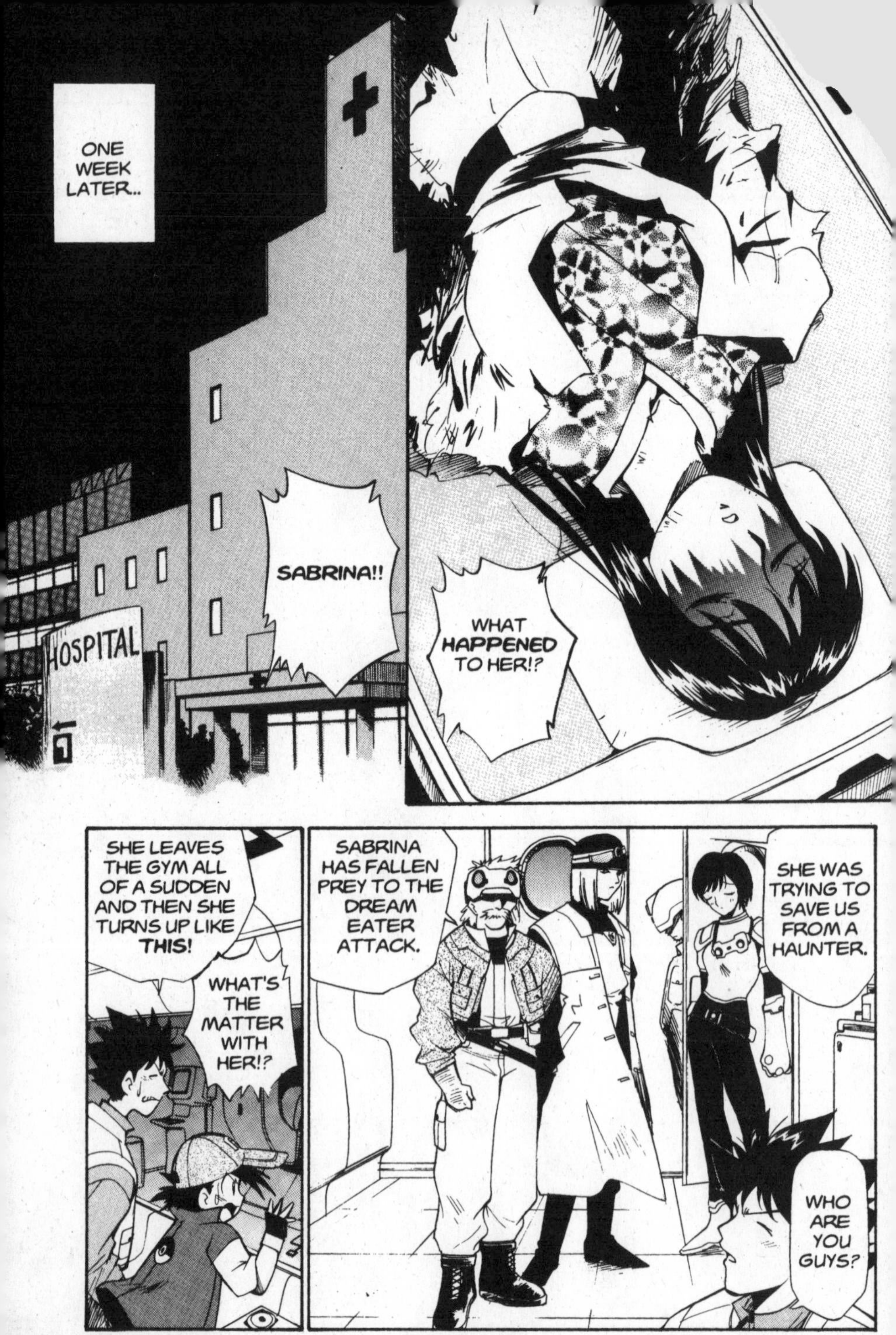

ONE WEEK LATER...
HOSPITAL
SABRINA!!
WHAT HAPPENED TO HER!?
SHE LEAVES THE GYM ALL OF A SUDDEN AND THEN SHE TURNS UP LIKE THIS!
WHAT'S THE MATTER WITH HER!?
SABRINA HAS FALLEN PREY TO THE DREAM EATER ATTACK.
SHE WAS TRYING TO SAVE US FROM A HAUNTER.
WHO ARE YOU GUYS?

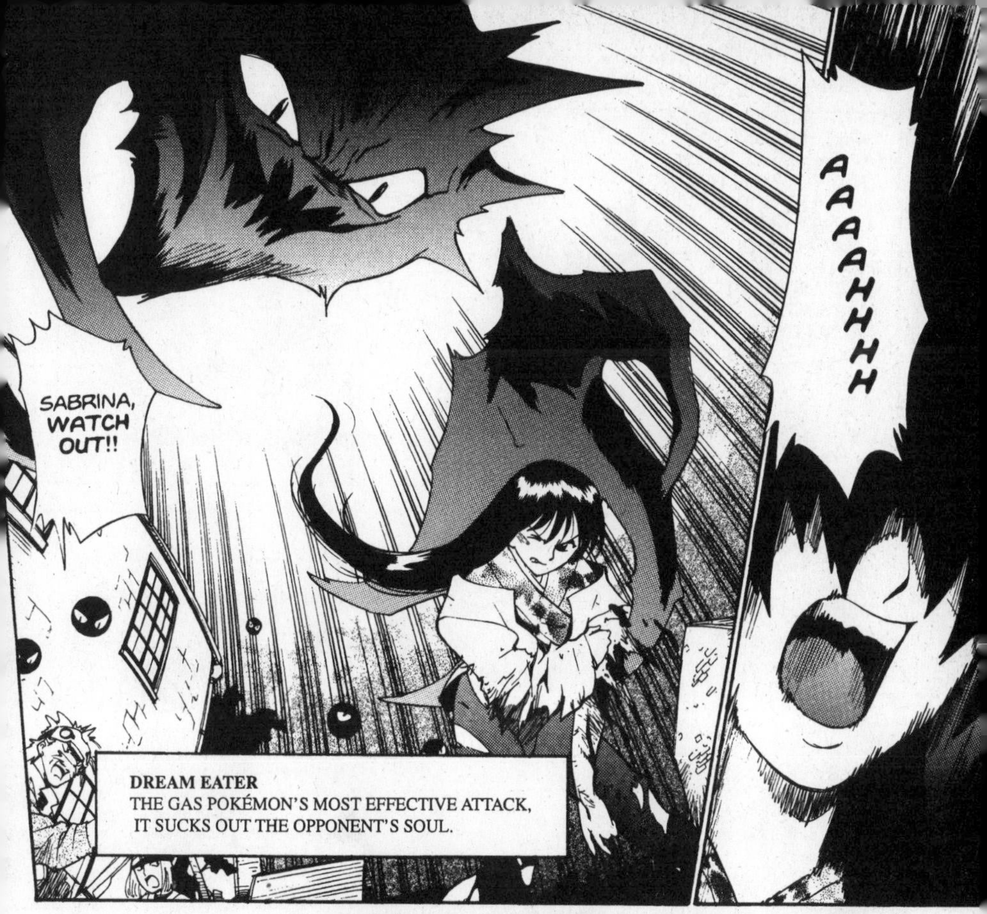
SABRINA, WATCH OUT!!
DREAM EATER
THE GAS POKÉMON'S MOST EFFECTIVE ATTACK, IT SUCKS OUT THE OPPONENT'S SOUL.
AAAAHHHH

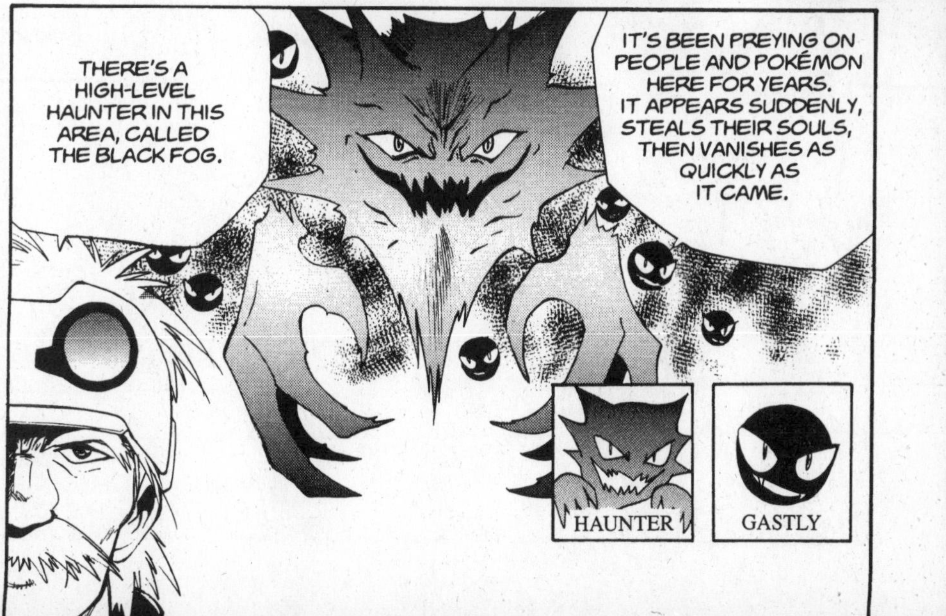
THERE'S A HIGH-LEVEL HAUNTER IN THIS AREA, CALLED THE BLACK FOG.
IT'S BEEN PREYING ON PEOPLE AND POKÉMON HERE FOR YEARS. IT APPEARS SUDDENLY, STEALS THEIR SOULS, THEN VANISHES AS QUICKLY AS IT CAME.
HAUNTER
GASTLY

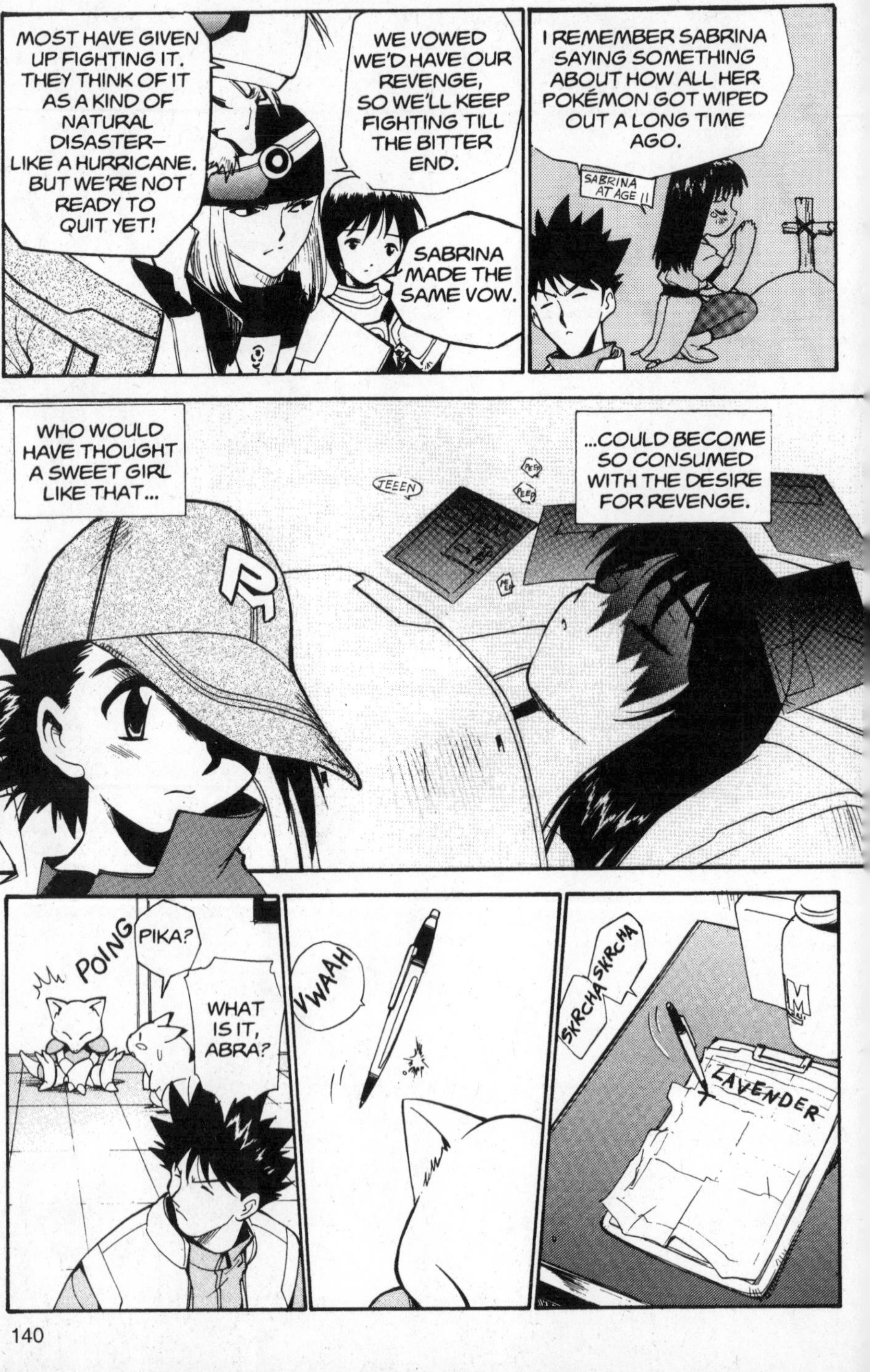
MOST HAVE GIVEN UP FIGHTING IT. THEY THINK OF IT AS A KIND OF NATURAL DISASTER— LIKE A HURRICANE. BUT WE'RE NOT READY TO QUIT YET!
WE VOWED WE'D HAVE OUR REVENGE, SO WE'LL KEEP FIGHTING TILL THE BITTER END.
SABRINA MADE THE SAME VOW.
I REMEMBER SABRINA SAYING SOMETHING ABOUT HOW ALL HER POKÉMON GOT WIPED OUT A LONG TIME AGO.
SABRINA AT AGE 11
WHO WOULD HAVE THOUGHT A SWEET GIRL LIKE THAT...
JEEEN
...COULD BECOME SO CONSUMED WITH THE DESIRE FOR REVENGE.
POING
PIKA?
WHAT IS IT, ABRA?
VWAAH
SKRCHA SKRCHA
LAVENDER

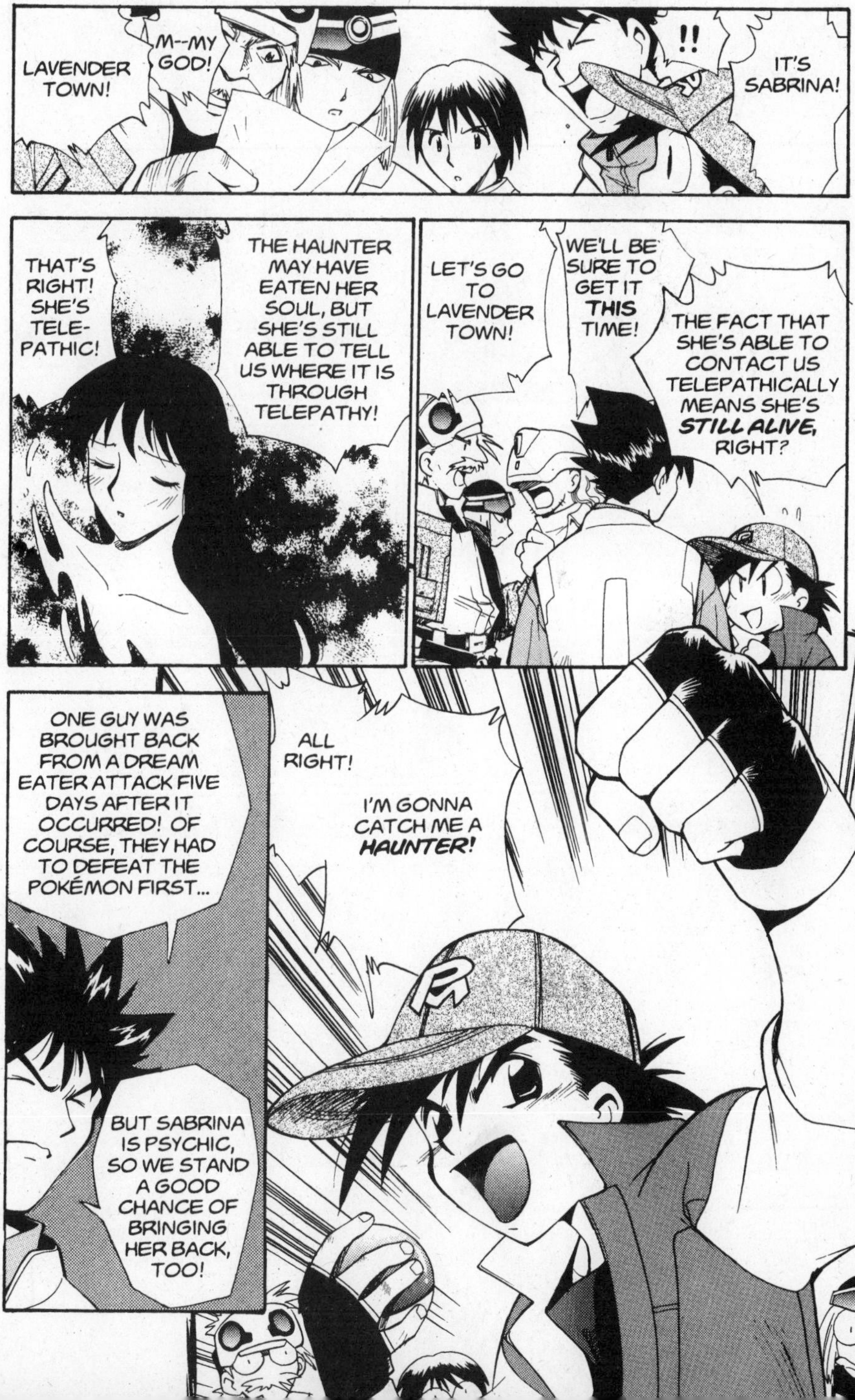
LAVENDER TOWN!
M--MY GOD!
!!
IT'S SABRINA!
THAT'S RIGHT! SHE'S TELE-PATHIC!
THE HAUNTER MAY HAVE EATEN HER SOUL, BUT SHE'S STILL ABLE TO TELL US WHERE IT IS THROUGH TELEPATHY!
LET'S GO TO LAVENDER TOWN!
WE'LL BE SURE TO GET IT **THIS** TIME!
THE FACT THAT SHE'S ABLE TO CONTACT US TELEPATHICALLY MEANS SHE'S ***STILL ALIVE,*** RIGHT?
ONE GUY WAS BROUGHT BACK FROM A DREAM EATER ATTACK FIVE DAYS AFTER IT OCCURRED! OF COURSE, THEY HAD TO DEFEAT THE POKÉMON FIRST...
BUT SABRINA IS PSYCHIC, SO WE STAND A GOOD CHANCE OF BRINGING HER BACK, TOO!
ALL RIGHT!
I'M GONNA CATCH ME A ***HAUNTER!***

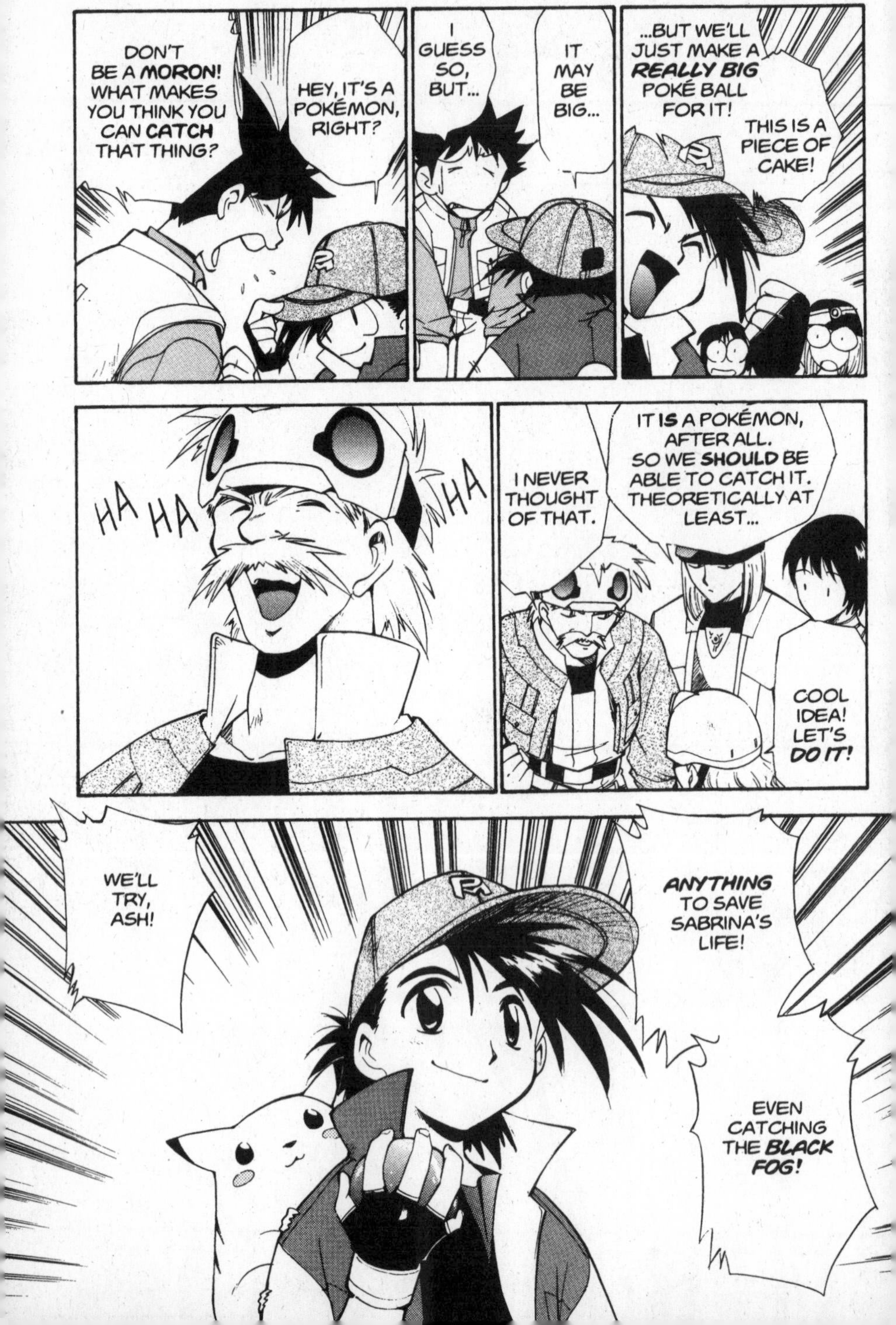
DON'T BE A **MORON**! WHAT MAKES YOU THINK YOU CAN **CATCH** THAT THING?
HEY, IT'S A POKÉMON, RIGHT?
I GUESS SO, BUT...
IT MAY BE BIG...
...BUT WE'LL JUST MAKE A ***REALLY BIG*** POKÉ BALL FOR IT!
THIS IS A PIECE OF CAKE!
HA HA HA HA
I NEVER THOUGHT OF THAT.
IT **IS** A POKÉMON, AFTER ALL. SO WE **SHOULD** BE ABLE TO CATCH IT. THEORETICALLY AT LEAST...
COOL IDEA! LET'S ***DO IT!***
WE'LL TRY, ASH!
ANYTHING TO SAVE SABRINA'S LIFE!
EVEN CATCHING THE ***BLACK FOG!***

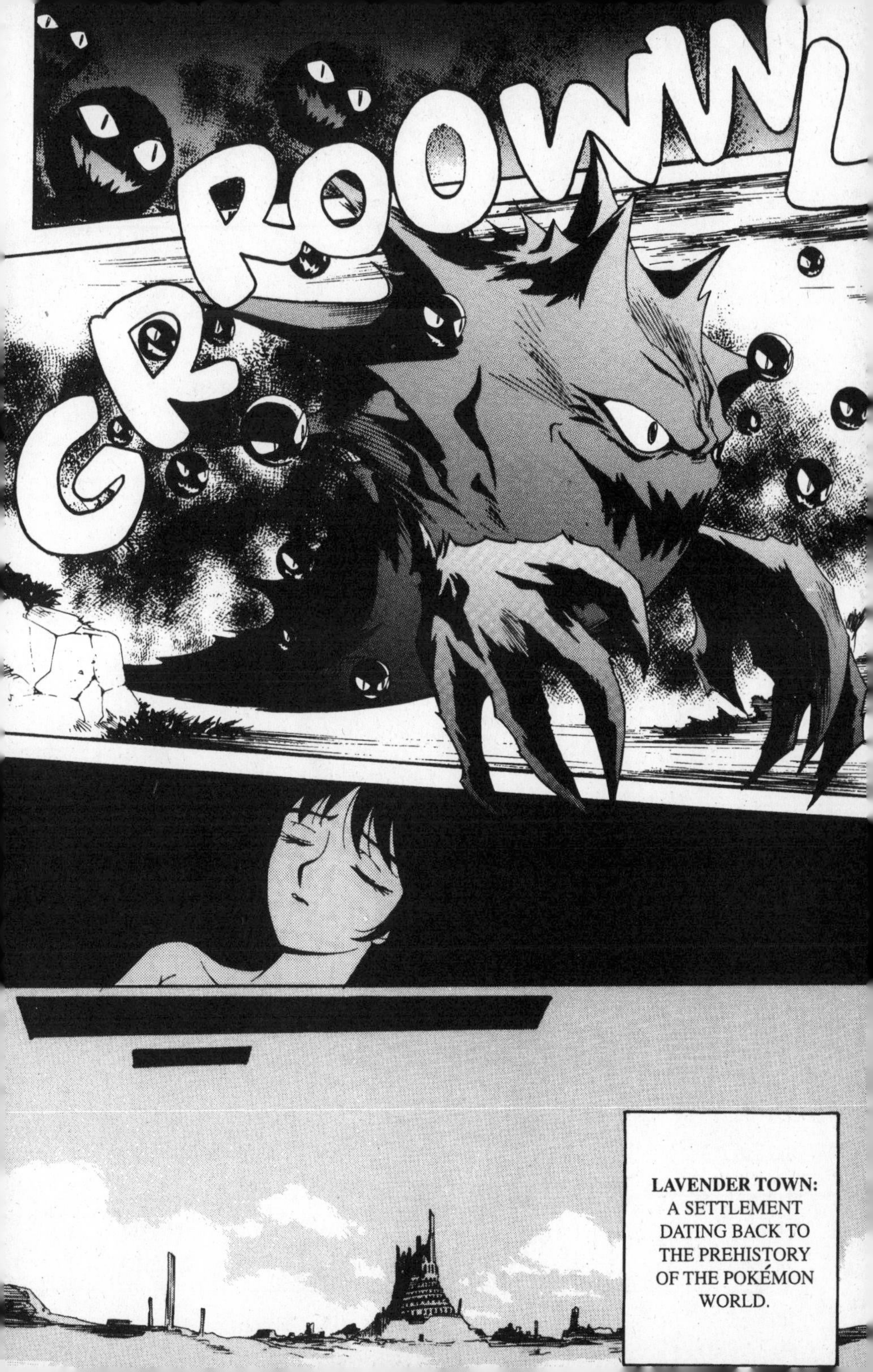
GRROOWWL
LAVENDER TOWN:
A SETTLEMENT
DATING BACK TO
THE PREHISTORY
OF THE POKÉMON
WORLD.

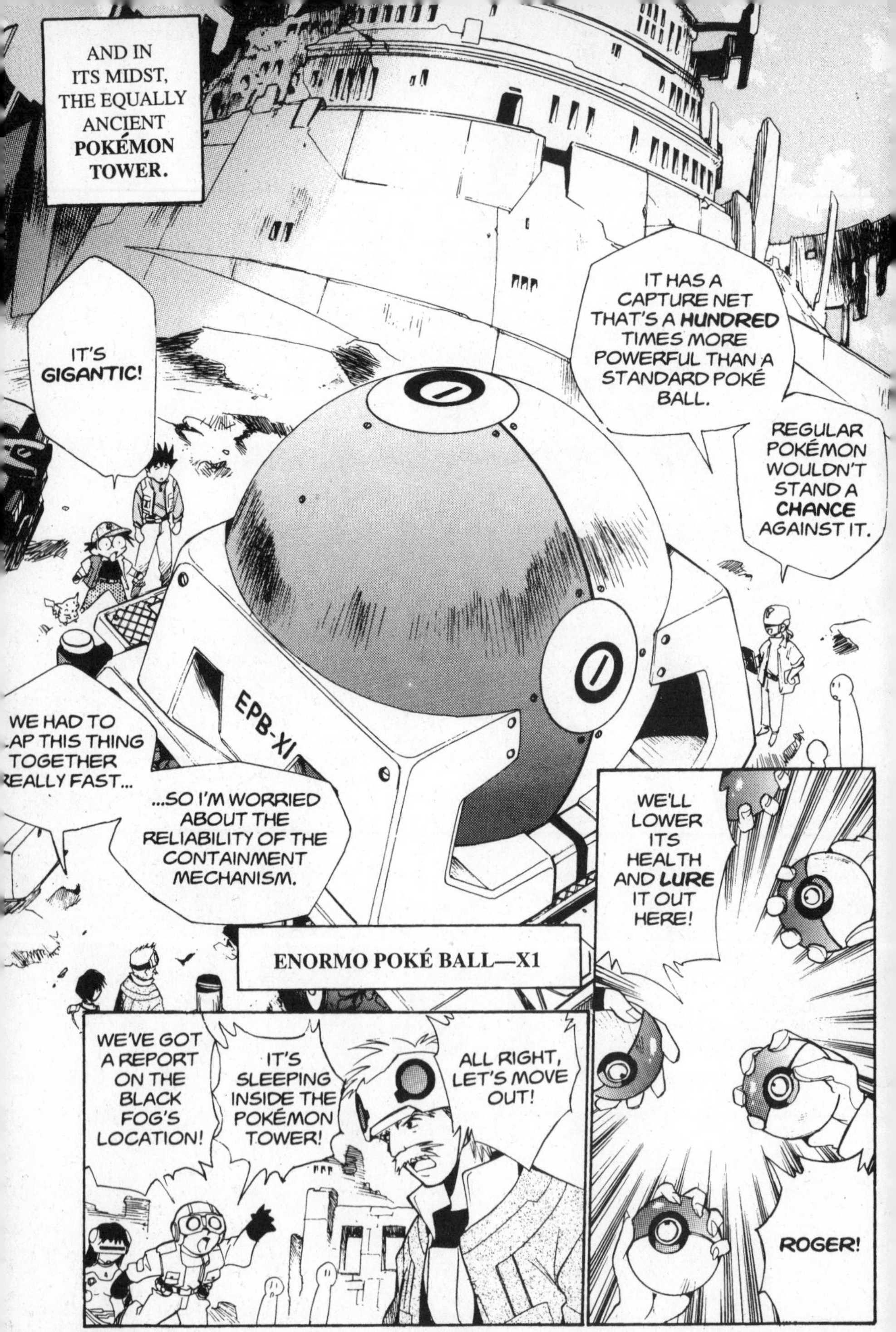

AND IN ITS MIDST, THE EQUALLY ANCIENT **POKÉMON TOWER.**
IT'S **GIGANTIC!**
IT HAS A CAPTURE NET THAT'S A **HUNDRED** TIMES MORE POWERFUL THAN A STANDARD POKÉ BALL.
REGULAR POKÉMON WOULDN'T STAND A **CHANCE** AGAINST IT.
EPB-XI
WE HAD TO AP THIS THING TOGETHER REALLY FAST...
...SO I'M WORRIED ABOUT THE RELIABILITY OF THE CONTAINMENT MECHANISM.
ENORMO POKÉ BALL—X1
WE'VE GOT A REPORT ON THE BLACK FOG'S LOCATION!
IT'S SLEEPING INSIDE THE POKÉMON TOWER!
ALL RIGHT, LET'S MOVE OUT!
WE'LL LOWER ITS HEALTH AND **LURE** IT OUT HERE!
ROGER!

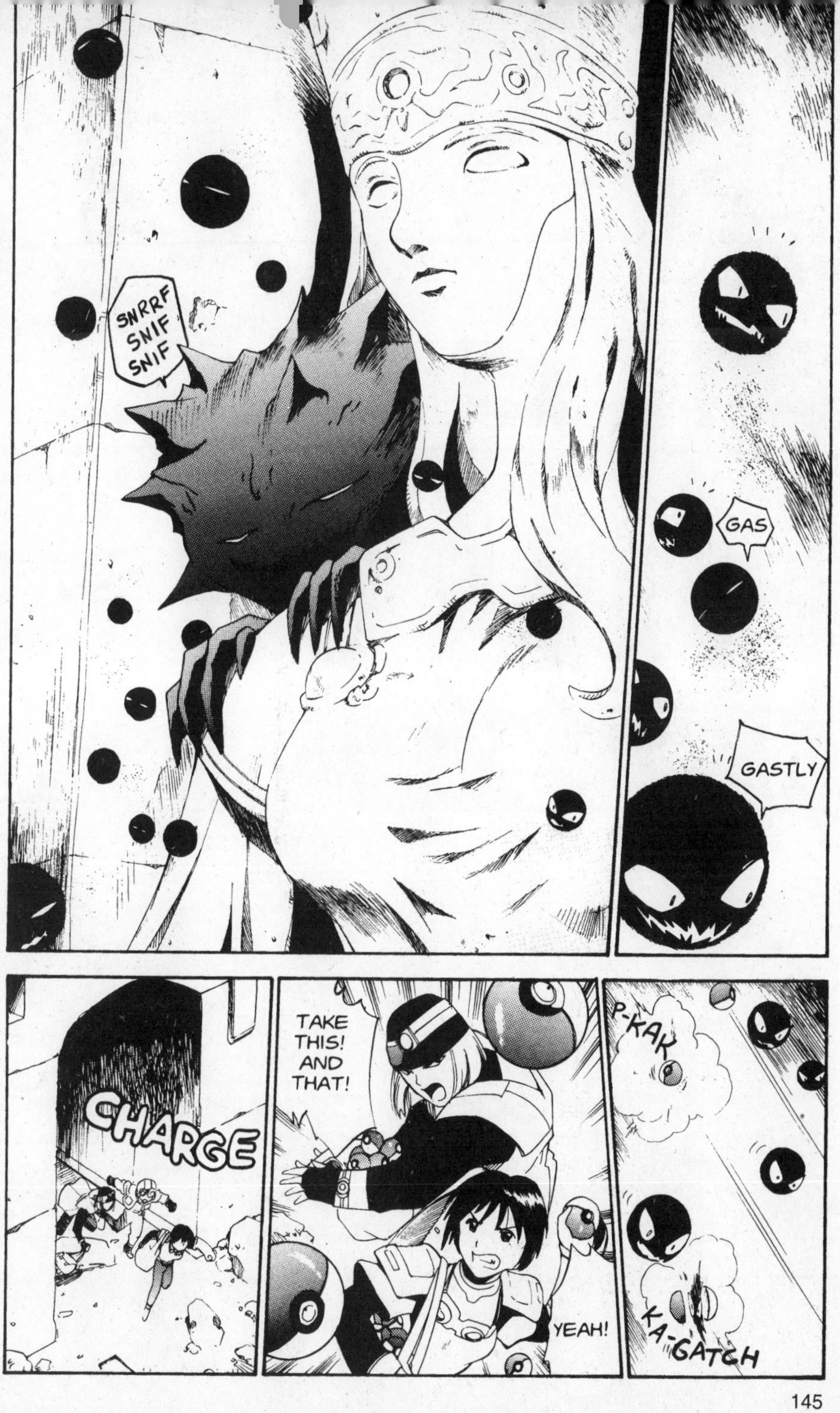
SNRRF SNIF SNIF
GAS
GASTLY
CHARGE
TAKE THIS! AND THAT!
YEAH!
P-KAK
KA-GATCH

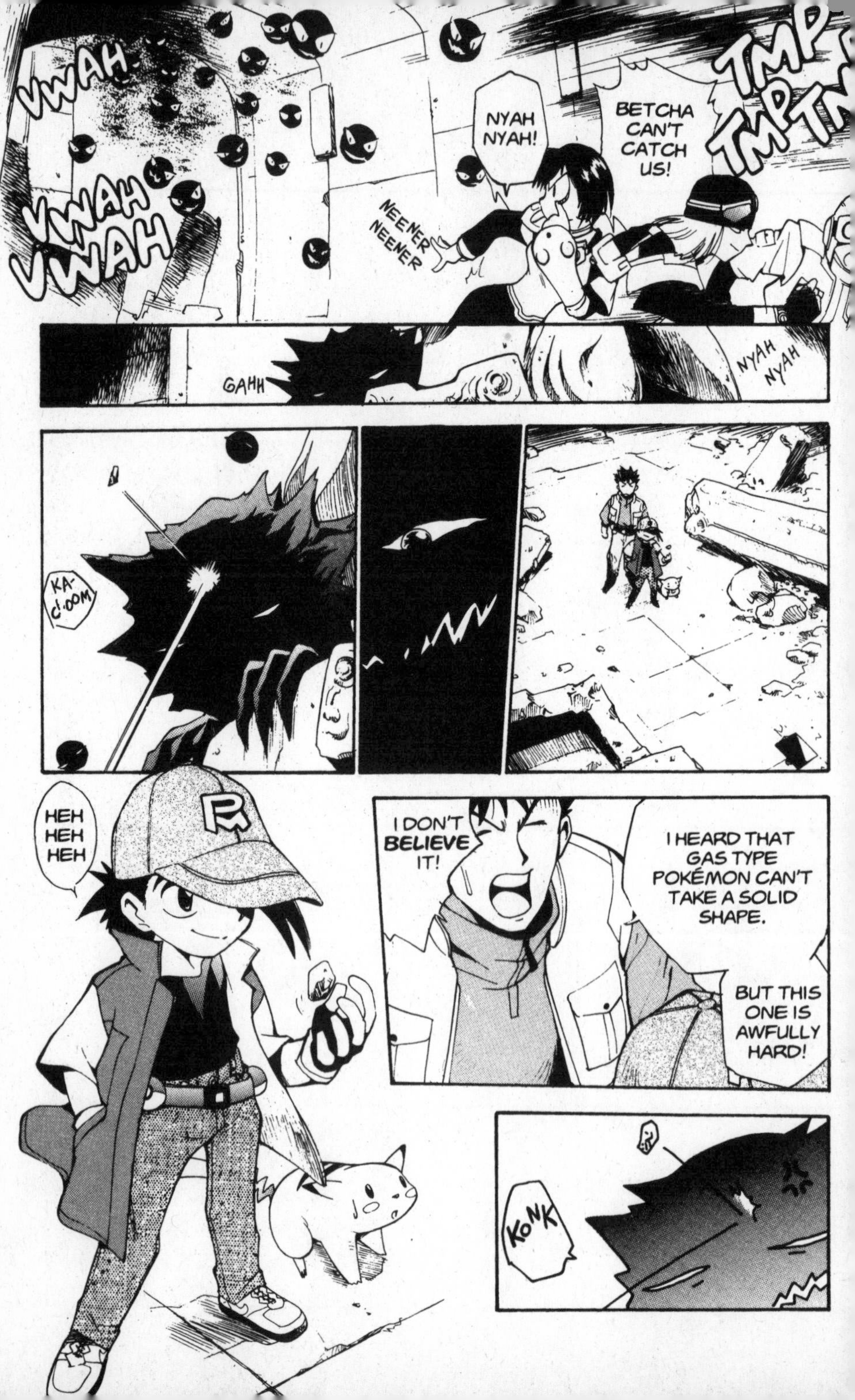
VWAH
VWAH VWAH
NYAH NYAH!
NEENER NEENER
BETCHA CAN'T CATCH US!
TMP TMP TMP
GAHH
NYAH NYAH
KA-C!OOM
HEH HEH HEH
I DON'T **BELIEVE** IT!
I HEARD THAT GAS TYPE POKÉMON CAN'T TAKE A SOLID SHAPE.
BUT THIS ONE IS AWFULLY HARD!
KONK

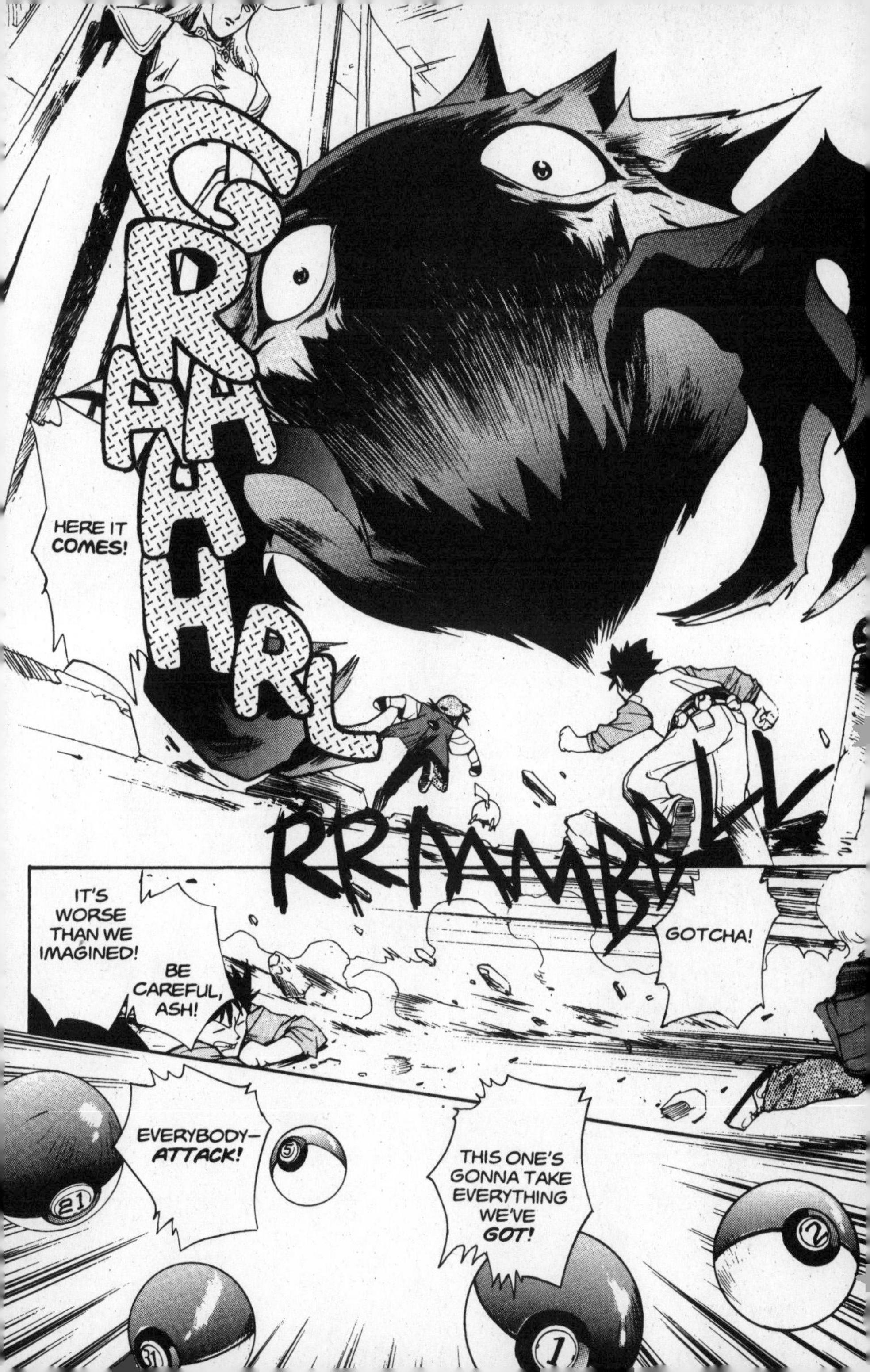
HERE IT COMES!
IT'S WORSE THAN WE IMAGINED!
BE CAREFUL, ASH!
GOTCHA!
EVERYBODY— ATTACK!
THIS ONE'S GONNA TAKE EVERYTHING WE'VE GOT!

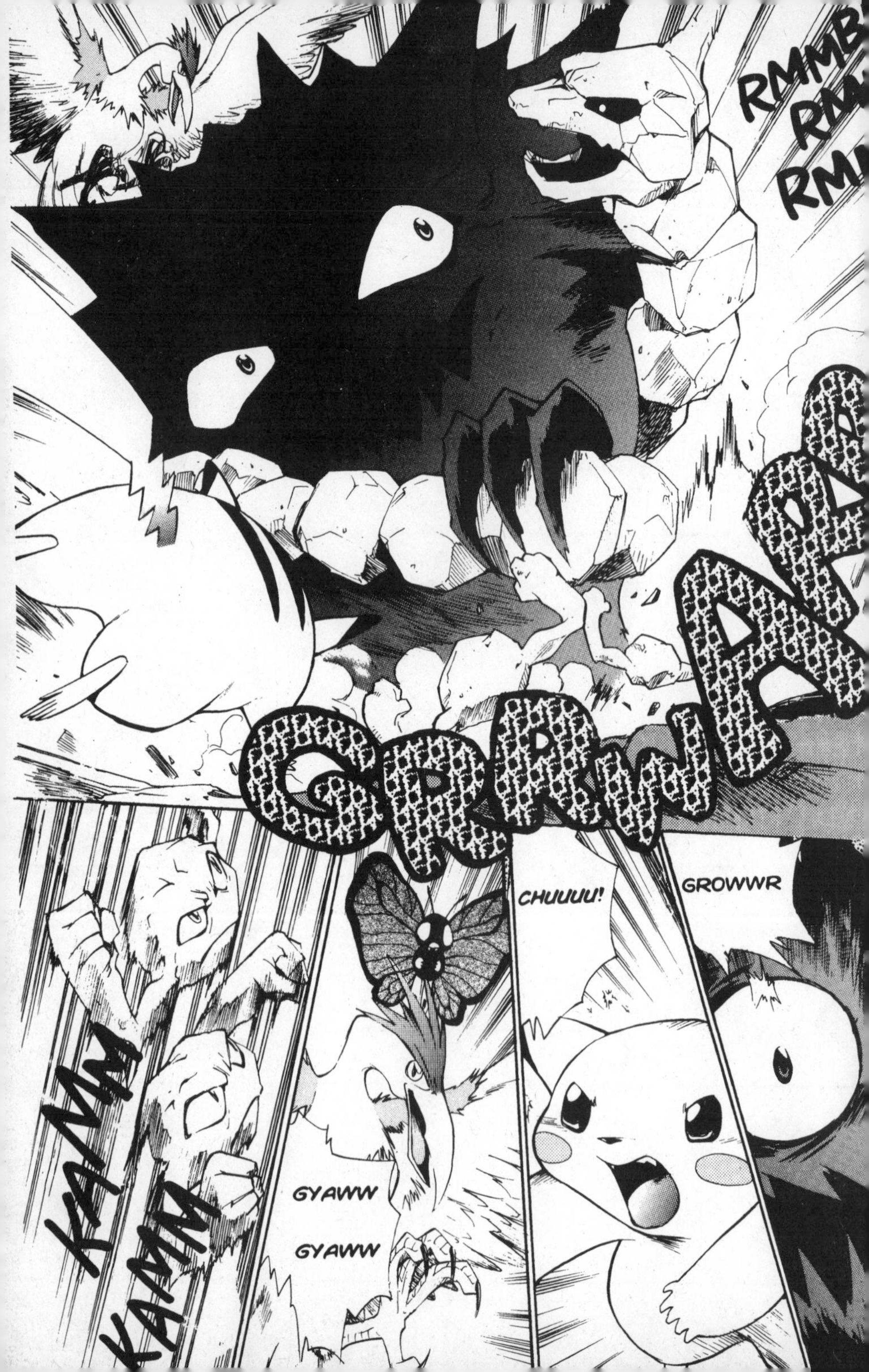
RMMB
RMM
RMM
GRRWAR
KAMM
KAMM
GYAWW
GYAWW
CHUUUU!
GROWWR

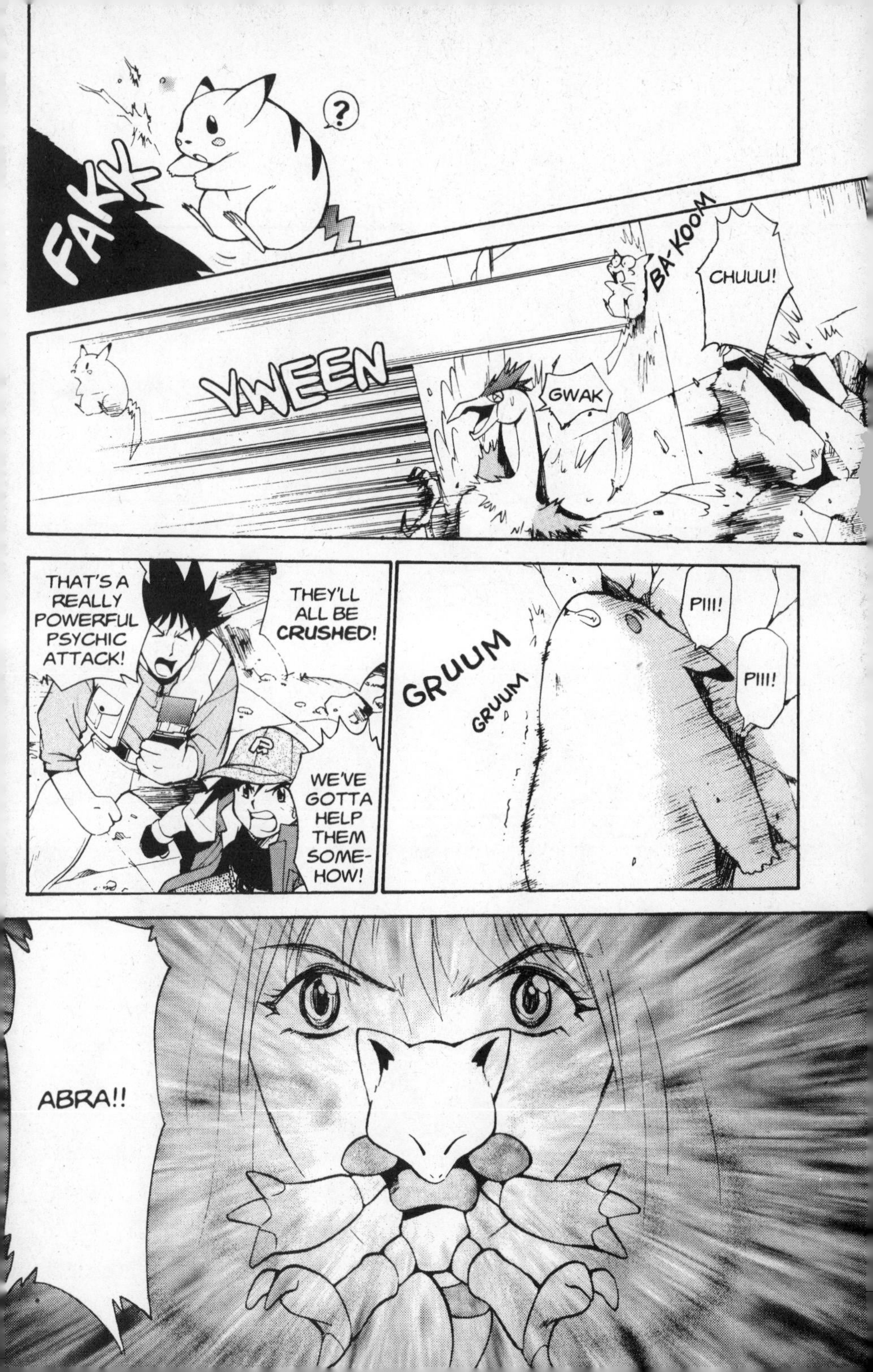
?
FAKK
BA-KOOM
CHUUU!
VWEEN
GWAK
THAT'S A REALLY POWERFUL PSYCHIC ATTACK!
THEY'LL ALL BE CRUSHED!
WE'VE GOTTA HELP THEM SOME-HOW!
PIII!
PIII!
GRUUM
GRUUM
ABRA!!

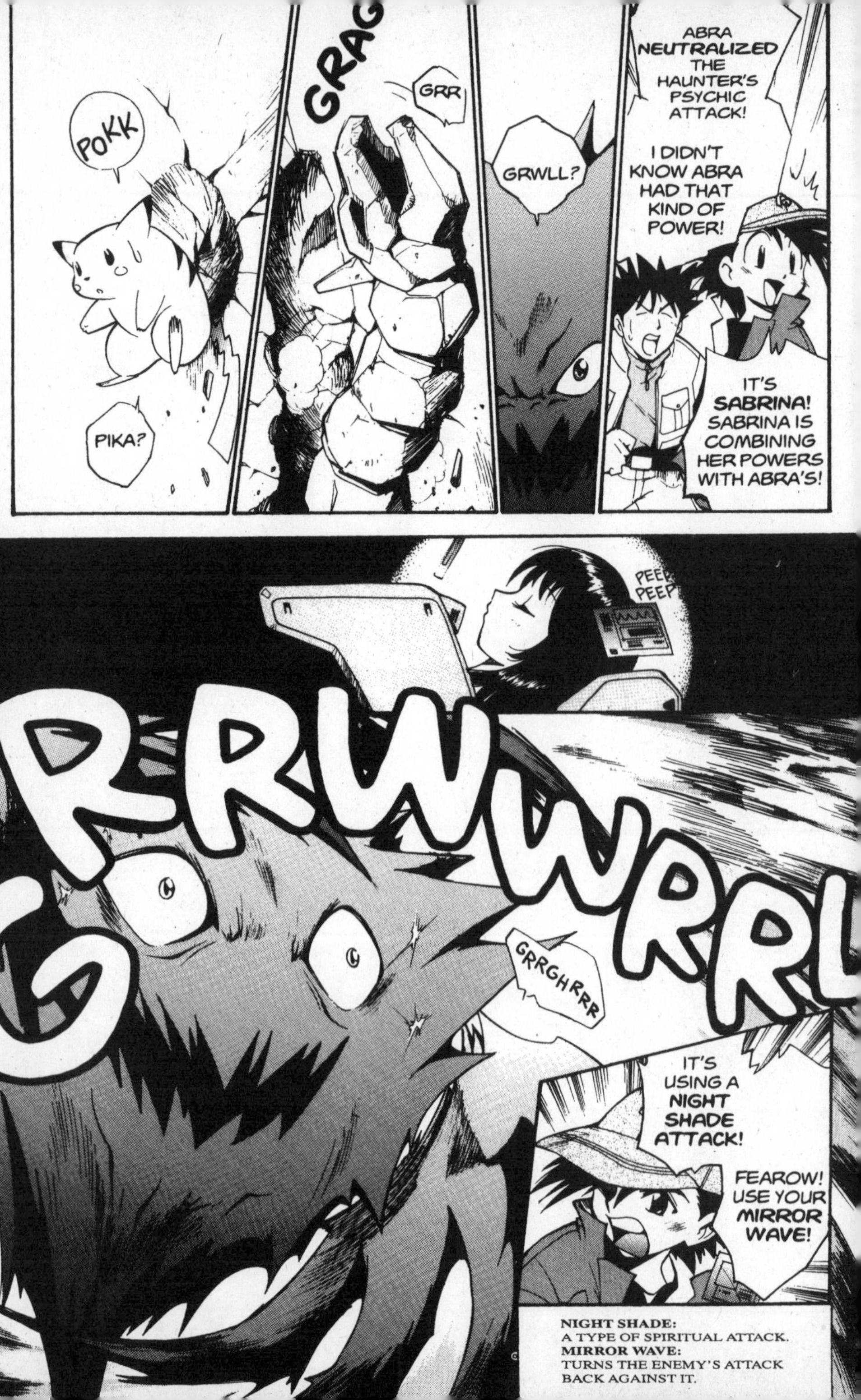
POKK
PIKA?
GRAG
GRR
GRWLL?
ABRA NEUTRALIZED THE HAUNTER'S PSYCHIC ATTACK!
I DIDN'T KNOW ABRA HAD THAT KIND OF POWER!
IT'S SABRINA! SABRINA IS COMBINING HER POWERS WITH ABRA'S!
PEEP PEEP
GRRGHRRR
IT'S USING A NIGHT SHADE ATTACK!
FEAROW! USE YOUR MIRROR WAVE!
NIGHT SHADE:
A TYPE OF SPIRITUAL ATTACK.
MIRROR WAVE:
TURNS THE ENEMY'S ATTACK BACK AGAINST IT.

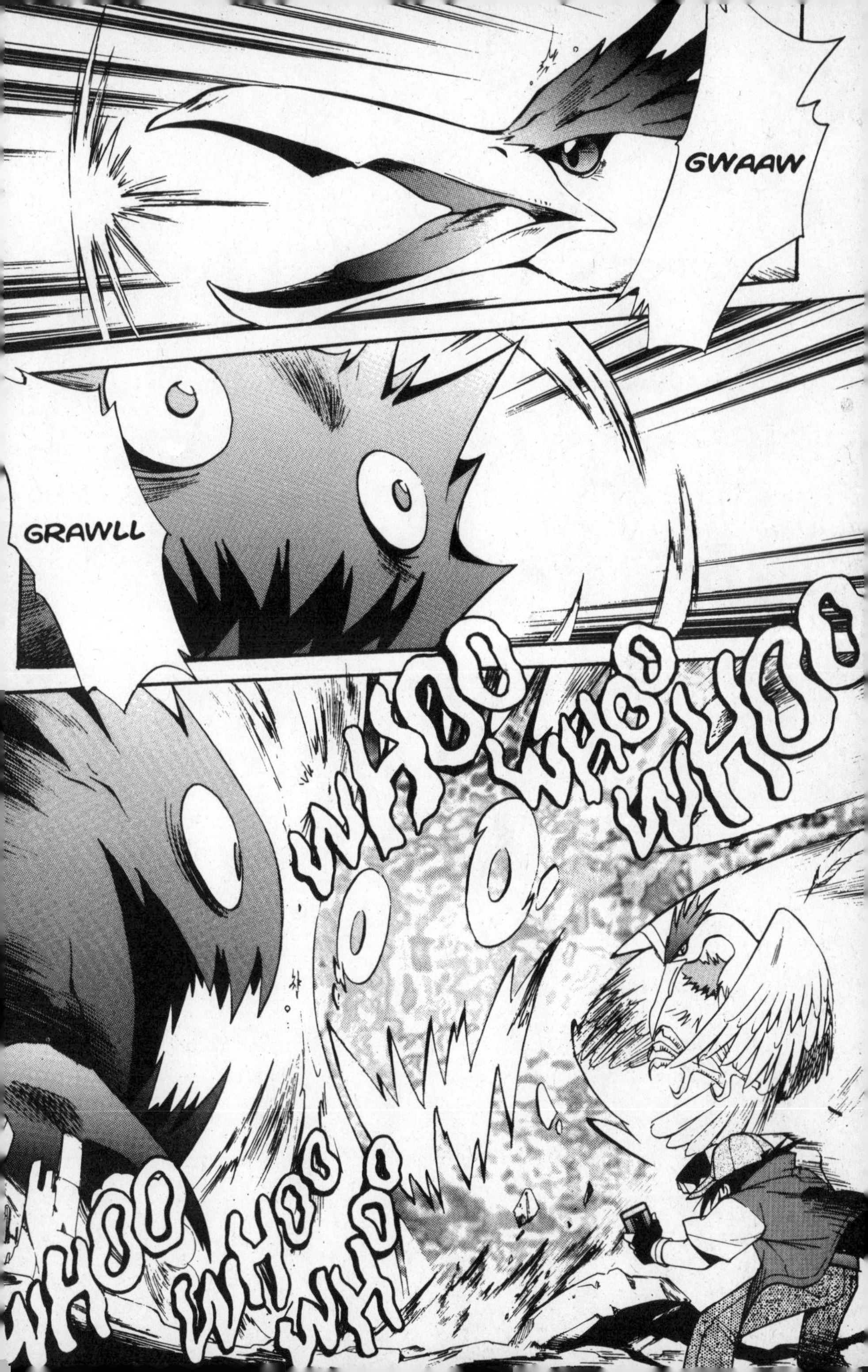
GWAAW
GRAWLL
WHOO WHOO WHOO
WHOO WHOO WHOO

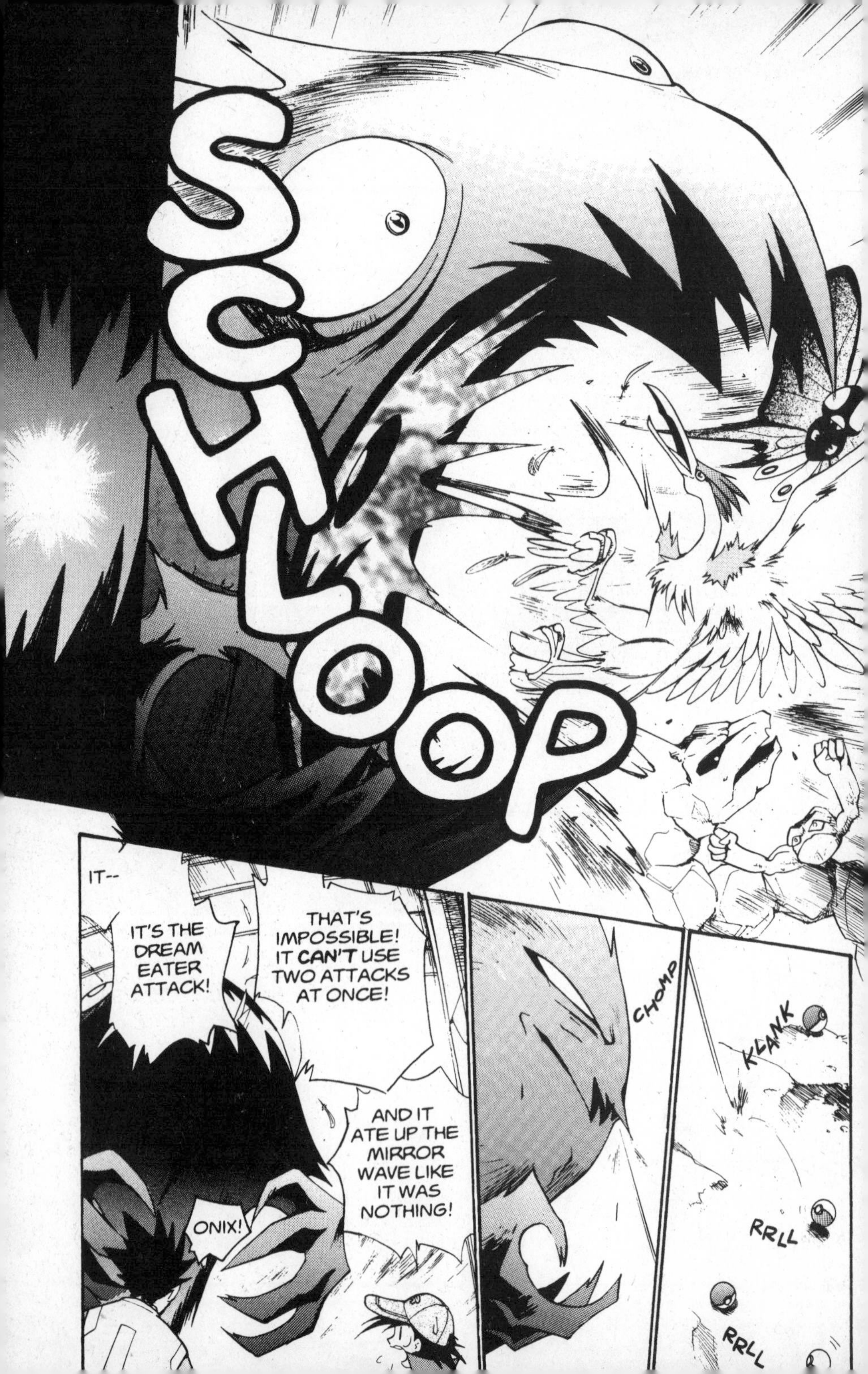
SCHLOOOP
IT--
IT'S THE DREAM EATER ATTACK!
THAT'S IMPOSSIBLE! IT **CAN'T** USE TWO ATTACKS AT ONCE!
AND IT ATE UP THE MIRROR WAVE LIKE IT WAS NOTHING!
ONIX!
CHOMP
KLANK
RRLL
RRLL

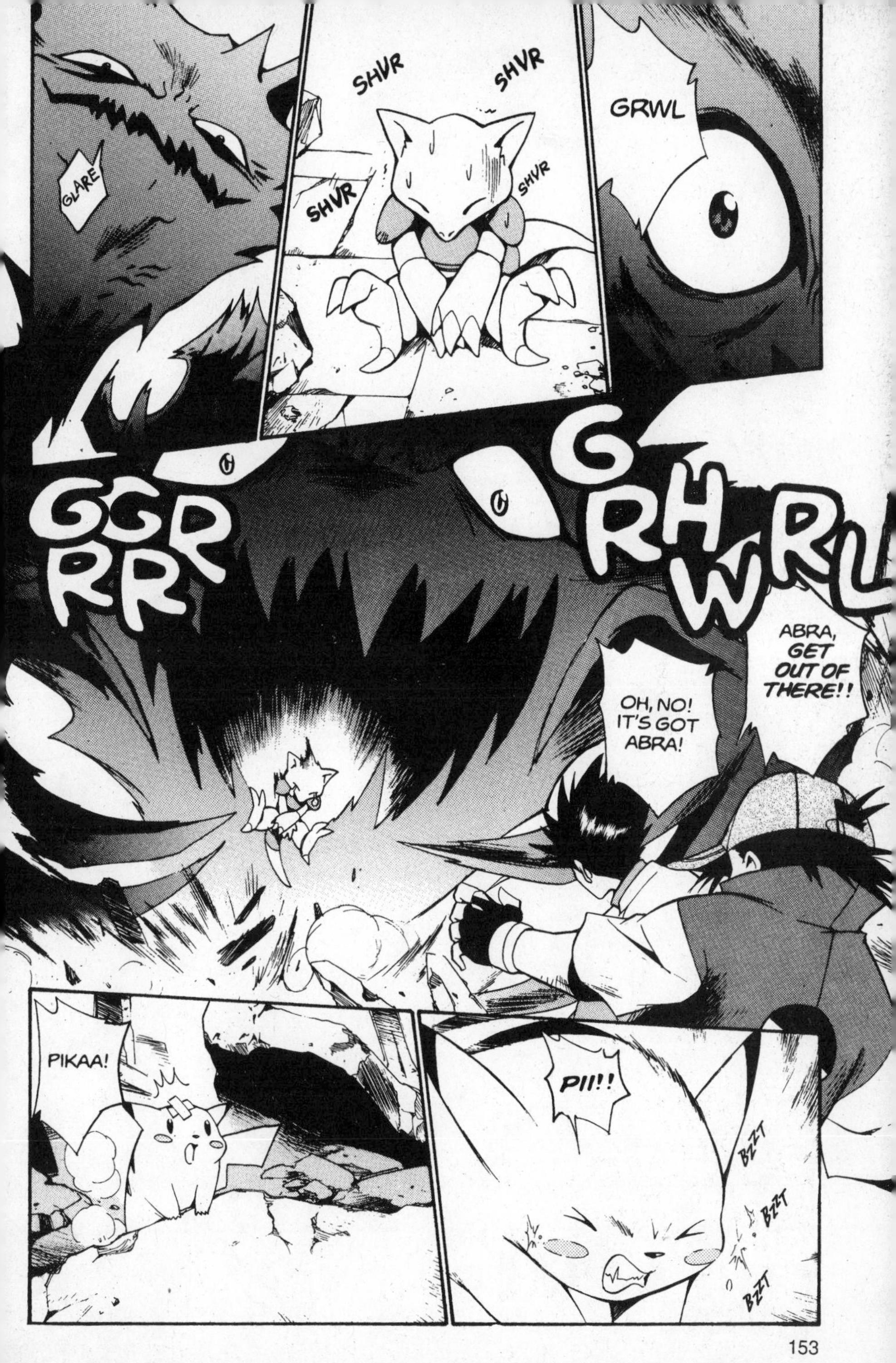
GLARE
SHVR
SHVR
SHVR
SHVR
GRWL
GGRRR
GRHWRL
OH, NO! IT'S GOT ABRA!
ABRA, GET OUT OF THERE!!
PIKAA!
PII!!
BZZT
BZZT
BZZT

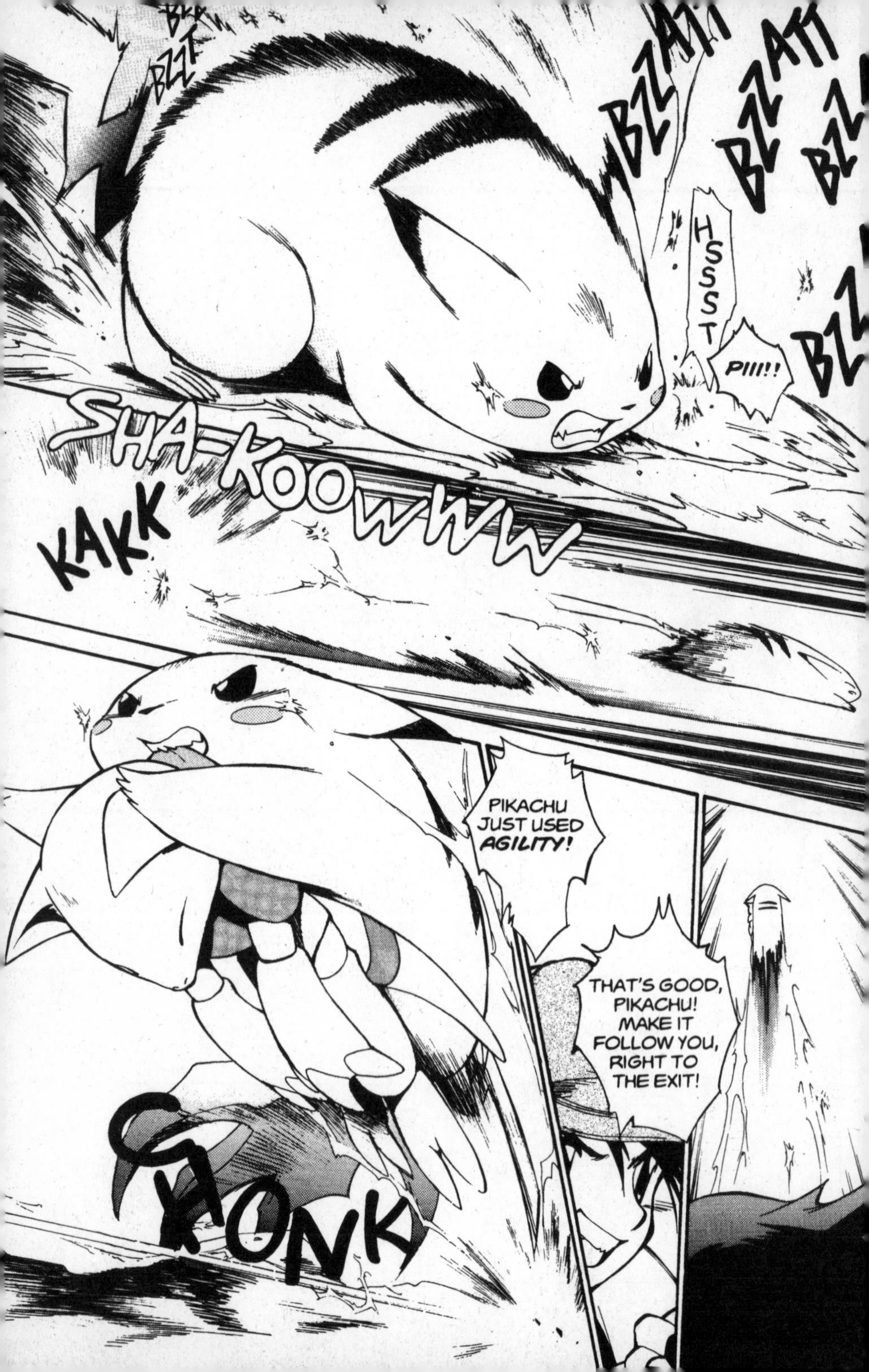
BZZATT
BZZATT
BZZ
HSSST
PIII!!
BZZ
SHA KOOWWW
KAKK
PIKACHU JUST USED AGILITY!
THAT'S GOOD, PIKACHU! MAKE IT FOLLOW YOU, RIGHT TO THE EXIT!
CHONK

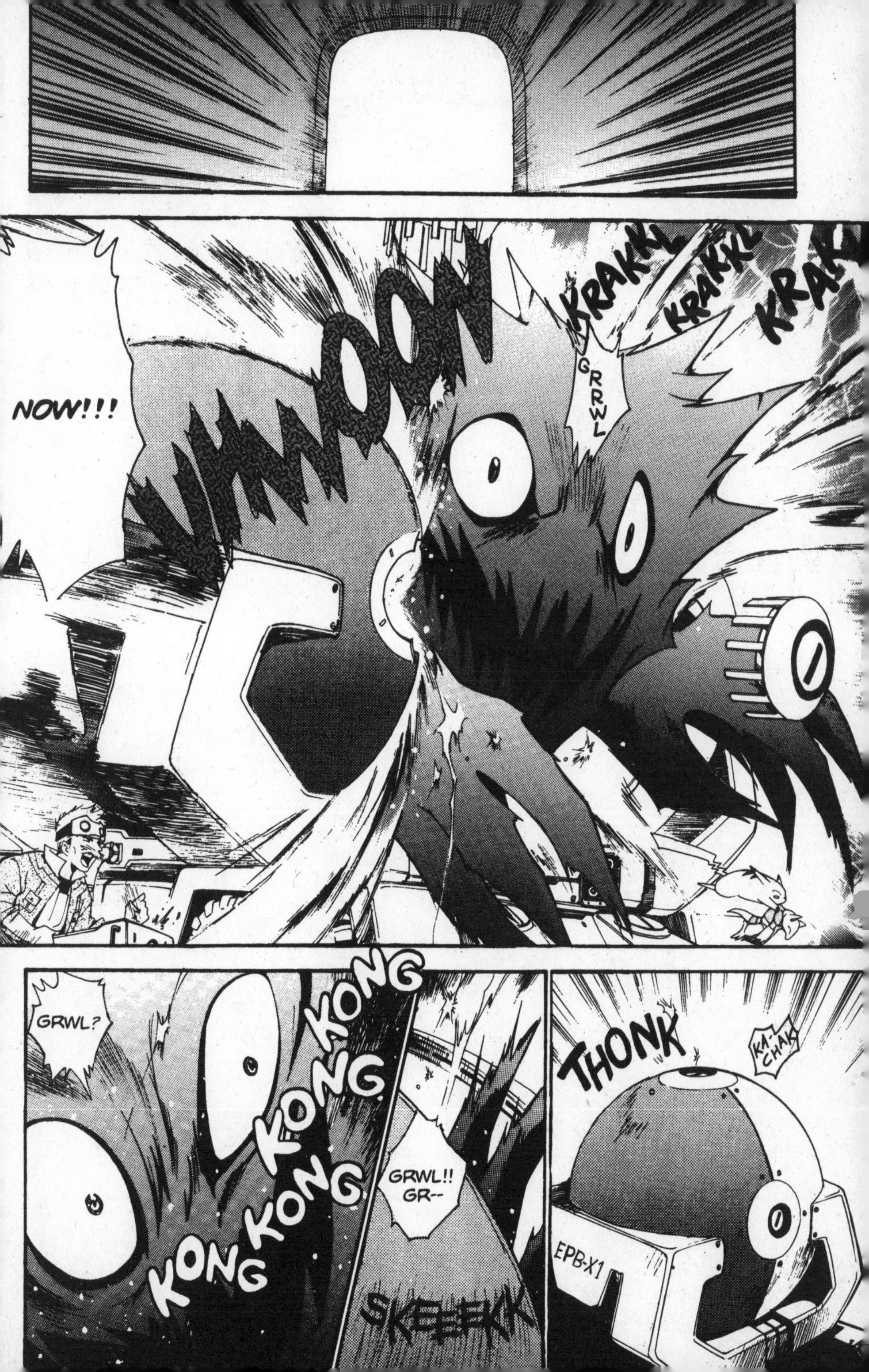

NOW!!!
VMMOOOM
KRAKKL KRAKKL KRAK
GRRWL
GRWL?
KONG KONG KONG KONG
GRWL!! GR--
SKEEEKK
THONK
KA-CHAK
EPB-X1

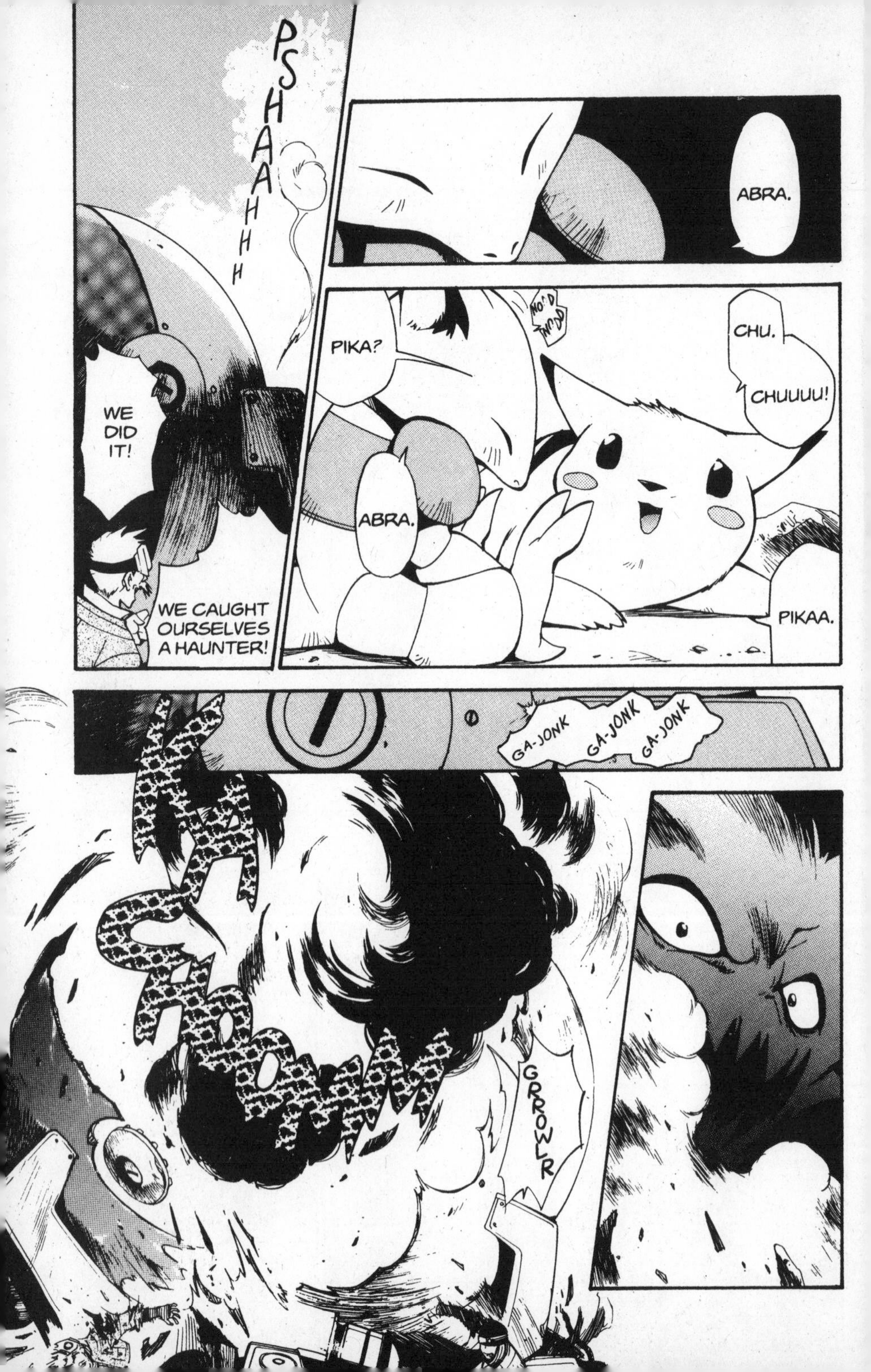
PSHAAAHHHH
WE DID IT!
WE CAUGHT OURSELVES A HAUNTER!
ABRA.
PIKA?
NOD NOD
ABRA.
CHU.
CHUUUU!
PIKAA.
GA-JONK
GA-JONK
GA-JONK
KA-CHOOM
GRROWLR

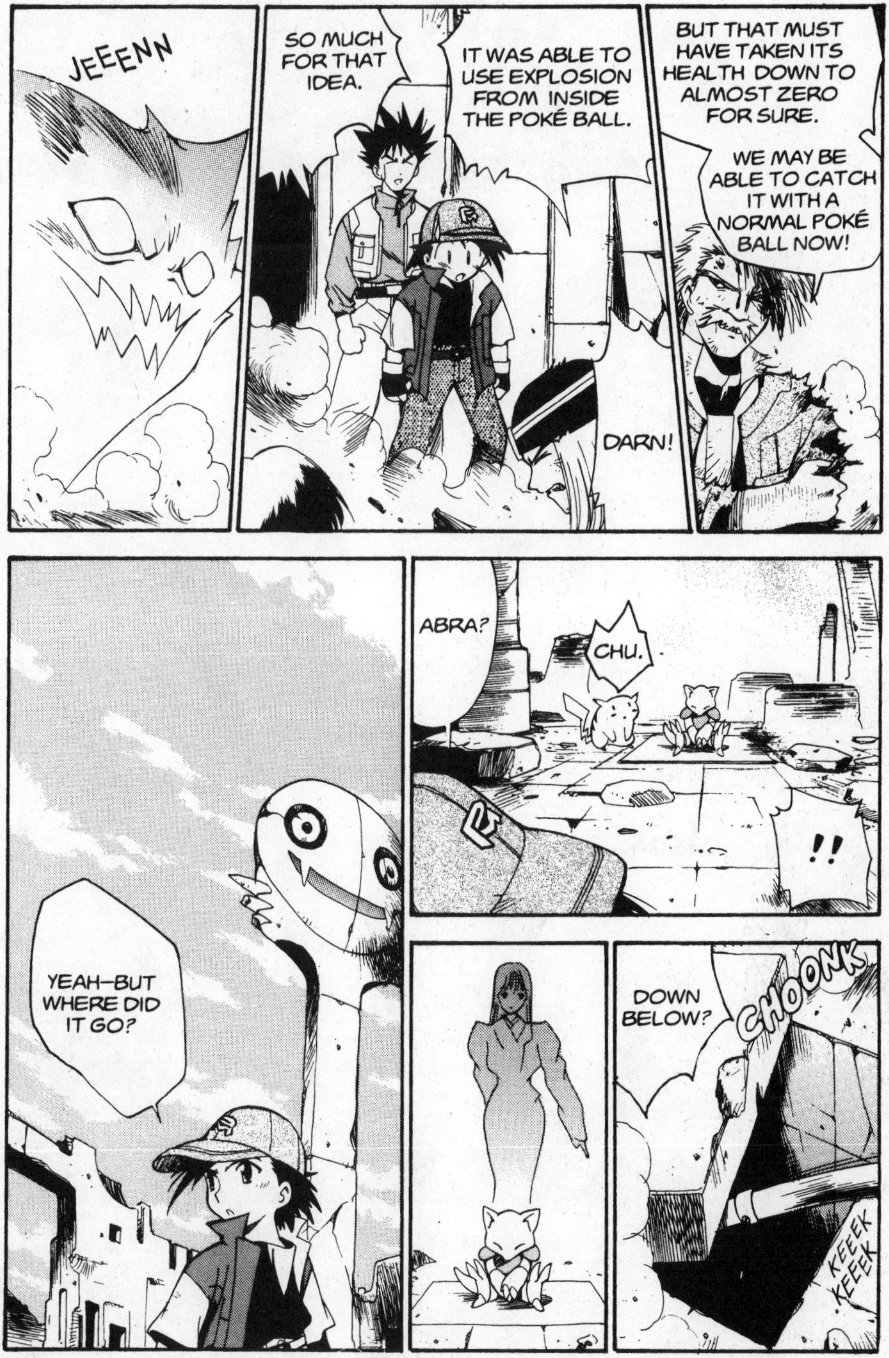
JEEENN
SO MUCH FOR THAT IDEA.
IT WAS ABLE TO USE EXPLOSION FROM INSIDE THE POKÉ BALL.
DARN!
BUT THAT MUST HAVE TAKEN ITS HEALTH DOWN TO ALMOST ZERO FOR SURE.
WE MAY BE ABLE TO CATCH IT WITH A NORMAL POKÉ BALL NOW!
YEAH—BUT WHERE DID IT GO?
ABRA?
CHU.
!!
DOWN BELOW?
CHOONK
KEEEK KEEEK

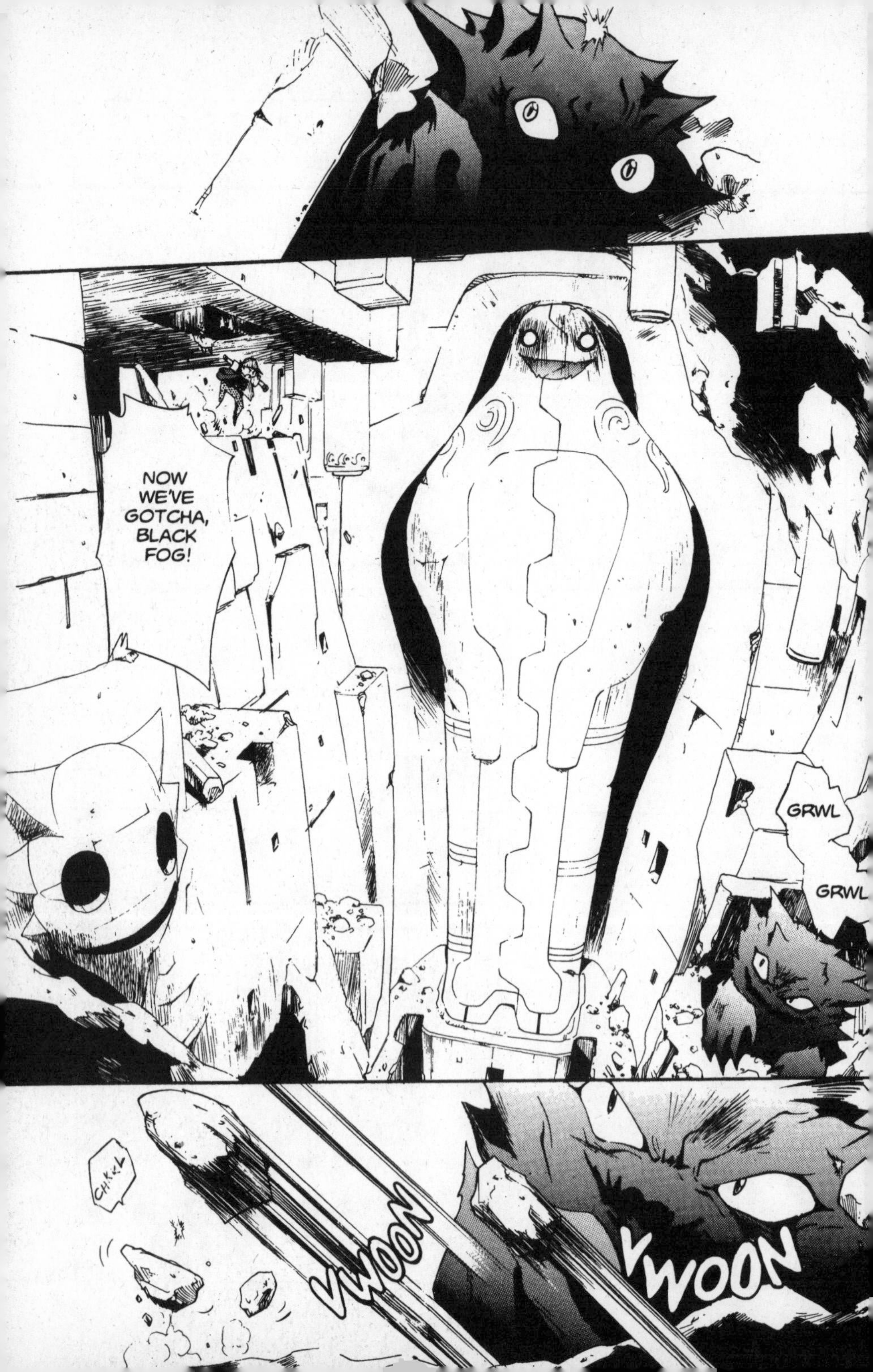
NOW WE'VE GOTCHA, BLACK FOG!
GRWL
GRWL
VWOON
VWOON

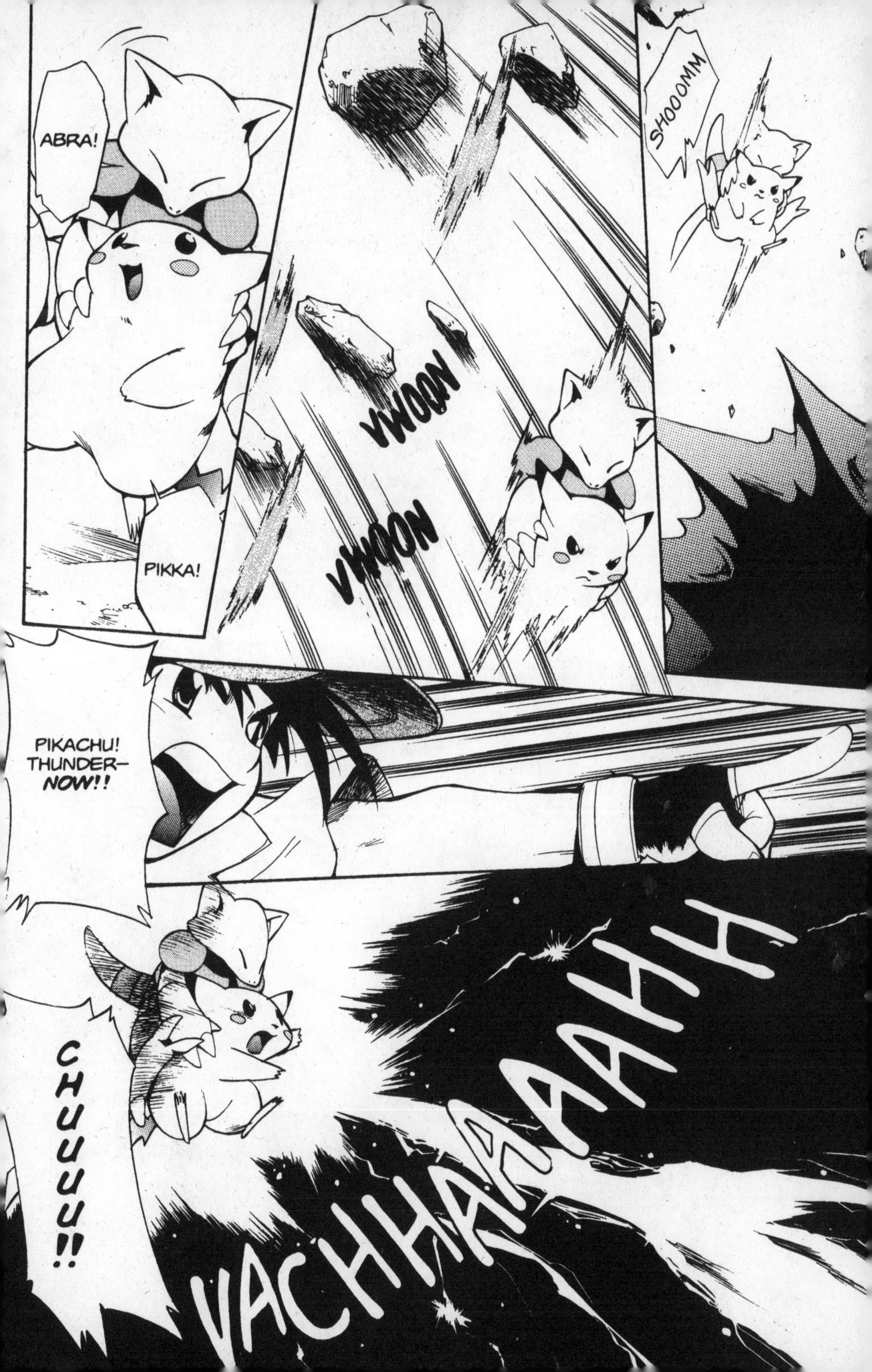
ABRA!
PIKKA!
VWOON
VWOON
SHOOOMM
PIKACHU! THUNDER—NOW!!
CHUUUUU!!
VACHHAAAAHH

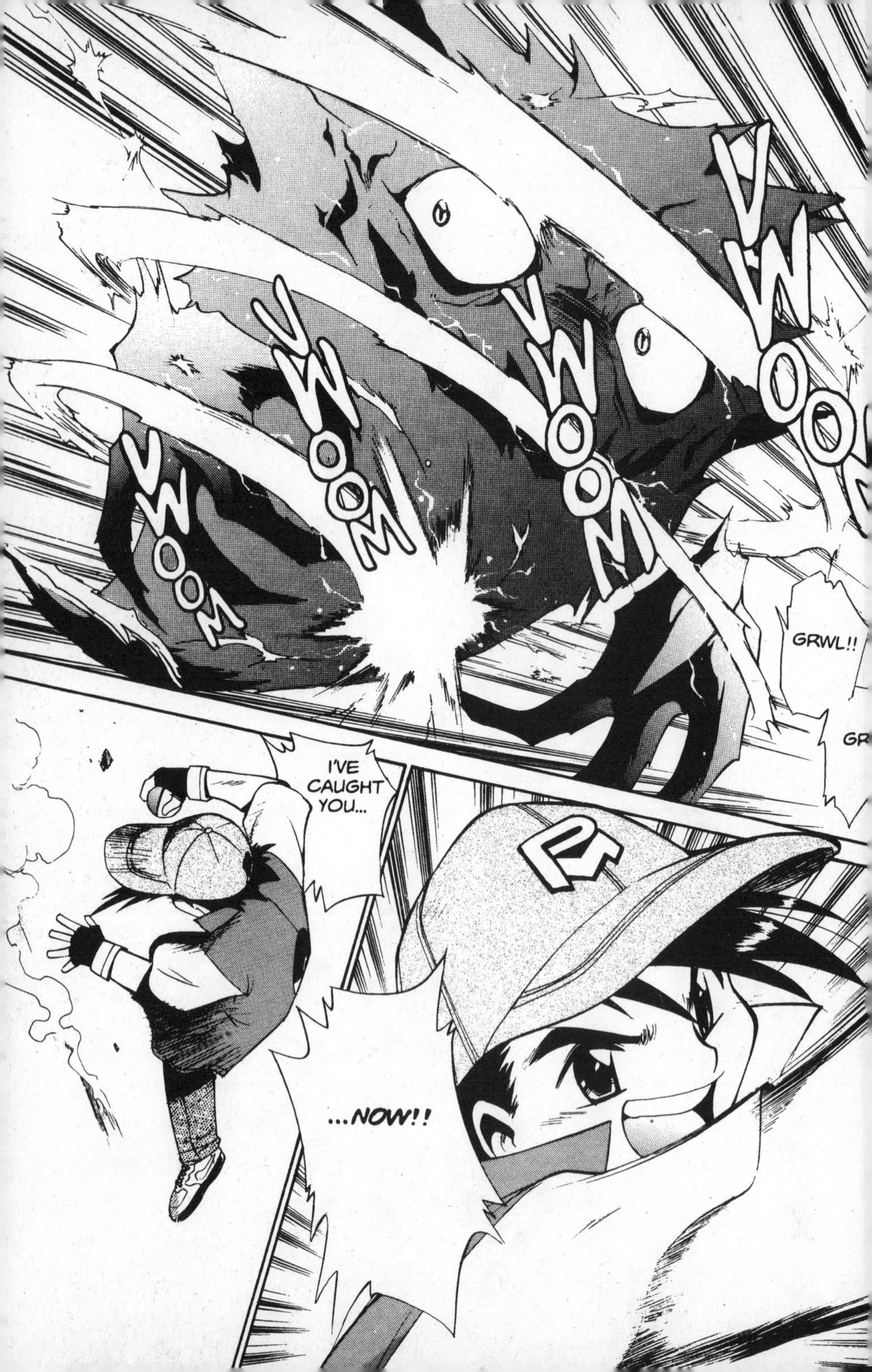
VWOOM
VWOOM
VWOOM
VWOOM
GRWL!!
GR
I'VE CAUGHT YOU...
...NOW!!

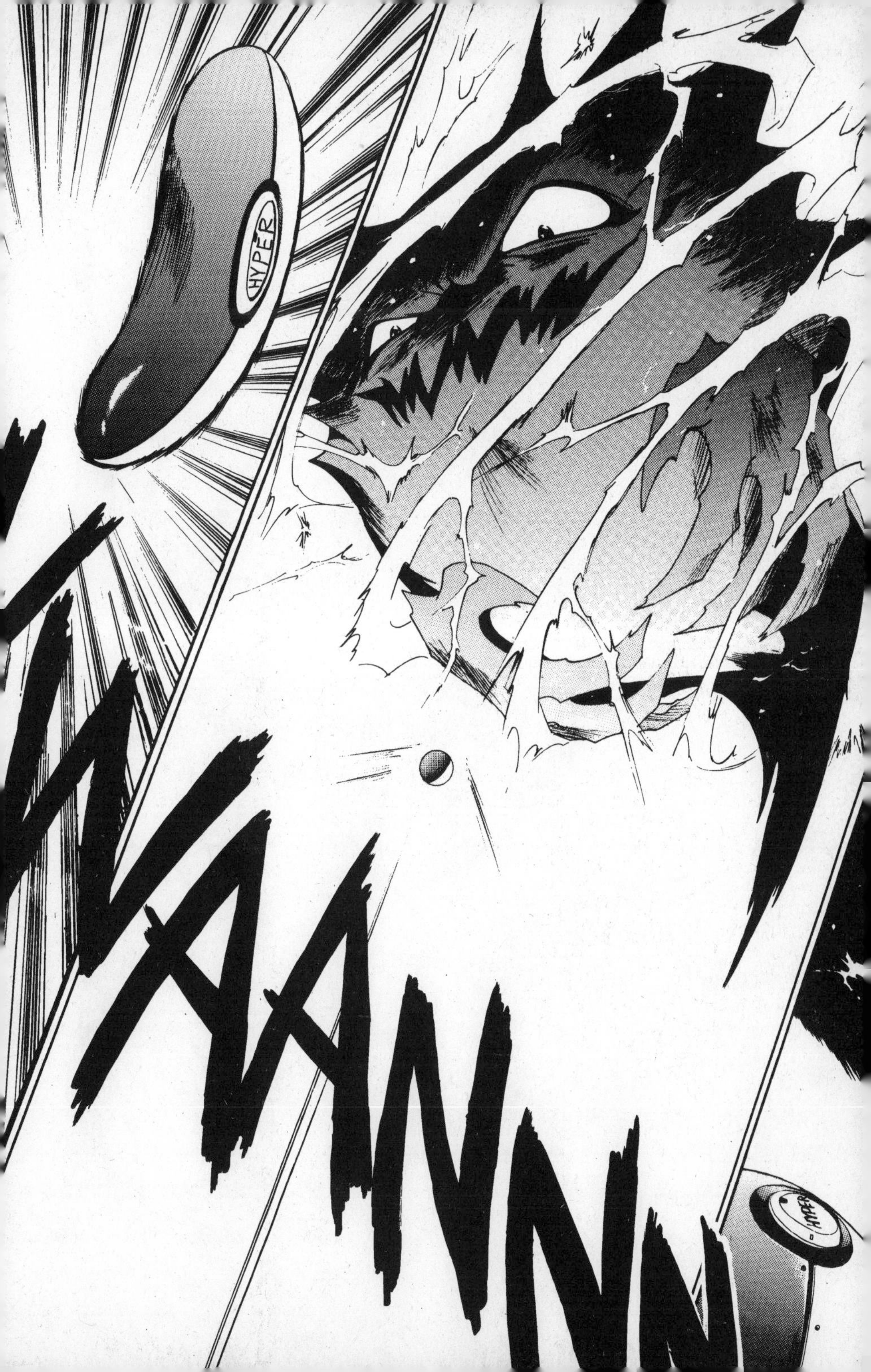
HYPER
ZAANNN
HYPER

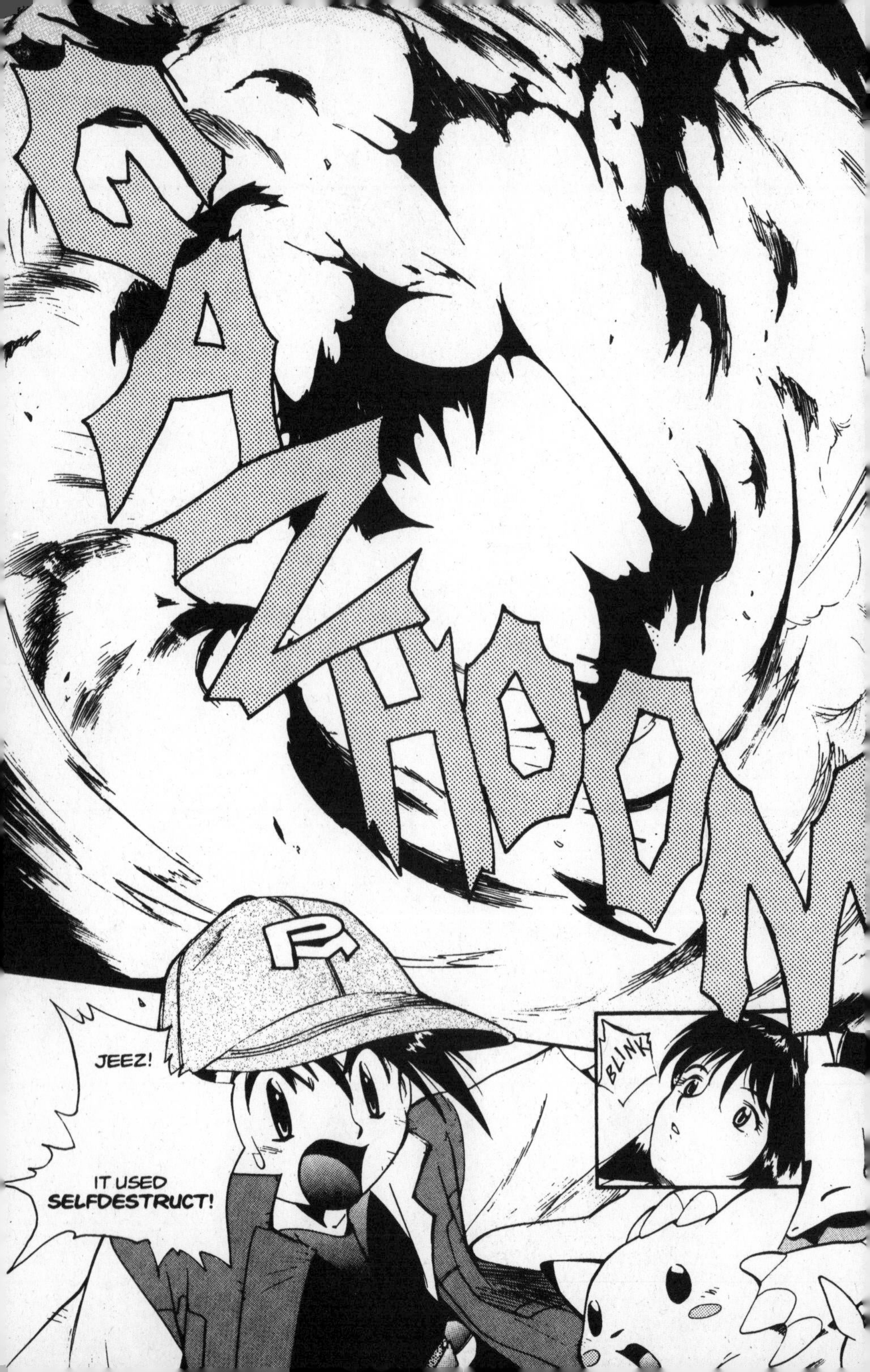

GAZHOOM
JEEZ!
IT USED **SELFDESTRUCT!**
BLINK

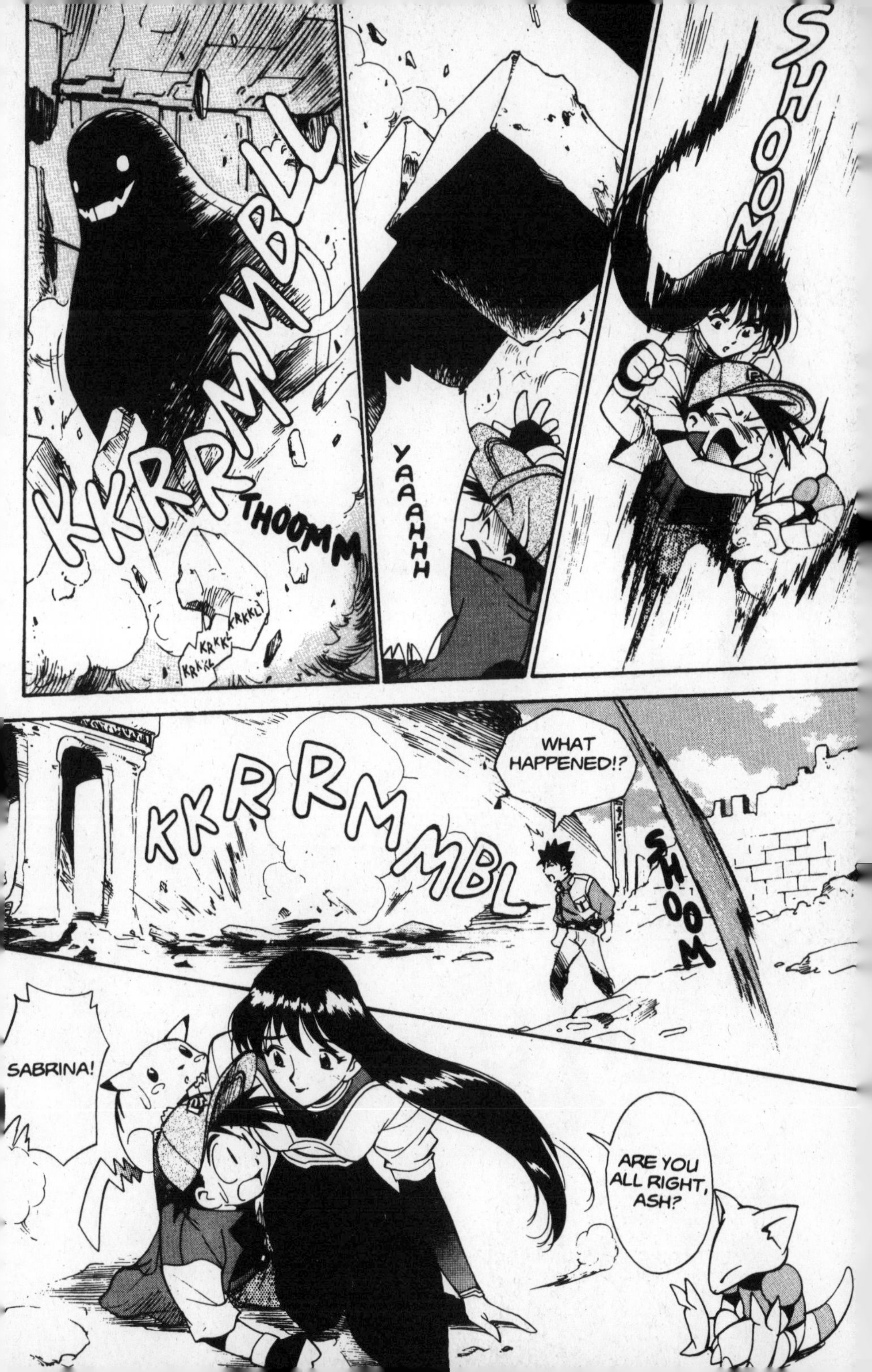
KKRRMMBL
THOOMM
KRAKL
KRKKL
KRKKL
YAAAHHH
SHOOOM
KKRRRMMMBL
WHAT HAPPENED!?
SHOOM
SABRINA!
ARE YOU ALL RIGHT, ASH?

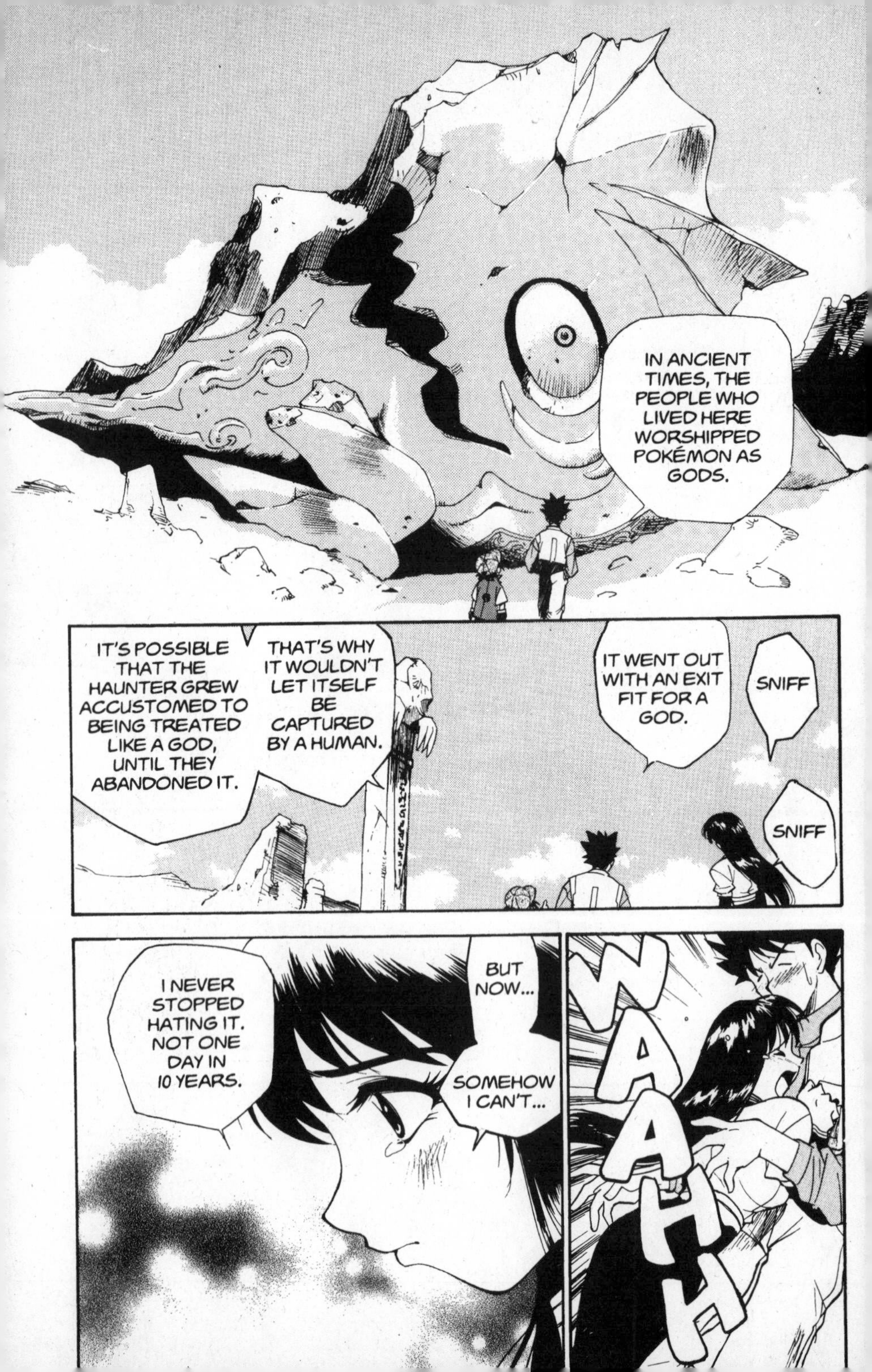
IN ANCIENT TIMES, THE PEOPLE WHO LIVED HERE WORSHIPPED POKÉMON AS GODS.
IT'S POSSIBLE THAT THE HAUNTER GREW ACCUSTOMED TO BEING TREATED LIKE A GOD, UNTIL THEY ABANDONED IT.
THAT'S WHY IT WOULDN'T LET ITSELF BE CAPTURED BY A HUMAN.
IT WENT OUT WITH AN EXIT FIT FOR A GOD.
SNIFF
SNIFF
I NEVER STOPPED HATING IT. NOT ONE DAY IN 10 YEARS.
BUT NOW...
SOMEHOW I CAN'T...
WAAAH

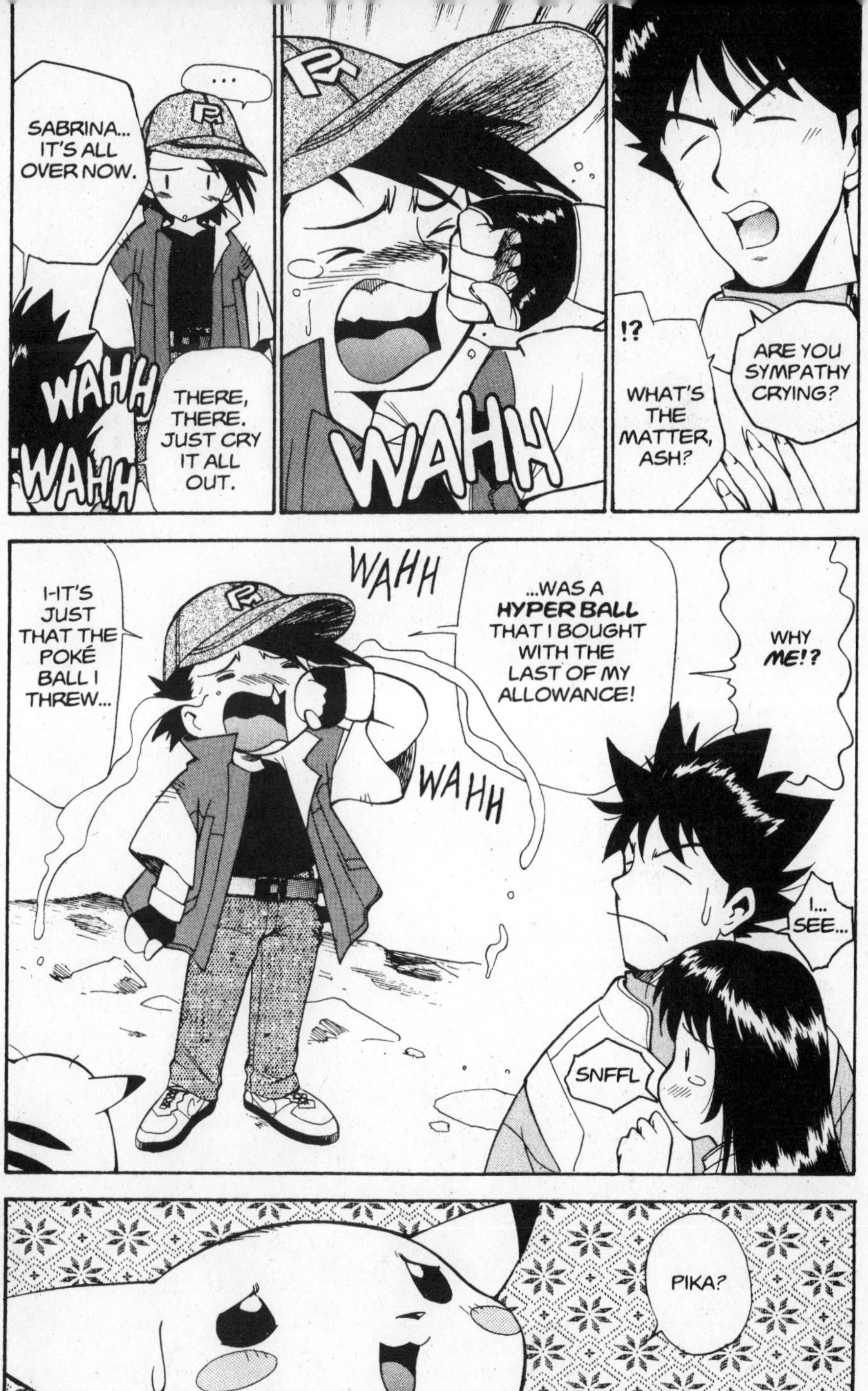
...
SABRINA... IT'S ALL OVER NOW.
WAHH
WAHH
THERE, THERE. JUST CRY IT ALL OUT.
WAHH
!?
WHAT'S THE MATTER, ASH?
ARE YOU SYMPATHY CRYING?
I-IT'S JUST THAT THE POKÉ BALL I THREW...
WAHH
...WAS A **HYPER BALL** THAT I BOUGHT WITH THE LAST OF MY ALLOWANCE!
WHY ***ME!?***
WAHH
I... SEE...
SNFFL
PIKA?

CATCH THE CONTINUING ADVENTURES OF PIKACHU AND ASH IN **POKÉMON: PIKACHU SHOCKS BACK**!

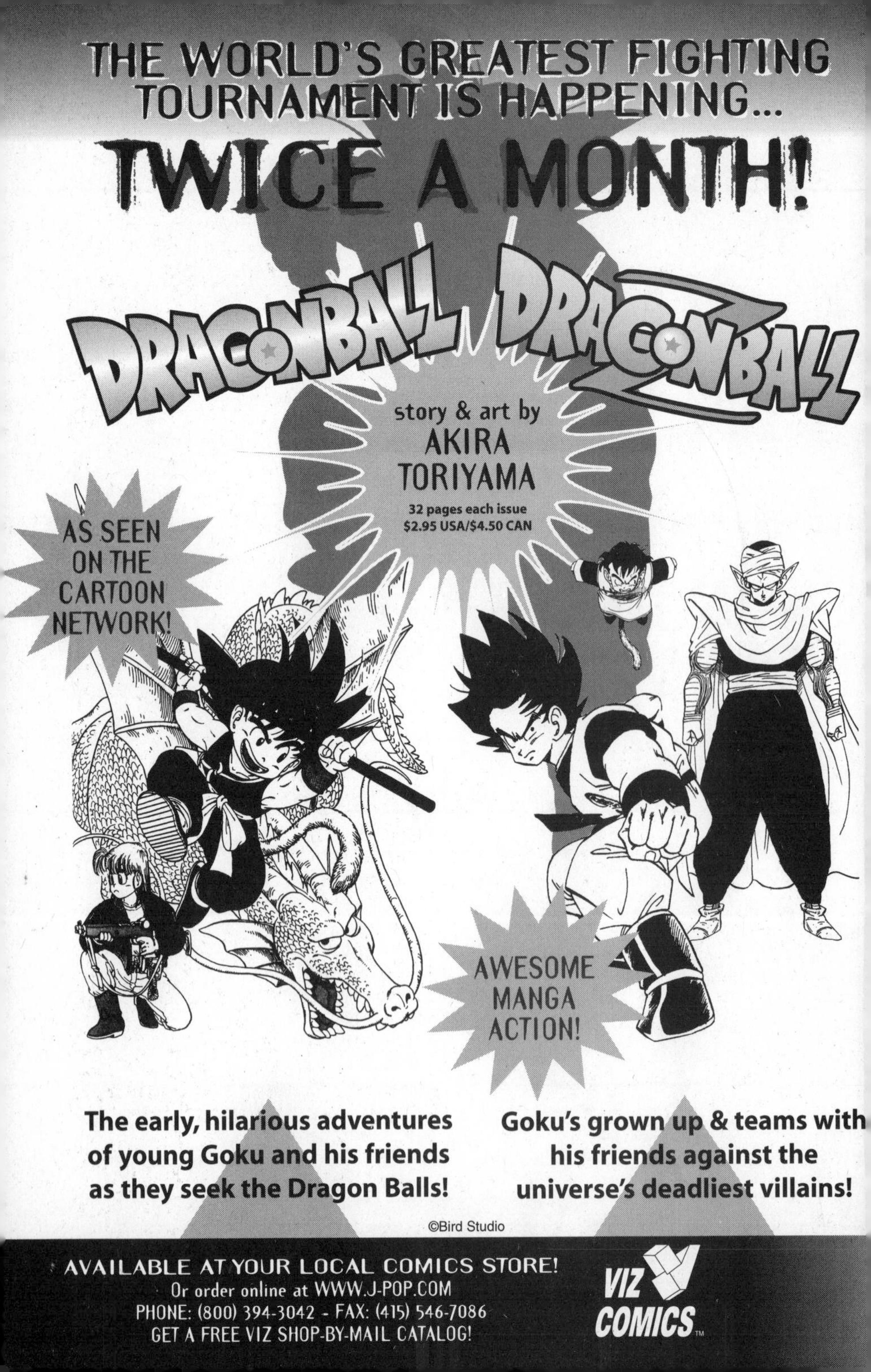
THE WORLD'S GREATEST FIGHTING
TOURNAMENT IS HAPPENING...
TWICE A MONTH!
DRAGONBALL
DRAGONBALL Z
story & art by
AKIRA
TORIYAMA
32 pages each issue
$2.95 USA/$4.50 CAN
AS SEEN
ON THE
CARTOON
NETWORK!
AWESOME
MANGA
ACTION!
The early, hilarious adventures
of young Goku and his friends
as they seek the Dragon Balls!
Goku's grown up & teams with
his friends against the
universe's deadliest villains!
©Bird Studio
AVAILABLE AT YOUR LOCAL COMICS STORE!
Or order online at WWW.J-POP.COM
PHONE: (800) 394-3042 - FAX: (415) 546-7086
GET A FREE VIZ SHOP-BY-MAIL CATALOG!
VIZ
COMICS